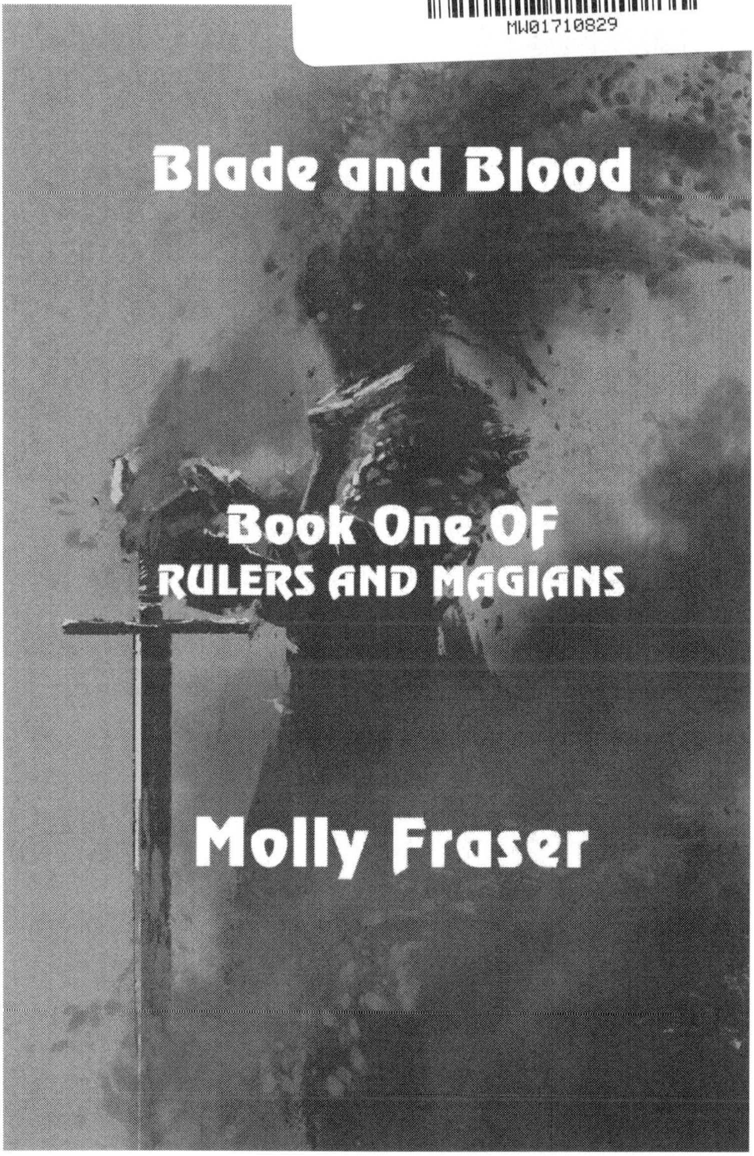
Blade and Blood
Book One OF
RULERS AND MAGIANS
Molly Fraser

Publisher's Note:

This is a work of fiction. All names, characters, places, and events are the work of the author's imagination.

Any resemblance to real persons, places, or events is coincidental.

Solstice Publishing - www.solsticepublishing.com

Blade and Blood

Of Rulers and Magians Book 1

Molly Fraser

Dedication

For Shannon who likes to use her imagination

Chapter One

Early morn was Lyta's favourite time of day. Her leather boots made soft scuffing noises on the damp stones as she crossed the castle courtyard. She paused as a dog howled once in the kennels near her. The only person in sight was Druck, her mother's commander, waving his thick arms as he spoke to a guard at oldgate. A grey mouse scuttled past on her right while to her left, white curls of mist rose into the clear sky from the fields in the outer ward. She sniffed the air: mingled with sweet baking scents from the nearby kitchen were heavy horse smells from the stables.

Then Obela's screeching voice disturbed Lyta's calm mood. The guard at the foot of her tower must have given her away. 'Kedie! Come back at once for your repast.'

Her nurse was always concerned about regular meals. She insisted that morn repast was essential to provide nourishment for the activities that followed. Lyta ducked behind a row of barrels, pushed the last bite of honeycake into her mouth, and wiped away the sticky crumbs. On her run through the busy kitchen, she'd grabbed two warm cakes from a long rack on a table. The cook had waved a dripping ladle in response to Lyta's hurried thanks.

Now she waited until she could be sure Obela had left the window. Her old nurse would reckon she was going to the stables to see Virr. Since he too was an early riser, Lyta could be sure he was at work. She patted the length of twine in her pouch. If she demonstrated the correct tying of yesterday's knot, Virr would show her a new one. Although he was now their gerentis, the officer in charge of the castle animals and workers, Virr had a nautical background. He'd learned the intricate skill of knot tying from his sea captain father.

'This knowledge might be useful one day,' he'd said as his capable hands twisted the twine. 'Kedie, never pass up the chance to learn something new.'

In the first section of the stables, horses snorted for her attention but Virr wasn't there. Lyta passed through the narrow stone archway that separated the old and new parts. 'Virr!' she called. 'I tied the widow knot.'

She'd started to run left when she skidded to a stop. She recognised the worn brown boots lying on the floor beyond her. Had Virr fallen and been harmed? With an icy sensation growing in her belly, Lyta edged forward and peered around the corner. Virr lay spread across the stones in a pool of bright red blood.

His throat had been cut.

Lyta clapped a hand over her mouth to stop the sour vomit spewing from her lips and swallowed hard several times. When she could keep down the contents of her belly, she drew in a ragged breath and yelled for help. Nin, the head groom, ran from the rear stalls. Stopping beside her, he gaped at the body of his master.

'Holy Serene!' he said. 'What wicked man would slay Virr?' Nin reached out a shaking hand to steady himself against the wall.

Lyta swallowed again and tried to forget that Virr was a friend. She looked more closely at his body. Virr had advised her to examine any difficult situation with detachment. Surely, this was the time to act on his words.

'Tears and complaints don't solve problems, Kedie,' he'd said. 'Find the things that are wrong and then search for logical answers.'

When Nin ran off to fetch the guard commander, Lyta bent down to examine the body. Although tears were close, she forced them back. She owed it to Virr to follow his instructions.

As she bent down, a fly buzzed past her and settled on the neck wound. It was joined by several others. The sight of these insects feeding on Virr's blood was too much for Lyta. She stood up hastily, turned her head, and vomited on the grey stones.

An hour later, Lyta took one sip of a foul potion and then pushed the cup away. Her nurse protested. 'You need to rest, Kedie. Your hands are still shaking.'

Lyta closed her mouth and shook her head. 'But I don't want to rest.'

Instead, she left her bedchamber to run down the tower steps to her workchamber where Tutoran Cordon was reading beside the window. 'I wasn't sure if I would see you this morn, Kedie.' He placed the book on a small table. 'You must be sore distressed by your friend's untimely death.'

Lyta was grateful that he acknowledged her friendship with Virr. Some folk at the castle thought it was unseemly for the daughter of the ruler of their demense to have such close ties with the castle gerentis, a man of lowly birth and a foreigner.

Lyta forced her voice to sound as calm as possible. 'Thanks for your words.' She moved to the window and noticed down below that people were moving through oldgate. 'Where will they take him?'

'His body has been placed in a cold cell. Do you know if he had family in Falga? They may wish to have him back.'

Lyta nodded. 'Virr told me he was raised in the port city of Naris.' Crossing to the large wall hanging, which depicted the five demesnes of Mondalia, she pointed to a spot on the coast.

'I'll pass on that information.' Cordon rubbed his chin where sprouting black hairs struggled to become a beard. 'Do you really want to work today? Under the circumstances, you may be excused.'

'I need to work.' When her knees began to shake, Lyta sank onto a stool. 'Some things weren't right with Virr's body.'

Cordon leaned forward, his face alight with interest. 'What did you note?'

'His amulet was missing. Virr always wore the Asteriki star around his neck. It might've slipped under his body but I didn't see the silver cord either.'

'Anything else?' The tutoran tapped his fingers on the table as he listened.

'His blade wasn't hanging from his belt. It too had a star pattern on the hilt. I wondered if his own blade had been used to cut his throat.'

At this bleak thought, tears welled in Lyta's eyes and she rubbed them away with the back of her hand. 'And I don't understand how someone killed him. Virr was so strong. He'd have fought hard against an attacker.'

'I can answer that question.' The commander told me Virr was hit on the back of his head with a heavy object. He was probably knocked senseless before he was slain.'

'I see.' Lyta took a ragged breath. 'Do you think he suffered?'

Cordon stretched a hand toward hers. 'Fear not. Death would have come fast, Kedie.'

'So who could have done such a wicked thing?' Her voice trembled.

'Mayhap that's something for you to ponder.'

Mayhap the tutoran was right. Lyta leaned her aching head against the cold stone wall and thought for a few minutes. 'Where would I start?'

'Who was in the stables when you arrived there?'

'I saw only Nin but the other grooms and boys must have been there too.' Lyta bit her lip as a thought occurred to her. 'The killer might be an outsider who left before I arrived.'

'True. Unless he waited to see who found the body.'

Lyta shook her head. Fourteen summers hadn't given her any experience with murder and murderers. 'Won't Druck be searching for the killer? He's the castle protector.'

'The commander will be the one to catch the man.' Cordon paused and shuffled his feet. His thin eyebrows knitted together. 'Kedie Lyta, I was too hasty in suggesting that you could study the matter. Let others do that work. You must not put yourself into danger.'

'I won't do anything rash.' Lyta stared at him in an earnest fashion.

The tutoran's frown lines only deepened. 'Please, leave everything to the commander and his men. I should not have put foolish ideas into your head.'

Although Lyta nodded in reply, his words came too late. She had already decided to investigate Virr's death by herself.

Each evening, Lyta visited her mother in the hour before supper when the kedura had completed her daytime duties. As Lyta entered her bedchamber, Halia waved her maids away and held out both white hands. 'I'm so sorry, child. Virr was a fine man and you'll miss him.'

Lyta leaned against her mother's silken side, breathing in the familiar citrus scent of her perfume. She let the tears roll down her cheeks. 'Why would someone kill him?'

'For many reasons. Greed for his possessions. Jealousy over his status. Hatred of foreigners. Who knows which one might be correct.' Putting one arm around her daughter's shoulders, Halia gave her a linen square to dry her eyes. .

Lyta sniffed and blew her nose. She slid her fingers over the smooth emeralds in her mother's bracelet. 'Will Druck find the murderer?'

'He's started the search already,' Halia said as she bent down to fit green satin slippers on her feet. 'Don't fret, child. He'll bring the killer to justice.'

'But how will he find him?'

'Druck's a capable man.' Halia turned Lyta's face to hers. 'You're very pale. Do you wish to dine in your bedchamber this evening?'

The thought was appealing but Lyta had a plan to follow. The guilty man might be eating in the great hall. Could she identify him by the shifty look in his eyes, the restless movements of his hands, and his lack of appetite?

'No, I'll come.'

'Then you'd best change from your grubby tunic.' Halia gave her daughter a gentle push toward the door. 'Go and find Obela. Then when you are dressed, go and visit your aunts.'

Jona and Vea were actually Halia's aunts. Both had come to live at the castle when their husbands died. Lyta found them both in Jona's chamber discussing the latest hanging they were stitching. The women looked up when she opened the door.

'Look at this, child,' said Jona. Her plump face was creased with a frown. 'Does the nose on this horse look right to you?'

Vea snorted. 'I already told you it was fine. And Lyta knows that black horse is obviously Midnight.'

Lyta bent down to examine the hanging, spread across the bed. 'You're making a hanging with horses?'

'It will show Midnight, Nighthawk, and your Silver,' said Jona. 'They'll be running through a meadow of flowers.'

'Trotting, not running,' said Vea.

As only the outline of a black horse had been stitched, Lyta was unable to give her opinion of the piece but she liked the idea of a hanging showing horses. Mayhap it could be placed in her workchamber.

***

During the meal, Lyta sat beside her mother at the head table, moving food around the platter. Even the handsome singer plucking his lute in a new song didn't interest her. Her gaze roamed over the faces of the diners. She knew everyone in the hall and had thought of them as friends. Now she observed a hall full of people who each looked capable of murder.

Later, Obela closed the thick velvet hangings tight around the bed but as soon as she left the chamber, Lyta yanked them back. She liked to watch the long threads of moonlight shimmering across the floor and walls. Her nurse said it was wrong to let Lady Moon shine onto a girl before she'd experienced her first moonblood. Obela had strange old-fashioned ideas which she'd collected from the tales she loved to tell.

Lyta's body ached with tiredness but when she closed her eyes, the grim picture of Virr's body lying in blood filled every corner of her mind. She opened her eyes again and stared at the dancing moonlight, remembering the first time Virr had come to the castle. He'd been standing outside beside the moat as mother and daughter trotted up the hill from a morn ride through the township.

When Virr stepped in front of her horse, Halia pulled on the reins. 'What do you want?' she asked in a sharp tone.

'Your horse, Kedura.' The man pointed. 'His right foreleg troubles him.'

Halia peered down at Midnight's leg. 'He's not been limping.'

'By tonight, that leg will be red and swollen.'

The newgate guard snorted as he jabbed at Virr with his short sword. 'Pay no attention, Kedura. He's a Falgan and you know how they tell lies.'

Halia watched the stranger in his shabby grey tunic and worn boots who ran a gentle hand over Midnight's leg. 'Are you sure of this?'

The man touched the sign around his neck. 'I swear on the Holy Stars.'

She nodded. 'Then follow me. If my horse becomes lame, tend him. But if you want a job in my stables, then you must cure him.'

That was how Virr came to live at the castle. By evening, Midnight's leg was indeed swollen and he was unable to put any weight on it. When the stranger cured the horse, he earned the kedura's gratitude as well as a position in the stables.

Lyta was entranced by Virr's special gifts. The new groom was able to tell if any horse ailed by looking closely at it or by talking to it. 'What did you say to your Courage?'

'I asked about his belly, Kedie.' Virr's eyes twinkled.

'And what was his answer?'

'It pained him.' Virr added a handful of green powder to a pail of warm water. 'This mixture will cure him by morrow morn, Kedie.'

When Virr told Halia that her daughter's pony should be replaced, the kedura listened to his counsel. No matter that Lyta had been begging for a bigger mount for two moons. Virr had fast become the master of all things horse.

Lyta had hoped to replace staid Frisky with fiery Nighthawk, one of Midnight's shining black sons, but Virr shook his head. 'You need a mount with a sweeter nature.' From a side stall, he led a grey mare. 'This horse will serve you well.'

The mare stood still with her eyes fixed on the cobblestones. Unlike Nighthawk, she didn't stamp her feet or toss her head.

Lyta frowned. 'She's as dull as my old Frisky. I want a mount with fire.'

'This mare has better qualities than fire in her belly.' Virr ran a strong hand down the animal's neck. 'Try her and see if I am right. If you are still unhappy in a sevenday, I will accept your judgment.'

Feeling like a fretful child, Lyta allowed Virr to boost her onto the mare's back. She stared down at the gerentis. 'Does this nag have a name?'

'Should you keep this mount, then you name her.'

Within the sevenday, Silver and Lyta became close companions. As Virr had promised, the horse was sweet natured but also resolute and responsive. She was also crazy for apples, nuzzling pockets for them whenever Lyta came to the stables. Even though she'd had grooms and stable boys to tend her horse, Virr had insisted that she learn to look after Silver herself. 'If you are without servants, then you must know what to do,' he said.

Although Lyta couldn't imagine such strange circumstances without grooms or servants, she learned to keep Silver in good stead.

Remembering Virr's care and attention made Lyta feel even more sorrowful. No other man at their castle possessed his wisdom and kindness. He had taken care of her from the second morn of his arrival, almost as if he'd come to Aldeton Castle to protect her.

Hot tears gushed from her eyes when she thought of the empty hours ahead without Virr's company and guidance. How could she manage?

Chapter Two

Next morn, Lyta rubbed her eyes, gritty from lack of sleep and swollen from weeping for Virr. She tried to ignore Obela's grumbles at the sight of the open bed hangings.

'You were sleeping in moonlight again, Kedie. What did I tell you? The Mother's beams are too strong for the young. You'll become a weak woman with trouble bearing children.'

Lyta stayed patient. After all, her old nurse was set in her ways. 'It wasn't moonlight that kept me sleepless. I was remembering Virr.'

Obela had always been scornful of Lyta's friendship with Virr. Halia had explained to her daughter that the nurse's father had been killed by a band of Falgans in a border raid. 'Of course, that raid was in response to an earlier one by an Aldean band but Obela still blames Falgans for his death.'

When Lyta began to visit Virr, Obela had growled, 'The only good Falgan is a dead one.'

Now, recalling that cruel comment, Lyta felt queasy. How many others would have this same reaction to Virr's death? Despite Obela's frowns, she pushed away the platter of fruit and cakes and told the nurse to take the food from her chamber. 'I don't want to eat this morn.'

Lyta also refused to dress. Curled in her nightclothes on a chair by the window, she thought about the stable workers. Nin was the first to be considered. When Virr had arrived at the castle, Nin's nose was put out of joint. He'd been the chief healer of horses and no foreigner deserved to take this valuable position from him.

Nin ridiculed Virr's potions and balms. 'These weak concoctions might work on the nags of Falga but in Aldea, our superior horses need special care.'

He complained about Virr to everyone until people started to avoid him. He was more circumspect with his words to Lyta because he knew of her regard for the Falgan. Things came to a head when Bold, Commander Druck's horse, fell ill.

Nin dosed the animal with his best remedy. 'That will do the trick, Sir. Every horse that has taken this potion has recovered quickly.'

But Bold didn't recover quickly. The horse looked close to death when Virr was called to his side. Lyta, who'd been in the stables at the time, followed him to Bold's stall.

Virr leaned down to talk to the horse and then listened to his reply.

'I understand,' said Virr. He spoke again to Bold.

When Virr stood up, he turned to Druck. 'You must have a plant growing in these parts called Talsy-Bright. It has a small blue flower.'

The commander frowned. 'I've never seen it. Is it poisonous?'

'Only in the spring. Bold has eaten some.'

'Can you cure him?' Druck asked. His bushy eyebrows joined over a pair of anxious dark eyes. 'I've never owned a better mount.'

Virr ran a hand down Bold's quivering hindquarters. 'I will try but he should have been dosed many hours ago.'

Virr saved Druck's horse and earned his appreciation and a purse of silver coins. He also earned Stron's position as head of the stables when the old man died twelve moons later. From there, Virr was awarded the position of gerentis, the officer in charge of all the outside workers and animals at the castle. He had proved to be just as knowledgeable about falcons and hunting dogs as he was about horses.

Recalling this history made Lyta wonder if Nin had continued to hold a grudge against Virr. He'd ceased his grumbling about Falgan remedies but his rancour might have been buried deep inside his heart. After all, he'd probably expected faster advancement in the stable because of his long service at the castle. Then Lyta recalled the groom's distress at seeing Virr's body. But what if that had been feigned? She decided to leave Nin at the top of her list of murder suspects.

Obela interrupted these musings. 'Kedie, your tutoran is waiting in the workroom,' she announced. 'What will I tell him? 'She faced Lyta with folded arms and tightened lips.

Lyta stood and stretched. 'I'll come when I'm dressed.'

Her nurse took a green striped gown and matching surcoat from the clothes chest.

'I'm not wearing that!' Lyta pushed the garments away. 'Get me a clean tunic and hose.'

'Not this day, Kedie.' Obela looked smug. 'Remember the chosen come here for testing this morn. Your lady mother wishes you to receive the children with her in the great hall and take dinner with them. '

Now the day was really spoiled. Lyta hated formal occasions that required good clothes. Giving an enormous sigh, she allowed Obela to remove her nightwear and hand her clean smallclothes. Then the nurse tugged the green gown over Lyta's head and shoulders. The nurse straightened the bodice and tied a ridiculous golden girdle around her waist. 'This gown is a little tight,' Obela said. 'Mayhap, you will grow hips and breasts at last.'

Her comment was the final blow to Lyta's unhappy mood. She knew her freedom to run around the castle would vanish after she experienced her first moonblood.

Her mother had said Lyta would stop being a child on that day. Halia had added, 'Then you'll learn how to rule so that you can be a kedura here or in another demense when you marry a kedir.'

Lyta knew those facts but remembering her mother's words this morn was difficult. Halia had become sole ruler of Aldea when her husband was killed in an early battle of the Freedom War. Since Lyta's mother was comely and young enough to bear more children, she'd received many offers of marriage. She turned them all down. Lyta was her only living child as an older boy had drowned in the harbour. Pushing unwelcome thoughts of ruling and marriage from her head, Lyta shoved her arms into the surcoat and dismissed Obela.

Tutoran Cordon was peering out the window when she entered the workchamber. 'I see that the children have gathered in the courtyard.'

Lyta joined him at his post. About three score children, all seven summers old, stood bunched together on the stones. The faces that she could see showed a mixture of fear and excitement.

'I remember this day well,' said Cordon. 'I'd lived my life in a small village in Delis and had never seen a town or a castle. When I was selected by Magian Domen and his prentices, I was terrified to come here. Older children told me wild stories about the fierce Aldean people and the painful testing.'

'That first testing does hurt,' Lyta said.

'Yes, I felt a stab every time the magian placed his hands on my head but the pain was exceeding brief.'

Lyta recalled her own day. Because of her status, Magian Domen had tested her separately. Halia had told Lyta the results. 'The magian says you have special gifts which could be developed with full training but I don't wish you to follow the path of magic. However you will have some private lessons.'

'Do you regret becoming a prentice magian?' Lyta asked Cordon. 'Ten summers is a long time to train. And you can't marry until you've completed the course.'

Cordon stared at the far wall, his eyes dreamy and unfocused. 'At seven summers, I didn't think about the length of the training. I was exceedingly excited to attend the Erudence for book learning. I was permitted to come home in midsummer for a sevenday.'

His mouth twisted as he recalled his past. 'At first the visits went well but over the next summers, I grew apart from my family. They were glad of the extra coin my position gave them but we no longer understood each other's ways.'

'When did you start your magian training?' Lyta asked.

'At the usual age of fourteen summers. Then Magian Domen selected me to start as your tutoran.' He turned back to the window.

Lyta watched as several prentices in their brown robes led the children from the courtyard. 'They're going inside for the first session,' she said as the group vanished from her view.

'Then we should start to work,' said Cordon. 'Let us continue with the study of the Freedom War when the five demesnes of Aldea, Sevvir, Delis, Parian, and Falga gained their independence.'

Lyta sighed. She didn't want to turn her mind from Virr's death even though the war was a vital part of her land's history. The struggle had begun when Aldea, Sevvir, and Parian rebelled against the tyranny of the ruler at Haven because of his excessive taxation demands. Falga and Delis took the king's side in the fierce fighting that followed. During the four summer conflict, the king and his entire family had been slain. At the peace council, each demesne established its own rulers known as the Kedur and Kedura. Their children were called Kedirs and Kedies.

These new names had been chosen to reflect the new order of governance. For the last ten summers, the land had been peaceful apart from odd skirmishes and border raids.

This morn, Lyta wanted to consider whether Nin could really be Virr's murderer. But that would agitate Cordon. Better to have him believe that she'd given up her own probing. She could ask her mother later if Archis Druck had made any progress.

At noon, Kedura Halia welcomed the children to the castle and bade them to enjoy their dinner. Many children stared open-mouthed at the bright hangings decorating the stone walls, at the shining battle shields hanging from the rafters, at Halia in her richly embroidered robe and shining tiara, and at the servants who handed out platters of meat, cheese, bread and fruit. Some were too over-awed to eat or drink.

While Lyta ate her own meal, she wondered how many of the tested children would be enrolled at the Erudence in Aldeton. After the final testing, those without sufficient talent would return to their own towns and villages. And not every gifted scholar completed book learning either. Some decided they'd rather become farmers, sailors, soldiers, or shopkeepers when they were older while others wished to marry their sweethearts, settle down, and raise families. Then not all prentices endured their next round of rigorous training. As Lyta glanced around the hall, she wondered if the little fair-haired boy at the table to her right and the dark girl beside him would ever become magians.

During the meal, her mother told Lyta that Archis Druck was questioning everyone who worked in the stables and anyone else who had reason to go there. 'He asked me if you could describe what you noticed about Virr. I said you may decide. I don't want his inquiries to distress you further.'

Lyta finished the cider in her cup. 'He can meet me. Did he say when?'

'He suggested the fifteenth hour today.'

Lyta agreed, hoping that during his questions, Druck might let slip some new facts. But before she saw him, she'd visit the stables and talk to the grooms and stable boys. As Lyta was on good terms with them, they might give her information that they hadn't mentioned to Druck.

When Magian Domen and his prentices came into the hall to collect the children, Lyta escaped to the stables. Nobody was visible in the old or new part. She left the stables and followed the pathway to the nearest outside storechamber, hoping to locate Ivil, a stable boy about her age. At the open door, she saw him, carrying a sack of grain. Tabir and Saxo were similarly burdened.

Ivil dropped the sack and wiped sweat from his flushed face. His voice was soft and concerned. 'Kedie, you must be sore upset about Virr.'

'Thanks for your words,' Lyta said shortly, not wanting to become tearful before him. 'Could you tell me where you were yestermorn?'

'We was here from sun up,' he said. 'This grain came in by wagons the morn before and we've been busy since.' He nodded toward the huge pile of sacks outside the open doors.

Lyta perched on a hay bale. 'Then you didn't hear anything or see anyone strange in the stables?'

Ivil shook his head as did the other two. 'Nothing, Kedie.'

'What about the grooms? Were they all here yesterday?'

Tibir wiped his nose on his sleeve. 'Not Regur. He fell from the hay loft and was tended by one of those healing prentices.'

'And mayhap, not Givis,' said Saxo. 'He's courting Rusa from the kitchen. They both slip out sometimes to be together.'

'Yint must have been around as well as Nin. '

'I think so, Kedie. We told these things to Archis Druck.'

Lyta stood up. 'If you think of anything useful, then please tell me.'

Ivil bent down to pick up the next sack. Then he paused with it on his shoulder. 'One of the wagon drivers was new to us.'

'Him with the big nose,' said Tibir with a grin.

'He spoke angry to Virr,' Saxo added, 'and then he drove away.'

A jolt of hope shot through Lyta. 'Did you hear their words?'

Ivil shook his head. 'They was talking out there in the yard. Too far for me to hear.'

'Did the stranger leave with the other drivers?' Lyta asked.

'Don't know, Kedie. Virr saw us watching and sent us back to work.'

Lyta started to leave them but then she turned back. 'Did you tell Druck about this new driver?'

'I didn't,' said Ivil. 'It slipped my mind until you asked about strangers.'

'What about you two?' She turned to Saxo and Tibir.

'No, Kedie,' they chorused, shaking their heads.

Later, Lyta was still thinking about the angry stranger when Archis Druck was escorted to her workchamber. He bowed low before her. 'Thank you, Kedie, for agreeing to receive me.' His broad smile showed a mouthful of square yellow teeth. .

Lyta inclined her head. She'd never liked the man. Her mother said he was thorough and conscientious but

Lyta thought his mouth smiled but not his eyes. And he smiled even more when Halia was nearby, another reason for her wariness.

'Kedie, if it won't distress you unduly, could you please describe what you saw in the stables yestermorn.'

Lyta told her story as clearly as she was able. Mentioning Virr's body brought a lump to her throat and she swallowed twice before she could finish her account.

'Kedie, did you notice if the Star Sign hung around his neck?'

She'd hoped to be the only one who'd observed this fact. 'Wasn't it under his body?'

'The cord had been cut and the sign had gone. Now about his blade, did you see it?'

'It had also vanished.' The commander was behaving like the conscientious man her mother considered him to be.

'I believe the murderer took both.' Archis Druck rubbed his hairless chin. 'When exactly did Nin appear, Kedie?'

'I yelled out and Nin came running.'

'Hmm,' said the commander with a frown. 'Did he seem surprised?'

'He was sore distressed and held the wall for support.'

'I have accounted for all the workers in the stables. Of course, some of them may be lying to save their necks.' When he leaned forward, Lyta drew back. 'Can you tell me anything else, Kedie?'

She shook her head. 'Will you be able to discover the truth?'

This time, his smile was cruel. 'I have ways of getting the truth, Kedie.'

After he'd left, Lyta stayed on her stool, staring at the large wall hanging before her. A lord in rich robes looked down at on a ragged man on his knees. . Both skinny hands of the peasant were clasped before him and his face was anguished as though he begged his master for mercy.

Lyta wondered how merciful the commander might be. She'd surmised that Druck was referring to using torture to gain a confession. But what if none of the stable workers had killed Virr? As a kedie, she was shielded from the dark happenings in the deepest dungeons but Lyta knew enough to suspect that sufficient pain might force a confession from an innocent man.

Chapter Three

Erit stood in the shadow of the whispering trees and peered along the trail. The Dark Forest was bleak and damp at this early hour and he shivered in the sharp breeze that stirred the leaves. He rubbed both hands together to warm them before tucking his frigid fingers into the opening of his leather jerkin.

Cett was late. The man had been reliable so far but this waiting was bothersome. Erit wanted to be sure that Virr was no longer an obstacle to his plans. At a meeting two moons earlier, Erit had tried to persuade Virr to leave the castle at Aldea by promising him a better position in Falga. Then he'd offered a substantial bribe. But the stubborn gerentis shook his head to all offers. As a last resort, Erit had asked Cett to talk to Virr.

Erit smiled as he thought about the lucky strokes that had led him to Cett. Needing an accomplice, Erit had searched for someone with links to Virr. Because he knew of Virr's association with the Star faith, the Asteriki Temple in Avridon had been his starting place. There, he met a skinny novice in a shapeless grey robe who told him an interesting tale.

'It was a real scandal when Virr left Temple,' she said. 'I'd just come here and didn't know what was going on. People were whispering and holding secret meetings.'

'Did Virr leave the priesthood because he did something wrong?' Erit asked. Information about any shady dealings might be useful.

The novice shook her shaved head. 'Nothing like that. They said Virr would be the Chief Star Priest one day. That's why folk were so shocked when he left here.'

'Do you know where he came from?'

'I heard tell it was Naris but I don't know if that's right.'

Erit prised open her hand and slipped a silver coin into it. She looked down at it with her mouth open. Then her body tensed as she stared over his shoulder. 'I must go. They don't like me talking to strangers.'

A tall man in a silver robe swept past Erit and grabbed the girl by the right ear. She flushed bright red and hung her head before she was tugged along the passage.

Erit journeyed next to Naris hoping to get more clues about Virr's background. There, he was fortunate enough to meet Sia, Virr's sister, who still lived in the port town.

Pretending to be an old friend of Virr, Erit tracked the woman down. He'd learned she was married to a prosperous wine merchant. Their house on a rise overlooking the water was large and comfortable and he was shown into a bright solar. Half a dozen noisy brats swirled around them as Erit talked with the woman. Sia was a little suspicious at first but she unbent when Erit spun a believable tale about meeting Virr in the days before he joined the priesthood at Avridon.

'Do you know Cett too,' she asked, swatting away a little girl who clutched Erit's robe with a sticky hand.

Erit nodded, hoping that he wouldn't be asked for details.

'His half-brother,' said Sia. 'Virr and I had the same mother but she died of a fever when I was six summers and Virr was four. Father married again and Cett is her son. He's obviously younger than us.'

'Is he close to Virr?'

Sia glared at two boys who were poking a fat tabby cat with wooden swords. 'Not these days. You see, Cett is exceedingly devout and he was so proud when Virr became a priest. He took it hard when Virr left the Temple. Cett said he dishonoured the family. He searched high and low for Virr to persuade him to return. But our brother had vanished into thin air.'

'So where's Cett these days? I'd like to talk to him about Virr.'

'Then you're in luck. Cett went to sea like our father but his ship has just docked. You'll probably find him in The Black Duck.'

She refilled his cup with wine and Erit thanked her.

Swinging around, Sia grabbed the wooden swords. 'Go outside at once!' She waited until the boys had left the chamber for the courtyard before she continued. 'Cett spends too much time and too much coin at that place. He needs a wife and family to set him on a straight path.'

Erit drank his wine and pushed the cat away with his foot. It was eyeing the last bite of cake on his platter. 'Where will I find the inn?'

As he followed Sia's directions, Erit thought that many a nagging wife had driven her husband to places like The Black Duck. The winding alleys near the harbour smelled of rotting fish and stale ale with a whiff of frying meat. As he trudged along watching where he placed his feet, Erit wondered why so many taverns had connections with birds. Ducks, geese, and swans were popular names for inns in every demesne.

The Black Duck was barely an inn. As Erit came through the door, he summed up the dingy place as a watering hole for seamen. The low rafters and dim light made it difficult to see anyone clearly. Sia had given him one useful clue in his search for Cett. 'We all have a touch of red in our hair like our father.'

Erit squeezed through a bunch of men gathered around an older man telling a story. The tale must have ended with a joke because the listeners all roared with laughter. At the back wall, Erit stopped and looked around, searching for anyone with reddish locks. He hoped Cett hadn't followed the latest fashionable trend of many seamen present and shaved his head.

In the far corner, four men were gathered around a narrow table barely big enough to hold their cups of ale and a flickering candle in a pot. Two men had shaved heads, one had long black curls and the fourth had short hair with a distinctly rusty tinge. That had to be his man. Somehow he had to get Cett alone to discuss his plan.

He took the only empty stool in the chamber and ordered ale from the over-worked barmaid. Although she was wide with a lumpy face, he tried to charm her. If Cett was a regular patron, she might know useful facts about him.

'Some information, my dear?' Erit slid an extra copper coin across the table and was amused by the speed with which it disappeared down the front of her grubby blue blouse.

'What about?' Her thick accent suggested an origin from Delis.

'That fellow in the corner with the red hair. Do you know him?'

The barmaid snorted. 'That's Cett and we know him too well. His temper matches his hair. Landlord's always throwing him out for starting fights. '

If Cett was fast to fight, he'd need special handling. And the man was tall and muscular enough to do some damage in a brawl. As Cett swung around to speak to someone behind him, Erit saw his large nose. Since that was a feature that Virr and Sia had not inherited, it must have come from Cett's mother's side of the family. Erit waited for a chance to get his quarry alone.

Two ales later, the opportunity came. Catt stood up from the table and took his leave along with many farewells and back slaps. Erit followed him out the door and trailed behind him as the seaman wove his way through several back alleys. Erit rehearsed in his mind what he would say to get Cett on his side.

He rounded a corner and was taken by surprise when Cett grabbed his neck and shoved him against a rough wall. 'Why are you following me? I told Ruat he could have his coin in a sevenday.' Cett glared into Erit's eyes and shook him.

As Erit was choking, his voice sounded unnaturally high. 'I don't know Ruat and I know nothing about any coin. I want to talk about your brother, Virr.'

When Cett relaxed the hold, Erit's feet touched the ground again. He rubbed his neck where the edge of his tunic had cut into the flesh.

'What about my brother?' Cett asked. His suspicious gaze had not vanished.

'If you still want to find him, I know where he is.'

Cett rubbed his bristly chin. 'Follow me and we'll talk.'

At the dock, they sat on two old boxes for their conversation, away from anyone who might overhear. Cett was willing to have another chance of changing his brother's mind. 'Once a priest, always a priest,' he said. 'It's not like being a seaman. I can quit my ship and live on land whenever I wish but Virr should have been a priest for life.'

'But what if you can't persuade him to leave his present position and return to the temple?'

Cett shrugged. 'I'll try not to get angry with my brother but I sometimes struggle to stay calm.'

Remembering those words and his recent actions, Erit knew he'd have to keep a close eye on Cett and his temper. He didn't want Virr to be slain, just removed from his role at Aldea castle.

Now he peered again along the misty road and noticed someone coming toward him. Erit's heart sank as he noticed the man's shambling steps and drooping head. Was Cett drunk this early in the morn?

When Cett came close, the reason for his state was obvious. His red eyes and dripping nose showed that he had been weeping for some time. 'What happened?' Erit asked.

For answer, Cett held out a Star symbol on a silver cord. 'He didn't listen to me. I told him that leaving the Temple disgraced our family but he just argued with me. Even said that the Chief Star Priest had given him leave to go. As though I would believe such a wild tale.' He swiped the sleeve of his tunic across his slimy nose and face.

Erit felt his heart sink. 'So what did you do?'

'I grabbed his blade and... The man broke into rasping sobs and buried his head in his large hands. The Star symbol fell to the ground.

Erit could finish the sentence for himself. Cett had killed his brother for the sake of family pride. He forced down a quiver in his body at the very idea of Virr's blood being shed. 'Why did you take the star?'

Between loud sniffs, Cett said, 'He wasn't worthy to keep it.'

Erit picked up the sign and studied the costly-looking piece. It was solid silver and heavily embossed. 'You should have left it with the body.'

Cett slumped against a nearby tree trunk and wiped his flushed face on the edge of his blue tunic.

Erit scratched his head. 'Did anyone see you?'

'The stables was empty.'

'What about the other days when you drove the grain wagon into the castle?'

Cett thought for a moment. 'One of those grooms saw me arguing with Virr. He had long black hair. But he was too far away to hear what we said.'

'We must be sure he heard nothing and said nothing.'

‘And I took Virr’s blade,’ said Cett. His voice shook as he pulled the weapon from his belt. ‘This belonged to my father and I wasn’t leaving it for those Aldean bastards.’

Erit placed a hand on Cett’s right shoulder. ‘You need a drink. Let’s drown your sorrows at The White Swan. The ale’s on me.’

Chapter Four

Lyta hadn't ridden Silver since Virr was killed. He'd always accompanied her along with four guardsmen on any outings. Her mother wouldn't let her ride alone with Virr in case they were attacked by men unfriendly to Falgans. This morn, Silver definitely needed exercise. Lyta found Regur brushing the horse's back and rump. The groom's eyes were puffy and rimmed in red.

'What's the matter?' Lyta asked. 'Does your leg still pain you?'

Regur shook his head.

Lyta looked for her usual groom. 'Where's Givis?'

'Gone, Kedie,' he muttered.

'Gone where?'

'I don't know, Kedie. When the guards came to take him for more questions, we found he left us in the night.'

Lyta chewed her lip. Had Druck decided that Givis might be the guilty man? She didn't believe it. She'd often seen Virr and Givis talking together and the groom seemed closer to his master than anyone else in the stables. What reason would Givis have for murder? But then, why would an innocent's man leave the castle under the shelter of darkness?

'Did Givis take his belongings with him?'

'No, Kedie.'

'Was Aldea his demesne?'

Regur sniffed. 'He came from Sevvir.'

And mayhap the groom was already on his way back there. 'Get Silver ready for me and inform Archis Druck that I wish to ride.' She thought of something else.

'Did you see a stranger around the stables two morns since?'

'No, Kedie, but Givis told us he saw a fellow who talked like a Falgan.' He sniffed again. 'I'll ready Silver for you.'

Two guardsmen rode before Lyta and two behind. Beyond the arched newgate, they made their way across the drawbridge and turned left through open pasture bordering the Dark Forest before following the track to her favourite glade. She blinked in the sudden sunlight of the open space. Several types of bright wildflowers and clumps of green ferns grew here and she often picked slender stems of Purple Salvan to decorate her mother's bedchamber. This morn, Salvan was not blooming and heads of pink Lady's Lips lay dry and withered on the grass.

Her ride was sad and solitary without Virr. In the past, Lyta had chatted about anything that entered her head and he'd answered in his deep steady voice. Even Silver seemed to miss him. She kept turning her head as though she expected to see Virr mounted on Courage, his big bay, riding beside them. Lyta wondered who would ride Courage now. As a horse with definite notions, he wouldn't easily tolerate a new owner. If she could talk to Virr's horse, mayhap she could explain what had happened to his master.

When the riding party returned to the castle, she went along the stalls to see Courage. He whinnied in welcome. Lyta stroked his smooth back; at least someone was still grooming him. Courage laid his large head against her shoulder. 'What will happen to you?' She didn't realise she had spoken the words aloud until the horse snorted in reply. Did Courage try to speak or was her mind playing tricks?

'You know Virr is dead?' Lyta asked.

Courage nodded.

'Someone killed him.'

The horse's large brown eyes stared into hers. 'Do you understand me?'

Her heart raced with excitement as the horse again nodded his head. Although she wasn't sure Courage understood, she was thinking of more questions to ask him when she heard footsteps.

'Courage misses his master,' said Nin, arriving beside them.

'Has anyone ridden him since Virr died?'

'We tried,' said Nin with a scowl. 'Regur, Yint, and me. He tossed us all off.' He frowned. 'I have the bruises to prove it.' Nin pushed straw back into the stall with his boot. 'I intend to ask your lady mother if we can sell him. He should fetch a good price.'

Lyta gasped. 'You can't sell Virr's horse!'

Nin's eyes were hard. 'Virr's dead, Kedie, and we can't keep Courage here if nobody can ride him. He's too expensive to feed and tend.'

He stalked along the row toward Midnight's stall.

Lyta drew her fingers along Courage's soft nose and whispered to him, 'I'll try to keep you here.' As she left the stable, she reflected that Nin was again at the top of her list of suspects for Virr's murder.

Tutoran Cordon was waiting in her workchamber. 'Did you have a pleasant ride?' He pushed Lyta's stool close to her.

'It was dull without Virr.'

'I have some news for you, Kedie. Magian Domen has been in touch with Magian Gila of Falga. Apparently Virr has a sister in Naris who wants his body returned.'

Virr had never mentioned a sister but then he hadn't talked about his life. All she knew was that his father had been a sea captain.

Her tutoran went on. 'Your lady mother is arranging to have Virr sent to his family as soon as possible.'

Lyta wished she could accompany her friend on his last journey but it wouldn't be appropriate. Virr had started as a groom at her mother's castle even if he had risen to a greater position. And Falga could sometimes be inhospitable to folk from her demesne.

Cordon pulled her mind back to her lesson. 'Kedie Lyta, we must work. This morn I'd like to finish our study of the war. Do you remember the order of the early battles?'

Lyta recalled the names from memory before agitated voices outside stopped her recitation. She rose and stepped to the window to discover the cause of the commotion. Four guardsmen were carrying something wrapped in a large canvas sheet. As she wondered about their burden, a white arm fell from the covering. 'It's a body' she said in a half whisper.

'A body?' Cordon joined her at the window. 'That certainly looks like one. Who else could have died?'

'Mayhap Givis didn't run away last night.'

Tutoran Cordon fingered his chin as he always did when he was thinking. 'I heard that Givis was missing but we don't know he's dead.'

When Archis Druck marched across the yard waving his arms, the guardsmen changed direction and made for newgate. Outside the kitchen, a cluster of workers huddled together watching the guards' movements. Lyta had to know who had died. Disregarding her tutoran's protests, she ran from the chamber. His shrill voice called her name as she jumped down the steps, taking two at a time.

Loud sobs came from a girl who lay against the shoulder of an older woman in a green kerchief. Other women gathered around the two were making noises of sympathy.

'Is Rusa here?' Lyta asked as she reached them. When the group parted, she could see a skinny brown-haired girl who was wiping her streaming eyes and nose on her apron.

She looked up. 'Yes, Kedie, I'm Rusa.'

Since Lyta didn't recognise the face, she assumed the girl must be a new worker in the kitchen. 'I'm sorry to upset you but was that Givis being carried across the courtyard?'

'Yes, Kedie. My Givis is dead. They said he was killed by a blade.' She crumpled forward in a new torrent of tears. Unable to think of any comforting words, Lyta patted her back. She noticed Prala, the head cook, striding toward the little group.

'Be gentle with Rusa,' Lyta told the cook. 'She mourns her friend.'

Prala snorted; her face was the same red as the kerchief on her greying hair. 'Kedie, she's too young to mourn for a groom. I told her to stay away from that Givis.' She turned to her workers. 'All of you, back to the kitchen. We have dinner to prepare.'

Lyta watched as Rusa was led away by two women. Then she sighed and returned to the tower.

Tutoran Cordon's face was pink with anger. His eyes flashed as he reprimanded his student. 'Do not concern yourself with bodies, Kedie. You must fill these hours with valuable learning.'

'But the castle folk are my concern. When I'm a kedura, I must know what is happening with my people'

'That morn has not yet come,' he said in a cold voice. 'I shall not report you to your mother this time but if you desert your studies again, I shall have no choice. Now back to our lesson.'

Lyta took great pains to please her tutoran for the rest of the time and he was looking less disapproving when he rose to leave. At the door he turned back. 'Remember your meeting with the magian after your dinner. Do not be late or let yourself be distracted by bodies or any other matters.'

Chapter Five

From the window of her workchamber, Lyta could just see the magian's dwelling, set beside the right wall. She hadn't forgotten about the lesson. Now, she enjoyed the hours with the magian but her first visit to his home was a trial. She'd walked through the gate and along the path lined with rows of fragrant herbs, with her stomach knotted with anxiety. Lyta raised her hand to the brass knocker shaped like a bear's head and swallowed hard. Obela's stories had given her a vivid picture of a magian's workchamber: a gloomy place with hanging cobwebs and rows of sinister purple potions in dusty flasks. Unseen creatures would scuttle in dark corners and strange smells would scent the air.

She should have known better. Obela's magians were ancient men with white beards straggling past their waists, blinking eyes and quavering voices. Magian Domen had an unlined face, sharp blue eyes, grey, neatly-trimmed hair and a hairless chin. His interior space was bright, lit by windows on two sides with the tools of his trade arranged neatly on wooden shelves. When she'd finally been brave enough to step into the workchamber, Lyta had looked for the mysterious hyala. She noticed only a dark cloth covering a large oval object on a table by the west window.

On that first lesson, Magian Domen motioned Lyta to a stool by the table and sat down opposite her. 'Kedie, I know you have talents and your mother has agreed to let me develop them.'

Lyta stared back at him, unsure of his meaning.

'You can move objects with your mind, an art know as lofting.'

Her eyes widened. She didn't think anybody knew about this power. She'd told only Virr her deep secret, sure he wouldn't tell another soul.

Magian Domen placed a white goose feather on the table. 'What can you do with this? Don't use your breath.'

Lyta concentrated on the feather until it lifted from the surface and then drifted into the magian's hand. He nodded before replacing the feather with a small wooden cube. This object was harder to move and took more willpower.

'Now try this.'

He placed a grey stone on the table. Now Lyta would need all her mental strength. She hardly breathed as she willed the stone to slide. It moved, stopped and then slid a little further. She looked up at the magian, expecting to see disappointment on his face but he was nodding at her.

'You did well, Kedie. Moving any of these objects without training shows a special gift.' He reached behind his stool and lifted a flask. 'You must be thirsty after that effort.'

How did he know? Lyta was always thirsty after she'd moved objects. She must have looked doubtful as he handed over a goblet filled with golden liquid. 'It's fruit juice and quite delicious.'

She sipped the juice. It was delicious, sweet, and tangy at the same time.

Since that first day, Lyta had studied regularly with the magian. Domen had taught her to move all manner of objects with her mind. One day, she'd asked if she could be taught to use the hyala but the magian shook his head.

Since Domen had remained close-lipped about the exact purpose of the hyala, Lyta asked her tutoran for more information. Cordon said the hyala was made from stone, ancient and special, mined from an extinct volcano in the central highlands of Aldea. Then the pieces were polished to a high sheen by trained craftsmen 'All the magians in our land must come here to purchase their hyalas. Then because the power of the stone starts to wane after ten summers, they need a replacement. Our demesne has profited from this trade.'

Magian Domen had said only that his hyala was exceeding heavy and had needed the strength of four men to move into his workchamber and then set in place. 'No man will ever take it from here but it's going to be a problem when I must get a new one.'

Although Cordon had not explained the workings of a hyala, Lyta suspected that it was used to contact magians in other desmenses. She often wondered how magians used their hyalas and what magic was involved.

This day when she knocked on the magian's door, his voice told her to enter. She glanced at the table but to her surprise it was empty. 'What are we studying?'

'Patience is a great virtue, child,' he said.

'Tutoran Cordon always tells me not to rush. But I hate to sit and do nothing at all.'

'Then this lesson may be a sore trial. You'll spend your time sitting and thinking exceeding hard. Get comfortable while I prepare my part.'

Lyta didn't dare say how much his words displeased her. Instead, she sighed inside, wishing that they were continuing any of her previous studies. While she waited for the magian to explain her new lesson, Lyta recalled her most recent study of herbs and basic healing arts. She'd learned the names and uses of all the herbs and flowers the magian grew around his workchamber. To test her, he held up a green sprig and asked for its name and healing qualities.

When she recalled them correctly by appearance, he made her close her eyes and identify them by smell and touch. That was difficult with some of the less fragrant herbs.

Lyta progressed to the stage when she could mix simple potions. Magian Domen told her the knowledge could be useful when she became a Kedura.

'All my prentices are well trained in healing,' he said, 'but you might want to be sure that an ailing person is receiving the correct treatment. Tell me what you would mix for a belly ache from eating too many green apples?'

'A combination of dried Well-Light and Salusy.'

'In what strength?'

'Two parts Well-Light and one part Salusy. Then I'd add a sprig of Caldan for flavour when I heated the potion.'

Magian Domen had nodded, the highest form of praise he gave her.

But this day, Lyta wouldn't be mixing and heating. Sitting and thinking sounded dull and tedious. Turning to face her at last, the magian said, 'I know you can loft objects. Some people with this gift can also loft and catch thoughts.'

Lyta regarded his face with sudden attention. This lesson might be interesting after all.

The magian went on. 'The training is difficult. We'll start with catching.'

He asked Lyta to close both eyes and empty her mind. This skill she'd been practising every time she lofted objects. 'Now I am going to turn around again and hold something in my mind. Its name may come to you.'

Lyta did as he ordered. Then she waited to receive his message. Nothing happened for a long time and she was ready to confess failure when she noticed a tiny spark flickering at the edge of her mind. She opened her eyes. 'Something happened. I saw a little light.'

Magian Domen nodded. 'This means your mind might be receptive but we will need to be exceedingly sure. Close your eyes again.'

This time, the spark was larger. 'I saw a flame,' she said.

'Are you weary?' the magian asked.

Lyta tried to smother a yawn. 'A little.'

'Then what should you take as a stimulant?'

Lyta stood up and traced a finger the row of flasks. 'This one. Green Grantax will revive me.'

Magian Domen handed her a little wooden cup. 'Take a small dose.'

After she'd swallowed the potion, she sat down and again emptied her mind. A flame appeared instantly and burned with a steady light. 'That message was definitely about fire.'

He nodded. 'It's one of the easier thoughts to send and receive.'

'Will I ever be able to understand words?'

'One day you might learn that skill.'

'What about understanding the thoughts of animals. Virr knew what they were thinking. And he could even understand birds and dogs.'

'Virr was exceeding gifted. He was once a priest of the Asteriki.'

Lyta shook her head. 'Then why did he come here to work for my mother?'

'He must have had good reason. Virr never did anything lightly.'

After the lesson, Lyta pondered the magian's words as she closed his gate. It made little sense for a priest of the Asteriki to give up power and position to become a simple groom. What had brought Virr to the castle? And did someone know why he'd come and prevent him from carrying out his true purpose? Once more, she wished she'd questioned Virr about his earlier life.

Instead of going to her chamber, she went to the stable storechambers. Ivil, Saxo, and Tibir were placing the last sacks of grain inside. Saxo ran a hand through his damp hair. 'Done at last. We can rest now.'

Ivil snorted. 'If Nin sees us doing nought, he'll give us new tasks.'

'Will he be the new gerentis, Kedie?' Tibir asked. He sank down on a hay bale and swung his dusty legs.

'That's my mother's decision,' she answered.

Ivil frowned. 'Nin's not half the man Virr was.'

'What can you tell me about Givis,' Lyta asked. 'When did he die and where was his body found?'

'The Commander thinks he died last night. His body was lying at the end of the grazing fields, Kedie. Past the Cold Spring by the outer wall.'

'Rusa said he was slain with a blade.'

Ivil nodded. 'Like Virr. But this blade went into his heart.'

'Was Givis a Star Child?' Lyta asked.

'No, Kedie,' said Saxo. 'He was one of us Moon Folk.'

Lyta still couldn't understand why Givis was killed. Was it because of his friendship with Virr? Ivil peered over his shoulder and then leaned closer to Lyta. 'Nin told us poor Givis killed Virr and then himself.'

'Is that what you believe?'

Ivil looked around again to see if anybody had come near. He shook his head. 'Not Givis. He didn't even like killing the rats in the storechambers.'

After Lyta left the stable boys, she went to talk to Rusa. The kitchen was its usual steamy, noisy place. Cooks yelled at kitchen boys and girls who scurried back and forth carrying food and pots. She couldn't see Rusa but Prala was standing at one of the long tables brandishing a knife. 'Where's Rusa?' Lyta asked.

Prala dabbed her sweaty face with the edge of her spotted kerchief. She waved the knife toward the open door. 'You'll find the little fool outside. She cried so much over the fruit pies that she made the tops soggy. Send her back here when you're done talking, Kedie.' She added as Lyta turned away, 'And command her to stop bawling in my kitchen.'

Rusa was a sad little figure huddled beside the row of barrels. The kitchen maid was sobbing loudly. When Lyta placed a hand on her shoulder, Rusa jumped and then raised a drowned face. 'You must have loved Givis exceedingly much,' Lyta said.

Rusa nodded. 'We was going to be wed next summer.'

'Did he talk about Virr?'

Although Rusa's tears had stopped, her next words were interrupted by muffled hiccups. 'All the time, Kedie Lyta. Givis wanted to be just like Virr, knowing about horses and suchlike.'

'Did he take up the Star faith?'

Rusa shook her head. 'Oh, no. Givis had joined Lady Moon to be like me and mine. But he said there was much good about the Asteriki when Virr telled him about it.'

Lyta hesitated before asking the next question. 'Did Givis mention a stranger who was asking for Virr?'

'Yes, Kedie. A rude man who spoke angry words to Virr.'

'Did Givis hear any of those words?'

'He didn't mean it, Kedie, but when the stranger spoke loud, Givis heard him talk about a plot.'

'A plot? To do what?'

'Givis didn't hear no more. They seen him near and Virr sent him to the old stable.'

Lyta's mouth dried suddenly. A plot was a serious matter. 'Was the stranger from Falga like Virr?'

'Givis said they talked the same.' Rusa clutched Lyta's arm. 'Do you think the stranger killed my dear Givis? And poor Virr?'

'I don't know, Rusa.'

Since the girl had stopped crying, Lyta sent her back to the kitchen. Sitting on a barrel, she pondered Rusa's words. Some solid facts about a plot would be helpful. What scheme was the stranger proposing? And was Virr slain because he wouldn't go along with the plan? And how were the Asteriki of Falga connected? This string of questions with no obvious answers made her head ache.

Next morn, Lyta raised the matter of Falga with Tutoran Cordon. 'I don't really know enough about this demesne. And it is our close neighbour.'

Cordon almost purred with satisfaction as he smiled at his student. Imparting information was his favourite activity. 'Ask away. What would you like to know?'

'Why is there such bad blood between us and Falga?'

'The main reason is that some Falgan lords still blame us for starting the Freedom War. Erle Rurrik for one has remained bitter. He made a false claim to your mother's throne through some obscure ancestor. Your grandfather was a prime mover in starting the conflict. He rode the land encouraging protest against the injustices of the old king. He was a fine speaker but also admired for his fighting prowess.'

'I've always liked his portrait in the great hall,' said Lyta. 'He looks exceeding fine in his silver battle armour.'

Cordon nodded. 'They say he was an impressive leader and your father was like him.'

Lyta reflected that she knew little about both men but now wasn't the time to ask more. 'I'd like to know about the Asteriki. Virr was a Star child.'

Cordon frowned. 'Kedie, you do realize it is not a true faith. Only Mother Moon can guide and protect us. Virr lived in error.'

'But he was a good man and I'd like to learn about his beliefs. If I am knowledgeable, then I may not fall into the same error.'

She waited to see if Cordon had taken the bait. He smoothed down his beard fluff and leaned back against the wall. 'Very well. The Stella Temple in Avridon is the centre of their so-called religion. That is where their priests are trained. I understand that there is a large map of the heavens on its ceiling. Those who have ventured into the building say the workmanship is quite fine.'

'Do the Asteriki worship all the stars?'

'Their faith regards the morning and evening stars as the main guides through life but the others have their special functions. For example, one star is said to promote healing while another assists children in their learning. Of course, we know that is all nonsense. No proof exists that stars do anything more than twinkle in the sky.' Cordon touched the shining Moon symbol that dangled from his scrawny neck. 'I hope that hearing these facts will convince you that the Lady Moon is our only true guide.'

While he talked, Lyta had been thinking that some Star believers might say that the moon did nothing more than shine and sail across the sky but she'd better not voice those thoughts to Cordon. They would provoke a torrent of arguments as he tried to make her understand her mistake. He was a fervent believer. Mayhap, the tutoran would have been happier as a Moon priest rather than a prentice magian.

When her tutoran left for his dinner, Lyta's mind drifted back to Virr. Did he come to Aldea to convert folk to his faith? She'd never heard of anyone at the castle changing their allegiance from Lady Moon to the Stars. Lyta had the nagging feeling that there was a connection between Virr and his faith, and the so-called plot. But what was it?

Chapter Six

When Lyta entered her mother's chamber, Amia was holding up two gowns. 'Wear the light blue with its dark blue surcoat,' Lyta suggested.

Halia raised her eyebrows. 'I didn't know you cared about gowns.'

'Well, I don't but I do know what looks good on you.'

Even though Halia was aged one score and eleven summers, she was still beautiful with her unblemished white skin and red-gold hair. It was hanging in loose curls now but when she was dressed, she'd wear her hair coiled on her head under a small crown. Amia slipped the blue gown over Halia's head. The maid added the embroidered surcoat, adjusted the fastenings, and then tied the braided silver girdle.

'Leave us,' the kedura told Amia. 'I wish to talk to my daughter.'

With a serious face, she drew Lyta close. 'Archis Druck has solved Virr's murder. The groom, Givis, killed him out of rage. Then in a fit of remorse, he took his own life.'

'Do you believe Druck?'

'The explanation sounds reasonable. The other grooms said that Givis was always complaining about the tasks that Virr gave him. He grew angry about being prevented from breaking in the young horses.'

Lyta knew that wasn't true. Virr had often commented to her on Givis's skill with horses. But now, she held her tongue, intent on hearing more.

Halia went on. 'Druck hasn't told anyone except me about the conclusive piece of evidence and I want you to be silent about it too.'

'What was it?' Lyta knew her voice sounded sceptical.

'Virr's missing Star sign was found in the groom's pouch.'

Lyta was surprised. Mayhap her theory had been wrong but she was not convinced that the groom was a murderer. Nothing she'd ever seen or heard supported this story. Givis was an excellent rider and she had observed him on several occasions calming a young nervous colt. Besides, couldn't Virr's murderer have placed the Star amulet in Givis' pouch after he'd slain the groom? The other grooms had concocted a tale to avoid suspicion falling on them. She wondered if Druck had asked the stable boys if they too agreed with the conclusion.

'I am glad the sad matter is settled,' Halia said as she patted her daughter's hand. 'And your friend Virr is on his way to his sister in Naris.'

'That's good,' said Lyta. She sat in silence for a while. 'Mother, have you ever been to Avridon?'

Halia glanced at her. 'Once, many moons ago when your father was alive. Why do you ask?'

'Tutoran Cordon said it's the home of the Asteriki priesthood.'

'Even though I'm not a Star child, I found the Temple was an impressive building and the ceiling is wonderfully made.' Her mother stood up. 'Now, child, put on a respectable gown for supper. And send Amia back here to arrange my hair.'

Lyta stood still. 'Before I go, I want to ask you again about Courage. Can't we keep him here at the castle?'

Halia frowned. 'We've already had this conversation. If nobody can ride the horse, then it's pointless to keep him.'

'When I grow taller, I'll ride him.'

'And what happens to the horse until then? No, Lyta, my mind is made up. We'll keep Courage until the next council meeting. One of our erles might want him.'

When Lyta didn't move, her mother waved a white hand. 'Off you go.'

Next morn, after repast, Lyta went down to the stables. Regur was brushing out Silver's tail. 'I hear that Archis Druck has decided that Givis killed Virr.'

Regur's fair-skinned face turned bright red. He kept his eyes glued to the brush and muttered some words.

'I didn't hear you,' Lyta said. She knew her voice sounded curt.

'It's a sad story,' he murmured. 'Poor Givis.'

'A story is exactly what it is. I know that Virr and Givis were friends.'

Regur kept his brown eyes lowered. 'With much respect, Kedie, you don't know everything what goes on down here.'

Although Lyta stared hard at him, the groom refused to look up. She sighed. 'Tell Archis Druck I'm ready to ride.'

Regur disappeared from the stables like a flash of lightning. She was glad to have made him feel uncomfortable. He needed to know that not everyone accepted the tale invented by the commander and the stable workers.

This morn, the riding party trotted toward the town. More people than usual were bustling about the grassy central square, setting up stalls and calling greetings and instructions to each other. Tomorrow was Moonfest, celebrated once at the summer solstice and again at the winter solstice.

At the edge of the square, a wiry fellow in a crimson cap pranced before Lyta's horse, juggling three apples. When she halted Silver, he added a fourth and then a fifth. The apples spun in the air in a mad red dance. He laughed when he caught her eye and threw an apple toward her.

She reached out but one of the guards snatched it instead. 'Kedie, you don't know if the fruit is good,' he said.

Lyta was forbidden to eat food outside the castle unless someone else had tasted it first. Just once, she'd like to be the girl with curly brown hair watching the juggler. That girl caught another of the apples and bit into it. But when Lyta looked at her ragged tunic and dirty feet, she decided it might be wiser to stay herself.

The riders moved through the township. The way was busy with carts and wagons full of goods coming for the Feast Day. Folk on foot were trudging along burdened with sacks and baskets. Amia had told her that clothes, trinkets, ribbons, and cooked food like pies could all be bought at the fair. Lyta imagined the fun she'd miss the next day. When she was kedura, she'd attend every fair, and sample all the food on offer.

Lyta pointed left towards the port and her escort changed direction. She always liked the sharp smells of seaweed and fish and the sounds of the place. This morn, men unloaded two sailing ships. The seamen worked with much yelling and laughing as they carried the containers ashore. What did those boxes and barrels contain? Food and drink no doubt but mayhap, spices from Delis and strong cotton cloth from Sevvir.

Shading her eyes, Lyta peered towards the coast of Falga and could just make out the outline of a row of blue hills. 'How is Falga from here?' she asked Borut, the head guard.

'About a day's sailing,' he replied.

Lyta gave the order to return home. Back at the stables, Yint helped her to dismount and took Silver. He was hurried and seemed anxious not to speak with her. Nin was nowhere in sight but she assumed that he would be equally unwilling to discuss the murders. Before she left the stables, Lyta walked along the stalls to visit Courage. The horse was listless and unresponsive to her greeting. Next time, she'd bring him carrots or apples. Her mind and heart were heavy as she left the horse.

As usual, Cordon was waiting in her workchamber. When he asked about her ride, Lyta described the fair preparations in the town.

He sniffed. 'Moonfests used to be holy times. Now people gabble fast prayers to our Serene Mother and then spend the rest of the day carousing and forgetting her.'

At times, her tutoran sounded like an elderly man and not someone only four summers older than Lyta. 'Do you want to become a magian one day?' she asked him.

Cordon frowned. 'If Mother Moon wills that to be my fate, then let it be.' He reached for a book. 'To our studies. Tell me the terms of the treaty at the end of the Freedom War.'

Lyta knew some of the terms of the treaty. The five demesnes had become independent and each Kedur and Kedura had sworn to keep the peace. They formed a joint council, which met every three summers to discuss any matters that might lead to conflict.

'What happened to those who fought in the war?' Cordon asked.

'The erles and their men at arms returned to their own estates. Then they took an oath to stay peaceful and loyal to their respective rulers. The lords of Aldea hold their own council with my mother twice each twelvemoon.'

Lyta enjoyed the council time when the four nobles arrived. Her two favourites were Lord Quilin of Highridge and Lord Wilus of Rellhaven. The former was young and handsome with an engaging smile, twinkling grey eyes, carefully arranged hair, and fashionable clothes. Erle Wilus was old and jovial. He wore plain grey tunics and wrinkled hose and his hair stuck up from his head in tufts. When Lyta was a child, he'd produce wooden toys from his waist pouch, and when she grew older, he plucked coins from her ears or hair. The other two, Trevin of Belltowers and Josik of Edgemere were serious men who bowed over her hand and murmured formal greetings. Lyta didn't attend the council meetings yet but she did attend the feasts and the jousting tournaments often held at the same time.

After her lesson, Lyta sat in the sun outside the keep. She reached into her own pouch where she felt the length of twine twisted into the widow knot. She pulled it out, undid the knot and tried to remake it. Lyta couldn't remember whether the length in her right hand went over or under the piece in her left hand. In disgust at her forgetfulness, she threw the twine down and ground it beneath her boot. Who would teach her useful things now that Virr was gone? The thought drew hot tears from her eyes. She'd never forget him and his kindness. Virr had been like a father and nobody else at the castle could ever take his place.

As soon as Lyta woke next morn, she sniffed the air, dense with the smells of Moonfest food. The special cakes dotted with sweet dried fruit and nuts were her favourite. Huntsmen had brought in deer and wild boar from the forest and she could smell the flesh roasting on the long kitchen spits. To celebrate the occasion, their main meal would be eaten at night instead of midday.

Before repast, Lyta joined her mother and her officers in the chapel where Elon, their Salvan, conducted the Holy Moon service. The priest resembled a magian in a tale with his long beard and squinting eyes. She knew that Halia sometimes grew impatient at the long prayers he conducted especially as he mumbled his words and often spat on people in front of him. However the kedura was unlikely to force the man to give up his position until he was too feeble to stumble from his chamber into the chapel.

After eating her moon cakes, Lyta went outside. Because of the feast, she didn't have to study. From the kitchen, she heard Prala's loud voice directing her army of workers. The head cook would permit half her staff to attend the fair this day while the others would go to the next scheduled one. Prala was careful to keep back enough workers to finish cooking the lavish food for the night banquet.

Ivil, Saxo, and Tibir waved at her as they hurried toward the gate. Each boy was wearing his good tunic and coloured hose. As gerentis, Virr had made sure that everyone under his care had special garments for feast days as well as everyday clothing. Ivil who came from a poor village in the north of Aldea had been overcome with delight at receiving special clothes.

'I never had two tunics at once in my whole life, Kedie,' he'd told Lyta once. 'Stron didn't notice until our bare bums showed through the cloth.'

The day dragged on. Lyta tried to read for a while and then gave up. After her midmeal, she strolled toward Magian Domen's dwelling where he was bent over plants in his garden. He bade her enter the gate. 'You can weed my Salusy, Kedie, if you have the time.'

Weeding wasn't Lyta's favourite task but it was better than doing nothing. She knelt down beside the herbs to yank out the straggly yellow weeds threatening to overcome the silver fronds of Salusy. She'd tidied almost all the rows of herbs before she stood up, stretching to remove the creaks from her back. After the magian thanked her for the hard work, she wandered into the courtyard and sat in the sunshine.

She was roused from her daydream of riding Courage through the Dark Forest when she heard the voices of workers returning from the fair. Lyta looked at her dirty arms and hands. She'd need a bath to meet her mother's standards for her appearance in the great hall. As she reached the keep steps, Lyta heard someone calling her name. She turned around to see Ivil beckoning to her. The excited expression on his face told her he had an urgent message to impart.

Since the stable boy had vanished through oldgate, she followed him into the dusty interior of a storechamber. Ivil looked around to see if anyone could overhear his words before he spoke. 'Kedie Lyta, I seen that driver with the big nose again. He was talking to a fellow in a red cap. Then they stopped their chat and went into The White Swan.'

'Did you follow them?'

'I peeped inside but they went up the stairs.'

Lyta leaned against the wall while she thought about this new information. If a plot actually existed, then more than one person might be involved in it. 'Will you tell Druck about these two men?'

Ivil shook his head. 'Just you.'

'But this news might be important.' Lyta tried to convey her concern.

Ivil shook his head again. 'I can't say nothing to nobody else.'

'This man might have killed Virr and Givis.'

'No matter, Kedie. I goes along with what the Archis said about Virr and Givis. To be a groom, I must keep in good with Nin.'

Lyta sighed, knowing she couldn't spoil Ivil's chance of advancement. 'I understand. Thank you for telling me this news.'

***

The noise in the great hall was so loud that it was impossible to have a normal conversation with the person beside you. Lyta sat at the head table along with Mother and her officers. The old Salvan nodded over his platter with his stringy hair drooping into the gravy on his roast meat. Druck was seated next to Halia, his head bent toward her, intent on every word she uttered. A red-haired singer finished his last bawdy song too much laughing and cheering and stepped back to allow another entertainer to take his place.

Lyta sucked in her breath as the apple juggler in his crimson hat ran toward them. He was tossing platters into the air, catching each one neatly by the edge. Dropping the platters into a tall stack on the floor, he pulled out a handful of shining knives from his pouch. As they spun high above him, the firelight was reflected in the sinister silver blades, a stark reminder of the weapon used for murder. Lyta wanted to shout a warning that this man might be dangerous but what would she say?

The kedura leaned forward smiling at the juggler. She threw a coin which he caught between his lips. He bowed low as he tucked the coin and blades into his pouch. 'Much thanks, Kedura.' His voice was low and clear with the ring of an educated man. Lyta wondered if the juggler could be a spy. Was he involved in a plot directed at her mother?

When a fight broke out between two guards at the back of the hall, Druck strode down to separate the struggling men. Halia stood up and turned to her daughter. 'This hall is no longer a suitable place for you,' she said. They left the high table.

Lyta said goodnight to her mother before following her guard, Jer, to her own tower chamber. The flickering light from the burning rush carried by him cast wavering shadows on the grey walls. Obela stumbled from her cot in the alcove by the door. 'You must be sore tired, Kedie,' she said with an enormous yawn.

Jer walked into the bedchamber and looked behind every hanging to make sure nobody lurked there. Then he nodded and left. Lyta heard his feet descend the stone steps and knew she could sleep safely with him on watch. He alternated guard duty with his brother, Kel.

Chapter Seven

Was the man always late? Erit looked up and down the alley. Surely an experienced seaman would have a strong sense of time. He needed this skill to plot a course on the high sea or even to board his ship before it sailed.

Other men and women passed him but there was no sign of Cett. Erit knew the groom from the castle had been killed. A bunch of stable boys had been discussing the sad news with two girls who sold roast meat from a stall in the square. Erit had bought some meat and then lingered within earshot. He was rewarded with the news that castle folk believed the groom had killed Virr and then taken his own life. A most satisfactory outcome.

Cett came up behind him and poked his right shoulder. Erit turned. 'There you are at last. 'What kept you?'

'An exceedingly comely girl.'

Erit snorted. 'Then hope she's clean.'

'I'll take my chances. Let's go inside.' Cett jerked his head at the open door of the inn.

They pushed their way into the crowded chamber, which wasn't a safe place to talk. Erit indicated the steep stairs at one side. 'Up here.'

He'd paid for the use of a tiny garret under the roof. The low ceiling barely gave the men enough room to stand and the place was just big enough for a lumpy straw cot. He pushed open the dirty window but the air outside was about as hot and dusty as that inside the chamber.

Erit turned to Cett. 'So you did the deed.'

Cett nodded. 'And that's my last body. You want more killed, then do it yourself.'

Erit forced down some queasiness. 'We have one more loose end.'

'It's your loose end, not mine.' Cett paused before adding. 'Who else knows about this matter?'

'I heard this morn that the groom was courting a kitchen girl. He might have opened his mouth too wide to her.'

'As I just said, that's your concern.' Cett sat down on the cot and yawned loudly. 'I got rid of the Star. Stuck it in the fellow's pouch to make it look like he'd taken it when he killed Virr.'

'The gossip indicated that the groom is thought to be was guilty of Virr's murder.'

'Now what?' Cett lay down on the cot. 'What great ideas do you have that don't involve killing anybody?'

'I'm getting into the castle tonight so I'll have a good look around before I perform. We still don't know how to take the girl. She always has at least one guard inside the gates and when she rides outside, she has four of them.'

Cett stretched both arms above his head and yawned again. 'Somebody will slip up and then we'll be ready.'

Erit sat on a wobbly stool. 'We need help to take her from that grey horse.'

'How long have you got this chamber for?' Cett yawned again and closed his eyes.

'Until next morn.'

'Then if you don't mind, I'll have a nap. I'm short of sleep. The other night while I waited for that groom, I had bloody great rats running over me.'

'Be my guest.' Erit heard Cett snoring as he descended the back stairs. He was still bothered by the groom's girl. From what Cett had said, Erit suspected Givis had heard something of the argument between the two brothers. When the girl was silenced, all the loose ends would have been tied up. Erit liked things to be neat and tidy.

Chapter Eight

The sole person stirring outside the keep next morn was Magian Domen. Lyta knew from previous Feast days that most folk would have aching heads and dry mouths. Since the magian drank very little, his head would be clear. When he beckoned, she followed him to his door. 'Would you like to study with me? I know it's not your usual time or day for a lesson. I will tell Cordon not to expect you.'

'Can we try more of that thought lofting?'

He raised his grey eyebrows. 'Didn't you find sitting and thinking a dull task?'

'Only before I knew what the task involved.' She sat down on a stool.

Then we will try another transfer.' He presented his back to her.

Lyta emptied her mind and let her body grow limp, ready to receive a message.

In the void, she glimpsed a silvery thread shining in the sun. 'Water? Are you sending me a thought about water?'

Magian Domen turned around. 'Correct. What type of water was it?'

'I need to see it again to be sure.' This time, she caught the notion of a large body of water with slight waves rippling its surface. 'Is it a lake?'

'I thought about Lake Peace. I grew up beside it.'

'But I've never been there. Does this mean that I can catch thoughts about places and objects I've never seen?'

'It would seem so. We'll have to test the idea further.'

Lyta sat still, thinking about the lofting. 'Could I catch thoughts that are sent by other people, not just you?'

'At the moment, I must concentrate very hard on the transfer. People without any training probably can't do that.'

'Hmm.' Lyta wanted to catch stray thoughts. If she could, then mayhap, she could track down the killer of Virr and Givis.

'Once we have refined your gift, we'll work the other way. I said earlier that it is more difficult to loft thoughts than to catch them.'

As Lyta pondered his words, a stab of pain shot through her head. 'Are you sending me a message about knives?' She rubbed her forehead. 'Something sharp jabbed me.'

'I'm not lofting,' he answered. Then he glanced at his hyala. A faint blue glow hung above the shrouded object.

Her gaze followed his. 'Is someone sending you a message?'

Magian Domen rose. 'We'll end our lesson for today.' He looked hard at her. 'How does your head feel?'

'Like someone stuck a long pin into me. Will the pain go away when I leave here?'

'It should vanish when you enter the keep but if it does not, then return here. I will give you an elixir.'

Lyta held her head as she closed the door and walked away. It wasn't until she was climbing the keep steps that the sharp twinge vanished.

Since the unexpected lesson had left her with many questions, Lyta went to her workchamber to think about them. Sitting on her stool in a shaft of sunlight from the window, she wondered about an object that was so powerful that it could send messages from a distance. Did magians experience pain from their hyalas? If so, they must learn to control their bodies as Magian Domen didn't seem to have been troubled by the blue glow. And what were the strong spells that bound magians to their hyalas?

Jer's boots sounded on the steps before he entered the workchamber. 'Kedie Lyta, your lady mother wishes to see you,' he said with a bow. 'I am to conduct you there at once.'

Lyta decided her present tunic would have to do. After all, her mother was accustomed to seeing her in crumpled and often dirty clothes. She followed the guard to the kedura's chambers where he announced her in a loud clear voice. Jer was always careful to use the correct protocol.

Halia dismissed him and her maids before she drew Lyta to a seat beside her. 'I have some exciting news, child. Kedur Baldus of Delis and his son, Kedir Firt, will pay us a visit.'

'How did you find out this news?'

'Magian Domen was sent a message from his fellow magian in Delis.'

Lyta nodded. So the hyala did glow when a message was being sent and received. 'Why are they coming here?'

'Kedir Firt is a little older than you. I suspect they're coming to see if you might be a suitable bride.' When Lyta frowned, Halia clasped her daughter's hands. 'You must marry one day but I want you to choose a husband who makes you happy at board and in bed. If this one is not to your liking, then we'll inspect kedirs in other demesnes. There are several boys of the right age.'

Lyta had been told often enough about marriage but it wouldn't take place until she had experienced her first moonblood. After she wed, her duty was to rule with her husband and to bear children. However, her mother was an exception to this pattern. She'd become a beloved ruler without a husband. Why couldn't Lyta follow in her footsteps?

'Of course, we'll have a large feast to welcome them,' said Halia. 'And since our council of erles is meeting at the same time, I'll stage a tournament. In his youth, Baldus was an excellent jouster and swordsman. His son might be equally skilled.'

'When is everyone coming?'

'In three sevendays. I have much to arrange before then. And you will need new clothes.' She touched Lyta's shoulder. 'No grubby tunics and shabby hose to meet Kedir Firt. We want him to see how beautiful you are.'

Lyta raised her eyebrows. She wasn't beautiful like Halia, having inherited her father's straight black hair, brown eyes, and skinny frame. Although she had few memories of the man, his portrait in the great hall was a constant reminder of their close resemblance. Lyta's looks wouldn't do well beside a kedie with the traditional white skin, blue eyes and golden locks.

'So, you will show us in a good light?' Her mother frowned.

'Of course, Mother.'

When she left her mother's chamber, Lyta returned to her tower. Her pleasant life was going to be disturbed. But at least Halia had made one thing plain. If Firt was an unpleasant person, she didn't have to consider him as a husband. And mayhap she'd find all the eligible kedirs in the land unsuitable in some way. One might be too fat, another too thin, a third too short, and a fourth one too tall or of low intellect.

Her mother wanted Lyta to be happy at board and in bed. She wasn't ignorant of the act to make children. She'd known how horses and dogs were bred but she hadn't seen people mating until one day three summers ago when she'd glimpsed two bodies in the straw in a storechamber.

She'd recognised Yint's skinny legs and long feet but couldn't at first see the girl beneath him. Lyta watched until their jerking and groaning ceased. As Yint sighed and rose on his elbows, she saw that the girl was Belia, one of her mother's maids. He leaned forward and kissed her rosy mouth then traced a path down her body to her white breasts. Lyta realised then that people might behave in a more tender fashion than animals did in the same situation.

On one of their rides, Lyta had asked Virr about people and their breeding. He looked at her with his usual serious expression. 'In people, there should be a difference between lust and love. Lust drives us to join with another but it is often temporary. Love is what makes two folk into true partners.'

'So animals don't feel love?' she asked.

Virr shook his head. 'I wouldn't say that. I've seen pairs of swans and geese devoted to each other. But with love and respect, a man and a woman can build a fine life together.' Then he smiled and added, 'Kedie, don't worry about this matter. Your mother will always have your happiness first in her mind.'

Next morn, Lyta was expecting to work as usual with her tutoran but he stopped her from taking a seat. 'Magian Domen would like to see you at once.'

Cordon sounded a little disconcerted at losing his student two morns in a row but Lyta knew he would never disobey an order from his master.

She was given a new lesson in thought lofting. Magian Domen sent her pictures with words attached to them. It was much more difficult to decipher the letters in a word than to catch pictures. After the last transfer about trees, she distinctly heard the words, 'Well done, child.'

When she glanced immediately at the magian's face, Lyta noted that his lips hadn't moved. Had she actually caught an unrehearsed thought?

She grinned in delight. 'You usually just nod so I'm never sure that I've done well.'

His eyebrows shot upwards. 'You caught my thought?'

'Quite clearly.'

'You're progressing fast.' He stroked his chin. 'Now, why did you catch that particular thought? Was it because I was praising you?'

Lyta jiggled on her stool. 'I don't care why. I'm just happy to succeed. Now can I practise lofting to you?'

'I want to think about today's lesson first.'

She had to be satisfied with his decision even though she longed to try the opposite messaging process. Both lofting and catching could be very useful.

Chapter Nine

The buzz of excitement about the guests started quietly and then grew as loud as a swarm of bees in flight. Everyone was involved in the preparations. Wea, the castle seamstress, came to Lyta's bedchamber with bright rolls tucked under her arm. When she spread the shimmering fabric over the bed, Obela fingered each one with a frown on her face.

This time, Lyta thought, her nurse wasn't going to choose for her. She'd behave like the kedies from the tales. Those girls spent their days planning their clothes, arranging their hair, and selecting their jewels. Lyta pointed to the colours she liked best and waited for Obela's objections.

'Not suitable,' her nurse snapped. 'Young girls wear white, pink or pale blue.'

'But I like these,' Lyta said, her mouth set in a firm line.

Wea cleared her throat. 'Kedura Halia selected each of these colours. She said that pale shades wouldn't suit the kedie.'

Folding her arms and setting her mouth into a frown, Obela sat down on a stool by the bed. She snorted several times as Wea took Lyta's measurements and then discussed the trimmings for each garment and the new small clothes necessary. 'You will also get matching hose and slippers,' she said.

Lyta tried to persuade herself that she'd feel more comfortable or more beautiful wearing the new gowns. But deep down, she knew that after the guests had left the castle, she'd slip back into her old tunics and hose.

Wea and her girls worked long hours to complete the stitching of her new clothes. When they were finished, Halia summoned her daughter and the seamstress to her chambers. She watched intently as Wea dropped the first gown over Lyta's head.

'Turn around,' Halia ordered as Lyta twirled before her. Amia stood nearby, her head on one side and her mouth screwed up in concentration.

'Hmm,' said Halia. 'The bronze goes well with her eyes. Show me the green one.' Lyta's face and body grew hot and sticky as Wea pulled and poked at her. Her initial smile became a scowl.

'I hope you won't wear that discouraging expression when Firt comes,' her mother said.

'How's this? Lyta forced her lips to curl upwards.

'Don't be difficult. You know perfectly well what I mean.'

As the new gowns and robes became a shining pile on the bed, Halia turned to Wea with a smile. 'You and your girls have done well. Amia, help Wea to take these clothes to Lyta's new chamber. She will be sleeping next to me while we have guests.'

After they left, Halia said, 'You need a maid to assist you dressing and arranging your hair. Obela will still take care of you but Caza, Amia's younger sister, will be here after dinner to attend you.'

Feeling pleased that someone younger than her old nurse would attend her, Lyta went to meet her tutoran in a small reception chamber off the great hall. Even her workchamber would be used to accommodate guests when everyone arrived at the castle.

Cordon's lesson was about Delis. 'I want you to be very knowledgeable about the demesne before Kedur Baldus and his son arrive. Tell me what you already know about their main cities and towns.'

Lyta couldn't imagine dazzling Firt with her knowledge of his demesne's geography but she submitted to the tutoran's boring questions and instruction. He smiled with satisfaction at the end of the lesson. 'Now, you are well versed and will not disappoint me.'

Magian Domen's lesson after dinner was much more to her liking. When Lyta arrived, he was standing before the west window in his workchamber with both hands clasped behind his back. 'Ah, Kedie, I've decided to let you try thought lofting. Instead of emptying your mind, you must fill it with the picture you wish to send. Any stray thoughts will mar the image and confuse the person receiving the message.'

Lyta sat down and made herself comfortable. At least his stools had cushioned seats. Since Cordon believed that comfort got in the way of learning, the stools in her own workchamber were unpadded.

'Choose something simple. And first, count backwards slowly from a score.'

What should she send? Something other than fire or water, and definitely, a picture without words. Lyta thought back to the day when Virr had taken her to the top of Stone Mountain. From the heights, they'd observed a small vale holding late spring snow. They climbed down to it and threw snowballs at each other until their ears and hands were scarlet and aching.

Lyta counted backwards from a score and then filled her mind with mounds of cold snow. She opened her eyes at the same time as the magian opened his.

'You sent a combination of mountains, snow, and Virr,' the magian said.

'I tried to keep Virr out of my mind but he wouldn't leave.'

Magian Domen nodded. 'That is understandable. The notions were strongly connected. You must learn to separate images.'

Lyta told him about the wonderful day when she and Virr ate a picnic midmeal on top of the mountain. They'd left the horses with the guards lower on the slope and then climbed on foot to the peak. 'That's one of my best memories. The view was magnificent and our meal of bread, cheese, and apples tasted better than any I've eaten since.'

'Did you happen to see an icecat?'

'Only the tracks. I've always wanted to have an icekit as a pet.'

'They are truly beautiful beasts but very fierce.'

'I wasn't scared. Virr was armed that day and he was teaching me how to throw a blade. I started out being unable to hit the castle wall but then gradually became more accurate.' Lyta hung her head to hide the tears from the magian's eyes. 'I miss him so much.'

'Of course, you do. However, you'll always remember him through the skills he taught you and the advice he gave.'

'That's true.' Lyta blotted her eyes with her tunic. 'Shall I try again?'

'Use the same snow thought but work hard to keep Virr out of it.'

Lyta focused very strongly on snow and not on the other memories. After two more attempts at lofting, she succeeded.

'A clean picture,' said the magian. 'Well done.'

Caza, the new maid, was waiting in her tower chamber to carry the rest of Lyta's possessions to her temporary quarters. When Lyta arrived, the girl was pressed against the wall as though she was trying to squeeze through the stones to escape from Obela. The old nurse had thrown open her press and was tossing gowns onto the bed and the floor. 'Look at all these beautiful clothes!' she yelled. 'I hope you know your work. The kedie always looked a picture when I was in charge.'

Lyta took a girdle from the nurse's shaking hands. 'You are still in charge. Obela, you and I have been together since I was a baby. Now you will have some help with your duties.' Lyta led Obela to a chair. 'Rest for a while. Caza will bring you spiced wine from the kitchen.'

When Obela sat down, the new maid slipped from the chamber. Lyta sighed. Having two people to assist her might be more difficult than she'd imagined. How did Mother keep a whole castle of servants happy in their work?

The erles of Aldea were the first guests to arrive. They brought with them squires, men of arms, and servants. Two of the nobles also brought wives and children. Sleeping in the small chamber next to her mother, Lyta missed the peace and freedom of her tower existence. The guest quarters were crowded too and tents were raised on the grazing grounds. The best guest chambers had been set aside for Kedur Baldus, Kedir Firt, and their retinue.

Dressed in one of her new robes, Lyta curtseyed and smiled at the right times and in the right places. She overheard Lord Trevin's wife whisper to Lord Josik's wife that the bronze robe was unsuitable wear for a young girl. She and Obela would have much in common. Lyta kept smiling even though the comment annoyed her.

The banquets and the tournament wouldn't begin until Baldus and his son arrived. Meanwhile Halia met with her erles to discuss the state of the demesne. Lyta suspected that a disagreement had developed when Lord Trevin stormed from the keep one afternoon with a scowl on his face. He called for his horse to be saddled and then galloped from the gate with his squire. Cordon said the erle had ridden through the Dark Forest for several hours. If her tutoran knew the cause of the disagreement, he didn't divulge it.

Lyta had begged her mother to keep Virr's horse without success. When she went into the stable after midmeal with apples for Silver, she found Lord Josik stroking Courage's nose. 'I always admired Virr's mount,' he said as Lyta came closer.

'They were very well suited.' A stab of resentment hit her as she watched the erle's actions. Courage seemed to enjoy the attention.

'Your mother has offered to sell him to me,' he said as the horse nuzzled his shoulder.

'But will you be able to ride him? Our grooms have tried and failed.'

Lord Josik laughed. 'I've never had trouble with a horse.'

'You do know that Virr could understand horses. Dogs and birds too.'

His thin eyebrows rose. 'Your head groom told me this tale.'

'It's not a tale. With my own eyes, I saw Virr both talk and listen to Courage.'

The erle's indulgent smile angered Lyta but she didn't get a chance to prove her words. His twin sons of ten summers rushed into the stables to greet their father. These boys had been causing havoc everywhere they went: stealing food from the kitchen, starting a contest to make all the kennel dogs howl at once, trying to take a falcon from its perch, and begging Nin to allow them to ride Midnight or Nighthawk. Lyta hoped Lord Josik wouldn't let the boys get on Courage's back. Although, on second thoughts, mayhap a sharp fall might calm one or both of them down.

'Father, will you have him?' asked the taller of the two boys.

'I'm considering it,' the erle answered.

'I should get that horse,' the other boy demanded. 'I'm a better rider than Jasim.' When he poked his brother's shoulder, Jasim turned and swung a fist at his twin's face.

‘Enough!’ snapped their father. ‘Out of here, hellhounds.’

Jasim tried to trip Menit as they ran from the stable and Lyta heard the sound of a scuffle outside. Then loud voices were added to the mix and Jasim reappeared. His eyes were wide. ‘Father! There’s a dead girl out here.’

Dead girl? Lyta’s heart missed a beat as she ran from the stables, closely followed by Lord Josik.

Chapter Ten

Four guards were standing around someone lying on the ground. Lyta pushed her way through the ring and then gasped. Water streamed from Rusa's long brown hair and clothes. Her open eyes stared blindly upwards. 'Did she drown?' Lyta knew this was a foolish question even as the words left her mouth. Of course, Rusa had drowned.

Archis Druck strode up to the group. 'Stand back!' he ordered, turning to an older guard. 'Was this the body pulled from the moat?'

The man nodded. 'Yes, Archis. I saw it from the tower.'

The Archis noticed Lyta and bowed low. 'Kedie, is she a kitchen wench?'

'Yes, she's Rusa. Givis's betrothed.'

Druck nodded. 'Ah, I understand. She jumped into the moat out of grief. Borut, inform the Kedura of the girl's death.'

Did she fall into the water or was she pushed? Someone might have thought that Rusa knew more about the previous killings than she'd mentioned. Now the last link in the murder puzzle had been eliminated. Rusa's death convinced Lyta that a plot did exist.

She couldn't bear the thought that a large crowd might gather to stare at poor dead Rusa. 'Archis Druck, have her taken away.'

He nodded. 'She'll be placed in a cold cell until we find her family.'

Rusa was wrapped in a sheet and carried away. Cook boys and girls who'd already heard the sad news were dabbing their eyes and sobbing as her body passed the kitchen door. Lyta stopped to talk to the head cook.

'What a pity!' Prala shook her curly head. 'No man is worth dying for.'

'So you believe she jumped into the moat because her heart was broken?'

'What other reason? Her little head was full of dead Givis.'

'Did she tell you that Givis killed himself?'

Prala raised both eyebrows. 'Her wild tale about murder came from her sorrow. Archis Druck himself came to the kitchen to tell us Givis killed Virr.'

Silver never did get her apples. Lyta's mind was awhirl with questions. With the crowds of strangers gathered at the castle, this was the ideal time for a murderer to slip back here. The man with the big nose could have been one of the many wagon drivers bringing in extra food for their guests.

To support her notion, she went to find Ivil. He was in the back stable grooming Nighthawk. He jumped when Lyta spoke. 'I didn't hear you, Kedie.' He stared at her new gown. 'You look very fine.'

She raised her skirt from the ground. 'And you look like a groom.'

Ivil's wide grin showed an empty space where a front tooth had been the last time she saw him. 'That's right. Nin said I earned this job.'

'What happened to your tooth?'

Ivil scowled. 'Saxo said he was better with the horses than me. You should see his black eye and torn ear.'

Lyta shook her head at him. 'Have you seen the big-nosed man again?'

'I thought I saw him yestermorn but when I got closer, he was gone.'

'What about the juggler?'

Ivil shook his head.

'If you see either of them again, send a message to Caza, my new maid.'

Ivil grinned again. 'I seen that Caza this morn when she came from the town. She's a right pretty girl.' He looked down at the ground. 'Kedie, your fine gown is getting dirty.'

Lyta pulled her skirt even higher. She didn't have this trouble with her old clothes. Fine gowns were not suitable for stable visits. Another good reason to wear tunics and hose.

When Lyta was back in her new chamber, Caza clicked her tongue at the sad state of the bronze gown's hem. 'Kedie, you smell like you been near horses.'

Lyta submitted to undressing and dressing. The maid adjusted the new red gown and matching surcoat and chose a golden girdle. 'Now your hair.'

Since Lyta was an unmarried maiden, her hair could remain loose. Caza brushed her locks until they shone and then arranged her hair down her back and over her shoulders. Her work was finished with the addition of a simple gold tiara.

Caza stood back and smiled with satisfaction. 'I seen a girl your age when I went to the kitchen. Your cook said she's Lord Trevin's daughter.'

'The Lady Adina. I haven't met her yet. She's been in bed with a fever.'

'She's out of her bed now and dressed very fine in a blue robe. But you look even better, Kedie Lyta.'

Lyta laughed. 'Enjoy it now. When our guests go, I'll return to my comfortable tunics.'

Caza's eyes opened wide. 'Oh no, Kedie. You have such beautiful robes.'

At the evening meal, the two girls were seated together at a lower table with the wives and children of the erles. Lyta hid a grin when she first saw Adina. She was the perfect kedie from the tales and songs with her large blue eyes, long golden curls, and white skin. Tiny pearls trimmed her pale blue gown. She greeted Lyta, absorbing every detail of the red gown. Then she spent the next minutes gazing at the head table. 'Don't you think Lord Quilin is handsome?' she commented. 'And Mother says he's an excellent horseman.'

'He is,' Lyta agreed. 'He was the winner at the last tournament. He handles a sword and battle axe very well too.'

Adina shuddered. 'I don't like swords and axes but riding in the lists is very exciting. Do you think he would accept my token for the tourney?'

'Quilin is older than he looks. And his wife died in childbirth. His son must be two summers by now'

'That's so sad and so romantic.' Adina sighed loudly.

The girl was tedious. And foolish. Lyta didn't mind talking about tournaments but her interest was in the way the riders handled their horses and their skill with weapons not in their looks and armour. She concentrated on her meal, leaving Adina to concentrate on batting her eyelashes at Quilin and at several comely squires in the hall.

Two morns later, a rider brought word that the ship carrying Baldus was near. The erles went to meet the Kedur of Delis, with colourful pennants waving from their lances.

Halia in her finest clothes and jewels waited in the great hall. After submitting to Caza's ministrations, Lyta was arrayed in an apple-green gown and darker surcoat with a golden chain hanging from her neck. Her hair had been brushed until her scalp burned. The castle officers stood behind their kedura along with the wives and children of the erles.

The clatter of hooves in the courtyard and the sound of voices heralded the arrival of their guests. Kedur Baldus was the first person through the door. He was a tall man proceeded into the hall by his huge paunch. Lyta could imagine what he looked like when he was young by glancing at his son. Firt, a step behind Baldus, was the same height as his father but much slimmer. Where the hair on Baldus' head had retreated behind his ears and was grey in patches, Firt's hair was dark brown, thick and wavy.

Baldus advanced on Halia with both hands outstretched. 'My dear Halia!' he said in a booming voice. 'I am exceedingly glad to be under your roof at last.'

The kedura was kissed soundly on both cheeks before Baldus reached back and dragged his son forward by the arm. 'This is Firt. Now, where's your little wench?'

Halia drew Lyta near. Up close, she had a clearer look at Firt. His pale blue eyes were too close together and stayed hard and assessing while his lips curved in a formal smile. Shuddering internally, she studied his mouth. It was too red, too moist, and ajar. Lyta added another reason to her list for the kedir rejection. Firt wasn't too short, too tall, or too fat but his mouth was too wet. She couldn't imagine it touching any part of her face or her body.

'Kedie Lyta,' Firt said. 'How delightful to meet you.'

Lyta turned her cheek to his lips. As he bent forward, his eyes darted sideways to fix on Adina. Lyta felt certain that the appearance of Lord Trevin's daughter was much more to his taste than her looks.

'Kedir Firt,' Lyta murmured. 'You are most welcome here.' She resisted the urge to wipe her moist cheek.

Halia's aunts were greeted by Baldus with resounding kisses and hugs. Jona blushed in response while Vea scowled. Adina curtseyed, smiled and dimpled as the erles and their families were made known to the visitors. A feast followed in the great hall.

Lyta always admire the hall at night. Flames from the giant log blazing in the wide hearth were reflected in the row of battle shields hanging from the rafters. The walls were adorned with the banners of the erles. She noted Josik's leaping salmon, Trevin's tall towers, Quilin's snarling ice cat, and Wilus's soaring bird. Her family was represented by the great oak of Aldea. To honour their guests, the coiled black serpent of Delis had joined the other banners.

Lyta was placed next to Firt at the High Table. While they made stilted conversation about jousting, hunting wild boar, and fighting, the kedir's eyes constantly roamed the hall, lighting on every young woman and serving maid. This boy was not the husband for her. She'd want someone who behaved courteously toward her in both public and in private places. Once she caught Quilin watching her. He smiled and raised his wine cup.

Mother's favourite black-haired singer entertained the diners with his lute and best songs. Lyta waited with some anxiety to see if the juggler had been hired for this feast. Suddenly, the man arrived. He bounded into the hall tossing a motley collection of objects in the air and was greeted with roars of approval.

When he arrived at the knife throwing part of his act, Firt reached into his belt and threw his own dagger at the man. 'Fellow, let's see how you deal with an extra blade!'

Adina and her mother both screamed and Lyta held her breath. The juggler reached out and grabbed the dagger without losing track of the knives in the air and in his other hand. The man was clever and exceeding nimble.

Firt clapped his hands. 'Well done, fellow!' he called.

Lyta detected disappointment in his tone and wondered if he'd wanted to see the blade draw blood. The juggler caught his knives and in the next quick movement flipped the dagger back to Firt. At the time, the kedir was half turned as a serving maid filled his cup. Without thinking, Lyta reached out and grabbed the hilt, halting the spinning blade in its path.

Her fingers throbbed from the contact as she stared at the weapon. Halia had gasped and Adina screamed again. Firt dropped his cup on the table where it bounced, spilling a stream of red wine. He yelled at the juggler. 'Stupid bastard, you could have killed me!'

Archis Druck pushed back his chair. 'Ignorant dog! You'll be punished for this treasonous act.'

But the juggler had grabbed his knives and was part way down the hall before anyone realised he was leaving. Guards rushed after him but the juggler passed through the door ahead of them. The next minute, Lyta heard confused sounds in the courtyard.

Firt turned to her, licking his thick lips. He spoke in a voice loud enough for the table to hear. 'Kedie Lyta, I was sore afraid for your safety.'

Baldus stood up. 'Good work, my dear. How did a girl learn to catch a blade?'

'Mother's gerentis taught me.'

'Then he did well.' He dropped a heavy hand on her shoulder as he leaned down toward Firt. 'Boy, you can thank Lady Moon that you were saved by a mere wench.' He roared with laughter as he swung a fist toward Firt who ducked away from his heavy arm.

When Lyta placed the blade on the table, Firt scowled. He picked it up and stuck it into his belt. For her ears only, he muttered. 'You made a fool of me tonight but never again. Play with your dolls, little girl, and leave knife play to the men.'

Lyta thought that mayhap, she'd prevented an injury but she hadn't endeared herself to a prospective husband.

Chapter Eleven

When the ladies left the great hall, Halia beckoned to her daughter and Lyta followed her. After dismissing Amia, the kedura sank down on a chair and rubbed her eyes. 'Child, I don't know whether to praise you or scold you for this night's work.'

Lyta moved a stool close enough to lean against her mother's knees. 'Firt has already made it clear he didn't like my action.'

'Men never like to look foolish. His pride was wounded.'

'Mother, can I speak openly about Firt?'

Halia nodded as she lifted the tiara from her head.

'Even though I've just met him, he can never be the husband for me. I find him distasteful. You must tell Baldus that a marriage cannot be arranged.'

Her mother sighed. 'I see that you two may not be well suited but Baldus made it clear tonight that he is strongly in favour of a wedding. In fact, your action made him even more certain that you'd make Firt a fine wife. He was full of your praises.'

'But Firt doesn't want to marry me. He would rather wed Adina or any other comely woman who smiles at him and says he is wonderful.'

'In the end, Firt will carry out his father's wishes. He has three younger brothers. If he displeases Baldus, one of those boys could become the heir in Delis. Their demesne laws allow a living kedur to appoint any child as a successor, not just the eldest.' She hid a yawn behind her white hand.

Lyta stood up and kissed her mother's cheek. 'Please convince Baldus that I'm entirely unsuitable to be Firt's wife. Do everything you can.'

'I will try to persuade him but Baldus is a stubborn man.'

Sleep did not come easy that night. Lyta tossed in her strange bed in the small bedchamber, listening to Obela's snores and Caza's sighs, wishing she was back in the tower. Her mind replayed the incident in the hall. Virr would have been proud of her for catching that blade. He taught her many skills that other kedies would never have learned.

As well as teaching her to throw and catch a blade, Virr had designed a light bow that she could easily draw. They practised in the grazing fields away from critical eyes. Virr set up targets and had her shooting so many arrows that her shoulder and arms ached for hours afterward. Although he was a stern tutoran, he praised Lyta when she was accurate.

The whereabouts of the juggler concerned her. The guards who chased after him had returned to the hall, shaking their heads. The man had vanished into the darkness. If he was still at the castle, he might have met up with the man with the big nose. Lyta turned the pillow hoping to find a cool place to rest her head. Enough worrying, she told herself. Go to sleep right now.

After repast in her chamber, Lyta went into the yard. Lord Josik and Lord Trevin were laughing together. As Lyta came near, she heard wagers mentioned. The two men stopped talking to greet her. 'Kedie, you must come to watch the contest,' said Josik. 'Firt is taking on all archers.' The erle nodded toward the grazing fields. 'The butts will be set up there.'

'We're counting on Quilin to defend Aldea's honour,' Trevin added.

Lyta thought that if she wagered on anybody, it would be Lord Quilin. She'd seen him demonstrate his prowess with many different weapons including the bow.

By midmeal, everyone knew about the competition. Squires were carrying bows and quivers of arrows down to the grazing field and then practising in preparation. Halia had ordered that the pavilion, which held the noble onlookers for tournaments, should be erected early. Servants carried lengths of timber and rolls of canvas to build the structure.

Adina's eyes sparkled. 'I like archery contests. There's no blood.'

'Unless an arrow goes astray,' Lyta said. 'Mother, will you enter the contest?'

Halia was known for her ability with the bow. She'd learned to shoot from her father and had often accompanied him on deer hunting expeditions. 'I'll leave this contest to our men. Adina, can you use a bow?'

'Father did not think it was a suitable activity,' the girl answered.

An excited crowd greeted the contestants as they lined up to shoot practise arrows. They were mostly squires attached to each of the erles as well as those who had come with Baldus. Archis Druck announced that two of his guards wished to compete and Lord Josik read out the rules. Each archer would shoot six arrows before his score was tallied. Then those with the two highest scores would have a final contest to decide the winner.

Baldus laughed a little ruefully as he took a seat beside Halia. 'I used to be a champion in my day but now I leave these matters to the young ones. Halia, are you willing to place a little wager on your erle?'

'Of course. I have great faith in Quilin,' Halia said. 'No doubt your coin will be placed on Firt.'

'He's very accurate as long as he stays calm,' said his father.

He leaned across the kedura to catch Lyta's eye. 'Are you as good with a bow as you are with a blade?'

'I have been instructed,' said Lyta.

'But she's not on display today,' said her mother firmly.

Lyta subsided into her seat, prepared to watch others shoot. She wished Virr had been present. He was an exceedingly competent archer.

Every contestant was greeted with cheers, which often turned to hisses and insults if the target was missed. Quilin and Firt had matching tallies at the end of the first round as did a squire attached to Lord Josik's household and Borut, the senior guard. The quartet took their place for the next round. When Borut was eliminated, a further round began. After that, Josik's squire left the contest and Quilin and Firt remained tied.

Baldus slapped his knee as he waited for the final round. 'Your man shoots well,' he said to Halia. 'But I'm sure my son will prevail in the end. Would you like to increase your wager, my dear?'

Halia agreed with a smile.

'Excellent news,' said Baldus. He leaned forward to yell at Firt. 'Make sure you win, boy. The state of the Delis treasury depends on your skill.'

. Lyta thought that Firt looked a little alarmed but he waved back and took his bow from a squire standing behind him.

Once again the score were even at the end of the round. Josik declared that each man would shoot arrows in turn until one missed the centre of the target. The contest came down to a final arrow. Quilin raised his bow. Then Lyta saw him catch Halia's eye. His eyebrows rose and she inclined her head slightly in response.

Quilin's arrow missed the target.

Baldus leapt from his seat, strode down to his son and clapped his shoulder. 'Well done, boy!' he roared. 'That's how we do it in Delis.'

Firt accompanied his father back to the pavilion and bowed low before Halia. 'I hope my shooting pleased you, Kedura.' His smug smile made Lyta want to hit him.

When Halia congratulated him on his victory, Firt's chest swelled like a turkey cock. He kissed Halia's hand and insisted on kissing the hand of every other woman present. His lips lingered longest over Adina's slender hand.

During the feast that night, the men at the high table planned a hunting expedition for the next day. Trevin said they might track down a large wild boar. 'I've seen some monsters there in the past. At the very least, we'll come back with a fine stag.' He turned to Halia. 'With the Kedura's permission, of course.'

Halia gave her consent. All the deer in the Dark Forest were under her control and poaching was punished by a heavy fine or even imprisonment.

'The ladies could have a picnic,' she suggested. 'The forest has some very attractive spots. One of the streams has its own waterfall.'

Lyta's gloom increased at the idea of a picnic. Even before the outing was suggested, she'd been unhappy with the way Firt was behaving. He leaned forward as though she did not exist and talked to Adina on her other side. If she needed any more convincing about Firt's unsuitability as a husband, she was by now quite decided.

Chapter Twelve

The hunting party set off at first light. Not that the morn was very bright under a grey and heavy sky. A noisy stream of talkative men on horseback and a pack of snarling and barking dogs and their keepers passed through oldgate and then newgate. Once the troupe had departed, the courtyard grew peaceful again.

Lyta found Halia in her solar working on the large horse hanging along with Aunt Vea and Jona and the wives of Lord Josik and Lord Trevin. Adina was plying her own needle competently beside them. 'Have you come to help us?' she asked Lyta. 'I've never stitched a hanging like this with horses.'

Lyta glanced at her mother whose lips had curled into an involuntary smile. Halia knew how much her daughter hated needlework. 'Not this time,' Lyta said.

'The preparations for the picnic are under way,' the Kedura said. 'Lyta, please visit Prala to see if the food is all prepared. And tell Archis Druck we will leave at midday.'

Lyta escaped from the solar with alacrity to carry out her errands. As she ran from the kitchen, she looked up at the sky. Darker clouds hung over the castle and the air was dense and damp. She wondered if the picnic should take place.

Archis Druck agreed with her assessment. He stared upward with his hands on his hips. 'The ladies will get very wet if they leave here. Another day might be more suitable for such an outing.' As he spoke, a few fat drops of rain grew into a steady stream of water and then a downpour.

Lyta retreated with the commander to the shelter of the gate where they both watched puddles form on the uneven stones. 'It won't be pleasant in the Dark Forest today,' she said.

'Kedie, talk to your mother about changing this picnic to another day.' Lyta didn't fancy being caught with Druck until the shower ceased. She took her chance when the rain slackened slightly and ran back to the keep.

Halia had already decided that eating under dripping trees was not a sensible activity. 'We will picnic inside,' she announced. 'We'll sit in the solar on cushions and eat here.'

Adina clapped her hands with pleasure and even Lyta thought it was a good compromise.

The rain did not cease; in fact it appeared to become heavier throughout the afternoon. Although the hunting party returned with only one deer, they were jovial and loud. Men, horses, and dogs were sodden and mud-covered. The servants were all busy, scurrying up and down the castle steps carrying containers of hot water.

As the rain ceased with sundown, everyone was hopeful that the tournament scheduled for the following day would go ahead. When Lyta studied the sky the next morn, she was not certain that all the events would be able to take place. The skies were streaked with red and gold and clouds were building over the forest. Virr had told her that seamen expected bad weather when the colours of the sunrise were bright.

Wagons of sand were brought from the shore to spread on the muddy ground where the tourney would take place. Other men were straightening the seats and canvas of the pavilion, which had been damaged in the previous day's rain. As Lyta stood watching the preparations, a deep voice spoke behind her. She turned to face Quilin.

He smiled. 'I must congratulate you, Kedie, on your quickness the other night. I've never seen a girl catch a blade like that. The young puppy should be glad you were watching.'

Lyta grinned; it was good to know that someone she liked also held a poor opinion of Firt's character. 'Unfortunately, he wasn't happy about it.'

'Never mind that,' said the erle. 'My squire tells me that Firt is boasting already about being the tournament champion after his great successes at the butts and the hunt.'

'Did you deliberately miss with that last arrow?'

'My lips are sealed. Kedie Lyta, if Firt hasn't asked for a token, might I beg one from you for this day.'

Lyta's cheeks burned. Nobody had ever asked her for a token at a tournament. 'I would be very happy to give one to you.'

'Then I will fight as your champion.' He raised her hand to his lips and kissed it. Then he smiled before turning toward his squire.

Lyta held both hands over her cheeks to cool them, surprised at the response to his kiss. Surely it was only a courtesy and nothing more on his part. The man was far too old to be interested in a girl of her age. As she watched him talk to his squire, a sudden thought hit her. Her mother and Baldus would both expect her to present a token to Firt for the tourney. She had better tell her mother what she'd done.

Halia frowned when she heard the news. 'I know you are inexperienced in such matters, Lyta, but you should have thought twice. I will talk to Baldus before the tourney to avoid any unpleasantness.'

After midday, everything was ready. Lyta stared up at a threatening sky, hoping the storm would hold off until later in the day. Unlike the solid rain they had just experienced, today could bring a sudden shower with loud claps of thunder and vivid slashes of lightning.

She joined her mother, Baldus, and the wives and families of the erles in the tiered seating of the pavilion. Folk from the town and castle lined both sides of the lists and the smell of savoury food hung in the air as sellers offered hot meat pies from large trays slung around their necks.

Adina was squeezed next to Lyta. 'This is such fun,' she said in her lisping voice. She examined the black scarf that Lyta held. 'Is that a token for Kedir Firt?' She was holding a silver and white scarf in her own hands. 'I'll give this one to Lord Quilin if he begs me for it.'

Lyta didn't correct the mistake. However her neighbour quickly learned the truth as both Firt and Quilin trotted toward the pavilion on their mounts. Firt, dressed in shiny silver mail, was riding a matching white horse while Quilin in black armour was mounted on a coal black destrier.

Adina's mouth opened in surprise as Firt reached for her white scarf. Baldus, with a scowl on his ruddy face, leaned out from his seat beside Halia to address Lyta. 'The Kedura told me she asked you to honour the erle from your own demesne. I hope that on the morrow, you will grant my son the chance to carry your token.'

'.Of course,' Lyta said quickly as Quilin accepted her black scarf and attached it to his lance. Before he turned away, he winked at her.

'He really is handsome.' Adina sighed.

The early bouts were between squires with little or no experience at tourneys. Some of them held their lances awkwardly and were soon unhorsed while others with more confidence scored points for hitting their opponents' chests or helms. Adina cheered when one of her father's squires won several bouts. As at the archery contest, the crowd beside the lists yelled approval for all the winners and hissed or called abuse at the losers. Baldus gave lengthy opinions on the dexterity and horsemanship of each entrant. Halia behaved with her usual dignity, making her own quiet comments. Adina judged the riders by their mail, pouring scorn on one young man for his dented armour and helm.

'It probably belonged to his father or uncle,' Lyta said. 'Young squires can't afford to spend much coin on their mail. That fellow is a good fighter and should go far.'

As each bout ended, Lyta glanced at the sky. Black clouds billowed like full sails on an enormous ship. Would the remaining matches finish before the storm arrived? She knew that her mother didn't allow jousting to take place in the rain.

Two squires had won their bouts. One of them would ride against Firt while the other would take his place against Quilin. Adina drew in her breath as Firt took his place and his opponent steadied his horse at the other end. The crowd was cheering for the Aldean squire while Baldus yelled instructions and encouragement to his son. Lyta couldn't see how Firt would hear anything with his helm closed.

The signal was given and the bout began. Adina sucked in her breath as the contestants came level with the pavilion. With a swift lunge, Firt unhorsed the squire.

Adina clapped her hands. 'Well done!' she called.

Baldus waved an arm in the air as he commented to Halia on his son's excellent sense of timing. Then it was Quilin's turn on his black mount to face the second squire on a grey horse. This time, Lyta felt her heart race as the horses galloped toward each other. However, before Quilin could find his mark, the other horse stopped abruptly. As the animal whinnied and tossed its head, yellow foam frothed from his mouth. The squire slipped sideways as the grey horse halted suddenly.

Then both rider and horse fell sideways. The squire landed on the grass. When the horse crashed down on top of him, the watchers gasped in unison. Quilin yanked on his reins to halt his own horse as men raced toward the fallen squire. Magian Domen and Archis Druck were among the first to reach the scene.

The commander yelled an order to guards who had been standing among the crowd. Druck grabbed a sharp lance from one of his men and drove it through the horse's neck. The animal shuddered once before lying still. Six men brought ropes which they fastened to the animal and dragged it off the squire and away from the lists.

Magian Domen knelt beside the injured man. One of his legs was bent at a strange angle and he screamed when a gentle hand was laid on his belly. The magian said something to Druck who gave further commands to his men. When they brought a wide plank, the squire was placed upon it and carried to a nearby tent.

Lyta had forgotten to watch the sky during this drama but now the spectators were startled by an enormous clap of thunder directly overhead. It was followed almost instantaneously by jagged lightning that lit up the area in an unearthly blue-green glow.

Large drops of rain fell from the sky. The crowd pulled sacks and hoods over their heads as they ran for cover. The pavilion roof would not be a protection for long if the rain stayed so heavy. Lyta noticed that the canvas was already bulging over their heads. Adina followed her gaze. 'We will be drowned.' Her voice rose to a shriek. 'And my best gown and robe will be ruined.'

'We should run for it.' Lyta scrambled from her seat.

'But I'm afraid of thunder and lightning. I feel safer here.'

As she spoke a second roll of thunder made them both jump. The accompanying lightning struck the pennant on the top of a tent to their right. It burst into flame.

Adina squealed. 'It's far too dangerous here.' Holding her long skirts up, she leapt from her seat and jumped down the steps to the ground. Baldus stripped off his cloak and held it over Halia in a gallant gesture. As

Lyta followed Adina, the rest of the pavilion party ran for the castle in a mad scurry.

By the time they reached the keep, everyone was drenched. Elaborate hairstyles had been replaced by dripping locks plastered to heads and clothes were glued to their owners' bodies. The only ones to enjoy the storm were Josik's two imps who danced around in the courtyard trying to catch rain in their open mouths until their father ordered them inside. Lyta hoped that Lord Trevin and Lord Wilus would be able to keep the boys in order in the days to come. The two erles were taking a twin each to be trained as squires.

Lyta reflected that the good thing about a thunderstorm was that it cleared the air.

Chapter Thirteen

Next morn, Halia declared the tourney could resume. Under blue skies, the sun and a stiff breeze were drying up the puddles. Lyta escaped to the magian's cottage before her mother could ask her to entertain their guests. She knocked on the door but Magian Domen did not answer. She wondered if he was tending the injured squire in another location. As she turned away, the magian appeared. His face was grave.

'How's the squire?' Lyta asked.

'He died an hour ago. His internal injuries were severe.'

'Poor lad. Lord Trevin will be grieved.'

'The boy came from Sevvir.I will inform their magian about his death.' He began to close the door.

'One moment, please. Do you know why the horse collapsed?'

'Nin says it was poisoned but nobody can confirm that. Trevin stated there was nothing wrong with the animal when it left his estate.'

Lyta was upset about the boy's death and disturbed to hear that the horse might have been deliberately targeted. The mount was grey, very similar in colour to Silver, her own horse. She made for the stables, needing to be sure that Silver was well guarded by the grooms and boys. Ivil was watering Midnight. He paused when he saw Lyta.

'I hope you're keeping our horses safe,' she said.

Ivil sighed. 'We're taking turns to sleep here. Nin's not sure the horse was poisoned.'

'So he might have been ill when he arrived here?'

'True, Kedie. How can we tell?'

Lyta visited Silver to make sure her mount was well. As usual the horse welcomed her. She stroked the soft nose, promising to ride Silver after the tournament was over.

Halia took Lyta to her meeting with the erles. 'You should start to learn what happens in our discussions,' she said.

The lords suggested that Firt and Quilin should have a final jousting bout and then, if they both agreed, continue the contest with weapons. Quilin was happy to accept their terms.

'Firt is also content,' said Lord Wilus. 'He intends to defeat you in the lists before trouncing you with a weapon of your choice.'

'Then I'll defend my honour with my short sword.'

Josik grimaced. 'The boy doesn't lack confidence. You should have won that archery contest and pricked his conceit.'

Quilin shook his head with a smile.

Before the tourney began, Lyta handed her token to Firt who grabbed it with an ungracious scowl. When Quilin accepted a token from Adina, he pressed his lips to her hand. She blushed and giggled.

After the unfortunate event of the first day, the crowd was more subdued as it gathered along the lists. When the two men took their positions, many folk yelled their support for Quilin while Baldus and his retinue called loudly for Firt to be successful.

Lyta held her breath as the two horses thundered toward each other. Neither contestant scored a hit. Each rider galloped to his own end to wait for the next signal. On the second pass, Quilin used a dextrous jab of his lance. Everyone gasped as Firt crashed to the ground. Lyta restrained herself from cheering but Baldus stood up, frowning until Firt stirred. Adina had shrieked and covered her face.

'The boy's fine,' Baldus said as Firt was helped to his feet. The horse and rider were made ready for another bout.

With a well-timed stroke of his lance, Firt unhorsed Quilin. Lyta gasped as the erle hit the ground. She breathed normally after she saw he was uninjured. Firt removed his helm and called out. 'Let's decide this hand to hand.'

Quilin removed his own helm. 'I agree.'

The horses were led away and each rider retired to his own tent. When Quilin and Firt reappeared, they were wearing tunics, hose, and soft boots and carrying swords. They came to the centre of the lists and faced each other, waiting for Erle Josik to give the signal to begin.

Adina moaned. 'Tell me what's happening.' She closed her eyes.

Lyta dug her in the ribs with a sharp elbow. 'I'll do no such thing. If you want to know what's going on, then watch.'

Firt was more heavily built than Quilin and his sword thrusts had more power behind them. However Quilin was more agile as he dodged every blow. He danced around Firt whose face soon became flushed and angry. Suddenly, Quilin darted forward and lunged at Firt's shoulder. His sword struck flesh.

Firt yelled, waved his arms in the air, and lost his balance. The sword fell to the ground, just out of arm's reach. The crowd laughed as he sat there, a large scowl creasing his features. Quilin should have asked his opponent to yield. Instead, he stood over Firt, looking down at him. Then the erle picked up the sword from the grass. He bowed and handed it to Firt. A roar rose from the crowd in approval of his courteous gesture.

Firt waved a fist in the air. He cursed, pushed himself onto his hands and knees, and before Quilin was ready, slashed at his opponent's leg. Quilin dropped his own weapon and sank to the ground. Bright blood ran between his fingers as he covered the wound with both hands.

Lyta's heart raced in distress as she tried to judge the seriousness of Quilin's wound. The crowd was shouting abuse at Firt while Baldus roared at his son. 'What are you doing?'

Firt frowned. He staggered as he rose and then stood motionless, staring at his sword as though it alone was responsible for wounding Quilin. Magian Domen was the first to reach Quilin. He was followed by four prentices carrying a large canvas sheet. The prentices wrapped Quilin in the sheet and carried him away.

Lyta swallowed hard. 'What a cowardly act,' she hissed at Adina. 'And to think I gave my token to that man.'

When a meat pie just missed his face, Firt seemed to realize what had happened. He shook his head before starting toward the pavilion. His father met him halfway and grabbed Firt's shoulders. The two held a hurried conversation before Firt nodded.

He trudged across the grass to Halia's seat. His head drooped as he spoke. 'Many apologies, Kedura, for my ungracious action. I didn't know what I was doing when I struck the erle. A wild rage overcame me.'

Lyta snorted when she heard his explanation. A wild rage indeed. He'd tried to win the contest by any means, fair or foul. Halia accepted his weak apology with a nod of her head. Her expression was stony.

An uneasy air hung over the great hall that night. Baldus had apologised to everyone in sight for his son's behaviour. 'He is young and headstrong, Halia. I hope you can forgive him. I've visited the magian and Domen is hopeful the erle will recover.'

Lyta heard this with trepidation. She must visit the magian herself to discover the full extent of Quilin's wounds. She felt uncomfortable when she was placed beside Firt at the head table but couldn't resist a comment to him. 'Don't people in Delis know how to behave? Our erle gave you time to recover but then you took advantage of him.'

Firt hissed at her. 'You are showing your ignorance of sword play.'

'I know enough about tourney rules to decide that you were a coward and a cheat.'

Firt's eyes narrowed to slits and his fists clenched on the table. 'Your words only prove your inexperience.'

Halia was leaning forward to catch Lyta's eyes. She must have overheard some of the exchange. 'Lyta, would you please serve Firt a portion of our excellent venison pie. Prala has made them especially for our guests.'

Lyta noticed for the first time that a golden-crusted pie had been placed before her on the table. Savoury smells and steam rose from it. She took a deep breath. 'Our cook makes delicious pies.'

Firt snarled as he slashed the crust with his blade. 'Then I hope she's cooked some humble pie as well. I'd be happy to serve you with a large slice.'

When the women left the hall, Lyta again followed Halia to her chamber. The Kedura sighed as she removed her tiara. 'What a dreadful day. I don't want to hear another apology from Baldus. He's almost smothered me with words.'

'I hope this shows you Firt isn't the husband for me.'

'Baldus agrees with you. He told me that his second son would be more suitable for you. Fultis has more spirit.'

Lyta regarded her mother with horror. 'Surely you won't support that idea! I'm not wedding any son of Baldus.'

'Don't get so upset, child. Baldus is leaving on the morrow and he won't return until the memory of Firt's actions has died away.' She frowned before adding, 'I have political reasons for keeping Baldus on my side.'

Lyta sighed. She was pleased that Firt was leaving so soon but the idea of meeting another Delis kedir didn't please her.

'One more thing to tell you,' Halia said. 'The erles will be depart the day after Baldus. Trevin has asked to leave his daughter with us.'

Lyta couldn't believe her ears. 'But, Mother, Adina and I have nothing to talk about. She'll be bored with me and I'm weary of her constant prattle of gowns, jewels, and hair styles.'

'This is what concerns many women so you should learn patience. Adina needs female company. She has no sisters and three more brothers at home. I've already told Cordon he will have another student.'

If Lyta had been upset before, she was more annoyed by the knowledge that Adina would not be leaving with her parents. What else could go wrong?

As soon as Baldus, Firt, and their retinue clattered from the courtyard, Lyta dropped her waving hand and breathed out in relief. She silently thanked Lady Moon for the sudden departure and asked her to prevent other members of the noble Delis family from visiting the castle in the future. Beside her, Adina was sniffing. 'I'm so sad they've gone. Do you think Firt will remember me?'

Lyta snorted in reply. Baldus had hugged her hard against his barrel chest, while Firt had kissed her hand in a perfunctory manner. However, he had kissed Adina full on the lips. While her father had glared at him for his audacity, her mother had smirked behind her hand. Did the erle's wife have marriage ambitions for her daughter in that direction?

Beside her, Adina gasped as she looked down at her blue surcoat. 'I've caught my hem on something sharp. It must be mended before anyone notices.'

'Talk to Wea, our seamstress.'

'Oh no.' Adina's voice was shocked. 'Only my maid touches my clothes.'

Lyta smiled as Adina ran up the steps. She'd been wondering how to get rid of the girl this morn to allow her to visit the magian alone. She needed to inquire about Quilin. When Lyta knocked quietly on the door of the workchamber, Domen opened it and waved her inside. She assumed that the erle would be occupying the sleeping chamber at the rear of the building. She'd never been in that space.

'He's resting peacefully after a very restless night,' said Magian Domen. He placed a finger against his lips to warn Lyta to speak in a low voice.

'Is the wound serious?' she asked.

'It's deeper than I thought at first and infection could be a worry. As well, some muscles have been damaged. I hope he will be able to walk normally.'

'Can I help you?'

Domen started to shake his head and then stopped. 'Yes, there is something you could do. Since you are here, you could mix more Jarse potion. Do you remember the receipt?'

'I do and I'd be happy to assist.' Lyta scanned the rows of flasks, shimmering in the sunlight before she collected the necessary ingredients. After checking her selection, the magian left her alone to do the work. When she left the cottage, Lyta walked more lightly, knowing she'd been a little helpful in Quilin's recovery. Now it was up to Lady Moon to get the erle back on his feet.

Chapter Fourteen

At first, Tutoran Cordon was pleased to have another pupil. He smiled broadly before questioning Adina about the history of her demesne. As she either didn't know or couldn't remember, his smile of welcome became a frown. 'Didn't your father employ a tutoran?' he asked in a despairing tone.

'Oh yes, but only one of my brothers listened to him. Tarr actually likes reading. I spend more time with Mother doing needlework and practising my singing and dancing.'

Cordon shook his head. 'I don't understand. Kedura Halia and her council passed a law that required all boys and girls to be educated equally. Your father was on the council at the time.'

'But he says book learning isn't needed for governing an estate and girls are better mothers and wives without strange ideas in their heads.'

Lyta was amused by her tutoran's shocked expression. Was he upset that Adina's father didn't believe in education or was he worried about the strange ideas that girls might be exposed to? She hid a grin behind her book cover.

Cordon cleared his throat. 'The Kedura wishes you to work with Kedie Lyta. As you are both at very different stages, I will instruct you separately.' He dropped the volume he'd been holding and searched through a pile on the table. He opened a dull-looking brown book. 'This should be a good starting point for you.'

Adina twisted her head to read the title. 'Is it a story book?'

‘It’s a basic historical record of Aldea. I will set Kedie Lyta to work and then you and I will begin on the first page.’ His new student sighed and yawned.

At morn’s end when the girls were both dismissed by Cordon, Adina was full of grumbles. ‘That was so boring. Do I really have to study every day?’

‘Except on Holy and Feast Days. I also have some lessons with Magian Domen.’

Adina’s eyes widened. ‘Oh no! I can’t learn magic. Mother and Father would never agree and I’d be afraid of being bewitched.’

‘Were you tested at seven summers?’

‘The testing hurt my head and the magian frightened me. Luckily none of us were chosen. Father was pleased to keep us at home.’

How could Lyta’s mother have imagined that the two girls might become friends? They couldn’t even discuss their lessons. Making a huge effort, Lyta asked Adina if she wanted to come to the stables.

Much to her surprise, Adina nodded. ‘I like to ride and Father said I have a natural seat. At home, I have my own horse and falcon.’

Before going to the stables, they collected carrots from the kitchen. Silver welcomed Lyta with many snorts and whinnies. She sensed reproach in the horse’s eyes as she hadn’t been ridden since Baldus and Firt’s arrival.

‘What a fine mare!’ Adina said.’ And with that shiny coat, she’s well named.’ She held out a carrot for Silver and smiled as the horse accepted it.

‘Tell me about your own mount,’ Lyta said.

‘She’s a deep chestnut colour. Her name is Star from the white markings on her head and nose. I miss her dearly.’ Stroking Silver’s nose, Adina added, ‘One of my brothers promised to exercise my horse. Father said he’ll make sure Tarr keeps his word.’ ’

Lyta watched Adina caress Silver; mayhap, they did have one interest to unite them. 'Our head groom will find you a good horse and then we can go out together. You can even ride my Silver if you wish.'

Adina's face lit up. 'You are very kind. I'd like that. Could we ride every morn instead of studying? '

Lyta laughed as she shook her head. 'Mother wouldn't agree. Let's find Nin and look at horses.'

The two girls and Nin walked along the stalls examining the horses. Lyta averted her eyes from Courage's empty stall. Lord Josik had bought the horse from her mother. He and the animal had already left. Losing Courage had meant cutting the last link to Virr.

They stopped beside Heart, a bay mare with a lively look in her eyes. Adina patted her glossy back. 'Your grooms really take good care of your mounts. When can we ride?'

They agreed to ride next morn after Adina's parents had left the castle. Nin said he'd arrange the usual escort with the commander.

'Then I'll have something to make me happy again,' Adina said as they left the stables. 'I've never lived away from home before.' When her blue eyes filled with tears, Lyta looked away, feeling uncomfortable.

Next morn, following repast, Adina clutched her mother and wept again. Her father detached the girl's hands and gave last instructions. 'Be a good lass and do as you are told,' he said, patting his daughter's head before mounting his horse.

As she watched her parents leave the courtyard, Adina sobbed. 'I should have gone with them. Now I have to stay here and study.'

The Kedura was standing on the castle steps beside Lyta and Adina. Now her eyebrows rose. 'Don't you like lessons?'

'I've never been good at schoolwork. But I am good at riding and Mother says my needlework is promising.'

Halia placed a hand on Adina's shoulder. 'Well, this morn, you and Lyta may be excused from schoolwork. I'll inform Cordon that you may ride instead.'

Adina's tears vanished. 'Thank you, Kedura. Riding will make me feel a little happy.'

'But only for this morn,' added Halia. 'It is important for girls to be educated.'

Later, Ivil and Nin led Silver and Heart from the stables. Both horses danced with pleasure at being out in the fresh air. Silver nuzzled Lyta's shoulder as she came close to her.

'She's so pretty,' said Adina. 'Almost as pretty as my Star.'

'Ride Silver this morn,' Lyta suggested, 'and I'll take Heart.'

'Really? Are you sure you don't mind?'

Lyta took a deep breath. 'I'm sure.'

Chapter Fifteen

Erit stared around the grubby chamber he was sharing with Cett. Cobwebs partially obscured the light coming in from the small window. He guessed it was better sleeping indoors than outside but not by much. The two men had decided to move further away from the castle to avoid being spotted by Archis Druck or one of his guards.

Yna, a relative of Cett, owned the inn which for once, was not named after a fowl. The place was called The Golden Icecat.

'She's a niece on my mother's side,' Cett said. 'You can tell by the nose.'

The niece didn't seem to care why they were in town so that was a benefit. Erit had juggled platters and knives the night before to great applause from the patrons of the inn.

'I like to provide entertainment,' said Yna, wiping her hands on a filthy apron. 'It brings in the crowds.'

Erit tried not to smile. The inn's main chamber didn't hold enough people to make a decent crowd.

'We're expecting a troupe of actors tonight,' Yna said. 'They come to town every twelvemonth at this time. Very popular they are.'

'What do they perform?'

'High class plays about kings, queens, and death. I do like a good murder.'

Erit reflected that he could do without more murders. He'd hoped to carry out his plan in Aldea without the deaths of Virr and the groom. At least he hadn't been directly involved in the acts. Nobody knew that he had a morbid fear of blood. Erit had successfully kept it a secret from his father, brother, and associates. Even drops of blood welling from a cut finger made him feel ill but strong self-control had prevented his inward reaction from showing on his face or in his body.

Cett and Erit went downstairs when they heard wagons and horses on the cobbles outside. The actors blew into the inn like a blast of wind, greeting Yna and her customers with yells and laughter. The troupe consisted of four men and a woman who appeared to be the daughter of the oldest man and the partner of another.

Erit sat in a corner, with a cup of ale before him, and watched the unfolding scene. He could tell they were actors and used to dealing in words. The white-haired man treated every sentence as a stately speech to be delivered at full volume, accompanied by numerous hand gestures.

Yna and her daughter bustled about, pouring ale and cutting hunks of bread and cheese. The daughter, who'd been lucky enough to avoid the family nose, was a buxom wench with flaxen hair and dimpled cheeks. She caught the attention of the youngest actor, a lively fellow with wavy chestnut hair and twinkling brown eyes. Erit was amused to note that Yna watched her daughter closely as the girl blushed and smiled in response to the actor's teasing remarks.

After a meal, the players vanished into the back of the inn to prepare for the evening show. Yna ordered her patrons to push the tables and stools against the walls to clear a space in the centre of the chamber.

With a flourish of his hands, the youngest actor bounded into the room. He was wearing a purple cape and carrying a wooden sword. He announced the play. 'The Tragic Death of the King and the Dreadful Events that Followed,' he declaimed too much cheering.

The young woman played the part of the queen with her father as the old king. The three other men were rivals for the queen's favour. By the end of the play, the entire cast was sprawled on the floor, murdered by stabbing, strangling, or poisoning. Erit had swallowed hard when dark red patches had bloomed on the king's tunic.

Amid loud clapping and whistling, the actors rose to their feet. They held hands and bowed low. The youngest man whipped off his hat and walked through the room soliciting coins. When he arrived at the corner, Erit held a silver coin over the hat. He asked, 'Does your acting pay well?'

The actor shrugged. 'Not so well. We don't starve but there are days when we tighten our belts and hope for a crust of bread.'

'I may have a paying job for you.'

'Then, friend, we'll drink together when I've given the old man our takings.'

He completed the circle of patrons before handing over the hat. Erit called to Cett who'd been swapping tall stories with two burly seamen and Cett joined him at the table.

The actor carried a cup of ale across the chamber and dropped onto a stool beside them. 'What's the job?' he asked. 'And, more important, what's the payment?'

'Do you know who you resemble?' Erit asked.

The man rolled his eyes. 'Of course. Everyone from Sevvir points out the likeness.'

'Are you actually related to Kedur Petrin?'

'According to my mother, I am. Unfortunately, the man has true-born sons and doesn't need me.'

'Well,' said Erit. 'I have two tasks in mind. One for a couple from your band and the other more for you. You can use your resemblance to play the part of Merik, the kedur's eldest son.'

The actor took a long swallow of ale. 'If the price is right, I'm all ears.' He rubbed his fingers together and leaned forward. 'Tell me more.'

Chapter Sixteen

When Adina was mounted on Silver's back, she gathered the reins with a practised hand. Silver, knowing she had a new rider, tried some unaccustomed pirouettes but Adina was well able to control her. Lyta watched her actions with approval. The four guards fell into their positions before and after the girls as their little party moved past the main gate.

The wind grew strong outside the castle. Both girls tugged their hoods over their heads as they trotted through the town. Folk bustled about their business in the square, the streets, and the alleys. Lyta kept a close watch for the juggler or the man with the big nose while Adina examined her new surroundings with interest. She laughed at the efforts of a child who was trying to remove a stubborn pig from a turnip patch.

Lyta asked Borut, the head guard, to take the road leading to the port. The harbour was always her favourite destination. When they halted their horses, she breathed in the familiar seaside scents of fish, seaweed, and salt. Only one ship was docked at the jetty and the last boxes were being loaded onto the deck as the one-armed captain shouted his orders.

The gangplank was rising when a skinny boy in a ragged tunic jumped onto the deck. A seaman lifted a hand to cuff the lad's ears but the latecomer ducked behind a row of boxes. The captain yelled a final order to untie the ropes and soon, the ship moved into the bay. Then, as the wind filled the striped sails, the vessel gathered speed, making for open water.

Borut tapped Lyta's shoulder. 'Kedie, the horses are getting cold standing here.'

'We'll take the high road home,' Lyta said.

Adina's cheeks were rosy and her eyes sparkled. 'This ride is wonderful. Can we do it again in the morn?'

'Next time we'll go into the forest.' Lyta pointed toward the trees.

'It looks gloomy.' Adina shuddered. 'Are there wild beasts?'

'Only pigs and deer. You'd like the wild flowers in the glades.'

They trotted along the track skirting the first row otrees. A loud horn blast beside Silver, startled the horse. She neighed, rolled her eyes, and rose on her back legs. A man rushed from the bushes on the other side of the road and made a grab for Adina. She struggled to avoid his hands and to control Silver. Borut drew his short sword while a guard helped Lyta as Heart also reared in panic.

When Borut leaned from his horse, he jabbed the fellow in his arm. The attacker ran off with drops of bright blood marking his path. Borut and one of his men followed the attacker and the party on the road heard yells and a short scuffle. Borut returned from the bushes, shaking his head. 'He had a horse waiting and got away.

Lyta had been expecting Adina to scream or faint or both but she did neither. Instead, she'd calmed Silver and was now stroking her neck and murmuring encouragement to her.

'What about the other man?' Lyta asked. 'The one with the horn?'

When the guards exchanged glances, she realized they'd forgotten about the horn blast that had frightened the horses in the first place. Borut waved at the youngest guard who slipped from his horse and disappeared into the thick undergrowth. The other three men formed a rough circle around the girls while they waited.

A few minutes later, the guard reappeared shaking his head. 'No sign of the fellow but I seen where he laid in the bushes.'

Borut ordered the ride to resume. The guards were now on full alert and rode with their weapons drawn. Lyta's mind was full of questions. Was the attack aimed at her or Adina? And why would anyone want to take either girl? She was relieved when they arrived at the drawbridge. Archis Druck was standing by the gatehouse to receive his usual report. Borut spoke to him in an agitated voice about the event and the commander instantly strode towards the castle.

By the time Adina and Lyta reached there, Halia was waiting in an antechamber beside the great hall. She frowned as she looked them over. 'Are you both unharmed?'

Lyta nodded but Adina burst into tears. 'I was so frightened,' she said between sobs. 'And my arm is bruised where that rough fellow grabbed me.' She buried her face against Halia's shoulder.

Lyta met her mother's eyes over the top of Adina's head. When Halia nodded, Lyta realized the discussion about the morn's events would take place without her companion. Halia summoned Amia. 'Take the Lady Adina to Obela. She will know what potion will best soothe her nerves.'

Once the maid had led the girl away, Lyta sat down beside her mother. 'Was Adina the target of this attempted kidnap?' Halia asked.

Her daughter explained about the hoods and the change of horses. 'I think the men were after me but I can't understand why.'

'It's a pity Borut didn't catch one of them. I'd have liked Druck to question him.'

'Do you think this is part of a plot?'

Halia's eyebrows rose. 'Why do you mention a plot?'

Lyta wished she'd kept her mouth shut but now it was too late. Instead, she took a deep breath and told her mother about the sightings of the man with the big nose and the juggler. 'I think Givis and Rusa were both murdered to keep them quiet. Someone thought they knew too much about Virr's death.'

Halia tapped her finger against her lips. 'Although your tale seems far-fetched, you might be right,' she said at last. 'But why was Virr killed?'

'If we knew that, then everything would make sense. Could Virr have come here to protect you or me?'

'It's possible,' said her mother, 'but since we can't ask him, this is speculation.'

When her mother left for her daily audience in the hall, Lyta went to ask the magian about Quilin. 'He's a little improved,' said Domen, 'but not enough for visitors. He was inquiring about you but I didn't tell him what happened this morn.'

'You already know about this event?'

'I met the commander after he'd talked to your mother. Did the incident upset you?'

'It bothers me because I don't know why someone would want to take Adina or me.'

'I'll ask some discreet questions in case people from another demesne are involved.'

'Since I can't solve this mystery, I'll try to put it behind me.' Lyta took a deep breath. 'Can I do anything to help you?'

'It's not your favourite activity but my herbs in the side plots need weeding. I can't ask just anyone because servants don't distinguish the weeds from the herbs.'

The magian was right about Lyta's dislike of weeding. However, she decided to complete the chore with a good heart. It would give the magian more time to tend Quilin.

By supper time, Adina had recovered her spirits enough to eat with Halia and Lyta. They had just begun the meal when they heard voices in the courtyard. Archis Druck sent a guard outside to discover the cause of the noise. When the man returned, he bent down to deliver a message in the commander's ear. In turn, Druck spoke to the kedura.

'Kedir Merik,' said Halia in a surprised voice. 'Is he travelling alone?'

'He has a squire and a man with him.'

'Bid him join us and arrange a chamber.' Halia looked thoughtful. 'I wonder why his demesne magian did not inform us of Merik's arrival. Never mind. He's here and if he's like his father, Petrin, he'll be good company for both of you.'

Adina whispered to Lyta. 'Where does Merik live?'

'In Sevvir. He's a son of Kedur Petrin, a kinsman of my mother.'

Merik was young and tall with glossy chestnut hair, dark eyes, and a most engaging smile. He kissed Halia's hand and apologised for his unheralded arrival. 'Father has reluctantly granted me leave to travel. I've been going wherever the wind blows. A northerly breeze has driven me here.'

When he was seated at the high table, he greeted the two girls. 'I am exceeding lucky tonight to be able to converse with three lovely ladies. Last night I had only two men and three horses, all remarkably silent and boring.'

Lyta smiled politely at him but Adina beamed so widely that Lyta wondered if the girl's previous allegiance to Firt was about to disappear. 'You are very kind, Sir.'

Merik was most entertaining. When Halia asked him to describe his travels, he had the whole table listening to his wild tales.

He finished a story with this line. 'And then the fellow ran off without the cow!'

The kedura joined in the laughter which followed. 'Merik, you are so much like your father. I haven't seen my cousin for many moons but I remember him as a fine teller of tales.'

Merik shook his head. 'My father is much better than me but then, he has the advantage of more summers to refine his art. I'm a mere beginner.'

After the meal, Jer escorted the girls from the hall. As they walked, Adina praised Merik in warm tones. 'He is so pleasant. And I laughed a lot at his stories. But I don't think he is as handsome as Firt or Quilin.' She turned to Lyta with a frown on her face. 'Which quality do you think is more important in a man? Good looks or a lively mind?'

Lyta was in no doubt. 'Good looks can change but a lively mind endures.'

'Hmm. I shall consider this problem,' Adina said as they reached her chamber. She said good night with a pensive expression.

Jer and Lyta continued to her tower where Jer took his position outside the door. As she got into bed, she thought that Merik was a welcome addition to their company. Mayhap the kedir and his two travelling companions could provide extra protection on any future rides. She was sure that as a kedir of Sevvir, he'd be well trained in the use of arms.

Early next morn, Lyta found Merik in the stables. He was grooming a horse as black as her mother's Midnight except for a little white sock on its right foreleg. 'You have a fine horse. Does he like apples?'

Merik sat back on his heels and laughed as Lyta held out one of the apples that she'd brought for Silver. 'Try to stop him from eating it. Apples are Gallant's favourite treats.' He watched his horse chew the fruit. 'You will be his friend for life.'

'He looks like a strong mount.'

'Gallant carries me all day without tiring. And he might even go all night.'

'That's mine.' Lyta pointed to Silver. The horse was watching from her stall further along the row. 'She's wondering why I'm giving apples to a complete stranger.'

'You'd better console her.' As she walked away, he added, 'Do you ride every day?'

'Whenever I can. But I have to study first.'

'Kedie, your mother might allow me to accompany you and the Lady Adina.'

The prospect was pleasing. 'We can ask her.'

But although Halia reluctantly agreed to consider allowing Adina and Lyta to ride with Merik, the weather was against an outing. A sudden downpour prevented them from leaving the castle after dinner. Instead, Merik taught them to play Brothers and Sisters, a card game from Sevvir and they spent the afternoon in gales of laughter. Merik said he'd won although Lyta didn't know how he could tell because he kept changing the rules to suit his hand. When Halia came to visit them at the end of her daily audiences, Merik persuaded the kedura to play a round of the game. Then he declared her the winner despite the fact that Lyta had gained the most counters.

Halia shook her head. 'I haven't played that game since I was a child in Sevvir. Merik, you are surely your father's son. He could charm birds from the trees straight into his open hands.'

Merik's talents extended beyond card games. He possessed a fine tenor voice and sang several songs after supper. Halia's singer performed a duet with him.

Adina sighed long and hard as she listened to the words. 'The lovers both dying in the lake was so romantic. But now I wonder if the man I marry should have a fine voice as well as a handsome face.'

‘If he sings like a crow, you can always hire a singer for your hall. ’ Lyta said. ‘Many things are more important than songs.’

‘Very true.’ Adina looked thoughtful. ‘In the morn, I shall make a list of the most important qualities in a husband. I must choose the right man.’

In her tower chamber, Lyta thought about her visit to Quilin earlier that day. The magian had actually permitted her to see his patient. Even though Magian Domen had said he was pleased with the erle’s progress, she was shocked by the change in Quilin’s appearance. His face was ashen and his eyes sunken in his face.

He spoke in a weak voice when she asked how he was faring. ‘I would do much better if this tyrant fed me a decent chop or piece of venison.’

‘In good time,’ said the magian. You must not run before you can walk.’

‘Walk? You won’t let me put my feet out of bed. How can I walk?’

Lyta laughed as she left the bedchamber. The erle might be weak in body but his spirit remained strong.

Chapter Seventeen

The riding party resembled a small army as it crossed the drawbridge. Halia had ordered Druck to make sure the guards understood their roles. 'If there's the slightest hint of danger along the road, the girls must be protected and then returned to the castle at once.'

Merik had said he understood the kedura's concern. He promised to take good care of Adina and Lyta. He'd looked solemnly at Halia. 'I'm a competent swordsman and my squire and man are both well-armed. We can assist your guards.'

After leaving the drawbridge, Adina grimaced, 'I thought we were never going to get away. Listening to all those instructions made my head ache.'

Merik leaned forward in his saddle. 'The Kedura was right to be worried about your safety. But don't be distressed, Lady Adina. No harm will come to you.'

Since Halia had told the guards to stay away from the town and the harbour, they turned toward the countryside and took the road that led into the Dark Forest. Once again, the kedura had decided the party should stay in the outer regions of the forest. 'Lyta knows several places where you can enjoy the wild flowers. Lady's Lips should be in full bloom.'

. When the road became narrower, they were forced to ride in single file. At the first fork in the way, Lyta called out to Borut to take the right hand trail. Merik sent his squire and guard ahead to make sure the way was safe and clear.

'If they see trouble of any sort,' he told Borut, 'they'll come back and report to you.'

Lyta was taking Adina and Merik to one of the larger glades. Virr had explained that a lightning strike had probably burned the trees and created the open space. The conditions were right for wildflowers that needed a little sun to grow. The riders came first to a smaller open area and Adina exclaimed at the clumps of bright pink flowers. ‘Can I pick them?’ she asked.

Lyta shook her head. ‘If you do, they’ll die. Each bloom lasts for only one day. If you want flowers, wait until we get to the Picnic Glade. Purple Salvan Capes grow there as well as yellow daisies and the ones we call Red Gloves from their shape.’

She was right. Salvan Capes bloomed there as well as the other wild flowers. Merik, Adina, and Lyta dismounted to admire the flowers at close range. As they walked from one patch to another, the guards held the mounts.

‘I’ll bring back a bouquet for the Kedura,’ said Adina as she bent down.

Borut smiled as he ordered two of the guards to help her in the task. They didn’t look very pleased to be commanded to pick daisies.

Merik took the bridle of his horse from the guard. ‘Gallant is very fond of that particular grass.’ He nodded toward a far corner.

Halfway across the glade, he paused and called to Lyta. ‘What are those white blooms? They are very small and delicate.’

‘Where?’ Lyta peered where he was pointing.

Merik took her hand. ’Over here. Around this tree.’

On the far side of the tree, he tugged her arm. Lyta lost her balance on the damp grass. Then before she could call out or stand up, he jammed a cloth into her mouth and dropped a rough hood over her head. It smelled of stale wine.

She swung both arms out until her fingers felt him and then scratched his flesh as hard as she could.

'Ow!' Merik said. 'That's enough!' He grabbed her hands and bound them together. Then he threw her onto a horse.

In panic, she twisted, turned, and kicked out with both legs. She knew her foot had hit him when he uttered a string of oaths.

When another man swung onto the horse, Merik tied the rope around her waist to connect her to the rider. Lyta's face was jammed against a broad back which smelled of sweat and onions. When Merik hit the horse's rump, the animal leapt forward.

The whole episode took only a few minutes. At first, Lyta wondered if Borut and the guards had even seen what had happened. Then she heard shouts and the sound of hooves and knew her guards were chasing them.

Suddenly, the noises became screams and yells. 'They've run into the ropes across the trail,' said Merik. He called out. 'Good work, lads. That will slow them down.'

The horses moved at a good pace through the trees as Lyta forced down the terror that was threatening to overcome her. Virr would have told her to control her emotions and try to think logically about her present situation. Where was she being taken? One of the trails looped through the forest and then reached the coast. Was that where they were headed? It was a deserted part of the shore away from settlements.

And who was the man claiming to be Merik? She didn't believe that the son of the Kedur of Sevvir would kidnap her. He had to be an impostor. Even so, why had she been taken? Her body jolted painfully against the rider and the hood and thick cloth made it hard to breathe. She hoped her head wouldn't be covered for too long. She was growing dizzy from lack of air. Swirling shapes dazzled her eyes before they were swallowed by a dense blackness.

The next thing she was aware of was rough hands pulling her from the horse. The hood and cloth were removed and she swayed as her feet touched the ground.

'Holy Stars! You weren't meant to kill the girl.'

Lyta blinked as she recognised the voice and the face. The juggler pushed her onto a fallen log. She stared at the circle of men around her. That tall fellow with rust-coloured hair had to be the man with the big nose. Then there was so-called Merik and his squire and the man-at arms who wore a bandage on his arm. She felt some satisfaction when she saw beads of blood on the long scratch down Merik's left cheek.

The juggler handed her a cup of water. 'Drink this,' he said. 'You'll feel better.'

She drank the water before addressing Merik. 'Who are you? You're certainly not a kedir from Sevvir.'

He flashed a cheeky grin. 'But I fooled you all, didn't I? Even your mother was taken in. This was one of my best acting roles.' He turned to the juggler. 'We want to be on our way. That castle commander struck me as the tenacious type.'

'Druck will track you down,' Lyta said. 'You're right to be afraid.'

'Ooh. I'm trembling in my boots,' he said. 'Come on, Erit, give me the purse. We're off to Delis.'

From his pouch, the juggler drew a cloth purse. He tossed it to the actor who caught it neatly before peering at the coins inside. 'Much thanks,' he said as he tucked the coins away. Then he nodded to his companions and they mounted their horses, which had been standing in the shade of the trees. .

Lyta had heard the juggler's name for the first time. He laughed as he turned to the man with the big nose. 'They'll be lucky to get to Delis. Kedur Baldus will lock them up good and tight if they do.' He took the cup from Lyta's hand. 'More water?'

She shook her head. The worst of the dizziness had passed but she still felt light-headed. And afraid of what might happen next.

Erit turned to the other man. 'Cett, see if the boat's in sight.'

'Aren't you afraid I'll able to identify you?' Lyta asked.

'We're not concerned. By the morn, we will be far from your mother's realm.'

That meant they were probably going to Falga. Surely the Kedur of that demesne wasn't part of this plot. It must be organised by one of the dissatisfied erles. Cordon had mentioned Rurrik's name. But what was his aim in kidnapping her?

Cett returned to report that their transport was in sight. Shortly after, a small battered boat with a green sail arrived. Erit waded through the light surf while Cett picked her up like a sack of grain and carried her to the boat. He dumped her onto a small deck. Then both men came aboard.

'No tricks!' said Cett, 'or I'll feed you to the fish.'

'No, you won't,' Lyta said. 'Rurrik wants me alive. Fish food isn't any use to him.'

Cett spoke in a low growl. 'Who told you about the erle?'

'Nobody.' She smirked at him. 'I worked it out for myself. And now by your blunder, you've confirmed I was right.'

Cett took a step toward her and raised a hand. 'You mouthy little brat! I'll teach you a lesson you won't forget.'

Erit jumped between them. 'Both of you shut up!' He flushed a deep red as he glared at Cett. 'As usual, you've said too much.'

Lyta wasn't sure if she'd helped her situation or not by discovering that Rurrik was behind her capture. .Cett pushed her into the tiny cabin as the ship began to move.

She wrinkled her nose at the strong smell of dead fish and ancient sweat. Falga was quite close to Aldea at this part of the coast and she calculated that it might take only hours to reach that demesne. Then where would they go? She didn't know the location of Rurrik's land.

Lyta searched her memory for any information Cordon had given her in the past. Rurrik was bitter about the war and its outcome as he was one of the erles with strong attachments to the old king. He also believed he had a claim to the Aldean throne through an ancestor. But why would it help him to take Lyta? Surely he knew that the Kedur of Falga and Halia would both be intent on rescuing her and punishing him.

When she smelled food cooking, she realised how hungry she was and hoped that Erit and Cett believed in feeding captives. She heard the sound of spoons on platters and felt relieved when Cett drew back the curtain and thrust a dish at her.

Cett saw her examining the meal. 'Not the food you're used to, my fine lady, but this is what regular people eat.'

Lyta didn't want to let him know that she was annoyed. 'It smells good and I'm sure it tastes good too.' She ate a large spoonful. 'Mmm. I like beans and vegetables.'

Cett snorted and left her alone to eat her meal. The food was warm and surprisingly tasty. The smooth shapes of the white beans went well with the crunchy slithers of carrot and red cabbage. She was tempted to lick the bowl but instead, she ran a finger around the rim to collect the last fragments. After all, she didn't know when she would eat next.

Chapter Eighteen

Lyta placed the empty bowl on the stained table. Eating the meal had reminded her of her mother's generous dinner table and she was blinded by a rush of tears. She wiped the drops off her cheeks with the back of a hand. No time to cry. She must concentrate on her predicament and use all her wits to escape from these men before they reached Rurrik's estate. She wondered how they would travel over land. Either Cett or Erit could probably catch her if she ran but if she was on horseback, she might have a chance to flee from them.

When she came ashore, she hadn't counted on being trussed up like a pig going to market and thrown into the back of an open wagon. She watched Cett closely as he tied her hands together, recognising the knot as one Virr had taught her. Although she might be able to wriggle out of it, she didn't want to show the two men that she had any skill with knots. Cett climbed onto the driver's seat and picked up the reins.

Erit clambered into the wagon beside Lyta. 'Don't even think of escaping.' He grinned down at her. 'I know what you can do. You should have let me nick that foolish puppy with my blade.'

Although Lyta agreed with him, she didn't want to say so. 'Why are you doing this?' she asked. 'Are you being paid like the actors?'

His grin vanished. 'I have my own reasons.'

'Were you behind the attack on the road? Mayhap, you blew the horn.'

'I gave that task to a troupe of idiots who didn't follow my instructions' He frowned. 'If you have a plan, it's best to carry it out yourself.'

Lyta shifted on the hard wagon floor. 'The rope is digging into my arms. Could you please loosen it for me?'

Erit pulled at the knot. 'Better?'

Lyta thanked him. It was useful to know that he had responded to a polite request. He had a more pleasant manner than Cett. The first time she'd heard Erit speak, she'd known he was an educated person. But how was he connected to Rurrik?

'Do you kidnap people often or is juggling your main occupation?'

Erit laughed. 'Juggling's a very useful skill. It allows me to get into castles and taverns. Everyone likes to be entertained. Besides, if the spectators don't like my knife act, I've plenty of blades to defend myself.' His face tightened. 'And kidnapping is not one of my normal activities. You are my first and last captive.'

At the risk of angering him, Lyta asked a question. 'Who killed Virr, Givis, and Rusa?'

The sudden blast of rage from Cett shook Lyta. She grabbed her head as a sharp pain stabbed her. Had she tapped into his thoughts because his feelings were so intense? Cett turned to face her and growled low in his throat. 'Even if I knew anything about that business, I wouldn't tell you.'

Lyta took a deep and shaky breath. 'I think you killed them. Virr didn't deserve to be murdered. And Givis and Rusa had families and friends who mourn them every day.'

'I had nothing to do with the girl.' Cett glowered at her, his light eyes fierce beneath thick brows. He dropped the reins and clenched both fists.

Lyta shrank back but she continued to probe. 'But you were responsible for Virr and Givis. How does it feel to be a double murderer?' She shuddered as another wave of anger hit her like a physical blow.

'Shut your big mouth,' Cett snarled, 'or I'll come back there and shut it for you.'

Erit moved between the two. 'That's enough, girl. It's over.' He waved at Cett to pick up the reins and continue the journey.

Lyta felt more bitter tears coming into her eyes. Knowing who had killed Virr and Givis didn't make her feel better about their deaths. And Rusa might have taken her own life out of sorrow and despair. Lyta choked down her own grief. She had to keep a clear head.

While Erit tapped the metal sides of the wagon in an annoying rhythm, Lyta peered into the gathering dusk to look for landmarks. Not that it made any real difference to her. She'd never travelled through Falga before.

They were moving on a bumpy track through open countryside with crops or tall grass on either side. She couldn't see any villages or houses but there were clumps of trees and a shimmer of water in the distance. 'How much further?' she asked.

Erit roused himself from his thoughts. 'Not too far now.'

When they reached a fork in the road, Cett called back, 'Which way?'

'Take the left.' Erit leaned forward as the wagon turned. His whole body tensed as he stared ahead. The wagon bumped along a much narrower trail. The gloom was accentuated by the shade of overhanging trees. Clumps of damp leaves brushed Lyta's hair and face.

'We're here,' said Erit in a strained voice.

A high wall faced Lyta and above it loomed a grey stone building. Was this Erle Rurrik's estate? Erit jumped from the wagon, walked to the iron door in the wall, and thumped it with both fists. 'Who's on watch?' he called.

A small window over the gate squeaked open and a shaggy-haired fellow leaned out to look at them. 'Open up,' said Erit.

The fellow disappeared and with many creaks and groans, the gate swung open. Cett drove the wagon through while Erit walked behind it. Lyta found herself in a courtyard lined with low buildings butted against the walls. The manor house in front of her was three storeys high with a low tower on each of the four corners. She swallowed hard to keep a knot of anxiety from rising into her throat. What dangers lurked inside this gloomy place?

Cett clambered from the driving seat and reached over the edge of the wagon. After grabbing Lyta, he dumped her on the ground. One of her feet had gone to sleep and she lurched forward.

'Steady,' said Erit, touching her with an outstretched hand. He pointed to the wide steps. 'We're going inside.'

Lyta stamped on her foot to bring it back to life and then followed Erit into the house while Cett stayed outside with the wagon. Burning torches lined the entryway, causing strange shadows to dance across the grey walls and high ceiling.

A tall figure in a black robe appeared from around a corner. 'So you have the girl,' he said in a deep voice.

Lyta stared up at him. She must not show that she was afraid. 'Lord Rurrik, I presume,' she said.

Rurrik turned to Erit. 'You told her?'

'He didn't,' said Lyta. 'I worked it out myself.' She glanced from Rurrik to Erit. They both had hair as black as raven feathers, and distinctive slanting eyebrows over dark eyes. Although the erle was taller than the juggler, the resemblance was noticeable. 'You're his son,' she said to Erit.

'Baseborn,' said Rurrik with a scowl on his face.

Erit flushed deep red. Taking Lyta's hands, he untied the rope.

'Come' said Rurrik. He set off at a fast pace. As Lyta stumbled after him, she hoped she'd soon learn why she'd been brought to his estate. The chamber she entered smelled smoky from a pile of smouldering logs on the hearth. The high ceiling was crossed by dark rafters. At one end of the hall was a musicians' gallery and at the other a long table set with platters, cups, and a single glass.

The erle pointed to a seat beside the high-backed chair. 'Be seated.'

Lyta slid into the place he'd indicated. When Rurrik clapped his hands, two servants in dark clothing appeared. One deposited a platter of steaming meat before Lyta while the next brought bread, cheese, and a flask of wine. 'Eat, Kedie Lyta,' said Rurrik. 'You must be hungry after your journey.'

Lyta ignored the food and turned to face him. 'Tell me why I'm here.'

'Your manners are very much like your father's and grandfather's, more the pity.' He gestured at the platters. 'Eat first and then I'll answer your questions.'

The roast venison looked juicy and smelled of spices and herbs. Lyta slid several slices of meat onto her platter and took some warm bread. The erle poured red wine into her cup. He drank his own wine and watched her over the top of his glass before taking meat, bread, and a small piece of cheese. After a few mouthfuls, Lyta felt the warmth flowing back into her chilled body. 'Now I've eaten something. Why am I here?'

'You are a necessary part of my scheme.' Rurrik stroked his chin with his long white fingers. A ruby ring glinted in the flickering light.

'And what's the scheme?'

'You will find out the details in due course. The end result is that I get my rightful place as ruler of Aldea.'

Indignation bubbled in Lyta's chest. 'But that's nonsense. My mother's the rightful ruler of our demesne.'

'Not if you examine your lineage closely.' The erle pointed at her. 'Your grandsire took the realm by force. The king had appointed a different ruler.'

'And the old king is dead and buried.' Lyta paused. 'So how do I fit into this absurd plan?' She focused intently on Rurrik's face. She might be lucky to catch a single word from his thoughts. She closed her eyes and emptied her mind. Then her eyes snapped open. 'Oh no!' she said. 'My mother would never marry you.'

His smile was cruel. 'Not even to save your slender neck?'

'I hope not.' Lyta swallowed. 'She'd never accept you in Aldea.'

Rurrik frowned. 'But how did you know I intend marriage? Did Erit tell you?'

Lyta shook her head. 'He didn't say a word about it.'

'Then one could almost think you read my mind.' When he stared at Lyta, she returned his hard gaze without blinking.

'If you have eaten enough, I will have you shown to your chamber. You are in a tower with a guard at the foot of the steps in case you have any foolish idea about fleeing.'

Chapter Nineteen

The erle clapped his hands to summon another servant who took a torch from its iron holder behind the table. 'This fellow will guard the steps. He is armed with a sharp blade and knows how to use it. A serving maid will attend you and sleep in your chamber. I will see you in the morn.'

Rurrik gestured to the guard who started from the hall. He took a winding passage and Lyta calculated that she was going toward the left tower at the rear of the erle's house. The stone steps of the tower were very steep and narrow. A young girl standing at the top dropped down in a low curtsey. 'I am here to serve you, Lady,' she said in a gentle voice. 'The Master has ordered water and clean clothes for you.'

The guard nodded at the girl before he closed the wooden door. Lyta didn't hear a key turn in the lock but she did hear the echo of the guard's feet on the steps.

Lyta smiled at the maid. 'What is your name?' She wanted to establish a friendly connection between herself and Rurrik's servants.

'Gova, Lady.' The girl was as slender as a sapling; her cheekbones sharp in a white face. 'Would you like to undress and wash?' She helped Lyta remove her outer clothes. Just as well Caza, Lyta's own maid back home, could not see the sorry state of the stained blue robe and surcoat.

Gova looked doubtfully at Lyta's clothes. 'I will try to mend and clean these,' she said as she laid them over a wooden chest by the window.

After the maid poured warm water into a large basin, Lyta sponged her face, neck, and arms. She would have welcomed a bath as well but tonight, sleep was more important. From a chest, the maid took clean nightclothes and helped Lyta into them. Then she pulled back the heavy curtains from the old-fashioned bed in the centre of the room. Lyta climbed onto it with the aid of a set of steps. The crimson hangings smelled so musty and damp that she wondered when someone had last slept in the bed. Mayhap Lord Rurrik didn't entertain many guests at his estate. 'Please leave the hangings open,' she asked.

Gova pulled them back before crossing to a straw pallet by the door. Lyta realized that leaving the chamber would involve stepping over the maid before she could tackle the guard outside. The erle was taking no chances.

Lyta lay on her back to contemplate the tumultuous events of the day. She tried to put aside her homesickness for Aldea to concentrate on her astonishing ability to catch thoughts and feelings from both Cett and Rurrik. Previously she had only been able to tap into images sent by Magian Domen. But these two men were strangers. Had she succeeded because of the emotion involved in her capture?

She wondered how Rurrik would inform her mother of the ransom demand. Unless he had some sway over the Falga magian in Toma, he would have to send an actual messenger. If he sent Erit, his bastard son, the juggler wouldn't get a very good reception in Aldea. Despite her best efforts, thoughts of home and her mother brought a lump to her throat but she refused to cry again. Tears would not help her. .

***

Weak rays from the sun crept across the floor of Lyta's chamber. Her nose felt cold to the touch and she imagined that her feet would feel even colder on the stones. Staying under the covers would be more comfortable.

Gova materialised beside the bed with a platter. 'Lady, would you like to eat your repast now?'

Lyta pushed herself into a sitting position. 'I'll eat in bed.' She reached out for the platter. The food included rosy berries and sliced green apples with steaming honeycakes. Obviously the erle didn't intend her to starve. She didn't think he intended to poison her either. Last night, they had both eaten venison from the same serving platter. For his plan to work, Rurrik must keep her alive and well.

She ate until she was full and then placed the platter on the end of the bed. She caught Gova staring at it. 'Would you like to finish the cakes?' Lyta asked.

Gova flushed. 'The Master wouldn't like it.'

Lyta moved the platter closer to the maid. 'The Master won't know. He will think I have an excellent appetite.'

Gova hesitated, one hand hovering over the platter, before she grabbed two honeycakes. As she stuffed them into her mouth, Lyta wondered how well the erle fed his people.

'Go ahead and finish them all,' Lyta said.

'I'll give these to my brother. Nol is guarding the steps.' Gova left the chamber with her honeycakes. When she returned, a frown creased her face. 'Nol says that the Master wants to see you at once. I'll dress you, Lady.'

She opened the carved wooden chest by the window. 'Which gown will you wear?' She pulled out a red gown and a dark green one.

Lyta stared at the garments. 'Who last wore these clothes?'

'They belonged to the Master's wife. She died many summers ago after a fall from her horse.'

'Both of them are ugly and old fashioned.' When she lifted the sleeve of the green gown, traces of a heavy perfume rose from its folds. The red gown smelled slightly better. 'I'll wear this one,' Lyta said. 'You should air the green robe outside.'

Gova pulled the gown over her head. The erle's wife was much fatter and taller than me,' Lyta said as the edge of the dusty skirt trailed over the floor. She bunched folds of fabric in both hands. 'I'll kill myself by falling over the hem. Are there any other clothes in that chest?'

Gova pulled out the remaining contents. At the bottom were a long brown tunic, a jerkin, and dark brown hose. 'I don't know how those got into the chest,' said the maid in a flustered tone as she dropped the garments onto the floor. 'They are boy's clothes.'

'And they are just what I intend to wear.' Lyta began to pull them on.

Gova's face crumpled. 'Oh Lady, the Master won't like it.'

'I'll tell him you tried your best to make me wear the ugly red robe.' Lyta touched the girl's shoulder. 'Don't worry.'

As Gova didn't look convinced, Lyta decided to make sure that Rurrik understood the clothing situation. The tunic and hose felt familiar and comfortable. She fastened her own pouch around her waist and allowed the maid to brush her long black hair.

When they heard a knock on the door, Gova opened it. Nol was standing there with a frown on his face. 'The Master grows anxious,' he said. 'I must bring you to him directly.'

Lyta followed him down the steps and along the passage to a small chamber near the front of the house. The walls were lined with books on shelves and the erle sat a table near the window. His chair was another high-backed seat with elaborate carving like a throne. Lyta noted that he liked the trappings of a ruler. When her host gestured toward a low stool, Lyta sat down.

'What in the Stars are you wearing?' Rurrik's face twisted in a deep scowl. 'I ordered them to find woman's clothing for you.'

‘If those were your wife’s gowns, then we are exceeding different in shape and size. The long skirts would have tripped me when I walked.’

‘I am sure that the maid could have tied them up with a girdle. I will have the clothes altered to fit you. You could have worn your own robe.’

‘My clothes are badly stained and torn but Gova will try to clean and mend them. Please don’t blame your maid. She tried to prevent me from wearing these.’ Lyta gestured at the tunic and hose. ‘This is what I wear at home.’

The erle looked down his long thin nose at her. ‘Then your mother is most remiss. That will change when I arrive. Your manners need improvement as well. I didn’t notice a curtsey when you entered my chamber.’

Lyta kept her voce steady. ‘I have been taught proper conduct but those rules don’t apply to acknowledging a kidnapper.’

Although Rurrik’s face flushed and his hands clenched on the table, he didn’t respond to Lyta’s words. He cleared his throat. ‘Can you read and write?’

Lyta nodded. ‘My mother arranged a tutoran for me.’

‘Good.’ The erle reached out for paper and a quill. ‘I require you to write a letter to your mother to assure her you are alive and happy here.’

‘Happy?’ Lyta’s tone was scornful. ‘How can I tell my mother I am happy when I’m a prisoner in a strange place?’

‘Then you will tell her you are being well treated. Bring the stool near the table and prepare to write. I will tell you what to say.’

‘I want to compose my own letter.’ Lyta folded both arms.

Rurrik gave a heavy sigh. 'When I am ruler in Aldea, I will marry you off as soon as possible. Preferably to a kedir in a distant demesne.'

'If such an unlikely event ever happened, I'd certainly move as far away from you as possible. I might even consider Firt as a husband.'

'Firt of Delis would be a most suitable match.' He pointed to the table. 'Now write. Obviously, I will read your letter. If I do not approve of anything, then you will start again.'

Lyta's mind was whirling. How could she send a hidden message to her mother in words that were acceptable to Rurrik? 'Should I say that I'm your prisoner?'

'You will write that you are my guest,' the erle declared.

When he leaned over Lyta's shoulder, she recoiled from his sour breath. Too much red wine. Magian Domen would recommend a Ryna potion to sweeten his belly and mouth.

Her letter was lavish in praise of the Rurrik and his hospitality. She described the generous amount of food that had been offered to her and the superior nature of the furnishing and clothing in her well-appointed chamber. She referred to the estate as being a country place not far from the coast. When she laid down the quill, the erle snatched up the letter. As he read it, his eyebrows twitched.

He put the paper down and turned to Lyta. 'It doesn't matter that you mention this location. I have other houses and if necessary, you will be moved from here to another.'

'Is Erit going to deliver my letter to Aldea?'

'That's not your concern.' The erle took another sheet from the table, folded the two together and sealed them. He stamped an impression on the wax with the design on his wide gold ring.

'You will now return to your chamber. For entertainment, you may select books from my shelves. I can suggest some volumes to improve your present demeanour.'

Lyta could imagine the dry books he might select. She'd try to choose some of her own. 'Erle Rurrik, I'm accustomed to exercise each day. May I walk outside?'

Rurrik's long fingers tapped the table as he considered her request. 'Very well. You may walk for an hour with Nol. But only inside the courtyard. And don't talk to my people to distract them from their work.'

Lyta slipped a book of tales about Falga into the pile of worthy volumes Rurrik selected for her. As she left the chamber, Erit arrived. Since Nol wasn't in sight, Lyta waited by the door. She wanted to hear what was discussed in the chamber.

'I said you could have land when the task was completed.' Rurrik's voice was low and controlled.

Erit shouted in reply. 'You said I could have it when I brought the girl.'

'I told you that we would discuss the matter when the task was completed. Now I have to hear back from Aldea.'

'Then you'll add another condition.' A loud thump on the table startled Lyta.

'Calm down. You will be rewarded in due course.'

Lyta slipped behind an open door before Erit charged from the chamber. She caught a glimpse of his scarlet face and angry eyes. She wondered if dissension between the two men might aid her cause. Lyta turned when Nol rushed along the passage to take the books from her arms and escort her back to the tower.

After a meal at midday, Lyta walked with her guard in the open air. She smiled at people as they hurried past her, performing their duties. They all refused to meet her eyes or return her smile. Despite their behaviour, Lyta felt that she'd gained a small victory in being able to get outside. While she wandered in the sunlit courtyard, she examined her surroundings. By using her wits and her skills, she could develop an escape plan. And if she was going to be moved from this estate, she'd have to hatch such a plan speedily.

Chapter Twenty

Rurrik sat back in his chair and stared at Erit. 'I am glad to see that you have come to your senses. You will travel to Aldea with all haste. And don't take that lumping clod with you. If they already suspect him of murder, it won't help my cause to have him with you.'

Forcing down more angry words, Erit tried to remain calm. He would not achieve his prize by shouting at Rurrik. 'I won't be any more welcome than Cett at the castle.'

The erle raised both eyebrows. 'Won't they believe that the actors took Lyta? You said that nobody saw you with the girl.'

'The commander might suspect I was behind the kidnapping.'

'How could he? You told me he has no proof.' Rurrik paused. 'Are you too cowardly to return to Aldea? I'll send a servant if you lack stomach for the task.'

Erit clenched both fists. 'I'm not craven.'

'Then take the letters and go. They won't lock you up if you make it clear I expect an answer as soon as possible.' He waved a dismissive hand.

Erit found Cett in the gatehouse chamber, throwing dice with two of the guards. Cups of ale and a pile of coins sat on the table. Cett looked up at him. 'So, what's happening?'

'I'm off to Aldea with the erle's demands.'

Cett grimaced. 'I don't want to go back there.'

'Then it's just as well you aren't coming. I'm to go alone.'

'So that's it?' Cett rose from his stool and followed Erit out the door. His whole face twisted in a scowl. 'Now that I'm no longer useful, you get rid of me.'

'Here's your price.' Erit tossed a cloth purse in Cett's direction. 'That's what you wanted, after all.'

The man tipped the coins onto his hand. 'I expected extra for the deaths.'

Conscious of the two guards listening in the chamber behind them, Erit kept his voice low. 'Killing Virr and the groom wasn't part of the plan. You're lucky I don't tell Druck what actually happened at the castle.'

Cett glared at him before he tucked the purse into his tunic. 'You keep your mouth shut and I'll do the same. Then we'll both sleep easier.' He shouted back to the guards. 'Now if you two will hand over my winnings, I'll be on my way. The sea with all its storms and serpents is a safer place than the land.'

***

Two days later, Erit was approaching the castle. For the last part of his journey, a knot of apprehension had been growing in his chest, making it difficult to breathe. Mayhap the erle was right and he didn't have the stomach to deliver the message. His heart flipped as he was challenged at the gatehouse.

'What do you want?' The guard's voice was harsh.

'To speak to the commander.'

'He's away.' The guard waved his sword in the air.

'Is Borut here?'

'He's the man in charge.' The guard peered at him. 'I thought I knew your face. You're that juggler fellow. They won't want to see you up there.' He nodded toward the keep. 'You caused a lot of trouble last time you was here.'

'I have a letter for the Kedura. If she wants to see her daughter again, you'll take me to her at once.' His steady voice was at odds with his jumping heart.

The guard frowned and tapped his sword. 'If you had something to do with that business, I should run you through right now. The place has been turned upside down since our Kedie Lyta disappeared.'

'Stop blathering and let me through.' Erit patted his brown pouch. 'Since I need to take back an answer to this letter, you would be unwise to kill me.'

When Borut came to see what was happening, the guard explained Erit's mission.

Borut's expression was stony. 'I'll escort him to the Kedura myself.' He nodded at Erit with one hand holding the sword hilt at his belt. 'And no tricks on the way. You go first.'

In silence, Borut followed Erit through newgate and past the storechambers. They went through oldgate, across the courtyard and up the steps. They entered the great hall where a group that included Lord Wilus and Lord Trevin was clustered around Halia. Borut coughed and bowed as he came up to the Kedura. 'Lady, this fellow has news of the kedie.'

Halia jumped to her feet. 'Is Lyta safe? Where is she?'

Erit held up the packet. 'Lady, I have letters here. I'll answer any questions when you've read them.'

Halia grabbed the packet and sank back into her chair. A serving man at her side gave her a blade to remove the seal. 'Lyta has written this.' Halia's hands were shaking as she read the letter. 'She says she's being well cared for although I detect a false note.in her high praise.' She bit her lip as she looked up at Erit. 'Is her lodging really so luxurious?'

'Your daughter's not in a prison cell. She's well cared for.'

Halia opened the second letter. She scanned the words and then laughed in a derisive fashion. 'This would be amusing if my daughter's life was not at stake. Here, read this nonsense.' She thrust the sheet at Wilus. He read it without speaking before handing it to his fellow noble.

Trevin's voice shook with anger. 'This is an outrage. The man must be raving mad to suggest such a thing.'

'Lord Rurrik is quite serious,' said Erit. 'He's asked me to wait for a reply.'

Halia rubbed her forehead. 'I must consult my council. You'll have an answer in the morn. Borut, make sure this man has food and a bed for the night.'

'I'll keep a close eye on him, My Lady.' Borut jabbed Erit's side with his thick fingers. 'Come along with me. I have a nice safe place for you.'

The nice safe place was a small damp cell in the gatehouse nearest the keep. At least Erit didn't have to share the confined space with anyone else or any rats. The food was bread and cheese, simple but adequate and not much different from the last meal he'd eaten at his father's house before he left Falga. He wondered about Halia's answer. She was in a very difficult situation and he wasn't sure how the two erles would advise her. He knew something of the nature of both men. Erle Wilus' advice would be thoughtful and considered while Erle Trevin's suggestions were more likely to be impulsive. He'd want action as once.

Erit was concerned about the whereabouts of the other two erles, the magian, and Archis Druck. Were they all on their way to his father's estate? If they'd caught the actors before they had left Aldea, the searching party might already know where Lyta had been taken. Cett had been foolish enough to mention the estate while the actors were in earshot.

Next morn, Halia's pale face was expressionless as she handed Erit a sealed package. 'Make sure this is placed directly into Lord Rurrik's hands.'

Erit bowed as he tucked the packet into his pouch.

'If you have any influence over him, make sure he treats my daughter like a kedie. If he mistreats her in any way, the same measures will be dealt to him when he becomes my captive.' Since her voice held a steely quality, Erit did not doubt the sincerity of her words. He reflected that the kedura and his father were well matched in determination.

Borut shoved the last gate open and pointed outside. 'Leave now and never show your poxy face here again.'

'I have no desire to return,' Erit answered. 'I hope this whole business is over soon.'

***

But soon was an optimistic wish. When Erle Rurrik read the kedura's reply, his wild rage made his serving man quiver and Erit dash from the scene. Fluttering shreds of paper from Halia's letter accompanied him through the door.

Chapter Twenty-One

On her first walk outside, Lyta had noticed the patches of greenery in the courtyard. At the left of the house were plots of herbs and vegetables for use in the kitchen. On the second morn, she bent down to identify the nearest herb. Capslon was an unusual choice for seasoning food but it did have the quality of promoting heavy sleep. Mayhap the gardener was prone to wakefulness at night. She glanced around to see if anyone was watching before picking a handful of sprigs, which she tucked inside her pouch.

Lyta added to her store of Capslon every time she went outside. She hung the bunches upside down in the window of her chamber and hoped that the dried version of the herb worked as effectively as the fresh variety. When Gova asked why she was keeping it, Lyta pointed out that the herb scented the air. As Capslon had a fresh citrus aroma, Gova seemed satisfied with the answer. Although Lyta didn't know when or how she would use it, she steeped some of the herb in water to make a potion and hid it in an ale container behind the wooden chest.

She'd been a prisoner of Rurrik for a sevenday before Erit returned from Aldea. She collided with the juggler as he shot from Rurrik's chamber like an arrow. 'What happened?' Lyta asked.

Erit plucked shreds of paper from his hair. 'Your mother's reply displeased him.'

'I told him she wouldn't accept his ridiculous demands, 'said Lyta.

'You'd better hope she has some sensible action in mind. When my father becomes really angry, he can be ruthless.'

At his serious tone, Lyta suppressed a shiver. 'How was my mother? Did she ask many questions about me?'

'Of course she did,' Erit replied. 'She's worried about you. She was glad to hear that you were safe and comfortable.'

As comfortable as possible.' Lyta gestured at the red gown which Gova had been forced to alter. Although, the red gown fit better than before and the hem no longer dragged on the ground, the robe was still an ugly piece of clothing. At night, she changed into her own blue robe. Rurrik kept old fashioned hours for his meals. He was served a light meal at midday and then his main meal at night.

Gova had done her best with the blue robe, mending the jagged rips in the skirt and cleaning the dirt from the bodice. Lyta had persuaded the maid to give her the tunic and hose instead of taking them away. The boy's clothing was safely hidden behind the bed hangings.

While she was talking to Erit, a serving man rushed into the house. His face was red and he bent over, gasping for air.

'Is there trouble?' Erit asked.

'Our Kedur is sending a party to speak to the master. They'll be here within two morns. And some Aldean nobles are travelling with them.'

Lyta stifled a cheer. Her mother would have contacted Kedur Ulit of Falga for help. And the Aldean erles would be an escort to deliver her home. The servant knocked on Rurrik's chamber door and was told to enter. The door closed behind him.

Lyta and Erit stared at each other. 'Now what?' she asked.

'Tell your maid to pack,' he replied. 'You'll be moving.'

Erit was correct. When Rurrik emerged from his chamber, he gave a series of sharp orders. Gova should gather Lyta's belongings together at once. They would be leaving early on the next morn. Other servants were told to place food and drink into wagons. Lyta asked Gova where they were going but the maid shook her head. 'I don't know, Lady. The Master has other houses.'

Lyta saved the boy's clothing by stuffing them inside the chest when Gova wasn't watching. She'd noticed that the gate had been left undone while the preparations to leave were continuing and tucked that information inside her head. This might be her best chance to escape.

She had to make sure Gova and Nol would not prevent her departure. She saved meat from her dinner plate. The pork was so strongly spiced that the addition of the Capslon potion wouldn't be obvious. If the herb worked, Gova and Nol would both sleep heavily after they had eaten.

All went well. The brother and sister had become accustomed to receiving extra food from Lyta and they both enjoyed the meat. Lyta felt guilty for deceiving them as they'd been kind to her but she forced down these tender feelings.

Lyta waited until the sound of heavy breathing from Gova's pallet reached her ears before dressing in her boy's clothing and creeping across the chamber. She stopped beside the maid and waited until she'd counted a score of breaths. Lyta stepped over her and reached for the door. She opened it slowly and silently before peering down the stairway.

Nol was sprawled on the floor below. By his snores, he was in a deep asleep. One step at a time, Lyta slipped down the stairs with her heart thumping in her chest. Nol was a large obstacle. His body reached from one side of the wall to the other. Holding her breath, Lyta stepped over him and then stood motionless in case she'd disturbed the sleeping guard. He gave an extra snort but didn't stir.

Lyta crept along to a side entrance. In their haste to pack for the journey, the servants had not secured it. She pushed at the heavy wooden door and when it swung open, she looked up to see where Lady Moon was placed in the sky.

The Lady was partially obscured by clouds enabling Lyta to move from one shadow patch to another. Near the gate, she held her breath. As she reached out to push it open, a hand grabbed her arm. Lyta gave a muffled shriek.

'Stay quiet,' whispered Erit. 'You don't want the guard to hear you.'

'Let me go!' Lyta tried to twist from his grasp.

'I can't let you leave. My father won't reward me if you escape.'

'But my mother will reward you if you help me.'

'That's unlikely. Halia isn't very fond of me.'

Lyta tried to kick him. 'She'd show mercy if you helped me.'

Erit didn't relax his tight grip. 'We're going back to the house and then to your chamber.' His voice sounded curious. 'How did you pass Nol?

'I gave him and Gova a sleeping potion.'

Erit chuckled. 'My father underestimated you.' He kept a firm hold on Lyta as they crossed the courtyard and entered the house through the side door. When Erit saw Nol, he shook his head. 'I'll get you to your chamber before I wake this idiot boy.'

Gova was still snoring inside the door. Erit waited until Lyta had crossed to her bed. 'Now, go to sleep.' He removed the key. 'I'll lock the door from the outside.'

Lyta heard the key grate and then his footsteps descending the stairs. She sighed as she stripped off her boy's clothing. If only Erit hadn't been in the courtyard, she might have been on her way to meet the erles. She covered her head with the bedclothes and wept from sorrow and frustration.

Next morn the servants gathered in the courtyard. Gova and Nol could hardly keep their eyes open as they carried bundles and chests from the house. Rurrik thrust a heavy brown cloak at Lyta as she was hurried into the same wagon she had travelled in earlier.

Erit hopped up beside her. 'After last night's events, I'm taking no chances with you.'

A servant took up the horse's reins while the remaining staff occupied another two wagons. Rurrik mounted a large grey horse and at his word, the party moved through the open gate.

In the daylight, Lyta was able to study the Falgan countryside. After passing through heavily cropped farmland and several hamlets, the way led toward low hills with a ridge of much higher hills rising behind them. Lyta reviewed her knowledge of the geography of the demesne. Those distant peaks could belong to the Red Mountains, a sparsely populated part of Falga. She was surprised that the erle owned an estate in such an inhospitable area. Surely, the land was unsuitable for raising crops or animals.

Since she was forced to ride with Erit, Lyta decided to ask him again about Virr's death. He hadn't been at all approachable earlier but mayhap now, he would answer her questions. 'Erit,' she began in a hesitant voice. 'Please, tell me about Cett. Why did he kill Virr?'

Erit's head jerked around. 'His death was an unfortunate mistake.' He turned away to stare at the passing landscape.

Lyta had to accept his terse words but she wasn't satisfied. She tried hard not to think about Virr, her mother, and Magian Dome but images of her previous life crowded into her mind. She blinked rapidly to stop the tears from falling. She would not weep in front of Erit.

The horse slowed as the track rose into the hills. Clumps of red, pink, and grey rock lined the path; some of them had unusual shapes and looked as though a sculptor had worked on them. Lyta pointed to her left. ‘Erit, that big rock resembles a head.’

He looked up. ‘It’s The Old Man. From the other side, he seems to have a long grey beard.’

‘So he does,’ said Lyta after turning her head. ‘Do you often come to this estate?’

Erit roused himself. ‘When I was a boy, we came every summer to get away from the heat in the lowland. The air is cool and fresh here.’

‘It’s certainly cooler now.’ Lyta shivered as she pulled the brown cloak around her and raised the hood. ‘The winter must be really cold.’

‘I hear they get quite a bit of snow but I’ve never lived here through a winter.’

The horse laboured as it climbed still higher. Surely they weren’t going much further up the mountains. Lyta stared ahead, watching for any sight of a house. She was surprised when the horse halted. Three men left the wagons and tugged at several large rocks on the right side of the path.

‘What are they doing?’ Lyta asked.

‘Wait and you’ll see,’ Erit answered.

Rurrik and the wagons started off again while the servants pulled the rocks back onto the path. Although Lyta stared downwards, she couldn’t see any sign of habitation.

‘Now look right,’ said Erit.

When her eyes followed his finger, she saw a green valley far below. ‘You can’t see it from the top trail,’ Lyta commented.

‘It’s well hidden,’ he said. ‘One of the reasons my father likes the place.’

As they slowly descended the hill, Lyta saw more details of their destination. Small buildings were clustered around a solid pink and grey house perched on a ledge above a river that shone silver in the sun. The sides of the valley were terraced and crowded with crops; however the upper sections were sheer rocky cliffs.

'What grows on the terraces?' she asked.

'Mostly grapes but other fruit too,' he answered.

Lyta looked around in pleasure as they moved lower. She would never have imagined such a magical place tucked away in the bleak Red Mountains. 'Do many people in Falga know about this place?' she asked Erit.

He shook his head. 'I hope not. My father likes his secrets.'

When the wagon reached the floor of the valley, the horse trotted over a stone bridge spanning the river. Then it turned toward the house. Unlike Rurrik's other home, this one was surrounded by a low wall. The coloured stone made the house look friendly and comfortable. If Lyta were not a prisoner, she might even enjoy living here.

Chapter Twenty-Two

At their first dinner together in the mountain house, Rurrik made sure Lyta understood his rules. 'You may go anywhere in the valley. You are unlikely to try to scale the cliffs but you must also stay away from the track. A permanent sentry stands there. And he's well-armed.'

Lyta didn't respond.

He stared hard at her. 'And if you managed somehow to leave the valley, you'd find other dangers. Wolves, bears, and icecats live in these parts.'

Her attention caught, Lyta leaned forward. 'Icecats? Have you ever seen one?'

'I've seen many. And when I was a boy, my father raised a kit after its mother was slain for her pelt.'

'Was the kit tamed?' Lyta asked.

'We thought so until one morn it broke a servant's neck. Icecats are unpredictable creatures.'

'But exceeding beautiful,' Lyta said.

Rurrik swallowed his wine. 'And never gentle.' He placed his glass on the table. 'Now, heed my words.'

Lyta and Gova had been given a chamber at the back of the house. The windows were large enough to give them a fine view of the vines on the rear terraces. With summer slowly waning, the grapes and the leaves were changing colour from shades of vivid green to deep purple and gold.

Since Gova didn't mention the sleeping potion she and Nol had been given, Lyta didn't refer to it either. As she walked between the vines and sampled the grapes, she kept an eye out for any useful herbs growing in this location. On one of the upper terraces, she noticed a low-growing yellow plant which looked like Altica. Magian

Domen had told her once that this herb caused belly aches and cramps. Although she couldn't see how Altica could help her, Lyta collected it. Rurrik's warnings about the mountain dangers hadn't eliminated her desire to escape and she waited for a suitable occasion to arise.

Within a sevenday, the grapes were ready for picking. The erle ordered everyone on the estate except the cook and one kitchen hand to work on the vines. Out of boredom and with a desire to be in the open air, Lyta persuaded Rurrik to let her join the pickers. Erit was also a worker and Lyta wondered if he was trying to remain in his father's good graces.

She found herself beside him one morn. 'Have you ever tried to juggle grapes,' she asked with a grin.

Erit threw a handful into the air and allowed them to fall into his open mouth. He chewed, swallowed, and then asked, 'How's that?'

'It's a wonder you didn't choke.'

'And just as well I wasn't observed. Rurrik doesn't like pickers eating his grapes. Or drinking his wine for that matter.'

Lyta laughed. She'd already noticed that Rurrik rationed his wine. He could drink as much as he wished but he poured Lyta and his son one glass each at meals before removing the jug from their reach. He encouraged them to drink weak ale instead.

One night at dinner, Lyta had entertained herself by moving the wine. She did it so carefully that nobody noticed and she held back her mirth as the container shifted just enough each time to be beyond Rurrik's fingers. Finally, he frowned and stopped drinking. When the jug slipped sideways to nudge Erit's right hand, he stared in surprise before pouring more wine into his cup.

This morn, since Erit was in a friendly mood, Lyta dared to ask him again about Virr's death. 'You told me Virr's death was a mistake. Why did Cett kill him?'

'You don't give up easily, do you? The quarrel was a private matter and I'm not going to discuss Cett's business.' Erit sighed loudly. 'Drop the questions. Taking about Virr won't bring him back.' He ripped a bunch of ripe grapes from the vine.

Lyta knew that wasn't the right way to pick grapes. She followed Rurrik's instructions to be careful not to damage the vines. When her wicker basket was full, she took it to the end of the terrace where a servant dropped the contents into a wagon. Each wagon was driven to an open air pit where the grapes were trampled by girls with purple legs and feet. The process looked like fun until Lyta realised how much hard work was involved.

She'd decided her basket was almost full when a whistle from above made her look up. 'What's that?'

Erit gazed toward the track. 'Someone's coming down.' A second two-note whistle followed the first. 'Ah,' said Erit. 'Not a stranger.'

'How did you know?'

'By the whistle the sentry gave.'

Lyta was intrigued by the signals. 'What if a stranger was coming?'

'That particular signal would have us all dropping our grape baskets and preparing for danger.' Erit was still watching the track. Then he frowned and sighed. 'By the Stars, it's Darik. He'll cause trouble.'

'Who's Darik?'

'The legitimate son.' A bitter tone coarsened his voice. 'Rurrik's heir. He comes to visit his father only when he wants something.'

'Does Lord Rurrik have other children?' Lyta asked.

'A daughter wed to an erle in Sevvir with a brood of children. She never visits him and he doesn't visit her.'

Lyta watched the track until she saw a tall man on a black horse nearing the bridge. He was dressed in red and black and accompanied by six men and a small pack of dogs. From her perch on the terrace above, she noted his dark hair. She'd have to see him close up to know if Darik's features were similar to his father's. 'What do you think he wants?'

Erit gave a short bark of laughter. 'I'll wager he's heard about your kidnap and he doesn't agree with Rurrik's plan.'

'How would he know?'

'He has many spies. Darik likes to know everything that happens in case his inheritance is affected.'

When the grape pickers finished for the day, Lyta went to her chamber to bathe and change for dinner. She was looking forward to meeting Darik. If he disagreed with his father's scheme, her situation might change.

That night, the meal was a more formal affair. Lyta was amused to see that silver plates and glassware had replaced the usual wooden platters and cups. And several jugs of wine had been placed on the table. Darik resembled his father closely with the same slanted eyebrows and sharp features. His eyes, however, were a light grey. The man was richly dressed in a crimson embroidered tunic with a thick gold chain around his neck.

Bowing low over Lyta's hand, he murmured appropriate words of greeting. She inclined her head in the gracious manner her mother had taught her. Rurrik sat in the centre of the table with Darik on his right hand side and Lyta on his left. Erit, seated next to Lyta, said in a low voice, 'Let's hope we'll get through dinner without any serious disagreements.'

Rurrik was playing the part of a gracious host. He served Lyta several choice slices of meat and poured her a second glass of wine. Darik was entertaining his father and the table with stories about the exploits of an eccentric neighbour. Since Rurrik also knew this man, a thin smile showed his amusement.

Then Darik leaned forward to address Erit. 'Little Brother, I hear you've been juggling in Aldea.'

Erit's fingers tightened on the stem of his glass. 'That's true.'

'You must have to keep many objects in the air to make your acts worthwhile.'

'True again,' said Erit. He set his glass down hard on the table.

'But if you offend your patrons, the rewards must be few.' Darik's grin held a keen edge of malice.

Erit flushed. 'Why don't you say what you mean?'

'Very well. I'm concerned that any goodwill between our family and Aldea might be altered by your actions.' His eyes slid from Erit to his father.

Rurrik turned to his son. 'If you have any question about Kedura Halia of Aldea, then address me. Erit merely carried out my bidding.'

Darik scowled. 'What nonsense drove your thinking? I'm glad you take the responsibility but what do you intend to do with Kedie Lyta? Keeping her here is plain foolishness. If I can discover her whereabouts, so can anyone else, including Kedur Ulit.'

'They won't get any information from the people I left behind,' said Rurrik through clenched teeth. 'Nobody will find the girl in this place.'

'How do you think I got here? Your people were very helpful.'

Rurrik's eyebrows drew together. 'Who talked?'

'I'm not saying. That's not your main problem. Even if Halia agreed to wed you to get her daughter back, what's to stop her refusing the match as soon as the girl's safely home?'

'I don't believe she would go back on her sworn word.'

'Then you're deceiving yourself. As usual.' Darik's fist thumping the table made the glasses jump. 'Halia may judge that an oath made to a felon isn't one she must keep.'

Rurrik glared at his son. He shoved his chair back and rose. 'I'm not discussing this matter any further. My doings are not your concern.'

'But, Father, this is my concern. As your heir, my character is tainted by this wide brush you're wielding. Both Falgans and Aldeans are sure to believe I was part of your ridiculous plot.'

. Rurrik raised his hand to point at Darik. 'Go back where you came from. I didn't invite you here and you're not welcome.'

Darik didn't seem worried by his father's words. He reached out to pour himself another glass of wine. Before his fingers had grasped the neck, Rurrik grabbed the jug from the table. He took it and strode from the chamber. Lyta put both hands to her head in an effort to diffuse the waves of anger that washed over her in his wake.

Darik sighed. 'His temper hasn't mellowed with age.'

'As usual, you provoked him,' Erit observed.

'The whole idea of marriage is foolish and dangerous. Our Kedur is most displeased. In an effort to create more harmony between us and Aldea, he appointed me as an envoy to Halia's court. We'd like to stop these persistent border raids.'

'Will you leave now?' Erit asked.

'I'm staying around. My armed men are more than a match for his grape pickers if things come to a fight.' Darik leaned forward to look at Lyta. 'Don't worry, Kedie. I'll get you home safe and sound.'

As he spoke, Darik seemed to notice Lyta as an actual person for the first time since they'd met. His eyes narrowed as they travelled from her head down to her waist. 'How many summers have you?'

'Fourteen.' When Lyta focused hard, she received a disquieting mind message from him about marriage. She was made even more uneasy by the intensity of his gaze.

'A charming age.' Raising his glass, he drank to her.

Erit's face tightened. He stood up and held out a hand to Lyta. 'Let me escort you to your chamber, Kedie. It's time you left this table.'

'You'll never pass as a nobleman however hard you try,' said Darik with another cruel smile. 'You will always behave like your servant mother.'

Clenching his teeth at Darik's mocking words, Erit grabbed a torch and clutched it. He marched ahead of Lyta to light her way.

She trotted to catch up with him to ask the question Darik's words and attitude had prompted. 'Is your brother a married man?'

Erit slowed a little. 'His wife died about twelve moons ago, leaving him with three daughters. The dead babe was a boy.'

Lyta stopped and placed a hand on Erit's arm to halt him. 'Would he ever consider asking for my hand?'

'I think the idea of marrying you just entered his head tonight. I'd be wary from now on. Darik isn't trustworthy.'

'And you are?' Lyta raised her eyebrows.

'I'd be a better husband than Darik.'

Lyta caught her breath and glared at him. 'Why would I want to be wed to anyone in your family? You're all despicable felons!' She stopped outside her chamber door.

Erit's voice rose. 'You could do worse than me.'

'I don't see how!'

Lyta jerked back the latch and swept into the chamber. She slammed the door in Erit's smug face.

Chapter Twenty-Three

Lyta placed both hands over her warm cheeks. She didn't speak to Gova as the maid prepared her for bed.

'Lady, can I help you further?' Gova's voice was more timid and higher than usual.

'You may leave me.'

In this house, Gova slept in a little alcove outside the bedchamber door. When the maid had left the room, Lyta sighed and forced herself to calm down. She needed to think in a rational fashion. Virr, Magian Domen, and her tutoran had all cautioned her about making a decision in an agitated mood. If Darik had wedlock in mind, she had more reason to escape from this place as soon as possible.

When Lyta turned her head to the window, she saw Lady Moon shining high in the sky. Her beams reached the grape vines on the upper terraces turning the purple grapes into bunches of gleaming silver. 'Help me, Mother Moon,' she murmured. 'I need a sure plan.'

And Mother Moon considered her request. During grape picking the next morn, Lyta noticed more Altica growing at the foot of a row of vines. She stuffed clumps down the front of her gown. Although she wasn't sure how she'd use the herb, Lyta was certain that Lady Moon had answered her plea.

That night Darik arrived at the dinner table as though he were an honoured guest rather than a banished son. Rurrik's fingers tightened around his wine glass as he drew a flask closer to his platter. Darik grinned, leaned back, and gave an order to the man behind his chair. The servant left the hall and returned with a jug of red wine.

'I see you ignore my commands,' Rurrik growled. 'What if I order my people to persuade you to go?'

Darik filled his glass to the brim. ‘I wouldn’t do that. My men have greater powers of persuasion than your puny grape pickers. I’ll leave when it suits me. After all, I am your true son.’ He shot a quick look at Erit.

‘Erit behaves more like a true son than you. He will be rewarded

Darik scowled. ‘Take care, old man. Don’t give any of my land to him.’

‘It’s my land until I die.’ A flush had grown on Rurrik’s sallow cheeks.

‘Then make sure your death arrives later rather than sooner.’

Rurrik pushed his plate away and stood up. He shook a finger in Darik’s face and his voice quivered with rage as he spoke. ‘Do not threaten me, boy. Take care of your own hide.’ With those parting words he left the hall. Lyta was prepared this time for the strong emotions he left in his wake.

Darik cleared his throat and turned to Lyta. ‘Don’t be disturbed by this little spat. Disagreements happen often between fathers and sons.’

When she didn’t respond, he said, ‘On the morn, I’m leaving for a day or two of hunting to allow my father to calm down. We may get a bear or even an icecat. If it’s a bitch with young, I’ll bring you a kit to raise.’

‘According to Aldean law, you can’t kill a mother icecat,’ said Lyta.

‘But you’re in Falga and subject to our laws.’ He smiled at her. ‘Then I’ll bring you a bear cub. I’m sure you’d make an excellent mother.’

His words sent sudden shivers down Lyta’s back and his sharp teeth reminded her of a wolf hunting its prey.

In bed that night, she thought hard. The grape picking would finish in two or three more days. If she feigned an injury, she could stay behind in the morn and ask to help in the kitchen. Then she could add Altica to the food. She had no idea of its strength although it was probably more potent fresh than dried. An entire household laid low with cramps, vomiting, and flux would give her an ideal chance to leave.

Lyta was unsure of the best direction to take when she left the valley. Should she go back or go forward over the Red Mountains? She needed to examine a map of Falga to confirm that once she crossed the Red Mountains, she could find a way to the coast.

Before she called for Gova in the morn, Lyta spent some time rubbing her right foot. When she got out of bed, she feigned a slip on the stone floor before falling back onto the bed with a cry of pain. When Gova came running, she examined the reddened skin with concern. 'What have you done, Lady? Your foot looks right sore.'

'I twisted my ankle.' Lyta tried to rise. 'Oh, I can't stand properly.' With the maid's help, she hobbled to the window seat. 'Fetch a bandage to wrap around it.'

Gova rubbed an evil-smelling green salve on the foot and then bound it tightly. 'I'll tell the Master that you can't pick grapes this morn.'

'Such a pity when we're almost finished.' Lyta placed her foot on a stool and took the platter from Gova. 'I could help inside the house.'

After repast, she limped to the little chamber that Rurrik used for reading. He frowned after glancing at her bandaged ankle. 'You must be more careful. I do not want your mother to believe we've mistreated you.'

'I'll tell her this injury was my own fault. Could I help with the dinner in the kitchen instead of working outside?'

'Kitchen work is not suitable for a kedie.'

'Neither is grape picking but you've allowed me to do that.'

Rurrik sighed. 'You may ask in the kitchen if you can do some light task but do not stand for a long time.' He stood up and moved toward the door. 'The picking is almost completed. I'll be supervising the final work.'

He waited until Lyta had limped past him. She leaned against the wall as though she were resting and noted he didn't lock the door. She waited until the erle had left the house before entering the chamber. Surely he had a map in his collection of books. With a sense of anxiety, she hunted through the shelves and sighed in relief when she found a map of the demesne in an historical record.

She traced a finger over the line of the Red Mountains. They almost cut Falga in half. But yes, if she travelled over the ridge, she would ultimately reach a strip of coastland on the other side extending toward Aldea. That would be her best route if she could avoid bears, wolves, and icecats. And Darik too.

Lyta made an elaborate pretence of resting her ankle until her maid left the house. Later, she limped to the kitchen for her midmeal and announced to the startled cook that she would help with dinner preparations.

The cook frowned. 'But, Lady, it's not fitting work for you.'

'Lord Rurrik has permitted me to assist you.' She sat down by the long table. 'I found an herb that also grows in Aldea. It's very savoury in a stew. Try this.' Lyta She held out a tiny frond of Altica. 'Tell me what you think of the taste.'

The cook chewed the Altica with a judicious expression on her plump face. Then she smiled. 'Very tasty. It would add good flavour to my stew.'

'Then I'll prepare it for you.' Lyta chopped her store of Altica very finely before adding it to the large kettle bubbling on the fire. She hoped she'd collected enough of the herb to affect the whole household. When the cook and her assistant were busy with other tasks, she helped herself to bread, cheese, and dried meat for her own dinner and for the journey ahead. On her way from the kitchen, she grabbed a leather bottle of ale.

When Gova returned at sunset, Lyta claimed to have a bad belly ache. She asked the maid to tell Rurrik that she felt unwell and didn't want to eat dinner. It might help if she'd claimed to suffer from sickness before the others were struck down. Gova passed on her message and reported that Darik hadn't returned from his hunting trip.

Lyta dismissed her maid. 'All I want to do is sleep. Why don't you eat with the other servants? Even the smell of food in this chamber will make me feel worse.'

When Gova had left, Lyta ate some bread and cheese and then placed the rest of her rations in her pouch. She wished she had a weapon but didn't know where Rurrik kept his blades. Could she search for an arms storechamber before she left the house? Her actions would all depend on how the effectiveness of the Altica.

Waiting was difficult. Lyta tried to read one of the improving books the erle had given her but the words danced before her eyes and she couldn't concentrate. She sat on her window seat and although Lady Moon was not yet visible, asked for her guidance and protection.

Lyta jumped into bed when she heard the maid's footsteps in the passage. Gova asked after Lyta's belly as she clutched her own mid-section. The girl's face was pale.

'What's the matter? Do you feel ill too?'

Gova nodded. 'I have a pain, Lady. Mayhap, I have got your sickness.'

'Then take care,' said Lyta. 'I am most uncomfortable.' She hoped that Mother Moon would forgive the lie.

An hour later when darkness had fallen, Gova bolted from the chamber holding her belly. 'I must leave you, Lady.'

After she'd fled, Lyta opened the chamber door to assess the situation in the house. She could hear groans and moans and smell the acrid stink of vomit and shit. Some servants must have been unable to reach the outdoor privies in time. She hoped that Rurrik was also laid low. Lyta waited while the sounds and smells in the house became even stronger. Gova's continued absence was a hopeful sign.

Dressed in her boy's clothes with a heavy pack around her waist, Lyta was ready. As she walked across the chamber, she grabbed the brown cloak which she'd worn on her journey to the present house. Knowing that the air would be cooler in the mountains, she slung it around her shoulders. Once through the door, she peered along the empty hall and then started toward the side door that led to the courtyard.

As she turned the last corner, a dark shape on the floor stirred. She stopped still with her heart hammering in her chest. Then a head rose from the body and Erit's voice said. 'Where do you think you're going?'

Chapter Twenty-Four

Lyta gasped. 'You startled me.'

'No doubt you're responsible for this mess.' Erit's voice was weak and ragged. 'What was in the stew?'

'An herb called Altica.'

'And, of course, you didn't eat any.' He stared at her legs. 'I see that a miracle has cured your bad ankle.'

Lyta stayed motionless while she assessed the situation. Was he strong enough to grab her and prevent her from leaving?

Erit sighed. 'Rurrik wasn't exaggerating about the beasts in the mountains. And Darik's out there too. He'd love to catch you.'

'I have to risk the dangers.'

'Then you'll need a weapon.' Erit pointed back down the passage. 'You'll find arms in a hidden closet in Rurrik's bookchamber. The opening is behind the first shelf of books.'

Lyta paused. 'I know you told me not to mention Virr and Cett again but this is my last chance to find out the truth. What was the quarrel between Virr and Cett?'

'You really know how to make me feel worse,' said Erit. 'Cett and Virr had the same father. Cett was angry when Virr left the priesthood. When he wouldn't return to the temple at Avridon, Cett lost his temper. Virr told him he knew about a possible plot.'

'I see,' said Lyta. 'What about Givis, the groom?'

'Cett thought he'd overheard words between the two of them.'

'And Rusa?'

'Who's Rusa? Nobody else was slain.' Erit groaned loudly. 'I'm off to the privy again. Last time I couldn't reach my bedchamber. Be off before someone else sees you.'

'Thank you for the information.' Lyta waited until Erit had staggered to his feet before she went to find the secret closet. She examined the bows hanging on the wall but they were all unsuitable. Instead, she chose a sharp blade which would fit in her pouch. Now she felt better equipped for whatever might lurk beyond the valley.

The passage was empty. She slipped through the door and then crept along the side of the house. From all corners, she heard noises from people in distress and felt guilty for having caused their pain and discomfort. She glanced up at a serene Mother Moon and sent a quick prayer for the afflicted folk to recover by morning. The magian hadn't told her how long the effects of the herb would last.

She stole up the track, watching for the sentry at the top. Had someone delivered his meal to him and if so, had he eaten it yet? She also listened for alarm signals from the house. When she was almost at the top, she heard the unmistakable sounds of vomiting coming from behind a large rock. The man was too preoccupied with the trials in his own body to be aware of her presence.

She reached the rising track and set off. It seemed wise to follow the path but not to actually walk along it. She stayed a few steps to the right side. Walking was hazardous there as the ground was uneven with clumps of grass and piles of slippery stones catching her feet. She had to be careful or she'd really twist her ankle.

In preparation for this journey, she'd plaited her long black hair. Now she stopped behind a boulder and drew her blade. Pulling the thick braid over her shoulder, she hacked through it. After undoing the braid, she let the breeze carry the strands away. Now, the rough edges of hair barely reached her shoulders. To be safe among people, she must pass as a boy with an unbroken voice.

In the morn, she'd look for a plant that grew in high places throughout the land. Known as the piss plant because of its smell, it was also used as a brown dye. If she rubbed juice from the cut stems over her face and hands, her skin would darken. And the stink should keep nosey folk at a distance.

Soon, she grew too weary to continue climbing. With the help of beams from Lady Moon, she searched for a safe place to sleep. A narrow crevice between two large boulders looked likely. She poked a stick into the opening to dislodge any small creatures. When nothing squeaked or stirred, she inserted her pack and then her body into the crack. It was a tight squeeze but she just fit. She curled up with one hand on her blade and fell asleep.

The sun woke her. Lyta crawled from her hole and stretched her cramped arms and legs. Then she ate some bread and cheese. She drank ale and reminded herself to search for a spring or clean pond. She peered down the mountain without hearing voices from any trackers. Were the erle and his people still recovering from the dose of Altica?

As she climbed over a low ridge of rock, she saw movement in a little vale below. In a patch of sunlight, four brown hares were dancing. They were leaping on their back legs with their long ears flapping with each jump. Lyta jammed her hand over her mouth to hold back her laughter. Was this a morn ritual for these animals? Then, while she watched, all four dropped down and began to graze on the grass.

That little display had cheered her spirits. Lyta set off uphill again, examining every plant to see if she recognised it. Other herbs, apart from the piss plant might be useful. When she did see the familiar thick stems, she gave a small cry of pleasure. After cutting a handful, she sat down to break open the stems and rub the liquid over her skin. What a stink! She hoped the smell would wear off a little before she reached a settlement or nobody would let her near an inn or a house. Not that she had any coin to pay for food or lodging. She'd be begging or working for both.

Staring at the ridge high above her, Lyta guessed that she might reach the summit in daylight in two morns if she walked steadily. She moved away from the path to search for water, watching for bright green grass or bushes which might indicate its presence. When Lyta saw a hopeful patch, she stumbled over the rough ground and sank to her knees beside a small spring bubbling up from the earth. She cupped her hands to catch some water. It tasted clean and cold. She finished the last swallow of ale and then swished out the bottle before refilling it. Lack of fresh drinking water might prove more hazardous than an encounter wild beasts or Darik.

As Lyta straightened up and wiped her wet face with the edge of her tunic she heard a cry for help. Her mouth dropped open in shock. The words had been clear. *'Hungry! Cold!'*

She turned in a full circle searching for a traveller in distress but nobody was visible. Then the haunting cry came again.

'Hungry! Cold!'

With a start, Lyta realized the voice was inside her head. The call grew louder as she climbed the slope. Ahead she noticed a dark opening in the hillside. Her steps slowed as she came closer and she clutched her blade. Who knew what might live in that place? Then she saw a large tawny beast sprawled half in and half out of the cave. At first sight, it appeared motionless but she still watched carefully to see if the chest rose and fell. No breathing was obvious. The great cat was still.

'Cold! Hungry!' The cry came from further inside the opening. Lyta couldn't ignore the distressed kit. As she came level with the cat, she saw an arrow deep in its head. The point had entered the right eye and then the brain. Had

the beast dragged herself back to the cave to protect her young one? She wondered if Darik or a member of his hunting party had been responsible for the death.

A sudden movement made her jump back. A furry body hurtled towards her legs, uttering its plaintive cry. *'Cold. Hungry.'*

Lyta took a deep breath. Then she sent a message back to the kit. *'Wait. Food.'*

Could the little animal receive messages as well as send them? Her question was answered when the kit wrapped itself around her legs and purred. 'Wait. Food,' it said.

Lyta shook her head. She'd never in her wildest dreams fantasised about seeing an icekit let alone talking to one. With care, she leaned down to ruffle the soft fur on its head. *'Wait,'* she said again. *'Food.'*

Remembering the hares she'd seen at play earlier, Lyta crept back to the spot where they'd been. She crouched down and peered over the convenient ridge of rock. Only one hare remained, chewing blades of grass.

She didn't want to kill the animal but the icekit's urgent demands for food came first. She drew her blade out and held her breath as she checked the hare's position. She aimed with care. The hare's body jerked as the blade pierced its heart. Then the animal flopped to the ground.

Lyta had been worried that the kit might not be weaned from its mother but her concern vanished as the little one's teeth tore into the hare's warm flesh. She waited until the first frenzied attack had slowed and the kit looked up at her with blood dripping from its muzzle.

'Good,' it said before settling on its haunches and cleaning its fur like any domestic cat. Lyta moved away from the body of the mother cat, which smelled bad and was attracting a horde of buzzing flies.

She sat outside the cave to ponder her new situation. Now what? She couldn't leave the kit to its own devices.

She didn't know if the mother had started to teach her young one to hunt. Since it had been very hungry, Lyta doubted that it had been given many lessons. She'd have to take the kit with her on her journey and deal with the complications.

The kit trotted from the cave and butted its large head against her legs, making a sound between a purr and a growl. Lying down on its back, it waved all four paws in the air.

That answered one of Lyta's questions. 'You're a female,' she said aloud. 'If we're travelling together, you need a name.'

She searched her mind for a suitable one. When she was very young, her nurse, Obela, had told her a tale about an icecat which became famous for saving some lost people. During a severe blizzard, the beast led the group to safety over a mountain pass. 'I'll call you Seta and hope you're a fine guide like your namesake.'

Seta purred and swished her long tail. Lyta continued her musings. The kit's head already reached the girl's knees and if she grew as large as her mother, she'd be a formidable cat. Would that make Seta a target or a source of protection? And while Lyta could get food with her blade, it would be better if the kit learned to catch her own dinner.

Lyta's first problem was to persuade Seta to leave her mother and the cave. She bent down to the kit to send her a message. *'Mother. Dead,'* she said.

So far, Seta had sent one word messages. Was that because she didn't know how to send longer ones or was it a natural limitation? The kit had a quizzical look on her face. She got up and walked back to her mother's body and pushed her head into the side. She nudged it three times without getting a response. Seta padded back to Lyta and did the same thing to her. Lyta responded by placing an arm around the kit's head and drawing it close. Her fur was warm in the sunlight and gave off a curious spicy scent. Unlike her mother's high circle of fur, the kit's neck ruff was short and fluffy.

'Mother. Dead,' Seta repeated.

'Dead,' said Lyta. *'Leave.'*

The kit seemed to understand. Seta padded forward and then stopped, looking back at Lyta. The girl rose and led the way toward the main track. She hoped that her new companion had keen ears and could warn of danger long before Lyta became aware of it.

The kit didn't travel in a straight line. Seta bounced sideways to bat at a blue butterfly and then leaped high in the air when a bird shot out of a nearby bush. She dropped to her belly to slither ahead and investigate. Lyta revised her plan. At the rate they were travelling, she wouldn't reach the mountain summit soon. Seta could make the journey twice as long. *'Come,'* she said in a sharp tone as the kit once more set off to explore the surrounding territory. *'Here.'*

Seta paused, one leg in the air as though she was considering whether she should heed the command or not. Then she tossed her head and rejoined Lyta who blew out a breath of relief. If she trained the kit to obey a few simple instructions, they might both stay safe.

The icekit heard the men's voices before Lyta did. She growled low in her throat and lifted her head to sniff the air. She bumped her body against Lyta's legs. Lyta listened hard for a few minutes until she, too, heard the same noises. A party of men was coming down the track. In desperation, she searched for shelter. A cluster of tall rocks on her left was the best choice. If she and the kit could hide themselves there, they could wait until the party had passed. She grabbed Seta's neck. *'Come. Fast.'*

They both ran toward the rocks. Lyta's heart sank as she recalled the hunting dogs that had accompanied Darik. She yanked Seta into a small opening ignoring the kit's whimpers and shoved herself in after her. If Lyta could send a message to the lead dog, they might have a chance to divert the whole pack. She had no idea if her transfer skills would also work on dogs.

She heard the dogs stop and howl and then Darik's voice. 'What have you found?' One dog barked in response and then the others copied it.

'They scent something over there,' said a second voice.

Before he could give a command, Lyta shut her eyes, focused harder than she ever had before and sent a message. *'Stop! Danger!'*

She waited without breathing, one hand on Seta's head.

'What's wrong?' The man's voice was puzzled. 'They're all sitting down.'

'That's the last straw.' Darik's voice was cold. 'When we return, kill them.'

'But, Lord…' the man sounded upset.

'Enough. All we have to show for our hunt is one wolf, too old to run. Move on. I need a hot bath and clean clothes.'

Lyta didn't let out her breath until the party had clattered down the track. She waited until the sounds of horses and men's voices became dim before scrambling from the shelter and dragging Seta out.

That had been close. And she had the discouraging feeling that it might be one of many similar situations before she reached home.

Chapter Twenty-Five

Erit raised his head from the pillow and then wished he hadn't bothered. He felt worse this morn than he did after a night of heavy drinking. What in the name of Stars had the girl said she put in the stew? He frowned as he tried to remember the herb she'd mentioned. Alta or some such. Whatever it was, the effect on his body had been powerful and unpleasant.

When he stood up, the chamber swayed around him. He clutched the bedpost for support but when he tried to take a step, his knees buckled under him. He stood still for a moment to get his balance before attempting to move again. This time he managed to reach the window where he fell onto a stool. After catching his breath, he peered outside. Near the privy wall, two men lay flat on their backs with their arms out flung. If they were still alive, he knew just how bad they must feel.

His lips curled in a wry smile as he thought of Lyta and her schemes. Rurrik didn't know what he was getting into when he'd decided to kidnap her. He'd considered that a girl of fourteen summers would have few defences. His father had certainly been proved wrong. And had he been laid low with the same spewing and shitting as the rest of his household? If not, he'd have sent out a search party by now.

Erit hoped Lyta could avoid the wild beasts and Darik on the mountain track and make a good escape. He'd admired the girl's pluck and skill from the moment she'd caught the blade at that dinner table back in Aldea. She certainly deserved better than craven Firt as a husband. Erit had sneaked back into the castle in a disguise to watch the tourney. Like most of the spectators, he'd been disgusted by Firt's cowardly behaviour.

His clothes stank. Stripping them off, he found a clean set in his chest and dressed. Now he needed water for washing and ale for drinking. Since his servant hadn't appeared, Erit went to see for himself the state of the house and its staff.

The whole place was a foul mess. He picked his way past splatters of green-flecked vomit and pools of runny shit and walked toward the kitchen. This morn, the place was dark and cold without the fires or the cook and her helpers bustling around making the repast. Erit filled a cup with ale from the barrel in a corner and sat down to drink it in slow sips. His tongue felt swollen and the inside of his mouth was coated with sandy dust.

Although his head swam a little when he stood, the ale had made him feel stronger. Was his belly ready to accept food again? Grabbing a crust of dark bread from one of the tables, he chewed it carefully as he walked into the courtyard. He crossed to the first body he'd seen from his window and recognised the back of his father's serving man. He poked the fellow with his foot. 'Sutt, move yourself. You'll have plenty of cleaning work to do.'

Sutt moaned as he sat up holding his head. 'Is the Master awake?'

'What do you think? If he was awake, he'd have been kicking you in the backside and threatening to whip you.'

Erit dug the second man in the side. 'Rise and shine as my old nurse used to say.'

'I don't know how you're so lively,' complained Sutt as he heaved himself up with the aid of a stone wall. He stared down at his clothing. 'Look at the state of my tunic and hose! I'll never get them clean.'

'Worry first about Rurrik's clothes. That's where your duty lies.'

The bread he'd eaten was staying in his belly where it belonged. Erit went to the pump and bent down to sluice his head and face with water. When he shook himself, drops flew off, sparkling in the sunlight. 'Stars!' The water was icy cold.

He walked back into the house passing people stumbling along passages, clutching their heads or bellies. A woman crept by, holding a stinking pot at arm's length, the other hand covering her nose. In the dining hall, two women were down on their knees with pails of water and brushes, scrubbing the floor. Had Rurrik given the order or were they starting to clean before he rose from his bed?

Rurrik's chamber was a large one in the back of the house. Erit tapped on the door and waited for the call to enter. When none came, he lifted the latch and went inside. The chamber smelled rank and the shutters were still closed. Erit slid one open before coming to the bed. Rurrik groaned and placed one hand over his eyes. 'Idiot! Who asked you to open the shutters?'

'I was worried about your health,' Erit said. 'Now, at least, I can see your face. You look terrible.'

Rurrik groaned again. 'I feel terrible. I've got a belly sickness like the one the girl complained about.'

Erit debated with himself as to whether he should inform his father of the true state of affairs. He decided he'd better explain or things could become worse for him. The cook would probably tell Rurrik about the extra ingredient in the stew.

'There's something you should know.' He told Rurrik about Lyta adding the herb to their food and the disastrous results.

'If I felt stronger, I'd wring her neck,' said Rurrik. 'She is the most annoying girl I have ever met.'

'There's more. During the night, she seems to have left.'

'Seems to have left? She is either here or she's not here. Which is it?'

'Lyta's not here. I reckon she's on her way back to Aldea.'

Rurrik drew in a shaking breath. 'Do we have men fit for searching?'

Erit shook his head. 'Nobody is strong enough.'

'Mayhap, she will meet up with Darik in the mountains. Although I am not sure what he would do with her,' Rurrik said.

'He'd return the girl to her mother and earn Halia's gratitude.'

'No doubt.' Rurrik lay still for a few moments. 'Send in my man now. I wish to rise from this stinking bed.'

Erit breathed out in relief. That had gone better than he'd hoped. He'd expected to be reprimanded for not preventing Lyta from leaving the house. Now he should pray that his father wouldn't soon notice that any weapons had vanished from the secret closet.

By the time Darik arrived back from his hunt, the house had been scrubbed from top to bottom. Even so, he wrinkled his nose as he entered the dining hall. 'What's the disgusting stink in here?' he asked. 'Did a dog die?'

'We all had a sickness,' said Rurrik in measured tones.

Darik glanced at the table. 'Where's the kedie? Is she sick too?'

Erit said. 'I'm surprised you didn't see her on the way. Lyta left the estate last night.'

'What!' said Darik. 'Father, didn't you send men after her?'

'They were otherwise occupied,' said Rurrik in a dry tone. 'As was I.'

Darik chewed his bottom lip. Erit suspected that his brother had intended to take Lyta home to Aldea. If Darik had returned the girl along with a concocted tale about her capture, he might have prevented dishonour falling on the whole family. In a strange way, his brother and Cett thought in a similar fashion. At least, in this case, nobody had been murdered.

'It's too dark now. In the morn, I'll take my men after her. Since we didn't see the girl as we came down the track, she must have retraced her steps.'

Erit didn't believe Lyta would have gone in that direction. He thought it was more likely that she'd climb up the track and go over the mountains. Then she'd make her way towards Aldea by following the coastline. He didn't voice that opinion to his brother.

Chapter Twenty-Six

Lyta soon found that an icekit made an exhausting companion. Seta's mother may have let her watch the process of catching prey but she hadn't instructed her kit in the finer points of hunting. Seta became so excited when she saw live dinner that she whimpered and whined, making enough noise to scare off the hares.

The girl ordered Seta to sit and stay, much as she would have trained a young dog. Then she added the command to be quiet using a warning finger to the mouth as a further signal. The kit was intelligent and soon understood these simple commands. She was also very affectionate and liked nothing better than curling up with Lyta. At night, Lyta was glad of the extra warmth as the air became colder the higher they climbed.

One morn when she expected to reach the summit by midmeal, Lyta was dismayed by a fall of snow. Seta was delighted by the white stuff and bounded through it, spraying snow in all directions. Lyta sat on a rock with her hood pulled over her head for warmth, and laughed, enjoying the kit's high spirits. However, she kept an eye on the track watching for people. She'd assigned the listening role to Seta.

Out of the corner of her eye, Lyta caught a glimpse of wings overhead. A large black eagle was soaring through the falling snow. She wasn't sure if the kit was too big for the eagle to attack but there was no point in taking chances. She threw back her cloak and grabbed her blade. If the eagle swooped down, she was ready. Seta had stopped her play and was also was also watching the path of the giant bird. Lyta wondered if the kit knew instinctively that it represented danger.

The eagle glided beyond them and then swung around until it was above Lyta and the kit again. Then it folded its wings and dived straight down. Seta growled as Lyta followed the bird's downward path, her fingers trembling a little on the hilt. Just before the eagle's talons reached her, Seta skipped sideways and Lyta's blade found the bird's head.

The eagle screeched once before tipping onto its side. Seta approached the bird by sliding forward on her belly. When she was close enough, she stretched out an exploratory paw to tap a wing. When the bird didn't move, she leapt onto it. She poked the bird's back before flipping it over. Somehow she knew that the only edible part would be the breast.

Lyta watched while Seta's white teeth tore at the eagle's flesh. The icekit found little worth eating. With a disgusted look on her face, she spat out a mouthful feathers before turning away.

'Hares. Better,' Lyta said.

The snow shower passed as fast as it had arrived and the sun returned. Calling to Seta, the girl started back on the path. When they reached the summit, Lyta stopped and stared at the expansive view below. In the sunlight, she could see well for many leagues. In the middle distance, spires and smoke rose from a good-sized town near a silver river while closer to the foot of the mountains, farmland and little houses dotted the landscape. Far to her left was a strip of shining sea.

Although the coast was her destination, Lyta wasn't sure if she should make her way there directly or not. Lack of food was her main concern. She'd eaten all the bread, cheese, and dried meat she'd packed. Would food be more available in the farm houses or in the town? And of course, Seta was her other concern. She might have been able to travel without much notice by herself but travelling with an icekit was another matter.

Most of the upward track was visible. Lyta sucked in a breath when she saw, far below, that a party of men and donkeys was starting upward. She wasn't sure how long they'd take to reach the summit but she did have some time to prepare. Seta had also seen the men and animals. She growled low in her throat as she watched. Was she identifying the men as a danger or the donkeys as food?

Lyta called the kit and set off along the top of the ridge. She needed to find another downward path. About half a league from the main track, she found the remnant of an ancient trail. Large boulders had blocked the way at about the half way mark but she might be able to skirt that obstacle.

Seta had bounded off to her right and Lyta turned her head to look for the kit. She was crawling on her belly. The girl stayed motionless, hoping that the kit was learning how to track without noise. Suddenly Seta leapt forward and grabbed something. She lifted the animal high in the air and shook it. *'Good!'* called Lyta. The kit had caught her first hare.

Seta seemed to smile as she crunched her meal. Now the only problem for Lyta was finding people food like berries or edible plants When Seta had devoured most of the hare, Lyta hid the remains under a pile of stones and called to the icekit. With great care, they began to descend the old trail.

The way was hard going. Stones of all sizes littered the path. Seta had fewer problems picking her sure-footed way through them. Four feet would be handy, Lyta thought. When something red caught her eye, she detoured sideways. Scarlet berries grew on a cluster of bushes. A bird flew up as she approached them and from the pips scattered on the ground, Lyta reckoned that the berries must be edible. She picked one and popped it into her mouth. Sweet at first bite with a touch of astringency around the pip. She couldn't name the berries, but they'd do until she found something better.

When snuffling noises came from nearby rocks, both Lyta and the icekit froze. A bear? A wolf? The two dropped to their bellies to crawl forward. Lyta peeped around the final barrier. She held a finger to her lips but Seta was already aware of the need for silence. A grey bear was pulling red berries from a bush using both paws and teeth. Lyta held her breath as the bear stopped eating and lifted its head. The white muzzle and milky eyes indicated an old animal. Lyta had seen castle dogs with eyes like that and Virr had explained that a cover had grown across the eyeballs. How blind was this beast?

The bear sniffed the air, swivelling its head from side to side. Lyta suspected its sense of smell might be better than its sight. She sent a message to the beast, hoping it too would be receptive. *'Danger! Leave!'*

With a sound between a grunt and a growl, the bear dropped down and ambled away from them. Lyta let out her breath with a whoosh. She didn't know whether the beast had received her message or if it had decided of its own accord to move off. In the end, the reason didn't matter.

Now that she'd hunted successfully, Seta was enthusiastic about catching hares. As if she knew Lyta must be hungry, the icekit presented the next dead animal to the girl. Lyta shuddered at the idea of eating raw flesh but she didn't dare light a fire. Smoke would alert people to their whereabouts. Taking a deep breath, she hacked off a thigh, stripped away the skin and then stared at the bloody flesh. She could do this. In fact, to survive she had to eat whatever became available. Memories of her mother's dinner table with its platters of succulent meat, savoury fish, soft cheeses, and warm bread flashed through her mind. She dismissed the images as she cut the thigh into bite-sized pieces on a nearby stone.

Lyta took a deep breath, speared a bit with her blade and brought it to her lips. She closed her eyes and shoved the flesh into her mouth. The texture was unfamiliar, the meat was tough, and the smell was unpleasant. Lyta forced herself not to gag. She chewed the mouthful until she could swallow it. Would it stay down? Somehow her belly accepted the food. By keeping her eyes shut and thinking of the meals she'd soon enjoy back at home, Lyta was able to eat the thigh. Seta, who'd finished the rest of the animal, was cleaning her face and paws. Lyta took a large gulp of water to wash the raw hare taste from her mouth.

She took stock of her position. Where were the men with the donkeys? She told Seta to stay while she crept back to a place where she could see the main track. The party had made fast progress and were about a third of the way to the summit. As long as she and Seta stayed out of sight on the old trail, they might arrive at the lowland without being spotted.

But when she reached the plains, what then? The icekit might be too excited by cattle, pigs, and dogs on the farms to heed Lyta. And how was the girl going to obtain enough fresh meat to feed a growing icekit? Lyta rubbed her head as she worried about these problems. In her memory, she heard Virr's voice. 'One step at a time. What is the first thing ahead of you? Overcome each obstacle as you come to it.'

When he'd said those words, Lyta had argued with him. 'But I can't ignore future obstacles. Shouldn't I think about them too?'

'Of course you have to plan ahead. But don't let worrying over future problems stop you from making a good present decision.'

The recalled words calmed her mind. Yes, she could make a present decision. Training Seta until she obeyed every command was a wise thing to do. Lyta took a last look at the climbers and then returned to the spot where she'd left the icekit.

Seta wasn't lying on her belly. She wasn't sitting on her haunches by the rocks either. In fact, she was nowhere in sight. Lyta climbed further down the trail but the icekit wasn't visible. Now Lyta grew alarmed. Had the kit wandered off in search of prey or had another beast like a bear or a wolf taken her. But surely that would leave signs of a struggle as well as noises. At the very least, she'd notice drops of blood.

After several calls, Lyta became more frantic. Seta had always responded before. The girl sat down with her back against a large rock, told herself to stay calm and ate a handful of berries. What were her choices? She could wait until Seta returned or she could continue down the trail and hope that the icekit tracked her.

Lyta decided to continue her journey. She came to the massive pile of boulders that was probably the result of a landslide. The only way past was to slide her feet sideways along a narrow ledge, staring straight ahead at the rock face. The drop was formidable and if she slipped, she'd land on jagged rocks below. She could understand why travellers had formed a new trail instead of trying to repair this one. Her hands were slippery with sweat and her knees were trembling by the time she edged past the obstacle. She sat down on the ground and tried to breathe normally.

The sun set and darkness dropped suddenly like a thick cloak. Lyta curled up in the middle of a circle of rocks and tried to sleep. Every time she woke, she called for Seta and the cold feeling in her belly grew larger with the continued silence from the icekit. The new dawn brought no answers with it and after eating the last handful of berries, Lyta stood up and started her descent again.

When sounds made by the climbing party reached her ears, Lyta hoped that Seta had the sense to stay well away from the main track. An icekit would be a trophy for them, either alive to be sold into captivity or dead for its pelt. Lyta stayed hidden with her heart banging in her chest until the noises made by the donkeys' hooves and the men's voices became faint. Once over the summit, they weren't a danger to her or to Seta. Lyta asked Mother Moon to make sure that no other party took the main mountain track before she reached the lowland.

She set off once more. Fortunately, the trail was easier to navigate beyond the rock pile. A combination of hunger and anxiety over Seta's continued disappearance nagged her. Every few steps, she called Seta but the icekit didn't answer. Before leaving the trail, Lyta rested against one of the last large outcrops of rock and peered ahead. What was the best plan to follow?

The two men working in the fields about half a league away couldn't see her yet but as soon as she set foot on the grassy trail ahead, she'd be visible. Smoke was rising from a cottage that she assumed was their home. A kind woman might be willing to give a dirty starving boy a crust of bread or a strip of dried meat. The thought of food made her mouth water. And she'd be thankful for some water too. She called the icekit one last time. When she received no answer, Lyta squared her shoulders, stepped from her hiding place, and left the Red Mountains behind.

Chapter Twenty-Seven

As she trudged toward the cottage, Lyta realized how weak she felt. Each step was an effort. She concentrated hard on placing one foot ahead of the next and found herself humming an old rhyme that Obela had taught her years ago. 'Left foot, right foot, off you go. Feet can carry you to and fro. Feet can carry you fast or slow. Left foot…' she could see Obela's wrinkled face chanting the rhyme as they walked along, hand in hand.

The words changed into something she couldn't recognise. She struggled to focus but the voice sounded hollow as though it came from the bottom of a well. Then it faded completely and she felt herself falling.

***

Lyta opened her eyes. The low white ceiling above her was unfamiliar as was the concerned face of the woman bending over her. 'What happened?'

'You swooned outside my house.'

'I did?' Lyta couldn't remember what she'd done. She recalled arriving at low stone wall but nothing after that.

The woman placed a hand on Lyta's forehead. 'You have a fever, child, and need to rest.' She reached out for a cup that she held to the girl's lips.

'What's that?'

'A good remedy for fever.'

'But what exactly is it?'

The woman looked surprised. 'You know about herbs? I've used a mixture of Salusy and Miuta.'

Lyta nodded and opened her mouth. The potion would reduce her fever.

'What's your name, child?'

Lyta was about to give it but she caught herself. After all, she was trying to pass as a boy. 'I'm Lytik.'

The woman laughed. 'I'm Berda and I know you're not Lytik. I took off your tunic and hose before I put you to bed. Why are you posing as a boy?'

Lyta's mind raced. She had to invent a story that would satisfy Berda's curiosity and yet keep the woman on her side.

Berda added. 'And you're wearing very fine smallclothes under that grubby tunic.'

'My lady gave them to me.' Lyta tried to sound like Amia or Caza. 'I was a maid in a noble household. The Master was trying to bed me but I'm a good girl and promised to a lad in my village. When the Master tried to take me by force, I ran away.'

Berda looked sceptical. 'Who is this noble lord?'

'I cannot say. If he sends his men after me, then you'll be safer if you don't know his name or my real name.' She was overcome by an enormous yawn as she finished talking. The potion was sending her to sleep.

Berda tucked a coarse blanket around Lyta's shoulders. 'Rest now. We'll talk more about your plight later.'

As she closed her eyes, Lyta wondered if she'd convinced the woman by recounting one of her nurse's romantic tales.

The chamber was dimmer when she awoke. When her belly rumbled, Lyta realized how hungry she was. The fever had lessened and her limbs no longer ached.

Berda entered the chamber carrying a bowl and spoon. 'I heard you moving. Here's some broth.' The aroma coming from the broth made Lyta salivate. She pushed herself against the wall as Berda handed her the bowl. 'Sip it slowly. How long is it since you've eaten?'

'I'm not sure. The last thing I ate was raw hare.'

'Then you'll be glad I cooked this one first.' Berda watched Lyta, her hands clasped before her. 'Are you going back to your village?'

'I have a long journey ahead. I come from Aldea.'

'Then how did you get to Falga?'

'My mother fell in love with a boy from this demesne but they're both dead. My aunt and uncle live in Aldea as well as my betrothed.'

Berda frowned as she studied Lyta. 'You speak like someone with schooling.'

'My mother was the daughter of a noble. It caused a great scandal when she ran off with my father. He was an actor in a troupe performing at my grandsire's estate.'

'Hmm.' Breda reached out for the empty bowl. 'On the morrow, you can have more to eat but this is enough for now.'

Lyta smiled and held out her hand. 'Thanks for your kindness.'

She fell asleep at once. Yells, growls, and screams woke her suddenly. What in Lady Moon's name was happening outside? The growls must surely come from a wild beast. A beast? Lyta sat up so suddenly that she almost hit her head in the ceiling. Had the icekit tracked her to this place?

She called Seta inside her head and was answered. Throwing back the blanket, she ran to the door and opened it. Berda was peering through the tiny window in the main chamber. 'Go back to bed, child. A wild beast is outside but my man and our lad will kill it or drive it away.'

'No!' shouted Lyta. 'Don't let them kill her. She's my companion.

The woman frowned. 'The fever has taken your wits.'

Lyta wrenched open the cottage door. The older man was advancing on Seta with a pitchfork while the younger one was holding a long branch. The icecat was growling in a threatening manner, her low ruff standing up around her neck. She stepped toward Lyta.

'Sit! Stay!' Lyta yelled this order aloud. The icekit obeyed.

The man turned. 'The beast understands you?' His eyes were wide with alarm and surprise.

'She won't hurt you.' Lyta ran barefooted across to her kit. Once she was close, she saw a long wound on Seta's right flank. Her fur was stiff with dried blood. *'Bear? Wolf?'*

'Wolf,' said Seta. *'Hurt.'*

Lyta sensed that the two men were still convinced that Seta was dangerous. They held their weapons ready as she knelt down by the icekit and touched her. Seta purred and pushed her head against the hand.

'Wait.' The girl turned back to the two men. 'You can go inside. I'll care for my kit.' She followed them into the house where they were talking excitedly with Berda The woman stood by the fire with her hands on her broad hips. 'They say the beast is your icecat. Is this true?' she demanded.

'It's true. She's been wounded by a wolf. I need water and cloths for cleansing.'

Without another word, Berda took a large bowl and two rags from a shelf near the fireplace. 'We'll add Pardew for healing. I'd like to see this icecat.'

Back in the courtyard, Lyta set down the bowl and knelt down to examine the wound. Berda joined her, carrying a candle and a small vial.

'Do you think the gash will close of its own accord?' Lyta asked. 'Some wounds need stitches to hold the edges together.'

Berda seemed to lose her fear as she too bent down. 'It should close without stitches but a scar will remain.'

Once the wound was cleaned, Breda suggested that Seta be placed in the small hut adjoining the barn. 'We'll bar the door to keep her inside until morn.'

Privately, Lyta doubted that a bar would keep Seta inside if she really wanted to escape. She'd order the icekit to go to sleep. But first she asked if the kit had eaten.

When Seta said she was hungry, Lyta asked Berda if she had fresh meat.

'Only a hare,' Berda said. 'Not very big.'

Lyta said it would be sufficient and then led the icekit to the hut. She piled some hay in the corner while Seta sniffed the walls and floor.

Berda's hare was received with enthusiasm. Lyta watched the icekit eat and then drink water from the pump. Berda placed a bowl of water near the kit and barred the door before the two returned to the house.

'You must be sore tired,' said Berda. 'I'll give you some more potion to let you rest.'

Lyta forced herself to stay awake long enough to ponder her situation. If tonight's episode with Seta was going to be repeated with other people, then she might have to avoid all towns and villages and travel through the most deserted areas to reach Aldea.

Chapter Twenty-Eight

As soon as Lyta woke, she called Seta. When the kit didn't answer the first time, she called her name again. Uneasy at the continued silence, Lyta dressed in her cleaned tunic and hose before going into the main chamber of the cottage. 'Berda?' When the woman didn't respond either, Lyta walked outside.

The first thing she noticed was the hut's open door, swinging on its hinges. With fear growing in her belly, Lyta ran across the courtyard and peered inside. The hut was empty.

'Berda!' Lyta yelled her name as she ran past the pig pen. She saw the woman stooped over a row of green plants in an enclosed garden. 'Berda, where's my icekit?'

The woman stared down at the ground as she answered. 'It's gone. My man and boy took it to Lord Havit.'

Lyta slumped against the wall. 'How did they manage to capture Seta?'

'I added a sleeping potion to her water bowl.'

Lyta felt close to tears. 'Seta was my friend. Why did they take her?'

'We need the coin,' said Berda in a low voice. 'Our harvest has been poor. We don't have enough grain to last the winter.'

Lyta opened her mouth to berate the woman and then closed it again. Her words wouldn't serve any purpose. 'Where's Lord Havit's estate?'

Berda pointed west. 'The far side of the town.'

'When did your husband leave with my kit?'

'Last night after you fell asleep. They loaded it on a wagon.'

Lyta looked up at the sun to calculate the hour. Since it was high in the sky, the men could be on their way home by now. She ran back into the little house to collect her pouch and then left without saying farewell to Berda. While she had been helpful, her kindness had been cancelled out by this treachery.

Beyond the cottage, the main way west was joined by a criss-cross pattern of roads and tracks. People on foot or driving wagons and carts moved toward the town with burdens of fruit, vegetables, and animals. One toothless old man grinned at her and patted the empty seat beside him. Lyta nodded back and took his hand to be hoisted into his wagon. The back was loaded with sacks. When he said something, she couldn't understand his words. Was he speaking in a strange dialect or was the confusion caused by his complete lack of teeth?

When he repeated himself, she guessed that he'd asked if she was going to the fair.

'Yes,' she said, hoping she sounded like a Falgan.

'At Toma, 'he mumbled.

She nodded, hoping that he hadn't noticed her twitch of surprise. Cordon had taught Lyta that Toma was the seat of the ruler of Falga, where Kedur Ulit's castle was located. She hoped that Darik had no influence at court. If he did, then her stay in Toma should be brief.

The old man hummed a tune as he drove along. Lyta fretted that Seta might already be in the erle's clutches. How did the man treat his collection of wild beasts? She hoped he was concerned for their welfare.

The high town walls were directly ahead. At the open gate, an armed guard was checking each foot traveller and wagon driver. Surely Rurrik hadn't been able to get a message to the town officials about his missing prisoner. Lyta clutched the old man's tunic in alarm.

'Don't worry,' he said. He reached down to grab a straw hat which he dropped on Lyta's head. She pulled it further over her eyes and waited with her knees trembling for the inspection. Running away would make matters worse.

The guard waved the family group ahead of them through the gate. Then he motioned the wagon driver forward. 'My old friend, Mirt,' he said smiling at the driver. 'What are you carrying this time?'

Lyta thought he said cabbages and her guess was confirmed when the guard opened one of the sacks. He took out two large cabbages.

'These will do nicely.' He placed them on the ground and then glanced toward Lyta. 'And who's this?'

This time the answer was clearer. 'Nak's boy.'

The guard peered at Lyta. 'He's grown since last fair.'

Lyta held her breath until the guard dropped his gaze and waved them through the gate. Once they were inside, she breathed out and touched the old man's arm. 'Thank you, kind sir.'

'Take care,' the old man mumbled. 'Here.' He bent down again and handed Lyta something wrapped in a large cabbage leaf. 'Food for you.'

She pushed his hand away. 'I can't take your meal.'

The man shook his head and pressed the package into her hands. He clicked his tongue at the horse, which had halted. 'You'd best leave now.'

Lyta slipped from the wooden seat onto the uneven cobblestones. 'Thank you again.'

Mirt lifted a hand in farewell and Lyta watched the wagon until it turned a corner in the winding street. After Breda's behaviour, she was glad some Falgans liked to help others without expecting a reward.

Lyta decided she could pass unnoticed at the fair. The place would be crowded with both townsfolk and strangers. She followed a group of women who were making their way along the streets. They were all headed for the sounds of people and animals.

When she turned a corner, the fairgrounds lay before her with the walls and towers of a large castle looming beyond them. The fair itself was situated in a large central square, a pleasant grassy space surrounded by trees. It was much bigger and better organised than the one she knew back at Aldea. Rows of stalls selling cooked food and other goods were grouped together while animals were arranged in pens in a separate section at the rear. Piles of fresh fruit and vegetables occupied another area.

Lyta lingered near the closest stall where fragrant meat pies were arranged on several boards. A young boy sitting on a barrel caught her eye and pointed to his wares. Lyta shrugged and patted her pouch, indicating that she had no coin to buy a pie.

The boy glanced around before pushing a pie toward her. 'Take it quick!'

Lyta grabbed the pie and stuffed it into her pouch as a burly man strode toward the stall. He scowled at her. 'No coin, no pie,' he barked. 'Be off.'

Lyta smiled before she melted into the passing crowd and the boy grinned back. People were sitting in the shade of the trees and Lyta found an empty spot beside a woman who was feeding her baby. The pie was delicious. She ate it fast and then wiped a hand across her mouth to remove any crumbs. Two young girls plumped themselves down beside her. Lyta ignored their chatter until some of their words caught her attention.

'I won't never go near no icecat,' said the girl in a bright red kerchief. 'Pa says they can't be tamed.'

Pink gown nodded in agreement. 'They're exceedingly fierce.'

Lyta leaned across to them. 'Did you see an icecat today?'

Red kerchief stuck her nose in the air. 'We wasn't speaking to you. Pa don't let me talk to strange boys.'

'But this one looks harmless.' Her companion giggled. 'Our master got a new beast.'

Red kerchief added. 'He's got many wild beasts. What's that word he calls them? A mena... something.'

'A menagerie,' said Lyta.

'Aren't you the clever one?' said pink gown in an admiring tone.

Lyta asked. 'Is the beast a full grown cat or a kit?'

'Half grown, I reckon,' said pink gown. 'You should hear it growl.'

'Where's this estate with the icecat?' Lyta asked.

'Take the west gate,' said the kerchief girl, 'and then follow the road.'

Lyta thanked them and made her way through winding alleys to the western gate. The guard there was allowing people to leave the town without checking their bags or wagons. She followed the winding road beyond the town. One side of the way was forested while the other was farmed. She wondered if this erle owned all the land from the town to his estate.

As she heard people travelling on the road before she saw them, Lyta had time to hide in the bushes and trees until they had passed. After she'd seen the third party, she decided to shadow the road but stay in the protection of the trees. She was worried that Darik might have followed her himself or sent out spies to track her whereabouts.

When she grew weary of walking, she sat down on a convenient log and opened the cabbage-wrapped package the old man had given her. Inside was a rough slice of black bread, a hunk of white cheese, and a red apple. With a drink of water from her bottle, the food made a satisfying meal. Lyta rested her head against a tree trunk and closed her eyes.

A shrill cry woke her. For a startled minute she thought it was Seta calling her before she realized the sound was human. Lyta shook herself and stood up. Someone seemed to be in trouble but she should be wary. The call for help might be a trap.

Creeping from tree trunk to tree trunk, she stole toward the sound which, as she drew closer, appeared to belong to a child rather than an adult. Ahead lay a small clearing. She peered around a large bush and saw a child sitting on the ground. Nearby a plump pony grazed on the grass.

Nobody else was in sight. Lyta straightened up and walked toward the little girl who lifted a tear-stained face. 'Who's there?'

Just in time, Lyta remembered her travelling name. 'Lytik,' she said. 'Who are you?'

'I am the Lady Terta,' answered the child. 'My father is Lord Havit.'

'And what are you doing here, all alone in the forest?'

The little girl's cheeks flushed. 'I was meant to go riding,' she said,' and then all the grooms went to look at the icecat. Nobody came to take me out the gate so I left by myself.'

Lyta squatted down. 'I think you fell from your pony. Are you hurt?'

'I didn't fall from Daring!' said Terta in an indignant tone. She pointed upward. 'That branch knocked me off.'

Lyta hid a smile. Daring was a most unsuitable name for the amiable pony beside her. No doubt, the little girl had named her. 'What is sore apart from your forehead?' The cut above her eye had bled a little but it was not deep.

'This knee and my elbow,' Terta said, pointing to the body parts.

Lyta pushed up the child's richly embroidered blue gown and then gently moved her leg sideways.

'Ouch,' said Terta. 'That hurts.'

'I think you've broken the skin but the bones are whole.' Lyta did the same thing to the child's arm. 'Your elbow will need soothing balm but your arm isn't broken either.'

A single tear slid down Terta's cheek.

Lyta stood up. 'Let's get you back on the pony and then I'll lead you home.'

'I can ride all by myself.' Terta's lip trembled. 'I just need to be know the right way to go. Daring made me get lost in these trees.'

Lyta tugged the girl to her feet and then cupped her hands to boost Terta into the saddle. 'Hold on tight. I'll take the reins and get you home.'

Chapter Twenty-Nine

They had travelled on the road barely a league before a group of men trotted toward them. From the shouts of joy that followed, Lyta guessed this was a search party from Havit's estate.

The man in front grabbed the reins from Lyta's hands. 'You're in big trouble, boy. Lord Havit will punish you for taking his daughter.'

'But I didn't take her.' Lyta's protests of innocence were drowned out by the voices of the men.

When one of them hoisted her onto his horse, the party wheeled around and moved west at a fast pace. 'Better keep your mouth shut,' said Lyta's captor. 'I wouldn't want to be in your boots when you see the Master.'

Lyta resigned herself to silence. She hoped that Terta would tell her father what had actually happened.

The mansion house inside the walls was bigger than Lyta had expected. The erle must be a man of some property and status in Falga. She heard Havit's voice before she saw him. It was loud and commanding as he approached them from the right corner of the house. When she saw the man himself, Lyta was surprised. The large voice belonged to a short squat man who reminded her of a toad. When his lady ran down the front steps with cries of concern, the slender woman towered over her husband. They made an incongruous pair.

The lady clasped Terta to her bosom. 'Just look at your forehead! Child, what did you do to yourself?'

'It was Daring's fault,' said Terta as her mother smoothed the hair from her eyes to examine the wound.

'This boy had captured the Lady Terta,' said the leader of the party. He pushed Lyta toward his master. 'I think he took her and then got scared and was bringing her back.'

Havit's grey eyes were cold as he examined Lyta from her head to her toes. 'Well, boy, what do you say for yourself?'

Terta wriggled from her mother's arms and tugged the hem of her father's crumpled red tunic. 'No, Pappy. Lytik found me when I was lost. He was bringing me home.'

'Is that so?' asked Havit.

Lyta nodded. 'Yes, my lord. A branch knocked her off the pony. But she's not badly hurt apart from some broken skin.'

Terta's mother swept forward. 'We'll soon have you better.' She took the child's hand to lead her into the house.

But the girl pulled away. 'Please, Pappy, I want Lytik to stay here. He was very kind to me when I was lost in the trees.'

Although the erle smiled at Lyta, his eyes remained hard. 'Are you afraid of wild beasts?' he asked.

'Of course,' said Lyta, 'but I'd like to help with the icekit.'

'So you've heard of it. I doubt you'll be much use. The beast won't eat.'

'Please let me try to feed it.' Lyta heard Seta growling from beyond the wall to her right.

Lord Havit shrugged. 'As you wish. If you fail, we'll feed you to the beast.' His short bark of laughter was mirthless. 'Follow me.'

He led the way around the house and stopped at an iron gate in the stone wall. 'This is the door to my menagerie enclosure.' From his belt, he took a large iron key and inserted it into the lock. 'Never stay in here by yourself.'

When he opened the gate, Lyta took in a sharp breath. The enclosure was large. Cages with iron bars were arranged in a circle around a central ring. She assumed this area was used to exercise the beasts. Above the cages at one side was a viewing platform with seats.

After this swift appraisal, her attention was riveted on the nearest cage. Seta sprang to her feet and stared at Lyta. *'Go,'* her message said.

'Wait,' said Lyta, going forward to the bars. When she reached a hand through them, Seta rubbed her head against the girl's fingers. She purred with pleasure. Erle Havit gasped and Lyta heard the startled exclamations of the men behind him.

'How did you do that?' asked the erle. 'She's been snarling and leaping at us and trying to get through the bars.

'I like icecats,' said Lyta, 'and they like me.'

'Then mayhap she will take food from you. We have several fresh-killed hares ready and a goat.'

'She'll be sure to eat the hares,' said Lyta, 'and if she's really hungry, she might try the goat.' A servant brought the meat on a plank. From above their heads, a system of pulleys opened the front part of the bars, just enough to slide the board through.

'Please open it wider,' Lyta asked. 'I want to go into the cage.'

Havit shook his head. 'I can't take that risk but I want you here to feed the cat. It's important that she gets healthy.'

Lyta was glad to hear that the erle was concerned about the condition of his beasts. Although Seta would hate being confined at least she would be well fed until they could both escape from the estate.

Lady Terta took a great fancy to Lyta. The little girl persuaded her father to give Lyta a new sky blue tunic and to allow her to stand behind the child at dinner. Lyta realized what it was like to be a servant as she shifted from foot to foot behind Terta's chair. Some of the adults snapped at her when she was slow to carry out their bidding. She'd even received a couple of cuffs on her ears. When Lyta returned to Aldea, she'd treat her own servants as kindly as possible. She suspected that Virr would have been pleased that she'd learned this particular lesson.

Lyta slept outside Terta's chamber. The little girl had ordered that a straw pallet be set there for her Lytik. In this household, everyone knew whose wishes were to be obeyed instantly. Lady Terta had only to smile at her father to be given whatever she wished although once when she wanted a new gown, she was forced to use tears to get it. Behind the erle's back, the estate workers called her Lady Brat.

Havit made it clear that Lyta's first duty was to feed Seta. Twice a day the freshest meat was prepared for the icekit. Every time, Lyta came near Seta's cage, the kit pleaded for freedom and every time, Lyta told her to wait. She could see how being caged was taking a toll on the beast's spirit. The kit ate her food but she was listless and slept most of the day.

Access to the enclosure key was the main difficulty in releasing Seta. Havit never handed it to anybody else and as far as Lyta could tell, he had the only one attached to his belt. Even Lady Nuna, his wife, never laid hands on it.

The menagerie workers followed every order concerning the beasts. One morn, they separated a wolf from his companions and placed it in a cage beside Seta. She took exception to the closeness of the animal and snarled at it.

When the wolf snarled in return, Havit laughed. 'That's what we like to see. Now build up the wolf with extra rations.'

Lyta had no idea of what lay ahead for Seta until the Lady Terta told her. The little girl liked to visit the menagerie with her father each morn and observe the feeding of the beasts. Terta wasn't bothered by the bloody carcases that were pushed through the cage bars or by the savage way they were torn apart.

'Pappy says they must both be strong,' she told Lyta. 'The icecat and the grey wolf.'

'Good meat keeps them healthy,' agreed Lyta.

'Which one is do you think is stronger?' the child asked.

'Hard to say.' Lyta answered. 'The wolf is older and bigger than the kit but she is very powerful for her age.'

'I will wager on the icecat,' Terta declared.

Lyta's heart almost stopped but she forced herself to ask, 'Why are you placing a wager?'

'For the battle.' A scornful expression appeared on Terta's face. 'You are foolish, Lytik. Everyone comes here to watch and place wagers. After the battle, we have a big feast.'

Lyta took a deep breath to steady her voice. 'So the icecat and the wolf will fight each other and people will place wagers?'

'That's what I said.' Terta hit Lyta's arm. 'Boy, you must listen better to me when I tell you something.'

'When will this battle happen?' Lyta forced herself to stay calm as she watched Seta gnaw the bones of a young goat.

'In a sevenday. That's why I needed a new gown.'

Chapter Thirty

Lyta was unable to sleep that night. She tossed on the pallet which seemed even harder than usual. How would she get Seta away before the battle took place? Even if she somehow obtained the key to the door, she still had to smuggle a large beast from the estate without being caught. The whole task seemed impossible.

Terta hadn't mentioned how the outcome of the struggle was decided but Lyta suspected that one beast killed the other. She asked a worker about it the next morn.

'Oh, they always fight to the death,' he said in a cheerful tone as he decapitated a hare. 'And these two beasts should give us a good show.'

'Does everyone place wagers?'

The fellow nodded. 'Last time I won a silver coin on the bear. The Master lets us wager and watch.'

Lyta felt ill as she watched Seta tear at the hares with her sharp teeth. What sort of man was Havit? She couldn't understand how he could collect wild beasts and then arrange to have two of them fight to the end.

Every morn she told Seta to wait for freedom and then she fretted about her inability to come up with a rescue plan. If she raised the bars of the cage, Seta would still be trapped in the enclosure. Getting the key was essential.

Two more morns passed. The estate workers were busy with preparations for the battle and the following feast. Lady Nuna was more distracted than usual as she gave orders for chambers to be opened and bedding to be aired for their guests.

Terta kept a close eye on the progress of her new gown. 'It will be very fine,' she announced to Lyta. 'And Pappy is giving me a golden girdle with a necklace to match.' She twirled around in delight. 'You need new hose, Lytik. Yours are quite shabby.'

But Lyta wasn't interested in new clothes. She kept a keen eye on the erle and his key. If the two were ever separated, she'd be ready to act.

Her first chance came at dinner that night. Lord Calid, one of Havit's close friends, had come early for the wild beast battle. Lady Nuna had remarked in a sour voice that this man always came before the other guests to eat and drink at her husband's expense. 'And he never invites us to his estate,' she added. 'Not that I'd want to go to his place. I've heard his wife serves a meagre table.'

During dinner, Havit Calid started a drinking contest, matching cups of strong red wine. Lady Nuna lasted through several flasks before she took Terta from the hall. 'You stay here, boy,' she told Lyta. 'They will both have to be carried to bed.'

First Calid and then Havit slid from their chairs to lie snoring on the cold floor. The steward nodded to Lyta and three other servants. They took an arm or leg each and carted the guest to his chamber where they dumped him on the bed. Then they carried their master. Lyta was not surprised that his lady wasn't in the bedchamber. No doubt from grim experience she was sleeping with her daughter for the night.

'Pull off his boots,' said the steward. 'I'll unbuckle his belt. He doesn't like other people to touch it.' He placed the belt on a nearby chest before laying a covering over his master.

Lyta followed him from the chamber. She noted that the steward did not lock the door. Outside Terta's chamber, she lay on her pallet waiting for the house to become quiet and still. Then she stood up and stole along the passageway. If anyone challenged her, she'd say she was on her way to the servants' privy outside. Luckily, she met nobody. Rumbling snores came from Havit's chamber.

Very slowly, Lyta lifted the latch and pushed the door. Something large prevented it from opening.

Through a slit in the door, she saw Havit's man servant lying on the floor. He stirred as he felt the door touch his body. 'Who's there?' he mumbled.

Lyta turned and fled. She hoped the man hadn't recognised her from his brief glimpse. She stumbled back along the passage with tears spilling from her eyes. This might have been her first and last opportunity to get the key.

The house was full of guests as the battle day approached. All the beasts in the enclosure were affected by the high level of excitement. Even the older and more lethargic animals prowled around their cages and growled. Seta was well aware that something was about to happen. Lyta tried to keep her voice calm as she gave the icekit her last meal.

'Make it a good one,' Havit called as he watched her with the hares. 'We want her to be really strong.' He tossed an extra chicken to the wolf.

The steward was in charge of the wagering. He sat at the back of the viewing platform with a small coffer of coins on the table before him. He entered names and figures into a long book and asked the person making the wager to sign his name or make his mark on the page.

'Lytik,' said a worker. 'Why not wager a coin on your icekit. She should fight well.'

Lyta couldn't even answer him. A permanent lump had grown in her chest and throat, making speech impossible. Silently, she called Seta to the bars of the cage and ruffled her silky neck fur one last time. The icekit turned her head for the girl to scratch behind her ears.

The viewing platform was full. Terta in her new finery had been brought there by her father but Lady Nuna was not present. Lyta and the estate workers were permitted to watch the battle from ground level. They stood just beyond the enclosed ring.

The crowd roared in approval when Havit ordered the bars of the combatants' cages to be raised. The wolf and the icekit stared into the open space. Seta took a few steps forward and the wolf did the same. They both paused. Then the wolf rushed at Seta.

Seta appeared taken aback by the attack. She jumped sideways to avoid the wolf's claws and stopped. The crowd roared encouragement.

'Bite him!'

'Use your claws!'

Lyta wanted to close her eyes but that seemed disloyal to her kit. For Seta's sake, she must watch. The icekit prowled behind the wolf as though she looked for a weak spot. The wolf turned to face her but he wasn't fast enough. The icecat leaped on the wolf's back and tore at his neck with her sharp teeth. The wolf howled and twisted his body from Seta's grip. Blood streamed from his wounds onto the sand.

With an enormous shrug of his shoulders, he dislodged the cat. Then he shook himself and sprang at Seta, seeking her vulnerable neck. The wolf was heavier and bigger than the icekit and Lyta knew that if he got her down on the ground, his teeth could rip open Seta's throat.

The crowd was yelling continuously with half cheering on the wolf and the others admonishing the icekit to fight back. Havit's voice was the loudest of all. 'Come on, icecat! You can do it.'

Somehow, Seta danced away from the wolf but he was determined despite his earlier wound. He leapt again and managed to sink his teeth into the side of her neck. Seta's blood gushed out.

That was too much for Lyta. From her pouch, she grabbed the blade. 'Freedom.' She sent this message to Seta. The icekit raised her head and looked straight at Lyta with her silver eyes. The girl threw her blade at the kit's head. Her aim was true. The point dug deep into Seta's brain and she crumpled onto the ground. Then the wolf's teeth tore at her flesh.

The people on the viewing platform were silent until they realised what had happened. Then they shouted with anger at the abrupt close of the battle. As soon as she knew her blade had gone home, Lyta had edged behind the ring of workers and until she was beside the gate. The workers were still gasping and pointing at Seta as the erle pounded down the steps from the platform. Lyta reached the enclosure gate.

Since she was the only one moving away from the ring, Havit noticed her departure. 'Grab him! Seize that boy!' he screamed. Calid echoed his calls as he followed Havit.

In the confusion, Lyta had a good head start. She had left the main gate before anybody could stop her. She dashed across the road and into the trees on the far side.

Chapter Thirty-One

Lyta had to hide. She clutched the trunk of an oak and clambered onto a low branch. Then she climbed higher until she was shielded by thick clusters of leaves.

She grabbed a wide limb and lay along it, hoping she was invisible from the ground. The erle's men had reached the forest and she heard feet rushing to and fro among the trees. Voices called and answered with Havit's loud commands rising above them all as he ordered them to look harder.

'He must have gone further into the forest.' he shouted. 'A purse of coins to the man who brings that damned brat back to me.'

Lyta lay motionless even though a yellow caterpillar crawled over her neck and face. She kept her mouth shut to prevent it from creeping between her lips. Even a slight movement might shake the leaves and be detected from below. She heard a worker suggest that the brat might have joined a band of pilgrims who were passing by on the road.

'Search them!' ordered Havit. 'He must be somewhere.'

Lyta stayed on her bough until she could no longer hear voices. She had lost all sensation in her legs and feet. If she didn't move soon, she might not be able to climb down. Gingerly she wiggled first one leg and then the other and relaxed her grip on the branch. She'd remain hidden until nightfall and then escape under cover of darkness.

Lyta hadn't realized how useful her blue tunic was until next morn when she joined a group of pilgrims trudging along the road. She'd attached herself to them after tracking their progress from the shelter of the forest.

She wanted to blend in with a band on its way to the holy temple at Avridon. Lyta hoped that Lady Moon would forgive her for passing herself as a Star child.

She glanced around at her fellow travellers. All were wearing something blue. Men sported blue kerchiefs around their necks; boys wore blue hose or tunics and girls azure blouses or gowns. She even saw a man with blue boots on his feet. But the prize for the most holy outfit went to an old woman riding on a donkey with blue reins and a blue blanket embroidered with stars covering its broad back. The woman herself was dressed entirely in blue from the kerchief on her head to the slippers on her feet.

The people walking with her were friendly. When they sat down to eat, women glanced at her empty hands and passed her a crust of bread or a piece of cheese and she was able to fill her water bottle from the many springs that dotted the way. Since all were well used, the earth around the bubbling water was muddy and wet. Lyta kept her head down most of the time and her words to a minimum as she wanted to be taken for a native Falgan. She did explain to the pilgrim next to her that she was an orphaned boy travelling to Avridon for guidance now that her parents had both died of a fever.

'You'll find comfort and help at the temple,' said the plump woman patting Lyta's hand. 'When both my babies died, I didn't want to live but a priest gave me hope and a guiding star. Now look what I have.' Lyta's eyes followed her pointing finger to a pair of lively boys wrestling each other on the grass nearby. The woman chuckled as she separated her twin sons with a practised hand.

At night, wealthy pilgrims slept in inns on the way while those with little or no coin bedded down in village squares or the countryside. They usually found protection under trees in case of rain. Her new friend gave Lyta a cloak to wrap herself in as she'd left her own at Havit's estate. Always, she kept an eye out for Darik or Erit in case one of them had used spies to track her.

The trip to Avridon took a sevenday. Lyta was almost sorry to see the towers of the city ahead as they rounded the final bend in the road. The routine of the walk had given her time to deal with the raw emotions caused by Seta's death. Although she knew she'd done the right thing in killing her friend, the dreadful end lingered in her mind like a nasty taste in her mouth. Would Seta have been better off left in the cave with her slain mother? Mayhap the kit would've learned to kill her own food and live freely in the Red Mountains? If so, Lyta had done the wrong thing.

Lyta recalled some of Virr's words. One day, when she'd been lamenting an unwise choice, he'd laughed at her worried face. 'Would have, could have, should have,' he'd said. 'Live with it. You'll never know what might have happened.'

The only consolation Lyta had was that she had given her companion a swifter death than she might have had in battle. On second thought, she wished she'd had another blade and the time to put the poor wolf out of its misery too.

The two guards at the gates of Avridon didn't check on anybody's right to be there. For the next sevenday, blue clothing gave anybody permission to enter the city and then to visit the temple. Lyta saw its twelve towers rising above the roof tops in the centre of the houses. Their silver spires gleamed in the light of the sun.

Taya, the woman with the two boys, had taken Lyta under her wing. As they walked the cobbled streets, she clutched Lyta's hand and pulled her to a stop. 'We cannot enter the temple in daylight,' she said. 'Only the Evening Star can light our way.'

'What should I know?' Lyta asked. 'I've had little instruction in the faith.'

'I noticed that you don't wear a sign or pray to the Stars,' said her companion. 'You can learn the right way at the temple where they give instruction. You'll get help too. The priest who guided me is a good man. Virr is his name.'

Lyta's heart missed several beats. Taya had actually met Virr when he was a temple priest! 'What did he look like so I might recognise him?'

'Tall and slim with dark hair, kept short like all the priests. I remember his eyes, as blue as summer skies. When he smiled at me, I knew things would be better. And of course his advice was very wise.'

Lyta swallowed twice. Taya's description had summoned Virr as though he stood alive before her. 'Mayhap he's left the temple since then.'

Taya shook her head. 'Oh, no. People said he'd be Chief Priest one day. I haven't been back for seven years so he might be in charge right now.'

Or he might be dead, thought Lyta. She rubbed her eyes hard to prevent tears from spilling down her cheeks.

'Don't fret, child,' said Taya, mistaking her sudden grief for anxiety. 'I'll show you what to do this evening.'

Many scores of pilgrims had settled down on the wide expanse of grass and trees around the temple. They were quiet and orderly as they waited. The noisiest children were peaceful and even Taya's twins sat without stirring.

A murmur rose from the crowd as they watched the sun set beyond the town walls. One of the western spires was the last to catch the rays and when they vanished, Lyta guessed that the time to enter the temple must be near.

A priest in a silver robe appeared at the wide doors. He stood at the top of the white steps and raised both arms as he chanted a prayer. The crowd repeated a refrain each time he paused. After the seventh refrain, the man lowered his arms and bowed his head. Then he gestured to the people and moved to one side of the door.

'We're going in,' said Taya as she hauled her sons to their feet. 'Now, boys, remember my words. No talking unless a priest speaks to you.'

Lyta followed the pilgrims up the steps, staying close to her friend. Inside the open doors lay a wide pool which divided the crowd into two. Each person dipped down and splashed a little water over their hands. Lyta wondered if this was an act of purification. She copied Taya as the woman showed her sons what to do.

Only the sounds of soft boots and slippers were heard as people moved in silence down a long passage bordered by tall arched windows. Those on the west still showed final streaks of red and gold across the sky.

Taya pointed ahead as they reached the centre of the temple. A vast roof curved far over their heads. Lyta craned her neck to admire the patterns of stars painted on it. She wondered what material made the shining surface. It couldn't be glass as she didn't see the sky beyond the ceiling.

As it had done every night on their journey, night fell fast. Gasps rose from the pilgrims when the stars above them suddenly glowed and twinkled as they did in the outside world. This was the wonderful ceiling that everyone who visited the temple remembered, even if like her tutoran, they didn't follow the Star faith. Now, Lyta understood how the fine workmanship impressed visitors and pilgrims alike.

When chanting rose from the walls around them, Lyta noticed the circle of silver-clad priests who had entered the space in a silent procession. The pilgrims sank to their knees on the white marble floor and Lyta followed. Since the floor was cold and hard, she hoped they wouldn't be required to stay in that position for too long.

Taya was waving her hands gently from side to side as she joined the prayers. Lyta couldn't catch all the words as the voices around her rose and fell. The sound was strangely calming and almost hypnotic in effect. Only the sharp pain in her knees kept her awake.

Taya nudged her as the service ended and people began to rise to their feet. Creaking of limbs and sighs accompanied their movements. 'Now we can talk to a priest,' she muttered into Lyta's ear. 'Ask for Virr.'

The pilgrims moved beyond the central dome. Corridors like the spokes of a wheel led in many directions and before Taya took her sons away, she indicated tiny chambers fitted with marble benches that lined the passage. 'That's where we talk,' she said as Lyta noticed priests waiting for pilgrims inside the chambers.

Lyta stopped and touched Taya's arm. 'I'll talk to that priest,' she said at the open doorway of a chamber.

Taya frowned. 'Virr is better,' she said.

'But he might be busy if he's the Chief Priest,' said Lyta.

'That's true.' Taya nodded. 'I'll be in the next empty chamber asking about my sons. The priest will tell me who should go to sea and who should stay on land.'

As Lyta stepped through the doorway, she wondered if all pilgrims had as much faith as Taya in the advice of the Star Priests. Surely some of them were not as skilled as others in giving guidance. When she paused inside the open doorway, the priest waiting for her threw back a silver hood. In the light from a torch on the wall, Lyta realised with surprise that she was a woman. Somehow she'd assumed that the priests were all men.

'Sit down,' the priest said. Then she stared long at Lyta. 'You are not what you seem.'

'I don't hold the Star faith.'

'Not only that,' said the priest. 'You're not a boy, you don't live in this demesne and while your clothes are plain, you're not of lowly birth.'

Lyta gulped. Would this priest reveal her many deceptions to others at the temple? Rurrik might discover her whereabouts.

'Don't worry,' the woman continued. 'Everything that happens in this cell is secret. Your heart and mind can be at peace.'

Lyta sighed. 'My heart and mind have been sorely tried since my friend died. He was very dear to me.'

'Virr tried hard to protect you but he didn't succeed.' The priest's voice was gentle as she leaned toward Lyta. 'He was much loved here and we also missed him very much.'

'How did Virr know I was in danger?'

'We hear many things. Your mother was also at risk. Virr asked permission to go to Aldea to keep the peace.'

'Then Rurrik wasn't the only erle in the plot?'

'Other men were waiting to see if his plans succeeded. Virr wanted to prevent an uprising in the land.'

Lyta sat for a time in silence while she thought about the priest's words. She didn't feel any happier about Virr's death but at least she knew what was behind it.

'And now you grieve for another friend,' said the priest.

Lyta realised that she knew about the icekit. 'I feel guilty. She was a beautiful beast.'

'And you were very lucky to be able to have her friendship, even for a little time.'

Lyta nodded. 'I'll never forget Seta playing in the snow.'

'Memories comfort us,' said the priest, leaning forward. 'What can I do for you?'

'You can help me return to Aldea.'

'Men are searching for you at this moment. We can give you sanctuary in the temple until all danger passes.'

Lyta breathed out in relief. At last she would be able to feel safe.

The priest bent down to pull out a garment tucked under the bench. 'Pull this over your clothes,' she said, 'and you'll be taken for a temple novice.'

Lyta tugged the grey robe over her present clothes. It was wide enough to cover her cloak, tunic, and hose.

'Cover your head with the hood, tuck both hands in your sleeves, and look down.' She waited until Lyta had adjusted the robe. 'If you are ready, then follow me.' The woman priest lifted the torch from its wall holder and walked swiftly from the chamber and along the passage. Lyta almost trotted to keep close behind her.

She glimpsed Taya waiting outside a chamber with her boys but knew she couldn't acknowledge her. She hoped the woman knew how grateful she was for their brief friendship. Mayhap one day, she could return to Falga and discover how Taya was faring.

When the priest turned a corner, a group of pilgrims surged toward them. The priest waited against the wall to let them pass. Lyta watched the people. At the rear, she caught a glimpse of a familiar face with two slanting eyebrows. She sucked in a frightened breath. Erit! How in the name of Lady Moon had he managed to follow her?

Chapter Thirty-Two

Lyta's shoulders lowered when she realised Erit had gone by without a look or a word. Her novice habit had made her unrecognisable. Why was he here? He could be attending the Avridon temple as a pilgrim but deep inside, she didn't believe this explanation. He was following her.

The priest turned toward Lyta. 'Stay calm,' she said. 'All will be well.'

Lyta took a deep breath and willed her heart to slow down. Would Erit question priests and novices? He needed to find only one person with a loose tongue to betray her.

The priest continued along the passage before stopping at a door in a side wall. She drew a key from her waist pouch and inserted it into the lock. When the door swung open, she guided Lyta through it.

They stood in a courtyard lit with flaming torches. Lyta peered into the darkness. She could see the dim outlines of flowering bushes, trees, and statues. She heard a gurgling stream and in the flickering firelight noticed it ran into a shining pond bordered by rocks. 'How beautiful!' Lyta said. 'Do pilgrims come into this place?'

'This is our haven,' said the priest. 'Here, we divest ourselves of the worries and cares laid on us by the pilgrims.'

Lyta nodded. She could imagine that the priests needed a private place after listening to the problems of so many worried people. 'I don't know your name,' she said.

'Call me Fana.' The priest pointed at a wicker chair. 'Sit here, child. I'll fetch soup and bread for you.'

Lyta rested her head again the back of the chair and closed her eyes. She must have dozed a little as she woke when Fana returned. Hot soup steamed in a wooden bowl.

She drank the vegetable broth greedily and ate the slices of rye bread on the tray.

Fana watched her with a smile. 'Now, you need rest' She lifted the tray as she continued. 'Follow me to your bed.'

The small white chamber was furnished simply with a low bed, a square table and a silver stool. Two empty wall hooks were intended to hold clothes. Fana pulled back a blue blanket on the bed. 'Get undressed, child, and lie down. I'll wake you in the morn.'

When Lyta woke, she had no memory of getting undressed and slipping into bed. This was the deepest night's sleep she'd experienced for many sevendays. Knowing she was safe had calmed her mind. After a tap on the door, Fana entered carrying a bowl of water and a tray of repast cakes with a cup of berry juice. A towel lay over her arm. 'Before you leave the chamber,' she said. 'Wash and then put on your grey robe. I'll take your other clothes away until you need them again.'

She picked up Lyta's tunic and hose and then paused at the door. 'Only the Chief Priest and I know you're here. When you've eaten, I'll take you to meet him.'

Pybik, the Chief Priest was the oldest man Lyta had ever seen. The skin on his face fell in so many wrinkles that they partially obscured his features. Only his eyes were young. They were piercing and grey as he observed Lyta and waved her to a stool before him. His chamber was as simply furnished as the one Lyta had occupied. The only difference was in the piles of books on the table and over the floor.

Lyta waited to hear his words. No doubt he'd spoken to Fana already and knew about her trials. She wondered what he was thinking and whether he would tell Erle Rurrik and Erle Havit where she was. They were all Falgans. She tried to search his mind for any clue.

The man laughed suddenly. 'Oh no, you don't. Everything inside my head is mine alone.' He leaned forward with both spotted hands on his knees. 'Child, who taught you this interesting skill?'

'Magian Domen.' Lyta knew her cheeks had flushed. 'I'm sorry to be so rude. I shouldn't have tried to invade your mind.'

'I can see when the skill might be useful but take care how you use it. Were you able to speak to your icekit in this manner?'

'She could send and receive only single word messages. But that was enough for us to become friends.' She swallowed several times. 'I feel so sorrowful just talking about Seta.'

'Of course you do. But you did the right thing.' One hand patted Lyta's shoulder. 'Now to other matters. You have been followed here.'

'I saw Erit, Rurrik's son last night. He was in a band of pilgrims.'

'Erit suspects you might be here and he has questioned other pilgrims and our people.'

'I don't know what Erit would do if he finds me. Take me back to his father or help me to get to Aldea. He seemed to like me but his father has promised him wealth and land.'

'The man is troubled and unsure of his true heart,' said the Chief Priest. 'Erle Havit suggested you'd probably joined a band of pilgrims.'

'Darik is also looking for me,' said Lyta.

'He is still on the far side of the Red Mountains. As for Erit, we'll let him believe you've left here. After he departs, we'll watch him.'

Lyta nodded. 'What's the safest way for me to go home?'

'I'll arrange an escort for you.'

'No. I am no doubt foolish but I would like to return on my own.' '

Pybik frowned. 'You are indeed foolish. There'll be more dangers ahead.'

'I wish to travel without an escort. I'd like to make Virr proud of me.'

Pybik swung around to stare out of his window into the courtyard. Then he turned back to Lyta with a sigh. 'I don't agree with you. However, at the temple we guide people to make decisions but we do not influence their future actions. I must respect your wishes.'

He stood up slowly. 'It would be most unwise to travel as you are. Erit and the others are searching for a boy. We must turn you back into a girl. I know Fana will have some ideas. She is very inventive.'

An hour later, Lyta sat on a stool while Fana walked around her. 'First, we must alter your hair.'

'Can you change the colour to brown?'

Fana smoothed Lyta's black head. 'An interesting idea.' She smiled suddenly. 'How about golden hair?'

'Golden!' Lyta had trouble believing her ears. 'Can you do that? '

'Older women use dyes to cover their silver locks.' She paused and lifted Lyta's chin toward the light. 'We will whiten your skin too. What did you use to get this colour?'

Lyta grinned. 'The juice of the piss plant. I was looking for more on the way here as it's wearing off.'

'Then we shall help it along.' Fana sat down on the bed and looked seriously at the girl. 'The trouble with being a girl is that men will regard you as prey if you travel without any protection.'

She stood up again. 'I'll worry about that problem later. Let's start with your hair and your skin.'

By midmeal, Lyta had been scrubbed, washed, rubbed, and rinsed. She hardly recognised herself when

Fana handed over a small looking glass. Lyta tipped it up and then down to get the full effect of the transformation.

The golden hair was startling. 'I'm not me now.'

Fana frowned. 'I should add some marks to your face. A girl of your age and birth would have moles or scars.' She used a dab of dark dye to give Lyta a large mole on her cheek and a small scar on her chin. 'All the dye will wear off in about two moons and by then you'll be back home.'

Lyta studied the effect of the marks on her face. She nodded.

'I've been thinking about making you less attractive to men,' said Fana. 'I've decided to give you a sickness.'

'But if I'm ill, how can I travel?' Lyta asked.

'Not a real illness but something that will keep people away.' She reached into her pouch and took out a small round box. 'A pinch of this in your mouth will make you cough. If it's bad enough, people will back away.'

'But will it damage my throat?'

'No. After you stop taking it, you won't cough again.'

Lyta opened the lid. Inside was a dark brown feathery substance. 'Shall I try it out?'

Fana nodded. She watched closely as Lyta picked up a pinch of the stuff between her thumb and finger and slid it into her mouth. At once, the girl's throat and chest went into paroxysm of violent coughing. When Lyta caught her breath again, she said, 'I sound like someone on a sickbed.'

'That's the plan,' said Fana. 'You can add fake coughs if needed.'

Lyta reached for a cup of water. After she swallowed, she said, 'I need a tale to go with my cough. What if my mother died of this ailment and I'm going home to tend my ill father. If people think my whole family is poorly, they won't come very close to me.'

'I like that,' said Fana. 'Now I have some girl clothes for you. Let's see if the gown is the right size.' When Lyta had undressed, Fana tried to pull a blue gown past her chest. 'Too small,' she said at last. 'You need more room around your chest.'

Lyta looked down at her body in surprise. She hadn't noticed her sprouting breasts. The loose fit of her tunic had obscured her shape.

'I'll find a suitable blouse and skirt. We keep many clothes here for pilgrims who need them.'

When she left the room, Lyta stayed on her stool. If her breasts were growing, she wondered whether she'd experience her first moonblood before she reached home. If so, she would have left Aldea as a girl only to return as a woman. The thought was unsettling.

Fana found a pink blouse and a green and white skirt. Both were slightly big. 'It is better if your clothing isn't tight to draw attention to your shape,' she commented as she helped Lyta with the front laces. Lyta twirled around. The skirt was long enough to cover the tops of her brown boots. 'Pybik wants to see you,' said Fana. 'He'll be here soon.'

The chief priest leaned heavily on his carved stick as he entered the chamber. Under his other arm, he carried a flat book. He smiled broadly as Lyta stood before him. 'You have done well, Fana. I wouldn't know this was the same scruffy boy who talked to me earlier.'

'Inside, I'm the same scruffy boy,' Lyta said, 'but I hope to deceive anybody searching for me.'

Pybik placed the book on the bed and opened it. 'This is a map of Falga, which also shows the borders of your demesne. When you reach Naris on the coast, I will have a ship waiting to take you home. I know you want to get there by yourself but it makes no sense to travel many leagues by land when you can get there much faster by sea.' His finger traced the route from Avridon to Naris and then from Naris to her home.

Lyta swallowed hard as she read the name of the city. 'Naris was Virr's birthplace and his body was sent there to his sister.'

'Sia still dwells there with her family,' said Pybik.

'But what about Cett? Does he live in Naris too?'

'Child, Cett will not trouble you. He's been hired on a ship bound for Parian and Sevvir. The voyage will last many moons.'

'Then I'll go to Naris and meet the captain of the ship. I want to get back to my mother as soon as possible.' Lyta shook her golden locks. 'But she may not recognise me when I walk through the gate.'

Chapter Thirty-Three

Erit stood beside his father as Darik prepared to leave the estate. He looked down at them from his saddle. 'I'll find that girl before the Aldeans catch up with her.'

'Will you return her to me?' Rurrik asked.

Darik grinned. 'Mayhap I will or mayhap I won't.'

'If you're wise, you'll bring her straightway here.'

But Darik merely shook his head. After he and his men had clattered over the stone bridge, Rurrik turned to Erit. 'Do you think the girl has gone back down the mountain?'

'She does have a name. Call her Lyta.'

Rurrik scowled. 'Then which way do you think this Lyta went?'

'I reckon she went north over the Red Mountains. And she is certain to be dressed as a boy. Her woman's clothing was left in the chamber.'

'I agree with you even though your brother is so sure of her path.' Rurrik stroked his dark beard as he thought. 'Follow the track over the mountains.'

Erit stared hard at his father. 'Why should I do anything else for you? You haven't rewarded me for my past errands.'

'Trust my words. I have promised both land and coin for your work.'

'What land and what coin? Words won't fill my belly and get me a wife.'

Rurrik sighed. 'Then let me be clear. You may have this estate and coin enough to govern it when you bring back that girl.' He paused. 'If you bring back Lyta.'

'I want your promise in writing before I leave.'

'Very well. After I write a document and we sign it, then will you carry out my wishes?'

Erit agreed. However he was surprised when his father actually produced a document. After reading it with care, he signed his name and Rurrik did the same.

When his father reached for the sheet, Erit grabbed it first. 'This stays in my possession,' he stated, noting the flash of anger in his father's dark eyes. Erit considered it very likely that Rurrik might conveniently mislay the document.

Erit met several groups of travellers as he climbed the Red Mountains. None of them had seen a lone boy travelling on the mountain or in the lowlands beyond it. When he reached the summit, he walked along the ridge. He thought he remembered an older path, which had been blocked by a landslide many moons ago. He found the track and noted the massive pile of boulders blocking it. Lyta may have decided the old route was safer for her even though it would have been exceeding difficult for her to navigate it.

He walked back to the main trail and followed it down to the plains wondering where he should stop. He stood still to judge the position of the old track. If Lyta had used it, the first habitation ahead of her would have been a small hovel in the distance. He walked toward it until he reached a woman who was digging turnips.

'Greetings,' Erit said. 'Have you seen a young boy passing here? Travelling alone.'

He caught a flicker of recognition in her eyes before she shook her grey head. 'No boy alone passed here.'

Erit knew she was lying. Then he thought again. If the woman had discovered Lyta was a girl then she might be telling the truth.

'What about a girl in boy's clothes?' Erit knew he'd asked the right question when she dropped her head to study the pile of turnips on the ground. Her weather-beaten cheeks held a faint tinge of red but she didn't reply.

Erit decided not to pursue the matter. He knew that this woman had seen Lyta. Mayhap their meeting had not been a happy one. He said farewell.

He'd gone only a few steps when feet sounded behind him. He turned to see the woman. 'She was going to the erle's house.'

'What erle?'

'Lord Havit.' She pointed west. 'He lives beyond the town.'

Erit threw a silver coin on the ground and the woman scrambled after it. Erit set off west. He had no idea why Lyta would be going to Havit's estate. Mayhap when he arrived there, he would discover the cause of her visit.

He'd been to Toma before when his father attended the kedura's council. At that time, it was also fair days and people crowded the streets and alleys. Now few people were entering the eastern gate. He stopped in the square beneath the towering castle walls and questioned people passing by. Nobody he met had any knowledge of a young boy journeying alone. He spent the night at a dismal inn by the west gate. By morn, he decided fleas were more numerous in the place than paying guests. He scratched his bitten arms and legs as he ate a repast of stale cakes washed down with tasteless ale.

Once through the gate, he followed the road for several leagues until he came to a group of substantial buildings. On the way he'd remembered some information about the erle. His father had told him once that Havit collected wild beasts and people visited his estate to view them. Had Lyta gone there to look at the collection?

When he was challenged at the manor house gate, he mentioned his father's name. The erle himself was standing in the courtyard and he slapped Erit on the back. 'I trust your father is well,' he said. 'I haven't seen his cheerful face for many moons.'

Havit invited Erit for dinner where he met the erle's family. The youngest was a pert child of about eight summers. She seemed to be the apple of her father's eye and he listened to every word she spoke. And her words were numerous. His lady was a nondescript woman who hardly spoke.

'You must view my beasts,' said Havit. 'I wager that you have never seen a giant snake from Parian or wild wolves from the highlands of Delis.'

Erit asked, 'Do you have an icecat?'

Erle Havit's face darkened. He slapped the table with his hand. 'I did have an icecat until a young wretch killed it. Right in the midst of a battle between it and a wolf. I lost many wagers on that match.'

Erit felt ill. How could the man collect rare wild beasts only to have them fight to the death? Then he had a sudden thought. 'How was the icecat slain?'

'With a thrown blade.' The erle sighed. 'And then the blasted brat escaped.'

Now, Erit was sure that Lyta had been involved. He was glad she'd got away but he had to discover where she would she travel next.

The Lady Terta had been listening to this exchange. The child leaned forward to fix her father with a steely gaze. 'Pappy, I miss my Lytik and you haven't found him for me.'

'Not for want of looking,' the erle muttered. 'I would dearly like to have your lousy Lytik back here.'

'I think he went to be a pilgrim,' said the little girl with a matching scowl on her face. 'And he wasn't a lousy brat.' These were her last words before her mother declared it was bedtime and swept her away.

'Is it likely that the boy became a pilgrim?' Erit asked as Havit refilled his wine glass.

The erle shrugged. 'The brat didn't wear a Star sign but he might have joined one of the bands. Herds of them were passing my gate at the time.'

'Is the pilgrimage over yet?'

Erle Havit frowned at him. 'Why are you so concerned about bloody pilgrims?'

Erit forced a smile. 'I don't care anything about them but I would like to see your collection of beasts.'

'We'll give you a bed for the night and you can view my menagerie in daylight.' He slammed his glass on the table and scowled. 'It's not the same without that icecat.'

Next morn, Erit viewed the wild beasts and felt sorry for them all. The giant snake was an enormous coil in a corner of the cage and it was impossible to tell if it was alive. From the foul smell, it might have been dead. The three wolves paced back and forth in their enclosure. The bears stood lethargically in their cage.

'I had to kill the wolf fighting the cat,' said Havit. 'It was sorely wounded. Those cats have formidable claws.' He led the way to the next cage, which held a bedraggled bear. If Erit had been able to wrest the keys from Havit's belt, he'd have released every beast. Instead, he thanked the erle for the viewing and said he had to leave.

If you see that damned boy on your way, send me word,' said Havit. 'I have an empty cage ready for him.'

Erit decided to take the road to Avridon. The more he thought about it, the more likely it seemed that Lyta had hidden from Havit in a group of pilgrims and travelled to the temple. Since she wasn't a Star child, he had no idea what she'd do there but her association with Virr might result in a friendly reception by the priests. He would try to locate the novice he'd met the first time he'd been in Avridon in case she was still talkative.

The trip to the temple was a miserable one. Heavy rain poured down on him and he was drenched to the skin after every day on the road. At night, he took a room in some grubby local inn and was almost dry and warm by morn. Then he trudged out into another downpour. Upon his arrival in Avridon, he asked questions of the people outside and inside the temple.

But he stopped talking when his throat burned and his head ached. Was he merely tired or was he coming down with a fever? Everything seemed to blur together. He followed a group of people along a passage but before he reached the central hall, he swayed and lost his balance. His last recollection was of the white marble floor somehow rising to meet him.

When Erit next became aware of his surroundings, he was lying in a long chamber. Lifting his head, he saw an old woman in a cot on one side and a child on the other. He must be in the temple infirmary.

A silver-robed priest glided along the row and stopped by Erit. 'I see you're awake.' She placed a cool hand on his forehead. 'And your fever is reduced.'

'What happened to me?' Erit croaked.

'You swooned in the passageway. Don't be concerned. We'll take care of you until you're fit to leave.'

Erit sighed. 'When will that be?'

'When we say so.' She smiled at him. 'Now rest yourself and then you can have a bowl of broth.' She smoothed the blue blanket, before moving to the next cot.

Erit wondered how far away Lyta would be when he was well enough to continue his journey. His only hope was to try to discover which direction she'd taken and catch up with her before she reached her demesne. Once she reached Lord Josik's Edgemere Estate on the border of Aldea and Falga, he had no chance of returning her to his father. Hiring a horse would make for a faster journey.

Several grey robed novices worked in the infirmary. Every time, one brought Erit food or washed his face and hands, he stared hard at the face. On his third morn, he was lucky enough to recognise the girl. Her face was a little plumper than it had been several moons ago but she was undoubtedly the same novice he'd met earlier. 'Do you remember me?' he asked.

She paused with the cloth dripping on his chest. 'I seen your face some place.'

'I met you when I was asking about Virr.'

The girl leaned down and whispered in his ear. 'And you gave me a silver coin. My mother was most happy.'

'Have you seen a boy? Mayhap he was a pilgrim.'

She grinned, showing a gap between her front teeth. 'We see lots of boys. They come with their mothers and fathers.'

'This one would have been alone.'

She frowned in thought. 'Fana was advising a boy by himself.'

Aha, thought Erit. This could have been Lyta. 'Could you find out where he went after he left here?'

The novice shook her head. 'All the dealings with priests are secret. We don't know what happens to the pilgrims.'

He clutched her hand. 'Ask some questions. I have more silver coins in my pouch.' He dropped her hand fast when he saw a priest observing them from two cots away.

Erit was declared strong enough to leave his sickbed in another morn. The priest brought him a stool and told him to sit outside the infirmary door in a sheltered place. 'The rays of the sun will help you to recover.' She said that when he could walk around the outside of the temple without resting, he'd be well enough to leave.

On the following morn, the novice appeared with his repast. From her excited face, Erit reckoned she had good news for him. 'I know where the boy went,' she said in a low voice. 'He's on his way to Lake Peace.'

'How did you find out?' Erit took the wooden platter from her.

'I heard Fana talking to the Chief Priest. He'd be the one to know the truth of the matter. When they saw me near, they stopped their talking. '

Erit thanked her and slipped two silver coins into her hand.

She flushed with pleasure 'Thank you, Sir. We're not allowed to keep money but my mother's in sore need with six young ones at home.'

When the priest in charge of the infirmary pronounced Erit fit to leave, Erit knew he'd tire more easily after his illness. He stopped at the first inn he reached and bought a horse. She was more of a nag than a mount but she appeared willing to carry him along the way.

When he came to a main fork in the road, he rejected the direction to the port town of Naris and followed the route to Lake Peace. He still hoped the delay caused by his illness hadn't prevented him from catching up with Lyta.

Chapter Thirty-Four

Before Lyta left the temple, Fana handed her a bundle of food. 'Put this in your basket. Virr's sister, Sia, may help you in Naris if you explain that you knew her brother.'

'I'll say he gave my family wise advice when we went to the temple on pilgrimage,' said Lyta. 'He did give me good advice at the castle so my words aren't altogether false.'

'Be very careful,' said Fana. 'Pybik wishes you well on your journey. He has sent you this and hopes you will be able to wear it.' She dropped a Star token on a silver cord over Lyta's head. 'This will be recognised by some people as coming from Avridon. We have Stellar Guides all over the demesne.'

'Thank you,' said Lyta, examining the image of the temple on the token. 'I am exceeding grateful for all your help.'

Fana hugged Lyta. 'I will pray to the Stars to send you home safely.'

She had reassured Lyta that they'd heard Erit wasn't on his way to Naris. 'We've convinced him you are taking the road to Erle Josik's estate. It's logical for a person on foot to want to reach Aldea as directly as possible.'

Pybik held her hand. 'One more thing,' said the chief priest. 'A friend of mine is returning to his holding. He'll give you a ride to the fork in the road.'

When Lyta opened her mouth to protest, he added. 'Now don't argue about it, girl. He'll be glad of the company and this will give you a good start on your journey.'

Lyta didn't need to eat the temple food as Pybik's friend supplied her with bread and dried meat from a barrel in his wagon. He wouldn't listen to her refusals. His soft voice commented on the countryside as they passed fields and forests and almost lulled her to sleep. She didn't use any of the coughing powder as it wasn't necessary to keep her distance from the kind man.

His face was creased with distress when he stopped at the fork. 'You're too young and pretty to travel by yourself. I'd better change my plans and take you to Naris.'

'Please don't,' said Lyta. 'I'll get to Naris without harm. Don't worry about me.'

The old man pursed his lips. 'Please take care. Some men may try to take advantage of you.'

Lyta waved at him and then watched his horse and wagon take the right fork. Now she had to use her own wits. Pybik had estimated it should take her three or four days to reach Naris. 'I've told the ship's captain to get word to me if he doesn't see you in a sevenday.'

The first few leagues were uneventful. Several groups on foot passed her going toward Avridon. Two young men on horseback greeted her and asked if she wanted a ride.

Lyta shook her head. 'I'm going the other way,' she said.

'Pity,' shouted the man with red hair. His companion made a remark which caused him to laugh loudly. Then they continued on the road.

When she heard the sound of wheels behind her, Lyta moved onto the grass at the roadside. She heard the driver call to his horse and then a yellow cart drew up next to her.

'Where are you going, my pretty?' The oily voice belonged to a fat balding man whose row of chins hung over the top of a stained tunic. His hairy legs were bare above his sandals. He stretched out a hand to pull her into the seat beside him.

This was surely the right time for the coughing powder. Behind her kerchief, Lyta took a pinch between her fingers and then popped it into her mouth. She doubled up at once into a fit of coughing.

When she glanced up, the fat man looked uneasy. 'Are you ill, my dear?'

Lyta tried to talk but failed. She bent over again with another violent spell of coughs. Without the man noticing, she scratched her arm and added the few drops of blood that seeped from the shallow wound to the kerchief.

When she removed it, she made sure the man saw the blood. 'I will feel better soon,' she said in a feeble voice. 'Give me a little time to recover.'

But the cart with the fat man was already moving away. Lyta waited until it travelled around the next bend in the road before she set off again. That had been most successful and the blood had certainly added to the effect of illness. With Fana's brown powder, she should be able to escape unwanted attention whenever it occurred.

When twilight fell, she looked around for somewhere to spend the night. She had been given coin to use for a bed in an inn but she thought it might be wiser to sleep in the open air. She walked from the road to search for a sheltered spot. Lady Moon helped her to find a rough hut. The door was hanging from one hinge but the back section of the roof was intact. She could use a large rock to keep the door shut.

Lyta dragged a log into the shed to serve as a seat and then opened her pack of food from the temple. The goat cheese smelled delicious as did the onion tarts and rye bread. She drank temple water from her leather bottle. Lyta munched her meal in the dark and thought she was reasonably content. Then she dragged a boulder against the door, wrapped herself in the cloak and fell asleep.

***

A loud voice woke her. 'This damned door is stuck!' A final push moved the rock and a shaggy head arrived in the hut. 'What are you doing in here?'

Lyta unwound the cloak. 'I slept here,' she stammered.

'Let's see you,' the man demanded.

Lyta stood up, grabbing her possessions. She blinked in the bright sun. She'd awakened far later than she'd expected. 'I'm sorry. I should have asked your permission.'

The stranger was far younger than she'd thought from his deep voice. He was more of a boy than a man. He rubbed a hand over his face. 'I didn't know this hut was even here. My uncle left the farm to me so I am looking it over.'

'I'll be on my way,' said Lyta. She wasn't sure if this was a situation where coughing powder was needed. The boy didn't look dangerous but her nurse had warned her that young men were unpredictable around women.

'Would you like a repast?' asked the boy. 'My aunt and I were about to eat. 'He pointed right. 'Our home is this way.'

'Many thanks but I have food.' Lyta was edging sideways as she spoke.

The boy reached out an arm to stop her. 'Why are you alone? You should be travelling with someone to protect you.'

Lyta told her story. 'My father is very ill in Naris. He has the same sickness that carried off my mother ten moons ago.'

She managed two fake coughs before she swallowed some powder. This time the fit was much worse. Lyta was unable to speak for several minutes and when she finally straightened up, the boy had moved toward the trees. He watched her with clear alarm on his face. 'You sound real bad too.'

'I'll feel better soon,' she said. 'Give me a few moments.'

The boy backed further away without speaking before he ran through the trees. Lyta grinned at his rapidly disappearing back. Fana would've been pleased at the effectiveness of her powder.

The sun was hot on her back as she trudged along the road. Lyta heard feet behind her and she braced herself for company. The feet were walking heavily but she couldn't tell until the person came beside her if she'd be meeting a woman or a man. Fortunately, this stranger was a woman carrying a heavy sack on her back. She wiped a large hand across her sweaty face. 'Hot out, 'she commented. 'What's your name, child? Are you going far?'

Lyta thought fast. 'I'm Mya, off to Naris.'

'Then Mya, you're too young to be alone,' said the woman. 'My name's Weira and you'll come with me to Naris.' Weira didn't look as though she was used to being disobeyed. She continued. 'I have five daughters and I'd never let them walk this road alone. What was your father thinking?'

'My father's ill.' Lyta could tell that Weira would insist on accompanying her. Mayhap that wasn't such a bad thing. Fat men in carts would be no match for this woman.

When Weira asked questions about her father's ailment, Lyta mentioned fever and coughing and the loss of flesh from his bones. 'My mother had the same sickness.'

Weira nodded. 'Sometimes it comes in families. You must take care that you keep yourself very clean when you tend your father. Always have hot water nearby to wash your face and hands.'

They continued on their way with the woman delivering information on the various illnesses in her family. When the sun was high in the sky, they moved off the road to the shade of nearby trees for midmeal. Weira mopped her red face. 'I'm getting too old to carry vegetables on my back. I'd arranged a ride to Naris but my friend's horse died.' She pulled a packet of food from her pouch. 'Have some bread and cheese, dear. You must be hungry too.'

Lyta unwrapped her own pack. 'You could share my food.'

Weira took an onion tart and bit into it. 'This is good. Did you bake it yourself?'

'The cook in the temple kitchen gave me food for my journey.'

Mention of the temple was the signal for Weira to recount the tale of her latest pilgrimage. She'd wanted counsel about her daughters. Her voice went on and on as she described the difficulties besetting each child. Lyta stopped listening after daughter number three's romantic troubles had been covered. Although her eyes remained open, her head was half asleep.

Weira stopped suddenly. 'Goodness! I've been boring you silly with all my woes. You'll be glad to hear that I received excellent advice from the priest and things are much better at home. I even have three prospective husbands for the oldest girls.'

That's good,' said Lyta, trying hard not to yawn.

Weira used a tree trunk to get herself up. 'We'd best be off. I want to be in my cousin's village before nightfall. You're welcome to share my bed.'

The rundown village consisted of a handful of shabby houses. The cousin lived with seven children in a two roomed cottage. Lyta couldn't imagine where they all slept in such a tight space.

'Her husband's at sea and every time he comes home, she gets another mouth to feed.' Weira muttered to Lyta as they ate a simple meal of vegetables and bread.

Weira's cousin gave up her own bed to the visitors. The children bedded wherever they could. Four curled up on the floor while the older two slept in hammocks slung on hooks from the kitchen ceiling. The baby occupied a large oval dish.

I'll never take a comfortable bed for granted again, Lyta thought as she tried to sleep next to Weira. The low cot was lumpy and narrow and the woman took up most of the space. She also snored.

The next morn, they resumed their journey. Weira glared at the grey clouds scudding above her head. 'We'll get rain by midmeal,' she said. 'You'll need that cloak of yours.'

Her forecast was accurate. Within three hours, the rain began. The two looked for shelter beside the road. When Weira pointed to a clump of trees ahead, they hurried toward it.

Lyta pulled her cloak around her body and raised the hood, while Weira used a length of sacking to cover her head and shoulders. She fingered the fabric of Lyta's cloak. 'That's a fine piece of cloth. Where did you get it?'

'The priests hand out clothing at the temple. Pilgrims leave gowns and tunics to give to the poor.'

The showers continued for an hour. They ate their midmeal before the rain slackened. Weira poked her head from her cover. 'I think it's passed.' She peered at the sky. 'And the clouds are breaking up.'

Once again, she had trouble standing up. Finally, she was upright and able to take a step. On the wet grass, her right foot slipped and she yelled out in alarm as she toppled over.

Lyta was too far off to prevent the fall. Besides, she was hardly strong enough to keep Weira upright. The woman lay on the ground, her face twisted in pain. 'My ankle! What have I done to it?' Lyta knelt down to run a hand over the ankle. It was swelling fast. Had Weira sprained it or broken a bone? The girl wished for Magian Domen's medical advice and his remedies.

'Roll down my hose and take a good look.' Weira moaned as she raised her hips for Lyta to reach the top of her hose. When the ankle was exposed, it was clear that the injury was significant. Weira wouldn't be able to walk on that leg. Lyta looked around for some herbal assistance and noticed a thick patch of sek. The magian had sometimes soaked the leaves and wrapped them around a limb to reduce swelling.

Lyta dipped a handful in a nearby puddle. Weira watched her movements with approval. 'Well, you seem to know what you're doing but right now, I wish you also had a potion for pain.'

'So do I but I can't find anything helpful around here,' said Lyta. She lifted Weira's foot onto a fallen log. 'Keep the ankle raised.'

Weira tried to smile. 'You're a good girl.'

'You can't walk to Naris. I'll go back to the road and stop the first wagon I see.'

Chapter Thirty-Five

The wait for another traveller seemed long but it was probably only twoscore minutes. As soon as Lyta spied the wagon turning the bend, she ran into the road and waved her arms.

The driver was a tall man with long black hair and a straggling beard to match. He was wearing a loose yellow robe with large golden suns embroidered on it. 'What's the trouble, child?' he asked in a high voice.

Lyta had already decided to tell the next stranger that Weira was her mother. People might be more inclined to help them both if they thought the two were related. 'My mother has hurt her leg. Are you, by chance, going to Naris?'

The stranger bent down. 'Do you wish me to carry you both there?'

Lyta smiled. 'Please if you will.'

The man paused for a moment before he nodded. 'Where is she?'

'By the trees. She slipped on the wet grass.'

The stranger left his wagon and followed her. 'Mother,' Lyta said as she reached Weira. 'This man will aid us.'

Weira struggled to sit up and then they both heaved her to her feet and into the back of the wagon. She lay down there with a groan and closed her eyes. Lyta mopped her own damp face and hands on her skirt.

The stranger dabbed at his face with a corner of his yellow robe. 'Now, little lady, you sit beside me.' He patted the stained wooden seat.

Lyta would have preferred to sit with Weira but the tray was loaded with boxes and barrels which they'd shoved aside to make room for the injured woman. Lyta scrambled onto the seat. After all, she still had the coughing powder if things became difficult.

The stranger clicked his tongue at the horse and they began to move. 'Tell me, little lady, do you know about Father Sun?'

Tutoran Cordon had mentioned that some folk in Parian didn't believe in either Lady Moon or the Holy Stars but she had never met such a person. She admitted that she was ignorant of this particular faith.

The stranger grunted. 'How can that be? But we have enough time before Naris for me to tell you about Father Sun and how he can change our lives.'

And he did. As the horse plodded on, he gave Lyta a long involved lesson about the ways of Father Sun who guided people from his home in the skies. She reckoned that he hoped to turn her from a Moon child into a Sun child during their journey but she was no more convinced of the rightness of his faith than she had been of the rightness of the Star beliefs. However, she nodded and agreed whenever the man paused for breath.

Once the clouds had passed, the sun shone brightly on them from a clear sky. The stranger smiled, 'We are being blessed. Sometimes, the Father is displeased by our wicked ways and he hides his face behind the clouds until we repent. When he shines again, we know we are back in his grace.'

Suddenly he dropped the reins and opened the fastenings of his yellow robe. With a shrug of his bony shoulders, the garment fell to his feet. He was naked beneath it.

Lyta gasped. 'What are you doing?'

'Worshipping the glorious Sun. Being open to his rays is the natural state for all earthly men and women.'

'Please cover yourself.' Lyta looked back for support from Weira but the woman was still lying on her back with her eyes closed.

The man reached out toward Lyta. 'Take off your blouse, girl, and let Father Sun shine on your breasts.'

When he grabbed a fold, Lyta pushed his hand away. Then she slid along the wooden seat. 'I'm not removing my clothes. Keep away from me!'

She was dealing with an obvious madman. When he continued to grope at her blouse, Lyta swung around. She clambered over the back of the seat and dropped into the tray of the wagon, narrowly missing Weira and two barrels.

Her patient opened her eyes. 'What's happening?'

'Nothing,' said Lyta. 'Stay calm, Mother, and rest. I'll sit beside you for the remainder of the journey.' She tugged her blouse back onto her shoulders.

The wagon driver sang in a croaky voice. From the words she understood, Lyta thought it was a hymn to the sun. She would put up with his songs and nudity as long as he stayed well away from her and continued to take them to Naris. But she wondered how far away the port town was. She didn't want to spend a night with this man when Weira was unable to offer any assistance.

When the Sun priest finished his hymn, he sat in silence. Lyta ventured to ask a question. 'How far to Naris?'

He glanced up at the sky to judge the position of the sun. 'We'll be there by nightfall.'

Lyta was delighted to hear this news. She bent over Weira. 'Where do you live?' she whispered. 'I should know the way since I'm meant to be your daughter.'

Weira roused herself to answer in a low voice. 'In Fishbone Lane. Tell him to make for the harbour and then it's easy to find.'

When Lyta passed on the information, the man nodded. 'I know it.'

Evening was falling when they came into Naris. Lyta was pleased to see that once the sun set, the priest put his robe back on. Light from lanterns shone from open shops and the windows of houses as they drove through the cobbled streets. When Lyta caught a glimpse of silver sea, she guessed that Weira's home must be close. The driver turned into an alley, just wide enough to take the wagon.

'You can drive right through,' Weira said with a tired smile. 'There! That green door. If you get out, Mya, the girls will help me inside.'

At Lyta's knock the door opened and the agitated face of a girl looked out. When Lyta pointed to Weira in the wagon, more girls flew out like a flock of clucking hens. They all talked at once and their mother replied. Within minutes, they'd carried Weira and her sack away. Lyta stood on the stones out of reach of the driver's hands to thank him for his help.

'You should let Father Sun into your dark life,' he said in a solemn tone. 'Then you will receive his many bright blessings.'

'I'll consider it,' said Lyta. She waited until the wagon had left the alley. Then a daughter rushed out to sweep her through the bright green door.

Weira was placed in her bed and a girl fetched bandages and a potion to decrease the pain. The woman insisted on telling her daughters about Lyta's sad circumstances before she would swallow the potion. 'Please help Mya. She was so kind to me.'

In the next room, the girls introduced themselves but Lyta quickly became confused by the names. The only one she remembered was Genia, the eldest daughter. In her mind, the others became Two, Three, Four, and Five. They were very much alike with fair hair and blue eyes. The oldest three were of an age to be wed.

As they plied her with food and drink, Lyta realised she had a problem. Weira would expect her to go to her father's house as soon as possible. She thought hard. Genia appeared to be the least talkative and most sensible of the group. Should she take the eldest daughter into her confidence? By the end of the meal, Lyta had made up her mind. She asked to speak to the woman alone.

Genia took her to a back storeroom piled high with turnips and carrots. She followed Lyta's gaze. 'We sell these vegetables in the market.'

Lyta took a deep breath. 'Can I trust you to keep a secret?'

'You have my word.' Genia's eyes were kind and steady.

Lyta started with the account of her kidnap in Aldea and continued to her arrival in Naris. 'The sick father was merely an invention to explain my journey.'

Genia stayed silent for a few minutes. 'We'd better get rid of him first. Shall we discover that he's already dead and buried? Otherwise, Mother will expect you to spend all your time at his sick bed.'

Lyta nodded. 'Then I must find the ship. It's called The Rogue and the captain's waiting for me.'

'Since at least one man is searching for you, I'll seek out the ship.' She smiled at Lyta. 'Don't look so worried. We'll get you safely home.'

When they returned to the kitchen, Genia told her sisters, she'd accompany Lyta to her father's house. 'I'll bring medicine with me.'

They pulled on their cloaks and left the house. 'Where are we going?' Lyta asked.

'I'll show you the way to the main square. Then we'll stay away long enough to convince the girls that you've learned about your father's death. I think a neighbour should tell us the sorrowful news.'

The other girls in the house were very solicitous when they heard the sad end to Lyta's journey. Two brought her a cup of red wine while Three and Four tucked a blanket around her knees and a cushion behind her back.

'I can't believe all his goods were burned,' said Five.

Genia nodded. 'That usually happens with the coughing sickness. It's a wise plan to avoid further infection.'

That night, Lyta was glad to share Genia's bed which was wide enough for two and soft enough for sleeping. Before they closed their eyes, Genia said that she thought Lyta should become a cousin. 'Your hair colour is similar to ours so nobody will be surprised.'

The other girls were delighted to have a new cousin Mya who explained that a cruel master was hunting for her. 'My friends in Avridon have arranged a passage on a ship to Aldea but I will have to take care getting to the port,' Lyta said.

'We'll keep you safe,' said Four.

Lyta reflected that it would be a great relief to return home where she didn't have to invent stories about herself. She went with Genia to her mother's bed. Weira had spent a restless night. Genia examined the swollen ankle which was dark purple and blue. 'You'll be off this foot for at least a sevenday,' Genia said as she rebandaged the limb.

Genia and Two went down to the harbour to discover if the ship was in port. While they were away, the other girls gave Lyta clean clothes to wear and washed her grubby blouse and skirt.

The two girls returned bursting with news. 'Naris is full of important people,' said Two. 'Nobles and suchlike.'

'A party from Aldea is searching for their Kedie,' Genia added. 'And Lord Rurrik and his son are also in town.'

Lyta felt her heart miss a beat. How had they traced her so quickly?

Two smiled at Three in a sly fashion. ‘And guess who else is back?’

The girl blushed. ‘Cett? But he left on a long voyage.’

‘The captain died and the first mate and the cook started to battle. When the cook locked himself in the storeroom with all the food and water, the ship had to return.’

Lyta’s head whirled. She certainly didn’t want to meet Cett again. And the only person missing from the search parties was Erit. By now, he might also have discovered that she took the left fork in the road and be on his way to Naris too. What should she do next?

Chapter Thirty-Six

Erit glared at the waters of Lake Peace, lying placidly on the border of Falga and Aldea. Lyta hadn't passed this way. The last farmer he'd met hadn't seen any solo travellers in a sevenday. Picking up a large rock, he hurled it into the gleaming lake just to disturb the calm reflections.

He'd been deliberately deceived by the priests at Avridon. Lyta must have gone to Naris. She might have encountered her erles from Aldea by now but just in case they hadn't found her, he should reach Naris as quickly as possible. He turned away from the lake and retraced his steps to a grubby little town on the coast. There a woman told him about the ferry to Naris. Since he had no need of the horse, he sold it to the innkeeper.

'You're in luck,' said the innkeeper, trying to hide his glee at the great bargain he'd made. 'The boat is due soon.'

Erit sat on a box beside the water. When the boat arrived, it was an old tub that looked more likely to sink than float. He suspected from his unsteady gait that the captain had started drinking early in the morn and hoped the fellow was sober enough to get them to their destination. Together with an old man leading a goat and a woman with a box of chattering chickens, he boarded The Pearl. The captain peered along the jetty.

'Are we waiting for someone?' Erit asked.

'My family,' the captain said. His frown cleared when an immensely fat woman waddled toward him. She was accompanied by four runny-nosed children. Erit took one look at their filthy hands and faces and moved further along the rail. A boy cast off and The Pearl's sail filled with a brisk wind. With much luck and a favourable breeze, they should reach Naris.

Since the boat followed the shoreline, Erit noticed clusters of houses and well-tended farms. He wondered which erle was lucky enough to own this fertile land. Loud squealing interrupted his musing. One of the children had poked a finger in the goat's eye and then been bitten by the animal.

A fierce argument erupted between the owner of the goat and the mother of the child. Both demanded compensation for injury. When Erit could no longer stand the shouting and screaming, he stepped forward and opened his pouch. 'Here,' he said, handing a silver coin to each adult. 'And I suggest, Mother, you keep your children away from goats.'

The old man nodded in a smug fashion. 'And you, Sir,' Erit added, 'should keep your goat away from children.'

The rest of the short voyage was uneventful. An hour after their departure Erit saw the opening to Naris harbour. The boat slipped between the headlands and made for the wharf. Erit contemplated his next step, unsure about locating Lyta in the town. The chief priest might have arranged a place for her to stay until the Aldean erles arrived to rescue her.

Since the only person he knew was Sia, Virr and Cett's sister, Erit decided to pay her another visit. She seemed like a person who would know the latest gossip and news. When he was shown into the house, he found Sia stitching a brown wall hanging in the sunlit chamber opening onto a courtyard.

Sia greeted him in a friendly manner. 'I am glad to see you again. Did you ever catch up with Cett?'

'I did and we talked about Virr and old times.'

She poured red wine for them both. 'Well, Cett's back again. The voyage he left on didn't work out. He's looking for another ship.'

'I'll try to find him.' Erit sipped his wine. 'What else is new in Naris?'

'The town is full of important folk. My husband told me there is a party from Aldea staying at our finest inn.'

'Are they visiting Falga?'

'Didn't you hear about their missing kedie? They've been searching for her more than three moons. Poor soul! She must be exceeding afraid and distressed.'

Erit thought of the last time he had seen Lyta in his father's house. Afraid and distressed weren't the words he'd use. But he nodded in agreement with Sia. 'Poor girl!'

Sia leaned forward and spoke in a low voice. 'They do say the kedie was kidnapped by one of our Falgan erles. What do you think of that?'

'Quite shocking, if it's true.'

'I believe it's true.' Sia waggled her head. 'Rurrik, the man who was meant to have taken her is in Naris as well.'

'Rurrik is here?' Erit couldn't imagine why his father was in town.

'And that son of his, Darik, came along with him. '

Holy Stars, thought Erit. How did he get here? Now we're all in one place. He wondered what tale Darik and Rurrik would spin about the capture of Lyta. Would Darik explain that his father was ill when he came up with the kidnap plot? And that now he'd realised the error of his ways and wanted to make amends by finding Lyta? That was a distinct possibility.

Erit finished the wine and placed the cup on a table. He was about to say farewell to Sia when the door opened and a whole gaggle of girls burst into the chamber. Sia laughed as she greeted them. 'I'm not surprised you've come. I think somebody must have heard that Cett was back in town.'

She raised an eyebrow at one of her visitors who blushed rosy red, giggled and stared down at her sandals.

Erit decided the golden-haired group must be sisters. He listened to their chatter about Cett for a few minutes. Some of the visitors seemed quite foolish but one, probably the oldest, was a sensible-looking woman with a warm smile.

Sia introduced the girls. Erit knew he'd only remember the first name. Genia was a suitably pretty name for a fine woman. Sia stopped when she came to the end of the row. 'And who's this little one?'

'Our cousin Mya,' said Genia. 'She arrived from the country with Mother last night.'

Erit noted that while Mya's hair was fair, her eyes were dark. The others had eyes in various shades of blue. Genia's eyes were azure like the sky on a cloudless day.

After the girls seated themselves on chairs and cushions, Erit edged around the chamber until he was next to Genia. 'Have you heard about this missing kedie from Aldea desmense?' he asked.

'The story's all over town. If she's here, then she hasn't shown herself to her erles.' Genia accepted a cup of cider and took one of the cakes a flustered maid had delivered.

'There's quite a crowd of you.' Erit said, glancing around the chamber.

'Mother despairs of getting us all married to suitable men,' Genia said. 'I tell her it's because we are very fussy about husbands.'

'What are your requirements?'

Genia lifted the fingers of her right hand. 'First he must love his wife. Second, he must be able to support her. Third, he must be kind and final, he should be able to laugh with her when something is funny.'

'That doesn't sound like a difficult list.'

'But he must have every quality not just two or three.'

Erit reflected that Genia would hardly consider a man who kidnapped a young girl to be kind. And he certainly wasn't in a position to support a wife unless he recaptured that same girl. He sighed as he realised that the first woman he might have even considered marrying would never want to wed him.

He rose to his feet and thanked Sia for her hospitality. Then he bid farewell to each sister, holding Genia's fingers a little longer than the rest. The last one he reached was the dark-eyed cousin. He stared at the girl's face with the strange sensation of having met her before. Then he shook himself and took his leave. He was off to find his father and brother and discover what foolish scheme they were hatching now.

He was half way to the town square when he stopped. He cursed loudly, startling a small child with a dog coming toward him. Of course he recognised those dark eyes. They belonged to Lyta.

Chapter Thirty-Seven

Lyta was in two minds about the proposed visit to Sia. While she wanted to meet Virr's sister, she didn't wish to leave the safety of Weira's house. The sisters said her doubts were senseless. 'Everyone will believe you're our cousin,' said Two. 'You'll be safe with us.'

'We'll never tell your master where you are,' said Four.

'And Sia is such a nice woman,' said Three.

'I know why you say that,' said her younger sister with a giggle. 'You're trying to persuade Sia that you'd make a good member of her family.'

And that was another reason for her doubts, thought Lyta. Weira might be in favour of her daughter's marriage to Cett but how would the mother feel if she knew the fellow was a murderer? Mayhap she should tell Genia the part of her story that she'd kept from her ears so that her younger sister could be protected.

In the end, Genia persuaded Lyta to come. 'I think you'd like to meet Virr's sister even if you can't explain who you are. She's a kind woman although she has a keen nose for the latest gossip.'

The shock of seeing Erit sitting so easily in Sia's chamber almost stopped Lyta's heart. After the first gasp of fright, she forced herself to breathe normally and hid herself behind one or two of the sisters. She felt a little better when Erit accepted her as cousin Mya from the country. She sat in a corner, sipping her cider as the girls talked, laughed and teased Three about Cett.

Sia appeared to be in favour of the match and said it was high time that her brother settled down with a good girl. 'I'd like him to give up the sea too but it's in his blood.'

With a combination of alarm and amusement, Lyta watched the interplay developing between Erit and Genia. He was obviously struck by her but it wasn't clear what Genia felt about him. Once again, Lyta wanted to warn her new friend that Erit had been part of the plot that took her from Aldea. Genia seemed to believe from Sia's comments that Erit was an old friend of Virr's and that he'd also met Cett on a previous visit to Naris. Don't lose your heart, Genia, Lyta thought. Erit is not what he seems.

With great relief, she saw Erit stand to take his leave. He said farewell to each of the sisters in turn, starting with Genia. He held her hand for several minutes, smiling at her. Then he worked his way around the chamber. He took Lyta's hand and stayed still, staring into her face with a crease between his slanted eyebrows. When Lyta tried to smile, the corners of her mouth seemed to have forgotten how to turn up in the regular way. She hoped he couldn't see her heart beating hard through the fabric of her blouse. Then Erit spoke and turned away and the danger passed.

On the way home to Weira's house, the girls had another object for their teasing. 'Did you see how Erit looked at Genia?' said Four. 'I think you've made a conquest. What did you find out about him, sister?'

'Conquest indeed!' said Genia. 'The man was simply being courteous. He asked about my life but I didn't discover much about him.'

I could tell you much about Erit thought Lyta but for the moment, she kept silent.

Weira had taken the opportunity of her daughters' absence to leave her bed. She'd hobbled to the kitchen where she was preparing a meal. With many cries and admonitions, Weira was moved into a chair with a footstool where she could supervise the dinner preparations.

'After midmeal, I'll go down to the port again and look for your ship,' said Genia in a low voice to Lyta. 'If I see the captain, I'll tell him you're here.'

Lyta thanked her.

'Are you really sure you don't want me to find the party from Aldea?' Genia asked. 'They would take you safely home.'

'I know it seems foolish but I want to walk through the castle gate on my own. I'd like Virr to be proud of me.'

Genia frowned. 'But the erles will be most concerned.'

'Then when I'm safely out of port, tell them I'm on my way home.'

'If that's your wish, I'll do it.' Genia sighed. 'But I don't agree with your decision.'

Genia left the house with Four. 'We're looking for the ship to carry our cousin home. Then she'll be out of reach of her cruel master. Don't let any strangers into the house.'

The other girls promised to keep Mya safe. Lyta was helping Three to sort turnips in the little storechamber when they heard someone knocking on the door. 'One of my sisters will answer it,' said the girl. 'We have a little window beside the door to show us who's outside.'

Lyta clutched the turnip she was holding. She had a nasty feeling that someone had discovered her whereabouts. Three came into the storechamber with a grin. 'It's not a stranger after all. Erit has come to pay his respects to our mother. I let him in. He and Mother are talking and drinking ale.'

Lyta grabbed the girl's arm. 'Please don't tell him I'm here. Say I've gone into town with Genia and your sister and you don't know when we'll be back. Please,' she begged. 'It's very important.'

The girl frowned. 'I don't know why you're worried. Erit seems very pleasant.'

'Last night I remembered that he knows my old master.'

The girl seemed reassured. 'Well, in that case, I'll say you're not here.'

She went into the main chamber to greet their guest while Lyta cowered among the vegetables. This visit was too close for comfort. Had Erit recognised her after all or was he visiting Weira because of his interest in Genia? She couldn't tell which reason was true.

Erit left the house before Genia and her sister returned. Weira had invited him back the following morn when everyone would be at home. When Lyta heard these words, she knew she had to reach the ship as soon as possible. She hoped Genia would have good news.

And Genia did have good news. For Lyta's ears only she said she'd met the captain and he seemed a trustworthy fellow. Lyta's passage had been paid by the Chief Priest at Avridon and the ship could sail the following morn as soon as Lyta was on board. For the benefit of her sisters, Genia said she had arranged passage for their cousin to Aldea with a captain whose ship was leaving port the next day.

'We'll be sorry to lose you,' Genia said to Lyta, 'but glad to know you'll be safe.'

Weira patted Lyta's hand. 'You're a good girl and welcome to return here any time.'

Lyta didn't doubt the woman's sincerity. Weira and her daughters had been kinder than she deserved. Now all that remained was for her to get to the port without being seen by Erit or his brother and father.

The sisters and Lyta sat down at the table to discuss how to leave the house without harm. 'If we go out together,' said Lyta, 'then I could walk in the middle.

'I know!' Two suddenly said in an excited voice. 'You know those cloaks Mother made for us last winter?'

'Blue with red trimming on the hoods,' Three explained to Lyta.

And she has one too,' said Genia. 'I see what you're suggesting. If we all wore the same cloaks, then people wouldn't know which one was Mya.'

'Exactly,' said Two. 'And we could even split into groups to make matters more confusing.'

Genia turned to Lyta. 'Would this plan work for you?'

Lyta had been listening with care. This idea was better than any she'd imagined. If Erit was watching the house, he could be tricked into following the wrong girl. She nodded in agreement. 'I like it. When did you tell the captain that I'd be at the ship?'

'Directly after repast. He said he would set sail immediately.'

'Then let's do it.'

Lyta spent a restless night. In her mind, she saw everything that might go wrong. Darik might catch her. Erit might have guessed where she was hiding and told his brother and father. And was she being foolish, as Genia had suggested, about not going to the Aldean erles? Was it pride in her own wits that kept her from contacting them? Virr had told her that pride often went before a fall. She might be in for a very large tumble.

Lyta could hardly swallow a small cake for repast. She forced herself to chew and swallow the dry crumbs. Then she sipped a cup of cider. The sisters fluttered around her as they pulled on the blue cloaks. When they were dressed, with hoods over their heads, it was almost impossible to tell the girls apart.

'Are we ready?' Genia asked and a chorus of yes answered her. 'Now remember, if anybody stops us, we scatter.' She pointed at her sisters. 'You two will go east and you two, west. I will go with Mya. We will meet up at the harbour. Do you understand?'

The blue hoods nodded. Then with Weira's blessing ringing in her ears, Lyta left the house with the sisters.

Chapter Thirty-Eight

Beyond the green door, the cluster of blue cloaks paused for a moment. Nobody was in sight. . The girls moved along the alley in a tight knot before stopping at the far end. Lyta couldn't see Erit lurking there or Rurrik and Darik. Would they be waiting at the harbour?

When Genia pointed south, they turned a corner into another twisting lane. This one was a busy thoroughfare with clusters of women and children on their way to meet the early morn fishing boats. The girls joined a chattering bunch. Another bend lay ahead. As they rounded it, Lyta saw Darik standing with two of his men, watching the passing women.

She clutched Genia's hand and muttered urgently, 'That man's watching for me!'

Genia motioned to her sisters. 'Scatter!' she said. Two ran east, two ran west while Genia and Lyta continued south.

'Follow her!' Darik yelled.

'Which one?' his man asked, turning his head in bewilderment.

A she hurried south, Lyta heard Darik call. 'You follow them and you follow the others. I'll take these two.'

Lyta didn't dare look behind to see if Darik was near. She scurried along until Genia suddenly stopped and pulled Lyta into an open doorway.

'What's wrong?' Lyta asked.

'Wait!' Genia said. 'This is my aunt's shop.' She opened the door and once inside, pushed Lyta behind a barrel of oil.

'Aunt? I need you.'

A woman who resembled Weira appeared from a red curtain at the rear of the chamber. 'Oh, it's you, Genia. What's the matter?'

'Can we borrow two cloaks?'

Although her aunt looked confused, she left the chamber and soon reappeared with a brown garment and a green one. 'Why in Holy Stars do you need these? You are both wearing perfectly fine cloaks.'

'I'll explain later.' Genia pulled off her cloak and handed Lyta the brown one, which she exchanged for her blue cloak. Then Genia donned the green one. 'Please hide these,' she said thrusting their blue garments into her aunt's arms. 'I'll come back for them.'

Genia peered out the door. 'I can't see that man. Let's go.' She tugged Lyta's hand and they left the shop.

Two women were trudging toward them, carrying heavy baskets. . Genia greeted them with a smile. 'May we walk with you? My sister is upset. She has been followed by a strange man who's trying to accost her.'

One of the women nodded in sympathy as she hooked Lyta's hand into her elbow. 'If that villain tries anything on you now, he'll be sorry.'

'Almost there,' said Genia to Lyta. 'Around the next corner.'

The safety of the blue sea lay ahead of them. Then Lyta caught a glimpse of Rurrik on his grey horse with Erit standing beside him.

She grasped Genia's hand with her free one. 'Please don't trust Erit!' she said. 'He's the man who kidnapped me. I'm sorry to tell you this fact.'

She waited as Genia swallowed hard and stared at Erit. He stared back. No doubt at all that he's recognised us, Lyta thought. What will he do?

'That's the man,' she said to the woman with the basket. 'He's trying to stop me getting on a ship.'

Genia roused herself from her trance. ‘That ship.’ She pointed at The Rogue bobbing gently at anchor.

‘He’ll have to stop me first,’ said the woman. She linked arms with her friend and with Lyta between them, the trio strode straight for the ship.

Genia called out to a man who was leaning over the rail. ‘Here’s your passenger, Captain. She must board fast.’

The captain sprang to the gangplank as Lyta, Genia, and the two women arrived at the ship. Rurrik and Erit were fast behind them.

‘Stop her at once!’ Rurrik yelled. ‘She’s a foul criminal who must be brought to justice.’

‘Untrue!’ Lyta yelled back. ‘He’s a kidnapper and a liar.’

‘I believe the Chief Priest more than you,’ called the captain as he dragged Lyta onto the ship. He pulled up the plank behind him and faced the angry noble. ‘You’re the wrongdoer here, Erle Rurrik, and your son too. I’ve heard your sorry tale.’

When he gave the order to cast off, a boy on the wharf untied the thick rope and threw it onto the deck. A seaman used a long oar to push the ship away from the jetty wall while two others raised the sails.

Lyta felt the deck quiver beneath her feet. She lifted a hand to Genia who was standing with a frozen expression on her face. She did have feelings for Erit, Lyta thought. And I believe he liked her. Then Genia waved back and the ship turned toward the headlands.

‘You’re safe now,’ said the captain, ‘and we’ll soon have you back in Aldea.’ He motioned Lyta toward the small cabin. ‘Please, Kedie, make yourself comfortable in here.’

Lyta thanked him as he opened the door for her to pass through.

‘Don’t get too comfortable,’ said Cett’s voice.

Chapter Thirty-Nine

Lyta's mouth dropped open in shock. She edged away from Cett until her back was jammed against a small table. 'What are you doing here?'

'I needed another ship and the captain needed another hand. Finding you here was a very lucky chance.' Cett's smile was menacing.

'You'll be taken by the guards as soon as we reach Aldea. Remember, I know what you did to Virr and Givis.'

'But if you can't tell anyone about me, then I'm quite safe.'

'What do you mean?' Lyta tried to keep her voice steady.

'You might have an unfortunate accident on board. A fall from the ship when you slipped on the deck. I tried to save you but, alas, couldn't grab you in time. And, Kedie Lyta, I might even shed a few tears at your death.'

Lyta swallowed hard. She could imagine such an accident. Before she could reply, the captain knocked on the door and then opened it. He glared at Cett. 'Why are you here, fellow? Get back to your duties on the sail.'

'At once, Captain.' Behind the man's back, Cett drew a finger across his throat as he turned to leave the cabin.

The captain asked if there was anything Lyta wanted. Too shaken to reply, she shook her head and he left. Lyta sat down on a rough stool to steady her trembling legs. How was she going to stay away from Cett on such a small ship? Although it wasn't a lengthy voyage, he'd have opportunities to try to harm her. She'd have to be resourceful. What advice would Virr have given her? He would have told her to make use of whatever she had in her possession.

She opened her pouch and spread its contents on the table. Three silver coins, one blood-stained kerchief, a piece of cheese, a crust of bread and a pink rock that she'd picked up outside Seta's cave. And last, the round box containing the coughing powder, her only weapon now that she'd lost the blade. Lyta forced down her mournful thoughts of Seta and the blade. Focus, she told herself. Focus on the situation at hand.

Another knock on the door brought her to her feet. The captain stuck his head into the cabin. He was carrying a plate of cakes and fruit. 'I don't know if you ate a repast, Kedie.'

Lyta thanked him as she took the wooden platter.

'And, Kedie Lyta, if you're weary, then please use the hammock.'

Lyta wanted to tell him to stay in the cabin to keep her safe but she knew the idea would shock him. He seemed to be a very proper man with a grave demeanour.

'Do you have a key for the door?'

The captain looked surprised but he crossed the cabin and opened a carved chest beneath the porthole. He rummaged inside it for a few moments and then straightened up, shaking his head. 'It's missing but don't worry. I'll make sure you won't be bothered again by my crew.'

I'm not successful at obtaining keys, thought Lyta after the captain had bowed and left the cabin. As she couldn't sit in ease, Lyta was pleased when the captain returned two hours later. 'I will escort you on deck,' he said. 'You need fresh air and you may have other needs as well.'

Since Lyta had been wondering about using a privy for the last hour, she appreciated his thoughtfulness. He pointed to a piece of sacking that had been attached to the railing on one side and the back of the cabin on the other. 'You will find what you want there. I regret it's not what you're accustomed to.'

Lyta was very grateful to see the pail and to use it. She was tipping the contents over the railing when Cett appeared. He reached out for her.

'Don't touch me!' Lyta hissed. 'The captain is right there.'

'But he's not right there. We've had a little trouble with the sail and he's gone to fix it.' He grabbed Lyta's left arm in a strong grip. 'This is where you have your unfortunate little accident.'

Using her right hand, Lyta dug in her pouch for the round box and twisted off the lid. Cett was so close that he would certainly catch some of the powder. As he laughed, she tossed a good pinch into his face. He dropped her arm at once and collapsed on the deck in a spasm of coughing.

Lyta had been careful to keep her own mouth closed. She backed away from the afflicted man and then ran. She could Cett gasping for breath as a second fit attacked him.

The captain turned from examining the rigging as she reached him. 'Is there trouble? Has someone frightened you?'

'That seaman is ill,' said Lyta, pointing in Cett's direction. He was still coughing and spluttering loudly.

'I'll attend to him, Kedie. You should go to the cabin in case he is ill with a fever.'

Lyta shut the door and leaned against it. That was a close call. She had no doubt that Cett would have tipped her overboard and then concocted a suitable tale to explain her disappearance. He'd already murdered two people. Another death would not distress him. .

Lyta was given midmeal and then dinner. The captain told her the ship would reach Aldea early the next morn. When he escorted her to the deck again, Cett did not appear.

'How is the ill seaman?' she asked.

'He's recovered,' said the captain with a tight smile. 'Sometimes, Kedie, these fellows fake an illness to escape their duties. I'll keep a close eye on him.'

Lyta was glad to hear his words. Now she had only to get through the night. As she settled into the swaying hammock, she placed the rock at her left hand and the box of powder by her right hand. If Cett entered the cabin she'd be ready. The motion of the ship lulled her to sleep.

The creaking door woke her. Lyta tensed as she saw a dark figure enter the cabin and then pause. With great care, she opened the box. Cett crept across the floor and then halted again. Lyta lofted the pink rock into her hand.

Two large hands rested on the edge of the hammock. Lyta hit first one and then the other with her rock. As Cett yelled in surprise and pain, she threw powder directly into his open mouth.

He'd swallowed more of the substance this time and the effect was immediate and powerful. He dropped down, gasping, wheezing, and coughing. As Lyta slid from the hammock, the captain rushed into the cabin carrying a lantern. Two other seamen followed him. He held the light high over the figure huddled on the floor.

'Not that fellow again?' he barked. Then he ordered his crew to drag Cett still wheezing and coughing from the chamber.

'Are you harmed, Kedie?' he asked anxiously.

Lyta assured him that she was fine. 'But please, lock up that man. He is guilty of crimes in Aldea as well as this attack on me.'

'He'll be placed in fetters.' said the captain in a grim voice. 'You have my word.'

Chapter Forty

When the captain told Lyta the ship was approaching the harbour at Aldeton, she hurried from the cabin. She'd imagined seeing the town so many times, but from land not from water. The little houses were shrouded in an early morn mist as though they were wrapped in filmy robes. The towers of the Erudence pointed above them all. Lyta pulled her cloak tighter round her body. She could hardly wait to see her mother again and she wouldn't even mind meeting Adina.

A solitary figure stood on the wharf watching the ship arrive. As she came closer, Lyta recognised Magian Domen. When she waved both hands at him, he lifted his right hand in a single gesture.

'I see someone's waiting for you.' The captain nodded his head toward the magian.

'I thought my mother would be there.'

'We're docking earlier than I expected thanks to favourable winds.'

The ship eased into the side of the wharf and a seaman jumped off the deck to tie up the thick rope. Then he hauled out the gangplank to allow Lyta to reach dry land. She paused as she reached Magian Domen. He wasn't the sort of person to give her a welcome embrace.

The magian nodded. 'I am glad to see you safely back.'

When Lyta leaned forward to hug him, she felt his start of surprise. 'That is how pleased I am to see you,' she said, releasing him.

She received a small smile in return. 'Your mother will be happy to have you back.'

The captain had followed her on shore. 'Thank you for your help,' Lyta said. 'The man in irons must face justice here. He murdered two of our people.'

'You can instruct Borut to send guards to escort him to the cells,' said the magian. 'Are you referring to the killer of Virr and Givis?'

'He tried to kill me too,' Lyta said.

The captain bowed. 'It was a great honour and privilege to return you to your desmense, Kedie. I will inform the Chief Priest that you have arrived.'

'No need,' said the magian. 'I will get a message to him.'

The captain bowed again before returning to the ship.

'I didn't come by horseback,' said Magian Domen. 'I thought you might like to stretch your legs after being on the ship.'

'I want to see everything.' Lyta said, her head moving from side to side. 'Oh, the town square looks just the same.'

'You were away for only three moons not a twelvemoon.'

'It felt longer,' said Lyta.

Early risers stared as they passed. 'It's my hair,' said Lyta. 'People aren't sure if they recognise me or not.'

'It makes a difference,' said Domen. 'Changing the colour was an excellent disguise.'

'Were the erles angry when I didn't go to them at Naris?' she asked.

'They were not pleased,' said the magian. 'And your mother was most concerned about your safety.'

'I didn't want to be brought home like a lost pig or a runaway child. I wanted to finish the journey without them.'

The magian nodded. 'I understand but you still caused worry. The erles and Druck will arrive later today. They waited for a ship large enough to carry their horses.'

At the castle gate, Borut looked twice at Lyta. 'It is you!' he said at last. 'Welcome home, Kedie. I am very glad to see you.'

The magian gave Borut directions about collecting the murderer from the ship and Borut nodded. 'We'll be right pleased to get that villain locked up here. I'll see to it at once.'

As the kedura walked from the door of the keep, Lyta dashed toward her. The two met on the steps in a tight embrace.

They were both weeping as Lyta raised her head from her mother's shoulder. 'You have grown so much taller,' said Halia. 'And what have you done to your hair?'

Lyta laughed through her tears. 'I became a golden-haired kedie.' She looked at the crowd waiting at the door to greet her. 'Where's Adina?'

'She was so unhappy that I sent her home,' said her mother. 'Now, please comfort Obela. She's wept constant tears ever since you were taken from us.'

Obela seemed older and smaller as Lyta put both arms around her. 'I thought I'd never see you again,' sobbed the nurse, clutching Lyta's hands.

Lyta gently twisted free to hug her nurse. When the other servants welcomed her home, she greeted each by name.

Halia hooked her arm through her daughter's. 'Come inside. You must be hungry.'

'You must eat a good repast.' Obela said. 'You know how important it is each morn.'

Lyta laughed. 'Now I really know I am home.'

Hours later, after eating, bathing and dressing, Lyta told the tale of her capture and escape to her mother and the castle officials. Privately, she had informed her mother about Cett's role in the matter. 'He must be punished for his villainy.'

'He shall be,' said Halia. 'And even though I'd like to bring Rurrik to justice, that won't be possible unless he steps on our soil.'

Next day before dinner, the, the Aldean search party reached the castle. They were weary and hungry. At short notice, Prala, the head cook, had prepared a feast for Lyta's return.

Caza selected Lyta's robe for dinner. She had exclaimed at the golden hair and wondered how long the colour would last.

'It should grow out,' said Lyta parting her hair in the centre to look for any dark hair. 'The magian may know of a potion to speed up the change.'

Lyta felt awkward at the table when she met the erles and Druck again but they soon put her at ease. She suspected that her mother had already told them about her journey through Falga. Lord Quilin's eyes twinkled as he bowed low over Lyta's hand. 'I am exceedingly content to see you back in one piece, Kedie. The castle was not the same without you.'

Lyta was aware of a blush sweeping across her cheeks. She'd forgotten how handsome he was and how pleasant his deep voice sounded. She swallowed before she responded in a voice that trembled slightly. 'I am exceedingly content to be home and glad to see you have recovered your health.'

Out of the corner of her eye, she noticed everyone at the table watching them. And her mother was nodding and smiling.

'I am most content to be strong again,' Quilin said. He lifted her hand to his warm lips. 'Welcome home, my Kedie. I trust on every future occasion, you'll leave the castle of your own accord.'

***

Two Summers Later

As their horses rounded the bend, Lyta noticed the little girl standing beside the road. She called in a high voice, 'Kedura, here's a flower for you.'

Midnight halted when Halia clicked her tongue. She bent down to take the bloom from a grubby hand. 'Thank you, child. That's a pretty flower.'

The girl grinned and bobbed a quick curtsey. Lyta watched her mother smile back and raise a white hand in acknowledgment before signaling Midnight to continue. The child scampered to the hut behind her as the commander of the guard drew level with Halia. 'Kedura, which road will you take to the castle?'

'The forest way.' At the fork in the road, Halia turned Midnight to the east and the riding party did the same.

Lyta on her mount Silver trotted beside her mother. They had not ridden together recently as serious matters had demanded Halia's attention. Increased raids by men from the neighbouring demesne had caused trouble for her folk in Aldea. Halia had convinced the ruler of Falga that he should take steps to stop the skirmishes or she would send in a formidable force of men at arms. For now, he'd convinced his people to stay on their own side of the border and cease hostilities but everyone knew they hadn't reached a permanent solution.

The sky above them was clear blue but in the distance, sullen grey clouds hung low over the far reaches of the Dark Forest. Lyta guessed there'd be rain before nightfall. The track curled around the outer ring of trees to meet the main road from the town and soon the familiar grey castle towers appeared, looming over the high stone walls. As usual, the drawbridge was down because nobody expected an attack on Aldea castle. Apart from the annoying border raids, peace had reigned in the land ever since the treaty ending the Freedom War had been signed.

The horses crossed the bridge and entered the gatehouse. Guards posted on both sides dipped their heads in respect and lowered their weapons as Halia, Lyta, and their escort passed.

The blaring sound of a bugle from the wall above startled everyone. Midnight neighed loudly and reared up on his hind legs. Halia was an experienced rider but when she pulled the reins to control her mount, somehow her left foot slipped from the stirrup. She toppled sideways.

With increasing horror, Lyta watched her mother fall further from the horse. Her head swung in a wide arc and struck the stone gatepost with a sickening thud. She dangled from the saddle, one leg still caught and a mass of golden hair falling from her cap. It became stained red from the blood that dripped into a pool on the grey stones. For a few seconds, Lyta and the riding party sat on their mounts transfixed with horror.

***

Lord Wilus of Rellhaven held Lyta's cold fingers in one warm hand. 'My dear, you must understand. At only sixteen summers, you are too young and inexperienced to step into Halia's slippers and rule Aldea by yourself. ' He patted the fingers with his other hand and smiled down at her.

Lyta studied the pattern of the grain in the wooden table top to avoid meeting the eyes of the five men seated around her. The sympathy from everyone who'd served her mother was overwhelming and she had no idea how to deal with it. Lyta knew the subject Wilus would raise next: which eligible kedir in the land would she choose as a husband. With her mother so recently dead, marriage was the last thing on her mind but the first concern of the council members. If she sat in this chamber any longer, she might dissolve into tears and disgrace herself.

Lyta cleared her throat and forced her voice to stay even. 'Forgive me, my lords, but I have developed an ache in my head. I can't discuss anything important right now and will retire to my chamber.' She rose to her feet. 'This meeting can resume in the morn.'

'Of course,' said Trevin of Belltowers, nodding at Lyta. 'We will meet again whenever it suits you.'

The erles and the magian stood up. Quilin, the lord of Highridge, moved around the table to take Lyta's arm. 'Kedie, I'll escort you. Are you still occupying the tower chambers?'

'Yes,' said Lyta, swallowing the lump in her throat. She couldn't even consider moving from her familiar quarters into her mother's state chambers.

Quilin opened the heavy door. 'You know, it will take time for your sorrow to pass,' he said in a low voice.

'But how long?' Lyta asked as they walked along the west passage.

His mouth twisted in a wry fashion. 'As long as it takes, Kedie. Grief consumed me for many moons after my wife died. Then it gradually became easier to bear.'

His wife had died in childbirth leaving a baby. The little boy must have reached four summers by now. Lyta had often wondered why Quilin didn't remarry. After all, he was certainly young enough at a score and four summers in age to take another wife.

Her guard followed them to the foot of the tower steps. Quilin nodded to him before releasing his grip on Lyta's arm and turning to face her. 'Kedie, I won't let them bully you into a sudden marriage,' he said. 'But when you're ready, you must make a decision about a husband.'

As Lyta ran up the steps, she sensed his grey eyes resting on her back; oddly, the feeling was both comforting and disturbing. Obela, her old nurse, waited at the open door. She clicked her tongue at the sight of the tears on Lyta's cheeks. 'Look at the state of you! I told you not to go to that there meeting. It's too soon to be worrying about matters in our demesne.'

Lyta rubbed her wet face. 'I had to meet with them. We discussed some urgent business.'

'And no doubt, those men bothered you again about a husband.'

Lyta nodded as she took a linen square from Obela. 'I don't understand why I can't rule Aldea alone. My mother governed by herself after my father was slain. And nobody objected.'

Obela began to unlace Lyta's grey gown. 'Well, you were too young to know such things but lots of folk objected when she refused every suitor. Some even talked about making Falga and our Aldea into one demesne under their kedur.'

The information surprised Lyta. 'I never read about that idea in my history books.'

'Such foolish talk went away fast when your lady mother showed she was both good and wise.' Obela lifted the gown from Lyta's body. 'Lie down on your bed and rest before supper.'

Supper was another public ordeal. And it didn't help that Lyta sat at the centre of the high table with Halia's portrait directly behind her. Did those good and wise blue eyes notice her daughter's poor appetite? The ability to eat well had deserted Lyta along with the ability to sleep soundly. Mayhap if she had another broken night, she should accept one of the sleeping potions Magian Domen had offered.

After supper, Obela tucked the bedclothes around Lyta as though she were only six summers old. 'Now don't lie awake this night. I've heard you tossing and turning. Your mother would expect you to eat well and get your rest.' She pulled the hangings tight around the bed to keep out the lamplight.

Easier said than done, thought Lyta. How can I make my body rest when every time I close my eyes, my mind behaves like a wheel, going over and over the whole accident? And it was such a foolish accident.

Halia had ridden Midnight for eight summers and had developed a close understanding with her mount. She'd always been able to control the high-spirited horse but that morn, something went sadly wrong.

As soon as Halia slipped from the saddle, Commander Druck leapt from his horse. He freed his kedura's foot, and placed her on the ground. Then he yelled to his guards, 'Find the magian and bring him here.'

Lyta had no memory of dismounting from Silver and reaching her mother. She did recall, however, cradling Halia's head in her lap and trying to staunch the bright blood with the edges of her green cloak.

Magian Domen had arrived quickly but he could do nothing. He held Halia's white wrist and waited. Then he sighed, closed her staring blue eyes and turned to Lyta. 'She is gone.'

A choking noise came from the commander's mouth. 'Can't you do anything to revive her? She can't be dead!'

The magian surveyed the scene and shook his head. 'I believe the kedura died the instant her head struck that gatepost.'

Lyta spun around to face Druck. 'Take Midnight away and destroy him. I don't want to look ever again upon a horse that killed my mother.'

She ignored the shocked expressions on the faces around her. 'That's an order,' she said. 'Do it at once!'

The crack of her mother's head against the post, the hot smell of her blood, and the sight of her staring eyes haunted Lyta's mind in the hours of light and became vivid nightmares in the darkness.

Next morn, after an argument with Obela about eating more at repast, Lyta left the building. Her guard, Jer, followed her to the magian's dwelling where she ordered him to wait at the gate. Domen answered Lyta's knock and ushered her inside his workchamber.

Sitting down on her usual stool, Lyta felt the familiar surroundings close comfortably around her. She knew each part of the workchamber: the orderly rows of blue flasks and crimson boxes on the shelves, each with its special potion or balm; the dried herbs hanging in fragrant bunches from hooks on the ceiling, the wooden stools by the table at the east window and above all, the mysterious hyala under its black coverlet by the west window. She'd learned its purpose over recent summers and knew now that Domen used it to communicate with the magians in other demesnes. However, she'd never been able to use the instrument. Only a magian had that power and skill.

When Lyta was seated, Domen took the stool opposite her. The magian was a spare man with hair shorter than the current fashion and a neat grey beard. He regarded her with his searching blue eyes before saying. 'You look tired.'

'I can't sleep properly. Mayhap I do need to take a potion as you suggested.'

'Then you can mix one yourself and take it with you. I'm sure you remember the ingredients.' He raised a thin eyebrow. 'What else troubles you?'

'Do you think I can rule Aldea by myself?'

The magian frowned. 'As we said yestermorn, you have no experience in governing.'

'I've attended all my mother's audiences with petitioners ever since I reached fourteen summers.'

'And how many decisions did Halia allow you to make?'

'None,' Lyta admitted, 'but Mother reviewed every case with me and asked for my opinion.'

'Were you always in agreement with her?'

'On two occasions, I was able to use my lofting power to catch thoughts from the people before her. Both men were telling lies.'

A blue flash from the hyala stopped their conversation. Lyta winced as a sharp pinprick in her head announced the arrival of a message. When she was younger, the pain was sharp and hard to bear but now she'd grown more accustomed to the hyala's strange force. Domen crossed the floor, removed the protective cover and then passed his hand over the glossy black surface. He muttered an incantation that Lyta could not hear.

His face was thoughtful when he returned to the table. 'That was a message from the magian in Falga. A delegation is on its way here and should arrive by nightfall.' He paused and looked directly at Lyta. 'It is led by Erle Darik.'

She gasped. 'But wasn't Darik exiled with his father and brother?'

'Apparently not. He must have persuaded his kedur that he had nothing to do with your kidnapping. His father and brother were certainly banished two summers ago and as far as I know are still in captivity on the Eastern Isles. But since he was named an erle, Darik must have inherited his father's lands.'

Lyta took several deep breaths to slow her galloping heart. 'I'm worried by this news. Darik wanted to wed me when I was kidnapped.'

'I suspect he isn't coming with his own proposal of marriage but with one from Kedur Ulit's son. Ardul would be the right age to be a suitor for you.'

'Along with the three other kedirs who've already staked their claim since my mother died.' Lyta sighed. 'And I don't want to marry any of them.'

Domen frowned. 'That's a matter for further council discussion. Right now you had better deal with this delegation. I do wonder why we weren't given proper notice of their visit. Mayhap it was because we might have objected to it.' He stood up. 'You should inform the erles as soon as possible and order your castlian to make preparations.'

Lyta sent Jer to gather the erles and then looked for her castlian. She found Godit supervising the servants who were replacing rushes on the floor of the great hall. She told him of the Falgans' imminent arrival.

'Kedie, chambers will be arranged and I'll instruct the kitchen to prepare a more suitable meal for this evening. How long will our guests stay?'

'I don't know. It depends on the nature of their business.'

Godit waved a meaty hand. 'No matter, Kedie. I will take care of everything. Leave it to me.'

Lyta thanked him before she hurried toward the council chamber. Outside the door, she met Quilin. After a glance at her face, he said, 'Bad news?'

'Are my thoughts so clear?'

Quilin smiled. 'Remember, I've known you since you were a little girl. I can read the messages in your eyes.

Lyta felt heat rise in her cheeks. 'I certainly hope not. Some of my thoughts are exceedingly private.' She told him about Darik and his delegation.

'I wonder what they're planning. We don't need trouble from Falga.'

'Are they likely to try to take over Aldea now that Mother has gone?'

'You know about that episode, do you? They certainly tried after your father was killed but we're much stronger these days and they're exceedingly unlikely to make that move.' He smiled as he opened the door for

Lyta. 'Let's see what the others think about this delegation.'

The others all voiced loud opinions. Wilus considered that Darik was coming to present a marriage proposal on behalf of Kedir Ardul. Lord Josik of Edgemere wondered if he was really coming to spy out the current situation in Aldea; Trevin felt sure that Darik was working on behalf of Rurrik, his exiled father. 'And we know that damned weasel wanted to marry our dear dead Kedura and claim the throne. Now he probably has designs on our kedie.'

Everyone talked at once until Wilus held up a hand. 'My lords, please. We won't know Darik's intent until we meet him.'

'And mayhap, not even then,' Trevin muttered. 'I don't trust the man. His whole family is rotten to the core.'

'Let's be sure to keep our eyes and ears open,' said Wilus. 'Our turbulent history with Falga demands our close attention now.'

Trevin banged his open palm on the table. 'I'd like to run a blade through Darik's body. We shouldn't believe any of them.' He sighed. 'Now, Kedie Lyta, don't let this visit bother your pretty little head. We'll protect you from all danger.'

His patronizing words annoyed Lyta. Had Trevin forgotten that two summers ago, she'd escaped from Darik's father and brother when she'd been kidnapped from Aldea. And she'd done that by herself without the aid of her lords.

She directed a cool smile at Trevin. 'I am not worried at all by this visit. We'll know soon enough why Darik is here.'

Chapter Forty-One

Lyta took a deep breath to steady her nerves before she entered her mother's chambers. The clean scent of Halia's perfume still hung in the air; its unique combination of citrus and musk was quite unmistakable. She choked back a sob as she surveyed the wide bed with its white silk cover and dark green velvet hangings, the chair with its gold cushion by the window and, along the walls, the row of carved oak chests that had stored Halia's clothes. Everything was arranged as though her mother had simply stepped from the chamber. Lyta still couldn't believe she would never return.

Amia, Halia's chief attendant, knelt beside the wooden chest nearest the bed smoothing the silken fabric of an azure-blue robe. When she heard Lyta's footsteps, she dropped the garment and sprang to her feet.

'Nobody told me you were coming, Kedie.' She dabbed her wet cheeks with a kerchief and sniffed. 'What can I do for you?'

'We're expecting guests from Falga for supper tonight and I wish to look regal and older. I thought one of Mother's robes might be more suitable than my own clothes.'

After measuring Lyta with her eyes, the maid walked around her. 'You are taller than my lady and you don't have her curved shape.'

Lyta grimaced. 'I'll never have Mother's breasts and hips. They tell me I resemble my father who was tall and lean.'

'You may not resemble the kedura her but you have your own beauty.'

'Thanks, Amia.' Lyta swallowed hard. 'Now, are there any garments you can suggest for me?'

Amia frowned as she thought. 'Hmm. Some of her colours won't flatter your black hair and brown eyes. Mayhap, the dark green silk would be suitable.'

She opened a long chest near the window and lifted a green robe. Then she replaced it with another garment. 'What about this one?' She stood up to reveal a shining golden robe and shook out its heavy folds.

'Oh, I remember that gown. Mother wore it when Kedur Baldus and Firt visited us. It had a matching surcoat.'

'It's here as well.' Amia laid both shimmering garments on the bed. She called for her sisters, Caza and Belia, who both hurried from the inner solar. 'Belia, unlace the kedie's gown,' Amia said. 'She wishes to don the golden robe.'

Lyta shivered as Amia and Caza drew the gown over her head. The fabric lay smoothly on her skin and it was suffused with the mother's perfume. She felt suddenly doubtful about using Halia's clothes. 'Should I wear this?'

Amia's reply was swift. 'My lady would like you to have her garments. They're much too good to be shut away.'

Lyta stood still as her arms were slipped into the richly embroidered surcoat. Amia tugged at the loose bodice. 'I'll pin this to fit you better.' She asked Caza to fetch the box of pins and clasps.

Bela found a matching golden girdle and then Amia used one of the brass keys hanging at her waist to unlock a jewel casket.

Lyta stared at the sparkling heap inside. 'Which ones did my mother wear with this gown?'

'These pieces.' Amia drew out a thin chain which she fastened around Lyta's neck and handed her two heavy golden bracelets.

Lyta selected a slender tiara. ‘Please arrange my hair around this.’

When Amia was satisfied with her work, she clasped her hands and gave a heavy sigh. ‘Oh, you look so fine. I wish my lady could see you now.’ She handed Lyta a looking glass and stood back with the other two maids, awaiting comments.

Lyta held up the glass to regard herself from several angles. She looked older. Tonight, everyone in the great hall would see her as a grown woman, not a child. ‘You’ve done well.’

Amia sniffed and felt for her kerchief. ‘You will surprise them all.’ She mopped her eyes as Belia folded the garments Lyta had been wearing and Caza answered a knock on the door. ‘Kedie, Lord Quilin is here to take you to the great hall,’ she said.

When he entered the chamber, Lyta stood still to observe his reaction to her changed appearance. Quilin blinked several times. His mouth opened but no words came out. With an obvious effort, he said, ‘For a minute there, Kedie, I didn’t recognise you at all.’

Lyta twirled around to show him the full effect of her glittering finery. ‘So, is that a good thing or a bad one?’

Quilin cleared his throat. ‘Good, of course. You look exceeding beautiful.’ He held out his bent arm. ‘Kedie, shall we go to dazzle Falga?’

Their entrance into the hall brought all diners to their feet. Clad in her mother’s garments, it was easy to copy Halia’s stately gait. With her head held high, Lyta sailed toward the empty chair at the centre of the high table.

She enjoyed the shocked looks on her lords’ faces before glancing at her guests. Darik’s jaw had also dropped open. Wilus cleared his throat and recovered his voice. ‘Kedie Lyta, you’ve already met Lord Darik of Falga. Allow me to present Captain Stor who accompanies him.’

Lyta smiled at the captain, a stocky man with a florid complexion, sharp black eyes, and grizzled hair. He made a deep bow to her and then stepped back beside Trevin.

Darik also bowed. When he reached out for her hand and kissed it, Lyta hoped the shiver of disgust that ran through her body was not obvious to anybody else. She nodded in return. 'How could I forget you? We met when your father captured me.'

Darik shuffled his feet uneasily. 'I was completely unaware of my father's felonious schemes. As you recall, when I discovered you were a captive, my only desire was to restore you to your mother.'

'That doesn't explain why I saw you and your father together at Naris when I caught a ship back to Aldea.' Lyta motioned for Darik to take the seat beside hers.

He had flushed bright red. 'I was at Naris with my father to prevent your recapture and to make sure you boarded that ship safely. My intentions were entirely honourable. Kedur Ulit understood the situation when I explained the circumstances.'

So that also explained his takeover of Rurrik's estate. Lyta didn't bother to respond. Out of the corner of eye, she watched him hold out his glass to be filled with wine. He downed half the contents in one gulp before turning with a look of relief to answer a question from Josik seated on his other side.

Lyta always thought the great hall looked its best at night by torchlight. The rafters blackened by smoke from summers of fires in the giant hearth seemed even higher in the flickering light. Flames from the fire were reflected in the shining battle shields hanging from the vast beams. Some of these weapons had belonged to her ancestors while others had been captured from enemies defeated in war.

She studied the banners placed at regular intervals around the walls. Each showed the emblem of a demesne in the land. The grey wolf of Falga, the tusked boar of Delis, the coiled black snake of Parian, and the majestic stag of Sevvir all waved in the heat from the fire and from the movements of diners and serving maids. She couldn't observe the largest banner of all which depicted the giant oak of Aldea, It hung behind her chair in a row of portraits of her ancestors.

As steaming platters of venison, pork, fowl, and fish were carried to the table, Lyta was impressed by the lavish feast that her chief cook and her workers had provided. Supper was ordinarily a smaller meal than the dinner they ate at midday. She must congratulate Prala on arranging such fine food on short notice.

Darik, who had recovered his composure, commented on the meat. 'This venison, in particular, is very tasty. Your cook has a clever way with sauces. I've never tasted the one he served with this venison.'

The erle's glass was filled often but Lyta drank little. She repressed a shudder every time his dark eyes roamed over her face and body, remembering the thoughts about marriage she had once lofted from his mind. This night, his thoughts were guarded and she couldn't catch any strong emotion from him.

Halfway through the meal, Darik leaned forward. With a flash of yellow teeth, he said, slightly slurring his words, 'Sweet lady, you have probably reckoned that I come here with a proposal of marriage from the son of my kedur. I wish to present the details to you and your lords as soon as possible.'

Lyta reflected that marriage to a kedir she had never met was preferable to one with this loathsome man. Honeyed words and wide smiles could never make Darik seem attractive. She answered briefly that he could meet with the council on the morn when the proposal would be discussed.

The diners grew louder and more boisterous as many jugs of wine and ale were circulated. When a fight broke out between her men at arms and some Falgans, Lyta left the hall with her guard. She could rely on her commander and his men to prevent any serious problems. Before she went to her tower, she visited her aunts. Because of their advanced age, both women preferred to dine at night in their own chambers.

When she knocked on her Aunt Jona's door, it was opened by her elderly attendant. 'Is my aunt still awake?'

'Yes, Kedie, she's been waiting for you.'

The chamber inside was hot and stuffy. Her aunt always complained of the cold. In fact, she complained about everything. Jona looked exceeding healthy with her compact round body and her plump face with its rosy cheeks but every time Lyta saw her, she had an ache in her head or her ears or her feet.

'Is that you, child?' Jona called in a high querulous voice. 'You are late coming to see me.'

'I'm sorry, Aunt. We were entertaining guests from Falga.'

'I heard that Darik was here. They once wanted me to wed his grandsire.'

'Yes, Aunt, you told me.'

Jona twitched the bedclothes nearer to her chin. 'Don't bother to visit Vea. She's taken a sleeping potion because of an ache in her belly. She only developed an ache after I told her my own belly pained me.' She waved a limp hand at Lyta. 'Child, you can go now. Leave me to suffer in peace.'

Lyta tiptoed to the door. Jona was an aunt on her mother's side while Vea was connected to her father. Both ladies had come to live in Aldea when they were widowed. They said they'd be chaperones for Halia after her own husband died. They were skilled needlewomen and spent their time stitching tapestries and hangings or adding fine embroidery to shifts and smallclothes. Lyta closed the door quietly, thankful for her own good health and went to bed.

The council chamber always impressed guests to the demesne. Bright banners representing each of the erles decorated the walls. Wilus's banner showed his dark brown rell while Quilin's snarling icecat was centred on his. Trevin was known by a black stallion and Josik by a leaping salmon. The next banner displayed Magian Domen's mortar and pestle. Behind Lyta's chair was placed the largest banner of all with its image of a majestic oak tree.

The highly polished table had been made from an enormous oak trunk that fell in the Great Forest during a winter storm. Matching chairs were arranged on the sides with a single high-backed chair at the head. When Lyta arrived for the meeting, the two Falgans were already present. Stor stood stiff and straight by the window while Darik lounged against a wall with one hand around a glass of wine, looking far too comfortable. He'd filled the glass from one of the jugs of red wine placed on a silver salver atop a large wooden chest. After Quilin led Lyta to the head of the table, she greeted everybody and then asked Darik to open the discussion.

He began with a flourish of his white hands. 'I have here a proposal of marriage from Kedir Ardul, the son of my esteemed ruler, Kedur Ulit of Falga.'

He frowned at Stor who handed him a sheet of paper. 'The kedir has reached eighteen summers and has been well schooled by a number of tutorans in a variety of fields of learning. His father instructed him in all matters of governance. He has ruled his own estate for three summers and is much loved and admired by his people.'

He lifted his eyes and smiled at Lyta. 'I am sure, Kedie, you'll be happy to learn that Kedir Ardul is tall and well-made with golden hair and blue eyes. He is very strong and skilled in weapon use and has been champion of tourneys in the demesnes of Falga, Delis, and Sevvir. And, of course, he sings, dances, and plays the lute exceedingly well.'

When he paused for breath, Lyta nodded.

'Kedir Ardul is most anxious to meet you here in Aldea and has charged me to arrange a suitable time for him to visit your demesne.'

Stor cleared his throat. 'Kedur Ulit has recorded here the details of coin and land involved in this marriage settlement. I will give it to your lords to read and consider.' He handed another sheet of paper to Lord Wilus.

Lyta felt a flash of anger that she wasn't considered wise enough to understand the information about coin and land. However, she controlled her feelings and replied in a steady voice. 'Lord Darik and Captain Stor, I thank you for presenting this proposal. I need time to consider it. '

Darik drummed his long fingers on the table. 'I expected a more positive and immediate response this morn because of the close bond between our demesnes.'

Wilus leaned forward. 'You heard Kedie Lyta's words. She will consider this proposal.'

'However my kedur has charged me to arrange a certain time for his son to visit you so that Kedie Lyta can meet him.'

'I think we all heard the kedie's reply. Let's set the matter aside.' Josik cleared his throat. 'In the meantime, we've arranged a hunt for you. You can be sure of bringing down a fine stag in the Dark Forest and mayhap, even one of our fierce boars.'

Darik stayed silent for several minutes as though he were trying to master his annoyance at not getting the immediate answer he desired. Then he smiled at Josik. 'I will be pleased to join you in a hunt.' Hs gaze switched to Lyta. 'I await your reply and will return promptly with it to

Kedur Ulit. He wishes me to point out that if you wed his son, you will have at your disposal a large army of well-equipped men.'

After Trevin and Josik had escorted their guests from the chamber, Lyta gave a large sigh and asked Wilus. 'Why did he mention this large army? Was it some kind of threat?'

Wilus snorted. 'If it was, then ignore it. You're not giving your hand to Ardul at the point of a lance.'

Domen and Lyta took glasses of wine from Quilin. 'No need for alarm, Kedie,' he said. 'Ulit knows we too can field a large army. The words were merely bluster on his side. He has no intention of using force.'

Lyta sipped her wine. 'I've been thinking about my four suitors. What if I ask for a span of six moons to consider marriage to one of them? Our next meeting will be held then in the winter at the time of the Moonfest. I could invite all the kedirs here and then make a decision. We could arrange banquets and provide some suitable entertainment.'

'Hmm. That might work.' Wilus tugged his shaggy beard, which had turned even whiter since Lyta had seen him six moons earlier. 'I have also been considering the question, Kedie. Before your marriage, some dissidents might want to take advantage of your youth and inexperience. Two of us could remain here during that next period to advise you whenever necessary. And our men would remain here to bolster your numbers if they should be needed.'

Quilin nodded. 'A wise plan, Wilus. We can decide later who is best suited to stay and who needs to return home.'

'I like this idea too,' said Domen. 'I will be happy to give advice on any matter, Kedie, should you ask for my help.'

Lyta already knew she would prefer to have the guidance of Wilus and Quilin but urgent business might require their attendance at their own estates. After all, they'd already stayed longer at the castle than usual because of her mother's sudden death and funeral. But she could also tolerate the advice of Josik and Trevin. Both men had the interests of Aldea at heart.

When she left the meeting, Lyta visited her mother's chambers. Last night, she'd decided that if she wished to be regarded as the rightful ruler of Aldea, she should move from her tower. It was difficult to take that large step. Lyta felt as though she was finally saying farewell to her mother by occupying her chambers. And what if Wilus was right and she was too green to step into Halia's slippers? Although her pillow had become wet with tears, she'd made up her mind.

She walked through the door from the antechamber that led into the solar. It was an L shaped chamber with a window at the longer end. Halia had been overseeing a building project to replace some of the old slit windows with modern frames fitted with glass. This new window gave sufficient light to a chamber that was primarily used for stitching and needlework.

Lyta greeted both her aunts who had their heads bent over their work. She inquired after Vea's health.

'I am exceedingly well,' she answered in a brusque tone. 'It's Jona who's always complaining about her head and body.'

Jona's opposite in appearance, Vea was tall and gaunt with a pinched face and large feet and hands. Lyta had once overheard her castlian refer to the two women as 'the long and short of it.' Amused by the phrase, she'd repeated it to her mother and had been rebuked by Halia for rudeness. However, Lyta had seen her mother turn away to hide a quick smile.

Lyta asked Godit to summon her mother's attendants. When they'd gathered in the solar together with Lyta's nurse, Obela, Lyta announced her intention to take over the chambers. Godit said he'd supervise the cleaning and the moving of Lyta's belongings. To avoid the dust, confusion, and the comments from her aunts, Lyta escaped to her tower workchamber.

She gazed around it, remembering the lessons with Tutoran Cordon. Although she'd ceased to study with him when she reached fourteen summers, she'd continued her other lessons with Domen. Her mother had wished her to develop her special gifts with the assistance of the magian. Lyta also wanted to improve her skills of lofting, a talent that enabled her to move objects with her mind and to catch thoughts from other people.

While Tutoran Cordon had been dry and stuffy at times, Lyta had never doubted his dedication to learning. He was a very serious man and she'd often thought he was more suited to the priesthood than to teaching. And in fact, when he'd ceased instructing her, Cordon had enrolled in the Salvance where devotees of Lady Moon studied her faith. If he completed the course, the man would become a salvan. Mayhap, as a priest, he would once again be assigned to the castle. Elon, the current salvan, was a very old man who was inclined to forget prayers and confuse rituals. Halia had tolerated the man's mistakes because he'd performed both her marriage and crowning ceremonies.

Lyta gazed at the wall hangings where her gaze had often wandered during history lessons. The closest depicted an orchard scene in spring with pink and white blossoms on the fruit trees and rabbits and hares playing in the grass. The largest one showed the whole country of Mondalia with each demesne marked in its own colour. Her Aldea was green while neighouring Falga was red. Delis was light blue and Parian next to it was depicted in gold. The last demesne of Sevvir was dark blue in colour. The names of the main towns in the entire continent had been stitched in black.

The Mercy hanging decorated the wall opposite the window. Lyta had never liked the expression on the erle's face as he looked down upon the poor peasant at his feet. She'd often wondered if he'd received mercy.

She grew melancholy from staring at the hangings. Halia, her aunts, and their attendant had been responsible for the making of each one. Lyta had provided few stitches as she'd never been adept with a needle or had the desire to develop the skill. Instead, she'd learned to ride a horse, throw a blade, and draw a bow. Her mother had understood her liking for the open air and the world outside the stuffy solar and had never ordered her to pick up a needle. She had, however, asked Lyta to help with the spring hanging as the subject was to her daughter's taste. After much effort, Lyta had stitched a hare.

A commotion outside drew Lyta to the window that overlooked the courtyard. Had the hunting party returned so soon? Then she saw Trevin and Josik walking beside a horse to support a figure slumped in the saddle. With a fast-beating heart, Lyta ran down the tower steps and then took the closest passage to the front door. The man on the horse was wearing the colours of Falga.

Chapter Forty-Two

By the time Lyta reached the courtyard, Magian Domen was already directing his prentices to lift Darik from the saddle. The erle's hose and boots were scarlet from the blood seeping from a rough bandage tied around his right thigh. When Lyta opened her mouth to ask how the erle had been wounded, Josik caught her eye and shook his head. She realized he didn't want to discuss the matters before other people.

Lyta waited for answers until Darik had been carried to the magian's dwelling with Stor following close behind. Left in the courtyard, Darik's men at arms had scowls on their faces as they muttered together. Lyta followed Josik and Trevin back up the steps into an antechamber off the great hall.

Josik sent a servant for the other council members and then he sank onto a stool and grabbed a jug of wine. He poured a full glass and took a large gulp before he sighed and said. 'Think we may be in a real coil here.'

'What happened?' Lyta asked as Quilin and Wilus hurried into the chamber.

'It's all my doing.' Trevin said. 'But I'll swear before Lady Moon it was nothing but an accident, no matter what that slimy bastard tells you.'

'Start at the beginning,' Wilus said, pouring himself and Lyta glasses of wine. 'From what you've said already, we might need this wine to ease our minds.'

Trevin took a deep breath and a further gulp from his glass before he said. 'It started out well. Darik seemed happy that the hunt was successful so quickly. We set him up to shoot a large stag, which really pleased him, but then he kept going on and on about getting a boar. Luckily, the dogs picked up a scent and we followed them to the Bright Glade.' He looked at Wilus. 'The one where we found that fine beast last summer.'

Wilus nodded. 'I know it. Go on.'

'After that, things got confused. Darik and I were both ready to strike. Then the beast gored the lead dog, rushed through the others in the pack and charged us. That damned dog flew through the air and knocked my lance sideways. The point pierced Darik and Josik had to step in fast to kill the boar.' He rubbed a hand over his eyes. 'As the Falgan fell to the ground, he yelled out that the wounding was a deliberate act on my part. Everyone in the party heard him.'

'How could he say that?' Lyta asked. 'You had many witnesses who will speak the truth if they are asked.'

Josik said, 'Everything was confused as Trevin said and everything happened very fast. I heard Darik's words but didn't see actually him get stuck by Trevin's lance. Stor was close to us but I'm not too sure if he saw the incident clearly either.'

Quilin had listened to both accounts, his dark head propped on one hand. 'But it may not matter what actually happened. Darik's men will believe his words, not yours.'

'I agree with you,' said Wilus. 'And we don't need any more bad blood between us and Falga. Our men and theirs are already brawling and scrapping. Last night, Druck threw several hotheads from both sides into the cells to cool them down.' He shook his head. 'Things could get worse after this incident is known.' '

'How serious is Darik's wound?' Quilin asked.

'Hard to tell. He bled like a stuck pig.' said Trevin. He stopped as he realised what he'd said and grimaced. 'Not an appropriate comparison under the circumstances. Domen will have cleaned him up by now. I'd better go and find out how the bastard's doing.'

'It would be much better if Quilin or I went,' Wilus said, 'since we weren't involved in the event.'

'Wilus, as the senior erle, you should go, and I'll accompany you.' Lyta added. 'I must show my concern for our guest.'

Within minutes, Wilus and Lyta crossed the courtyard to the magian's dwelling and knocked on the door. A flustered prentice in a blood-stained gown answered and bobbed a curtsey. 'The master is busy, noble lady and sir. The Falgan lord is sore wounded.'

'Ask Magian Domen to see me as soon as he can leave his patient,' said Lyta. 'And if Captain Stor is still here, tell him that we were inquiring about the erle's health.'

'Captain Stor is here. He's in the chamber with Lord Darik. Do you want me to fetch him?'

'No, please don't bother him,' Lyta said. 'Just pass on our message.'

As they returned to the keep, Lyta stopped and placed a hand on Wilus's sleeve. 'Are you quite sure that Trevin didn't injure Darik on purpose? I heard him earlier threatening to use a blade on him.'

'I don't think he was serious but I can't really be certain,' said Wilus. 'The two have been enemies ever since Darik married Trevin's niece. The Falgan treated her so badly that Trevin's never forgiven him.'

'Didn't she die?' Lyta asked. 'I remember hearing the tale. I thought she had a child.'

Wilus lowered his voice. 'Darik said the babe she was carrying caused her death but Trevin heard another tale from a member of the household about a beating and a fall down some stairs.'

'That is a complication in this matter. I suppose all we can do now is to hope that the magian's remedies are successful.'

Wilus nodded. 'An unsuccessful outcome could be a disaster for us if Kedur Ulit believes that his envoy was deliberately targeted.'

Lyta was concerned by his words. Back inside, she visited the chapel. Quite often these morns, she missed attending the usual services. As she bowed before the shining Moon altar, she recited the prayers of intercession and supplication. Even though Darik was sure to be a Star Child holding the Asteriki faith, Lyta believed that Lady Moon was powerful enough to intervene on his behalf. 'Make him well, dear Lady, for the sake of both our demesnes.'

She sank on her knees on the cold stone floor. Was it the darkness of the place, the smell of the heavy incense, and the flicker of the guttering candles that caused a sudden wave of dizziness? Or was it the memory of kneeling in this very spot beside her mother's body in its ebony coffin only sevendays ago?

Halia had looked beautiful. Amia chose an azure robe the same shade as eyes of her mistress while Lyta picked the bouquet of blue Remembrance flowers to place in the white hands crossed on her mother's breast. With the drone of prayers in her head and an empty belly because of the required fasting for the dead, Lyta's thoughts had whirled like leaves tossed in the wind.

Her mother could have been sleeping and it was easy to imagine her opening her eyes and smiling. She would ask what foolish games the Salvan and her daughter were playing. But of course, her mother's eyes were closed for ever and she was lying deep in the silent Resting Ground outside the western wall of the castle where her husband and all Aldean rulers were buried. .

Now Lyta shook herself and stood up with the aid of a nearby stool. Such sorrowful recollections would neither bring her mother back nor cure Darik. She had to rely on the skilled hands and potions of the magian and his prentices. She dipped her head once more in reverence to Lady Moon and left the chapel.

***

Magian Domen attended the council chamber next morn. Dark circles under his eyes testified to his lack of sleep. Wilus pulled out a chair for him and when Lyta nodded her assent, the magian sank into it and bent his head. Trevin poured some wine and handed the glass to him.

'How goes your patient?' Wilus asked.

'Right now, I cannot tell you exactly how he is faring. The wound itself was not life-threatening but last night, he developed a high fever. If I can reduce that, his body might start to heal. If not…' the magian shrugged and sipped from his glass.

'Of course, Darik's health is our main concern,' said Josik 'but while it is in the balance, I'm concerned about the level of ill feeling between his men and ours. Druck had to throw more brawlers into the cells overnight.'

'How do we reduce the ill will?' Trevin asked.

'What if both sides burn up some of that emotion in a tourney of sorts,' Quilin suggested. 'We could stage various contests for the men.'

Josik leaned forward with his face intent. 'Wrestling is always popular among men at arms.'

'Archery too,' said Trevin. 'We have many fine bowmen. And what about that sport the Falgans like to play, where they take turns throwing large rocks. A few rounds might content them. Especially if they win.'

All eyes turned to Lyta. 'What do you think, My Lady?' Wilus asked. 'If you graced the tourney with your presence, these contests may stay courteous and some of the ill-will could vanish.'

'I'd be happy to attend any or all of them,' Lyta said. 'How soon could this tourney of sorts take place?'

Josik stood up. 'Kedie, with your permission, Trevin and I will consult Druck at once and then let you know what we can arrange. The sooner the tourney starts the better it will be for all of us.'

Lyta turned to the magian when the two erles had left. 'Is Darik's condition really that serious?'

Domen grimaced. 'I have treated many with fevers. And despite my potions, a point always comes when the patient's body wins or loses the battle. Darik is a strong man and his body is fighting the infection. I believe his fate will be decided in two more morns.' He stood up. 'And now, I must return to his sickbed. I have been away too long. Incidentally, the contests are a good idea.'

Quilin waited until the door had closed. 'I asked Druck if he knew this Captain Stor and he said the man isn't a mere captain at all but actually the commander of Ulit's guards.'

'And what's more,' added Wilus, 'I've remembered his history. Ulit's first wife bore only daughters. When she died a score of summers ago, the kedur married again and this one bore four boys and at least two girls. Stor is the brother of Ulit's second wife.'

'And no doubt with a direct line to Ulit's ear,' said Lyta. 'We need him to report accurately to his kedur.'

'We do,' said Quilin. 'Let's hope it goes that way

A hastily constructed pavilion was erected in one of the broad fields outside newgate on the flat stretch of land that was reserved for sporting contests. The area was also the site of jousting tourneys. Trevin reported that men at arms from both demesnes were eager to show off their skills and already boasting about the possible results.

'We'll start with the archery contest,' he told Lyta, 'and then go to this rock throwing and end with the wrestling. You can award a prize of coin to each winner.'

'I've never seen this stone contest,' she said. 'What happens?'

'They call it The Stones in Falga. It's an old game and very popular. The rocks have to be a certain weight and shape so that's caused problems here. In Falga, the stones are ancient and kept safe under lock and key. As we speak, a group of Falgans and our men are out with a wagon, scouring the countryside around Aldeton for suitable rocky candidates.'

'Then the Falgans with their experience should win that contest,' said Lyta.

'They certainly have the edge but our men will do well in the archery and wrestling. I'm hoping that both sides will put their minds on the contests and not on rumours and fighting.' '

Several preliminary rounds had been conducted in archery before Lyta watched the finalists take their places. She invited her aunts to attend. Jona said she was in too much pain with her head to watch archery in the bright sunlight but Aunt Vea had graciously agreed. Lyta asked her to award the archery prize. Vea grew almost pink with pleasure as she took a seat in the pavilion beside Lyta. This competition had drawn the highest number of entrants and the score of men at arms lined up to decide the championship all possessed keen eyes and steady hands.

Folk from the town and castle were clearly in favour of the three Aldean men but they also cheered the fine shots of the other contestants. After three more rounds, Captain Stor, an Aldean from the castle guard, a Falgan man at arm, and a man from Trevin's estate were left as contestants in the final bout.

Lyta knew where her heart lay but she clapped politely as each man performed. In the end, Borut from their guardhouse was the winner. With a thin smile and a few gracious words, Lady Vea awarded him a purse of silver coins.

The crowd became quieter as the unfamiliar game of The Stones began. Three large black stones were placed at one end of the lists and five Falgans and two brave Aldeans took their places beside them. After each man had thrown a stone, a small boy placed a marker at the spot where it had landed. Each contestant had his own coloured wooden peg. When the three stones had been tossed, one marker was left at the position of the longest throw. Two Falgans went first and then the first Aldean stepped up to the throwing line.

His muscles rippled as he stretched both arms above his head. Then he bent down, picked up the stone, and tossed it. The object landed far short of the two Falgan markers and his remaining shots were no better. His supporters murmured uneasily to each other.

The next man from Aldea performed a little better and received a loud cheer but all eyes were on the last burly man from Falga as he stepped forward. He flexed his muscles, spat on his hands, took a large breath, and heaved the first stone. It went past any of the others and beyond any of the last two stones. Lyta thought that this man must be a champion in Falga. And now he had become a champion in Aldea. She gave him the next winning purse.

Wrestling was the last event and as in the archery competition, the finalists had already been decided. Three pairs of contestants with a Falgan and an Aldean in each were ready. The crowd yelled advice and criticism of the technique of each man. By the time the last pair faced each other, the noise was deafening. The two men were evenly matched in size and skill and either could triumph.

Lyta held her breath as the man from her castle pinned his opponent down. Could he maintain his hold for the required length of time? Druck counted loudly and the crowd chanted along with him. Then the commander raised his hand and announced the winner. He pulled the man to his feet and turned him toward Lyta to receive her praise and the prize.

Afterwards, nobody knew who made the first move but suddenly the lists were full of fighting men. The Falgans were shouting that the contest was unfair and the Aldeans were shouting equally loudly that the best man had won. A confused mass of struggling men filled the ground.

Quilin grabbed Lyta's arm and yelled, 'Let's get you two out of here.'

He pulled Lyta from her seat and lifted Vea to the ground. Then suddenly the mob of fighters fell back and a voice yelled, 'Foul play here!'

Lyta turned to see a man had fallen on the grass with blood staining his green tunic. She knew at once he was the winner of the archery contest. Borut had been stabbed.

'Wait!' she said to Quilin. 'You can escort Lady Vea. One of my men has been wounded. I want to make sure he is helped.'

'Then I'll stay here with you,' Quilin said. 'The mood here is ugly. You may not be safe.' He looked across the grass. 'Wilus is on his way over here. He can escort Lady Vea to her chamber.'

Chapter Forty-Three

Iben looked like many men in his demesne, wiry, on the short side, with dark hair and eyes and an olive complexion. The other inhabitants of the country of Mondalia said there were ways other than appearance to identify someone from Parian; he'd be slow to spend coin but swift to take offence.

On this particular morn, Kedir Iben was living up to this reputation as he haggled with an innkeeper over the fee for the night's lodging. 'Your filthy chamber was not worth ten coppers. My arms and legs are covered with bites from damned bugs. And surely you must have filled that grubby mattress with rocks. I'll give you five coppers if you include a repast of ale and bread.'

The innkeeper scratched his head, provoking Iben to attack his own head in response. 'I'll settle for eight coppers.'

'Six is my last offer.' Iben's right hand casually touched the hilt of the short sword at his belt.

The innkeeper caught the movement as Iben had intended. 'Six coppers seems about right, Sir.' He bowed low. 'I'll have the ale and bread brought to you. And I'll throw in some of our special cheese.' He called to his wife and then vanished into the kitchen.

Iben's companion had observed the proceedings with a wry smile. 'You can afford to pay ten coppers, Kedir. What was that nonsense about?'

'I believe in getting full value for coin.' Iben lowered his voice. 'Remember, Nirk, I'm not your kedir on this journey. Use my given name when you speak to me in front of strangers.'

Nirk grimaced. 'I'll try to remember but I've been your man for twenty summers. It's only natural for me to call you kedir.'

The innkeeper's scrawny wife brought their repast. Iben took a tentative bite of the cheese and left the rest of the lump on the platter. It was hard and rancid. After they'd eaten the dry bread and drunk the weak ale, the two men collected their horses from the stables and went back on the road.

'We should reach my sister's estate by nightfall,' said Iben as he tugged a thick grey cloak around his body. The morn was chilly with a stiff easterly breeze that was ruffling his hair.

'How long will we stay there, Kedir?'

'Long enough to send a message to Father so he thinks I'll be visiting her for at least two sevendays. Then we leave for Aldea.'

Nirk shook his head. 'I still think this journey to Aldea is foolish, Kedir. You're invited there in six moons' time to view the girl. Her appearance and nature won't change much in that span of time.'

'I want to get a good look at her ahead of the others. Then I'll know whether or not to make a proposal.'

'You'll propose marriage if it's your father's command,' Nirk commented. 'And that's likely to be the case.'

Since Nirk's words were true, Iben flushed but did not reply. The main reason for his journey was not to visit his sister or travel to Aldea but to escape from his father's heavy hand. The Kedur expected Iben to attend every function and then to listen to a long lecture on the mistakes of protocol he'd committed. His public words were also censored and every action examined. He'd become weary of the constant attention.

Iben was shrewd enough to know his father was failing in health and he was being groomed to become the face of the throne. He had two younger brothers. Netin, the closest to him in age, had been born with a crooked back. His mind, however, was blade-sharp and when Gerit had realized his quickness, Netin had been placed in charge of raising taxes and dispensing of the coin in the demesne. The youngest brother who was strong and skilled in arms would no doubt become Parian's commander when he was older and more experienced.

Iben had begged leave to visit his sister. After three moons of pleading, he'd received reluctant approval. Continuing to Aldea to catch a glimpse of Kedie Lyta was a spur of the moment decision. He was more than ready for an adventure in another demesne instead of leading a constricted and boring life at home.

After a long day with only one brief stop to eat and water the horses, Iben and Nirk reached their destination as the sun set behind a row of deep- blue hills. Tela had married an erle from the demesne of Delis, settled down on his land, and produced seven children in nine summers. Iben and Tela were ten summers apart in age. She'd raised him after their mother had become frail. Two more girls had quite destroyed the kedura's health and the woman had died when Iben reached five summers. Because of this background, he'd always been closer to Tela than to his other brothers and sisters.

When they reached the estate, a groom took the horses and a servant escorted the two men into the house, Tela was waiting for them in her solar. As she hadn't seen her brother since her marriage, she embraced him tightly. Then she held him away to study his face.

'You look so much like Father,' she said. 'I thought when you were young, you resembled Mother and, mayhap, you did inherit her nose.'

'Lucky for me,' Iben said, 'considering Father's great beak. You look well, Tela. I expected you'd be a worn-out drab after bearing seven children.'

'And number eight is on the way.' Tela smiled as she patted her rounded belly. 'Unlike Mother, I am very healthy and have no trouble carrying babies. You must both be cold and hungry. I'll have you taken to your chamber to prepare for supper.' She nodded to Nirk and then called for a maid.

Tela's lord was gruff-speaking but good-hearted. During dinner, he said little but he smiled tenderly at every word from his talkative wife, making Iben certain that Tela would produce even more children in the future. He was glad that the two were so happy with each other and that the estate was prosperous.

The rabble of nieces and nephews was delighted to meet an uncle. Unruly children swarmed around Iben tugging at his hands and clothes and demanding rides on his back and wild games of hiding and throwing balls. After two morns, he was tired and grumbled to Nirk about being constantly pestered.

'That's your own fault, Kedir. With children, you have to set limits.' He spoke firmly to a little boy who was jumping up and down and yelling for Iben to play a game of skittles with him. 'That's quite enough noise from you, lad. Sit down on the floor and behave or you'll see the back of my hand.'

To Iben's annoyance, the child did as he was bid.

The estate was located near the border of Delis and Aldea. In three more morns, Iben was more than ready to leave. While he was sorrowful to be parted from his sister, he was delighted to be separated from her rowdy brood.

He begged his sister to say that he was still with her if their father inquired about him and Tela agreed to his plea. 'I can quite understand why you want to see Kedie Lyta ahead of time. She might be exceeding fat and ill-favoured with warts on her face. You don't want to be surprised by her looks.'

Iben intended to travel to the town of Aldeton where he would wait for a chance to see Lyta. Surely the kedie visited her people or rode nearby. He knew that the town lay on a snug harbour close to the castle. To explain his cultured accent, he'd pass himself off as the youngest of six sons of a Parian erle. He'd tell people he was down on his luck because his father lacked sufficient coin and he hoped to be hired as a man at arms.

As they rode into Aldeton, Iben observed that it was a prosperous-looking town with several streets of tidy houses and a fleet of fishing boats in the harbour. The two men took lodgings at The Grey Goose, an inn beside the busy town square. The place seemed clean and the landlord was a smiling talkative fellow. He gave orders for their horses to be fed and watered and invited them for a drink. Iben suspected that despite the ordinary clothes he'd acquired from one of Tela's servants, the innkeeper suspected he was a nobleman with plenty of coin. He resolved to keep tight hold of his pouch.

The main chamber of the inn was crowded with men talking to each other in agitated voices. 'What's the matter with them?' Iben asked, gesturing at the noisy drinkers. 'Everyone seems angry.'

The landlord shook his head. 'That they are. One of our own was murdered up at the castle.'

Iben pricked up his ears at the mention of the castle. 'What happened?'

The man leaned closer. 'Some Falgans came here to see Kedie Lyta and they held a tourney of different games. Our man, Borut, won the archery contest but this Falgan villain killed him and stole his winning purse.'

'That's bad.' Iben shook his head. 'Was the culprit caught?'

'Yes, he was. But what made things worse is the castle lords are doing nothing about the matter. We need the man punished right soon.' He nodded at a tall fair-haired fellow waving his arms in the corner. 'Yalt over there wants action. '

'To do what?'

'I don't know what he has in mind but everyone always listens to him. He's a leader in this place.' He paused as Yalt pushed through the crowd and came near them.

'We need more ale.' He turned to Iben. 'Passing through town?'

'We'll stay here a few morns. My name's Iben and this is Nirk.'

'I'm Yalt.' His blue-eyed gaze surveyed them. 'You came here at a difficult time. There might be trouble.'

Iben frowned. 'What sort of trouble?'

'We're off to the castle to demand a murderer be turned over to us. Our man, Borut, was killed by a Falgan villain, We want the fellow hanged in full view in the town square.'

'Will you be armed when you go to the castle?' Nirk asked.

Yalt grimaced. 'Blades mainly but some will carry pitchforks or whatever they can find.' He waited as the landlord poured several cups of ale. 'We'll be ready to leave in an hour.'

Iben's hand went to his sword. 'Another weapon might be useful.'

Nirk said, 'I'm guessing that you plan a show of force and not an attack on the castle.'

Yalt regarded him with an interested look. 'You sound like a man with some fighting experience. You're right. If we show we're serious enough, I might get an audience with Kedie Lyta. I trust she's like her mother who was always straight with us.' He lifted the tray to carry it back to his friends. 'At least, that's my hope.'

'What a stroke of luck,' Iben said to Nirk. 'If we go along with this mob, I may see the kedie even sooner than I thought.'

'You're assuming she'll come to talk with the townsfolk. What if her advisers tell her to ignore them and their demands?'

Iben shrugged. 'I'll take that chance. And think of another idea if this one doesn't work out.' He pointed at Nirk's cup. 'Finish your ale. You must always be on time for a riot.'

Chapter Forty-Four

Wilus had hurried to the pavilion. When he arrived, Lyta placed a hand on his arm. 'Please make sure my aunt goes back to the castle. I must stay to see what happens here.'

'You should accompany her.' Wilus wore an anxious expression.

But Lyta was firm in her desire to stay and Wilus took Vea's arm to lead her away.

While they were talking, two brown-robed prentices had run from the crowd. The taller one knelt beside Borut and lifted the guard's wrist. Lyta was painfully reminded of her mother's accident as she watched the young man checking for signs of life. When the shorter prentice left the field at a trot, Lyta assumed she was going to fetch the magian.

Druck ordered all the men at arms to line up and hold out their blades. He asked Josik and Trevin to study each weapon and each tunic. The guilty man might have wiped the blade on a garment to get rid of blood stains. Then Druck took two guards to the edge of the field where the grass was longer. With their heads down, they searched the ground. Lyta guessed they might be looking for a blade that had been tossed away.

When Magian Domen arrived, he confirmed what she had suspected. Borut had been knifed through the heart. Since all the men present were experienced soldiers, everyone would have known the best place to strike for instant death.

Suddenly Druck stopped and waved a blade above his head. 'I have it,' he called out. 'Which man does not have a blade on him?'

Three men were not carrying weapons: two Aldeans and a Falgan. As suspects, they were marched from the field and Lyta assumed they'd be taken to the gatehouse. Borut's body was wrapped in a canvas sheet and carried off as well. Lyta saw tears on the face of the man nearest her. Borut had been a much respected man and Druck's second in command.

Lyta told herself not to weep. She'd always liked Borut, a rough and ready man, built like a bear but with a kind heart. He'd often been in charge of the party that had accompanied her on rides outside the castle. When she was younger, he'd always noticed if she'd become tired or cold. He'd given Lyta his own cloak when the wind grew strong. And one morn, he'd even picked wild flowers for her to take back to her mother.

She stopped Druck as he followed his friend's body. 'Does Borut have family nearby?'

'His mother and sisters live in the town, Kedie.'

'Can you make sure they get the purse he won today? I hope it's still in his pouch. If not, I will provide another. The coin may be needed to bury him.'

'It will be done, Kedie.' He bowed and strode away.

Quilin offered his arm to Lyta. 'Now it's time you returned to the castle.' He nodded at the group of Falgans who were walking back to their tents at the far end of the field. 'I don't like the look of that lot. If one of them killed Borut, then we are in for more trouble.' He grinned wryly. 'My tourney of sorts wasn't such a good idea after all.'

'You didn't know this was going to happen.'

Quilin sighed. 'I should have been more aware of what could go wrong.'

Back in her chamber, Amia unlaced Lyta's green robe. Obela fussed around her, trying to persuade her to drink hot wine for her nerves.

'You've had a nasty shock seeing that poor man slain before your very eyes. Just sip a little of this.' Her nurse held out a cup.

'My nerves are fine,' Lyta snapped. 'I don't want the wine. All I need is a little peace before supper.'

'I saw rells sitting in a row on the wall this morning,' said Obela, wagging her grey head.

'That's not unusual,' said Lyta. 'People often feed them down there.'

'But there were three rells. The old ones knew they were birds of omen.' Obela's tone was heavy with dread. 'And so far, we've had two deaths. Will the Falgan lord be the third?'

'I certainly hope not,' Lyta replied as she lay down. 'Magian Domen will do all he can to save him.'

Later after she was dressed, Amia announced that Druck had come to report. He was shown into the solar.

'What news?' Lyta asked.

'My Lady, the blade in the grass belonged to one of the Falgans in custody. He confessed to the crime. And he had Borut's purse in his pouch.'

'Was this man also in the archery contest?'

'He was the one Borut beat in the final round.'

Lyta thought for a moment. 'Then the killing might have been from simple jealousy and greed, not something more sinister.'

'Mayhap but the bad feeling between them and us has got worse. I have ten men already in my cells for fighting.'

'What do you suggest we should do to keep the peace?'

Druck sighed. 'Pray to Lady Moon for Lord Darik to survive his wound so they can all pack up and go home.'

Although Lyta had never liked the commander as a person, she felt sorry for him now. His face was drawn and pale and he seemed to have aged ten summers since her mother died. Of course, he'd served Halia since her wedding and respected her greatly. In fact, Lyta suspected he'd even loved her.

'Sit down and tell me what we should do with the guilty man.' Lyta pushed a glass and a flask of wine close to his hand. 'I can't keep calling him the murderer or the guilty man. What is his name?'

Druck sat and drank before he said, 'Kedie, he's called Trul and I know exactly what I'd do with him. Chop off his head tonight and stick it on the wall first thing in the morn.' He frowned as he continued. 'That might make matters worse, with Falga but he must be sentenced and punished. Nobody in Aldea gets away with murder. My Lady, after you discuss this matter with your lords, I'll carry out whatever punishment you decide is fitting.'

After Druck had left, Lyta pondered her dilemma. He was right. An execution might make things worse. However, she didn't believe murder would be sanctioned in the demesne of Falga either. She wondered how much force had been used to extract the confession from Trul. And then she wondered what her mother would have done in this situation.

Quilin sat on one side of her at supper and Wilus on the other. They had both heard about the Falgan's confession. 'Now what do we do with the man?' Lyta asked.

'Let's discuss it tomorrow morn in council. There are other matters we should talk about as well,' said Wilus. 'And we must consult Stor. He can speak for Darik.'

That night, Lyta finally slept after her usual period of wakefulness. She had an extraordinarily vivid dream. Her mother called her name and Lyta went into the solar. Seeing Halia in her usual spot by the window, Lyta burst into tears.

Her mother held out both hands. ‘Don’t be sad, child. I was sorry to leave you but I’m with your father now.’

Through her sobs, Lyta tried to say that she needed her mother’s advice. ‘I don’t know enough to be a good ruler like you.’

‘Well, I didn’t either at first. The lessons were hard to learn and I spent many sleepless nights. But, child, you must have confidence in yourself. You have a resourceful mind and good advisors.’

Lyta clutched her mother’s hands. They were warm and comforting. ‘I miss you dearly.’

Halia smiled. ‘I wish we’d spent longer together. But you must rest. The morrow will be hard.’ She smoothed Lyta’s hair. ‘Sleep now, my child.’

In the morn, Lyta woke, feeling more rested and for once, hungry for repast. Obela smiled with satisfaction as she removed the empty platter. ‘You will feel much better for this food. What did I always tell you about repast?’

‘That it is the most important meal of the day.’ Lyta mimicked her nurse’s tone of voice. ‘And it sets you up for your work.’

Obela snorted. ‘I am right. You don’t need to mock me.’

Her lords were in the chamber when Lyta arrived. Trevin and Josik were talking with their heads close together. Trevin’s face was serious when he turned to greet her.

‘Is something else amiss?’ Lyta asked him.

‘Last night I received a messenger from home. My wife and my eldest son have both been stricken with a sudden illness and may not recover.’

‘Then you must return at once,’ said Lyta. ‘I am much saddened by this news. Take heart. I’ll pray to Lady Moon for them and you.’

‘Thanks for your kind words,’ Trevin said. ‘I don’t like to leave you here in such uncertainty. And I hate to give Darik the chance to accuse me of running away from him. If he gets better, he will repeat the charge that I deliberately wounded him.’

‘Let him,’ said Josik. ‘I will deny it loudly and as often as necessary. And I’ll find others who saw what really happened in that glade.’

Trevin rose from the table. ‘Then with your permission, m

My Lady, I will leave you. Send word of any further business.’

‘And you must send word about your family,’ Lyta said. ‘We all hope they will be recovering their health when you arrive.’

After Trevin had left the chamber, Josik said, ‘He is also worried about Firt who’s been causing trouble at the estate. That marriage to Adina was an unfortunate match since it gave Trevin a treacherous son-in-law. His own boy is not as forceful as his father. He likes books more than horses and reading more than governing.’

‘I wouldn’t trust Firt either,’ said Quilin. ‘I still remember his cowardly actions when I fought him and have the scar on my leg to prove it.’

‘If his father restored him as heir in Delis,’ said Lyta, ‘he’d go back to that demesne and make Trevin’s life more peaceful.’

‘Never going to happen,’ said Wilus. ‘Baldus was disgusted with Firt’s behaviour in that fight with Quilin. He won’t restore him. After all, he has other sons and Fultis, the next in line, is a suitor for your hand, My Lady.’

Lyta nodded. She didn’t want to be reminded of Firt whom she detested or of the kedirs waiting on her doorstep. ‘Now, what do we do about Trul?’

In the discussion that followed, Wilus and Josik said the man should pay for his crime by being beheaded immediately. 'This is our usual punishment for the crime and it demonstrates that murder is not acceptable in Aldea.'

'But he's not from Aldea,' said Quilin. 'And we know things might get worse with his death.'

'They'll get worse if he doesn't die,' said Josik.' My men tell me folk in the town are demanding his life for Borut's. If tempers rise further, we could have an uprising on our hands.'

'Then we are at an impasse,' said Quilin. 'We must decide one way or the other. Indecision will be seen as a sign of weakness.'

Lyta wondered once more why she'd wanted to rule Aldea alone. These three men with many summers of wise governing under their tunics were still having trouble making up their minds. What chance did she have?

'We could stone him,' said Josik with a wry smile. 'That would be an appropriate sentence under the circumstances.'

Quilin raised an eyebrow. 'I hope that wasn't a serious suggestion.'

'It would involve more people.' said Wilus. 'And it has been done here.' He nodded at Lyta. 'In your grandsire's time, for crimes that affected a whole community, the perpetrators were punished that way.'

'I could never agree to stoning,' said Lyta. 'If Trul must die, then it should be a quick and sure death.'

'I really don't see the point in any more debate,' said Josik. 'The man has confessed his crime. He must appear before us and hear his sentence. Then he must lose his head. End of tale.' He banged both open hands on the table.

A sudden rap on the door made all heads turn. Quilin opened the door and spoke briefly to someone standing outside. Then he closed it and returned to the table. 'Druck is on his way to see us.'

'I hope it's not more bad news,' said Josik, pouring wine for himself and the others. 'We've had enough.'

Druck's eyes were hard and he had high colour in his face when he entered the chamber. He stood by the door. 'My Lady, I've just received information from one of my men who was in Aldeton. A mob from the town is on its way up the hill. They are carrying pitchforks and blades and are in an ugly mood. They want us to hand over Borut's killer to be hanged in the town square.'

Lyta couldn't imagine the peaceful townsfolk behaving in this way. They'd never shown any hostility to her mother or to her. 'Are they really a threat to us?'

Druck nodded grimly. 'I believe they mean what they say. I have ordered the drawbridge to be raised and our gates to be closed.'

Chapter Forty-Five

Archis Druck nodded to Lyta. 'With your permission, Lady, I'll return to the battlements. You'll be quite safe here in the keep. I will send word of any further developments.' He departed with a swirl of his green cloak.

The councillors looked at each other. Wilus tugged his beard. 'Why are the townsfolk rising up like this? Someone must be leading them.'

'And I reckon I know who,' said Quilin to Josik. 'Remember two summers ago when there was a riot in the square? The man behind it was called Yalt. If he's still in town, I bet he's the culprit.'

'What happened?' Lyta asked. 'I must have been in Falga at the time.'

Josik turned to Lyta. 'The fellow complained that some merchants charged too much for their wares. Your Lady Mother brought him and the merchants together and they struck a deal. Halia said Yalt had a strong sense of justice. But since he was too quick to take action, he should be watched.'

'So should we talk with this Yalt?' Wilus asked.

'Not until we've decided what to do with Borut's killer. We are the rightful ones to dispense justice not some rabble from the town.' Josik snorted loudly and drank the rest of his wine.

'We face an unusual situation,' Quilin said. 'Kedie Lyta is the heir of Aldea but until she's crowned in a sevenday, she's not the actual ruler. Under our laws, she's not yet able to pronounce sentence on anybody. So who makes the decision about punishment in the meantime?'

'The council,' said Wilus. 'By vote.'

'Majority or unanimous?' Josik asked

'I've read much of the history of Aldea,' said Wilus. 'And I recall that in the time of Kedie Lyta's grandsire, he became the heir when both his parents died of the fever. Since Alik had reached only ten summers, the council acted on his behalf. They used majority voting.'

'Then let's do the same,' said Josik downing his wine. 'Domen has sent a message regretting his absence so we'll vote without him but I suggest that Kedie Lyta should cast a vote and have her opinion noted.' He dipped his quill into the silver ink flask.

When the others nodded in agreement, Lyta felt a chill settle deep in her bones. She didn't want to be responsible for the death of any person, even a murderer. What would her mother have advised? She recalled Halia's words to act with her mind and not be swayed by her heart. Lyta straightened her spine against the high back of the chair. 'I will vote,' she said in a clear voice.

Wilus' voice and face were grave. 'I declare that Trul of Falga, the confessed murderer of Borut of Aldea be brought before us to hear his sentence. His execution shall then be carried out at daylight the next morn. All those in favour of this decision raise your right hand.'

Josik's hand shot up and more slowly Quilin and Wilus followed his example. When the three men turned to her, Lyta took a deep breath and raised her right hand as well.

Quilin nodded to Lyta as though he recognized her inner turmoil and lifted a flask, poured wine, and handed her a glass. 'Drink this, Kedie,' he said. 'I'd like to tell you that governing gets easier with time but I'm afraid it doesn't. You will always be faced with difficult decisions.'

Lyta sipped the wine. Then she placed the glass on the table and said, 'As my mother did, we must deliver the sentence in the great hall with witnesses. I think it would be wise to include some of the townsfolk.'

Josik frowned. 'That might be dangerous, Kedie.'

'Not if they leave their weapons outside the gates.'

'And the Falgans?' Quilin asked. 'What if they object to the sentence?'

Wilus leaned across the table. 'As the Falgan spokesman, Stor must hear our judgment. And if Darik is well enough, he must also be informed.'

Lyta smiled briefly. 'Before our meeting, the magian told me Darik's condition has improved a little.'

'Some good news at last,' said Wilus. 'Let's send for Stor and speak to him first. We can't announce anything to the townsfolk unless we get his co-operation.'

Stor took the news of their decision with an expressionless face. Then after a short silence, he said, 'I must be satisfied of the man's guilt. Kedur Ulit will need proof and the assurance that he confessed of his own accord. If Lord Darik and I are clear about these two things, we will accept your judgment.'

'Druck will take you to Trul,' said Wilus. 'Is Darik well enough to understand this matter?'

'He is better this morn. Your magian is an excellent healer.' Stor stood up. 'After I've seen your commander and Trul and reported to Lord Darik, I'll return with our word.'

The door shut behind him with a decisive clunk. Josik cleared his throat and said, 'How confident are we that Trul confessed of his own accord? Druck's methods are sometimes…' His voice trailed off as he looked at Lyta.

'I understand your meaning.' Lyta forced her voice not to tremble as she thought about torture. 'But aside from questioning Druck's methods, Trul had Borut's winning purse in his pouch.'

'True,' said Quilin. 'Let's hope nobody placed it there.'

Lyta sighed. She wondered if anything was ever clear. Rather than being black or white this whole situation had become several discouraging shades of grey. 'While we wait to hear from Stor, I need to know what's happening at newgate.'

'I'll go and see for myself, Kedie.' Quilin pushed back his chair.

Wilus and Josik decided to accompany him. When Lyta stood up, Wilus looked alarmed. 'You must stay here, My Lady. You cannot be placed in danger.'

The inaction annoyed Lyta. If she were kedura, she'd go to the gate no matter what her advisors thought. But she didn't wish to provoke conflict with them now. 'We'll meet again after our meal.'

***

Lyta ate her dinner with her aunts in the solar. Neither Vea nor Jona had been informed of the mob at the gate. She kept it a secret so as not to alarm them. The maids were clearing the napery when Wilus arrived in the antechamber. Lyta left the solar to speak to him.

'First of all, the townsfolk are still at the gate. As I suspected, they are led by Yalt. I can't see them staying long without food and water but I could be wrong. Druck has taken Stor to see Trul. The commander told me that several guards saw the coin purse in the culprit's pouch. So, we await for Stor to come back. '

When Lyta returned to the solar, she tried to smile brightly at her aunts as though nothing was wrong.

Vea frowned. 'When she brought our meal, Fulia, told us about the Falgan murderer and the anger in town. What's happening now? Are they about to storm the gate?

Jona clutched her bosom. 'Will we be slain in our beds?'

'Don't be ridiculous, sister. Our dear Lyta will calm the townsfolk down.' '

'It's true that I'd like to talk to them. But don't be worried, aunts. Druck has everything under control.' Lyta hoped this was a correct statement. .

The council meeting resumed when Stor sent word that he was ready. He entered the chamber and spoke without sitting down. 'Lord Darik would rather take Trul back to Falga to be sentenced by Kedur Ulit. However, since the man is guilty of committing a crime in your demesne, we will abide by your decision.'

Wilus thanked him for understanding the situation. Then he added in a more hesitant tone. 'Will your men understand this judgment and stay calm?'

'They will,' Stor answered. He bowed to Lyta before marching from the chamber.

Josik let out a long breath. 'I wouldn't dare to disobey him.'

Quilin turned to Lyta. 'We must pronounce sentence tonight before supper. Would you like us to take care of the procedure, Kedie?'

'Thank you. Godit will know how the hall should be arranged. Send word when you want me to attend.'

Lyta went to her bedchamber. When she was certain that her lords and her servants were occupied, she opened the door of the antechamber and beckoned to Jer. 'I wish to get to newgate without being observed.'

He regarded her doubtfully. 'My Lady, everyone will know you in those fine clothes.'

Lyta darted inside the chamber. Amia's plain grey cloak lay folded in a corner. She grabbed the garment and pulled the hood over her head. 'Come with me but walk beside me.'

'Kedie Lyta, that don't feel right.'

'Quick, now. We must get there before anyone misses me.'

Lyta kept her head down as they hurried through oldgate. She wondered how she could avoid Druck and his company of guards. Then she stopped and reconsidered her position. She was not the kedura yet and could not pronounce sentence but as the kedie of Aldea she had precedence over the erles and everybody else in the demesne. That gave her the right to speak to her townsfolk without asking for permission.

Lyta didn't believe the people of Aldeton would harm her. Since Yalt had listened to Halia, then surely he'd be willing to talk with her daughter without any violence. Lyta threw back her hood and took the last steps to the gatehouse. One of the guards on the wall saw her first. He coughed loudly to gain Druck's attention and then pointed behind him. Druck whirled around and opened his mouth.

Lyta called out to him before he could utter a word. 'I wish to speak to Yalt.' She entered the gatehouse and climbed the inner steps to join Druck on the wall. 'Which one is he?' From her present position, she saw people bunched together on the far edge of the moat.

Druck frowned and stayed silent for a few minutes. Lyta concentrated hard, hoping to catch any of his thoughts. Aha! Druck was uncertain about his tenure as commander if he disobeyed her order. Then he bowed. 'Of course, Kedie. Even though I think this may be unwise, I will instruct the man to come closer.'

He took a few steps until he was directly opposite the townsfolk. 'Yalt, step forward.'

A tall fair-haired fellow raised both hands above his head 'I'm Yalt. What do you want?'

'Your Kedie wishes to speak with you.'

The man laughed. 'Is she going to leap over the water or shall I swim across the moat?'

Druck spluttered with rage as he started to answer, but Lyta cut him off. She called out, 'I will have the bridge lowered if you swear to leave your arms behind and tell your companions to remain peacefully on that side.'

'My Lady, this is most unwise.' Druck's face was flushed and his hand grasped his sword hilt.

Yalt placed a hand over his heart and replied, 'I will swear to it.'

'Archis Druck, please lower the bridge.' Although Lyta's voice was steady, her heart thumped wildly in her chest. Was she doing the right thing in speaking to this townsman face to face? Would it have been wiser to order the bridge to be lowered for him to cross and then asked for it to be raised it again? Mayhap, but she didn't want to change her mind. That could be seen as assign of weakness and distrust.

Druck sighed but he gave the order to the nearest guards who slowly pulled the chains to allow the bridge to fall. Lyta waited in silence as the bridge creaked into place. Yalt spoke to the people around him before striding to the far edge. He held up two empty hands to indicate he carried no weapon.

Lyta knew this was her chance to restore the traditional friendship between the castle and the town. But would she be able to find the right words?

'Please help me, Mother,' she whispered as Yalt crossed the bridge.

Chapter Forty-Six

Lyta placed her trembling hands together. She must present herself to all the observers of this scene as a calm and collected person. Yalt paused after he'd climbed the steps to the wall and spoke to Druck. 'Do you want to check me for weapons or do you believe I come unarmed?'

Before Druck could give an order, Lyta stepped forward. 'No need,' she said. 'This man gave me his word.' She smiled at Yalt. 'Let us walk away a little in order to speak in private.'

Yalt's eyebrows shot up but he remained silent as he joined Lyta out of earshot of Druck and his guards. Jer stood behind her, shuffling his feet. 'You can go too,' she said to him. 'I will be quite safe.'

Yalt grinned. 'My Lady, do they really think I'm likely to attack you?'

Lyta looked hard at him. 'These men are all sworn with their lives to protect me. You have not taken that oath.' She gestured at the ledge, which was wide enough for sitting. 'Let's talk here.'

She studied the man as he waited for her to sit first. His voice and actions were those of an educated person. 'Did you mayhap train at the Erudence?'

Yalt shrugged. 'I put in seven summers there, Lady, and then decided it was not the life for me. I wanted to do more than teaching and healing.'

'What is your work now?' Lyta asked.

'I craft precious metals. Mainly gold but also silver and copper. It gives me satisfaction to make something beautiful and coin to feed my family.' He pointed at Lyta's silver necklet. 'I made that for your mother three summers ago.'

Lyta touched the delicate chain of intertwined flowers and blinked hard to prevent any tears from falling. Then she cleared her throat. 'I understand your desire for justice to be carried out in the town but my council has reached their decision. The Falgan, Trul, has confessed to killing Borut. He will be sentenced to death this evening in the great hall. The execution will take place tomorrow morn.' She focused intently on Yalt's face. Would she be able to catch this man's thoughts?

To her surprise, she met a blank wall. Somehow, Yalt could stop her from entering his mind. Was he aware that she had even attempted the act? Once when she'd tried to catch the thoughts of the chief priest of the Star Children, the man had known of her intrusion and rebuked her. Lyta forced her own mind back to the present. Concentrate on what's happening now.

Yalt's eyes were steady, displaying no signs of distress. 'Forgive me saying this, Lady, but your council is taking too long to decide the man's fate. We already heard that the Falgan confessed to the killing and we believe in swift justice.'

Lyta's voice grew cold. 'You are totally unware of what matters had to be considered first.' She had no intention of explaining the complicated situation to Yalt. Her tone softened a little. 'If you support this sentencing, then choose ten folk from the town to accompany you to the castle to witness it. Of course, they will attend without any weapons as is our custom on these occasions.'

Yalt paused. His blue-eyed gaze regarded Lyta gravely. Then he seemed to make up his mind. 'Many thanks, Kedie. I will come and bring ten with me. Will your commander inform us of the correct time to arrive?' He smiled suddenly. 'Do we have to swim or will the bridge stay down?'

'The bridge will remain lowered. I never believed you and your fellow townsfolk posed a threat to me. And I do understand their concern for justice. Borut was one of yours but he was also one of my men.'

Yalt stared again at Lyta as though he was assessing the level of her truthfulness and then he nodded. You are very like your mother, Kedie.'

The compliment pleased Lyta. If she became only half the ruler her mother had been, she'd be content. She pointed toward Druck. 'It's time for you to leave. My commander grows anxious.'

Yalt bowed and then walked away. Lyta waited until he had crossed the drawbridge. Before Druck could order it to be raised again, Lyta called to him. 'Let the bridge stay down. There will be no more trouble.'

Druck frowned. 'Then, Kedie, I will post extra guards just in case.'

'Ten townsfolk will come with Yalt for the sentencing. I have told him they must be unarmed.'

'Let's hope their word is good, Kedie.'

Let us indeed hope so, Lyta thought as she descended the steps. She'd have to defend her actions when she met the erles back at the castle. After all, they'd warned her about meeting Yalt. From their brief talk together, Lyta could understand why her mother had said Yalt should be watched. He was a clever man with an engaging manner but she sensed a forcefulness behind his manner.

As she made her way back to the castle, Lyta realized she must inform her lords at once of this meeting. It would be politic to do it before Druck spoke to them. She took a deep breath at the thought they might condemn her action taken without any consultation. However, to her mind, this had been a step in learning about governance. And then she must visit her aunts to make sure they weren't agitated. Mayhap attending the sentencing tonight would calm their fears.

Chapter Forty-Seven

The townsfolk charged along the road to the castle, waving pitchforks, blades, and makeshift lances. Iben even saw a garden hoe. Nirk, who'd taken part in real battles, was hard put to belong to this unruly mob. He shook his head at their lack of organization. 'What would you father say if he could see you now?' he muttered to Iben.

His kedir laughed. 'For once, Father would be struck dumb.'

Since the drawbridge had been raised, the crowd halted beside the moat. Yalt strode to the edge of the ditch and called to the row of guards on the other side. 'I want to talk to Druck.'

'That's Archis Druck to the likes of you,' a guard yelled back.

Iben pushed his way forward until he could see what was happening. Nirk followed him. 'The commander would be the one on the wall, wearing the long green cloak,' he whispered to Iben. 'He looks like a hard man.'

Iben nodded, his gaze intent on Yalt.

The green cloaked man strode forward. 'Return to your homes. If you disperse peacefully right now, we will take no action.'

'Ooh, we're trembling in our boots,' shouted a voice from the back of the crowd. 'Give us the Falgan murderer. He will hang in the town square for what he did to our Borut.'

'You have no authority to dispense justice,' Druck stated in a loud clear voice. 'That authority belongs to the Kedie and her lords.'

Yalt stepped forward a pace and shouted, 'Then why isn't the Falgan's head already stuck on the wall beside you? That would show true and visible justice. If the erles lack the balls to kill the man, then we'll do it for them.'

Loud cheering followed his pronouncement. From his vantage point, Iben noted that the commander flushed deep crimson and his right hand clutched the hilt of his sword. He said something to the three guards nearest to him before leaving the wall. Mayhap, he was off to the castle to inform the kedie and her lords about the noisy trouble at their gate.

'Stay calm,' called Yalt to his people. 'We don't want them shooting at us.'

'I'd like to stick this here fork into one of those there guards. I have my eye on the big fat one,' said the man who'd made the earlier comment. 'That would make him stop laughing at us.'

'No matter,' said Yalt. 'Their arrows can do more damage than our sharp sticks. Let's see what message Druck brings back.'

When Archis Druck returned, he walked through the gatehouse to speak to Yalt. Iben used his elbows to push his way even closer to hear their words.

'Justice will be served. The kedie and her lords are in council right now debating the matter,' the commander said.

'What's there to debate?' shouted the burly man. 'The blasted Falgan killed poor Borut so now we will kill the blasted Falgan. Debate ended.'

'There are matters to consider that you people can never understand,' said Druck, sticking his large nose in the air. 'Leave the dispensing of justice to those with wisdom and experience. Return to your homes at once.'

A chorus of boos greeted his words. A piece of horse dung flew through the air. It hit the fat guard on his helmet before dribbling down his face. Someone yelled, 'Shit to the shits!' and the townsfolk roared with laughter.

The guard yelled and lifted his bow. Yalt whirled around. 'No more chucking dung!' he called. 'We must show them we are also men of wisdom and good sense.'

When Druck spoke to the guard, the man dropped his arm and glared across the moat. After he'd wiped his face, his mouth shaped silent curses.

A white-haired man standing near Yalt tugged his arm. 'Now what do we do, boy? We can't stand here all day and night waiting for a response?'

'Stay calm, Grandsire. They will respond. If Kedie Lyta's like her mother, she'll come down to speak to us.'

'You can't be sure of that,' said the old man. 'My feet hurt with all this standing around. Let's all go home.'

Iben edged close enough to talk to Yalt. 'What if the girl is not like her mother?' he asked. 'She might stay up at the castle and ignore you.'

'Then I've gambled and lost,' said Yalt. 'Have you never wagered all on one last roll of the dice?'

Iben laughed. 'The only time I did that I was very young and lost all my coin. Now I make more cautious wagers.' He noticed some movement beside the gate. 'Look, somebody's coming.'

Yalt sighed in relief. 'It's Kedie Lyta. She's seen sense. Now we must talk if that bastard Druck will let me reach her. We can hardly converse across the moat by shouting.'

Iben saw a slender figure in a brown cloak, the hood pulled over her head. She was accompanied by a single guard. The girl was too far away for him to discern her features. He hoped Druck would escort her to top of the wall. Then he would have a clearer view.

The crowd murmured as they watched the kedie and her commander appear on the battlements. Lyta threw back her hood.

Iben felt as though he'd been struck in the chest by a heavy blow. By the Sun of Suns, this was the most beautiful girl he'd ever seen in his life. He sucked in his breath as he gazed at her shining black hair and perfect features. Nirk nudged him in the ribs but Iben's gaze was unable to turn from the kedie. His mind was decided in that instant. Lyta must become his wife.

Druck walked away until he was directly opposite the townsfolk. 'Yalt, step forward.'

'I'm Yalt. What do you want?'

'Your Kedie wishes to speak with you.'

Yalt laughed. 'Is she going to leap over the water or shall I swim across?'

Iben leaned forward to hear Lyta's answer. Would her voice be as lovely as her face? She said, 'I will have the bridge lowered if you swear to leave your arms behind and tell your companions to remain peacefully on that side.'

Iben breathed out in relief. Her words were sensible and her voice was low and sweet. He was jarred by Druck's harsh tones. 'My Lady, this is most unwise.' The commander's hand went once again for his sword.

Yalt placed a hand over his heart and called out. 'I will swear to it.'

Lyta's words were clear. 'Archis Druck, please lower the bridge.'

Druck gave the order to the guards below him. They slowly pulled the chains to allow the bridge to fall.

As the chains groaned and the bridge creaked down, Yalt spoke to the old man. 'Don't fret, Grandsire, I will be safe over there.'

Both sides waited in silence for the bridge to drop into place. Then Yalt strode over it and disappeared into the gatehouse. Within minutes, he appeared on the wall near Druck and his men. Iben couldn't hear what was said but he saw Lyta draw Yalt away from the others and then dismiss her own guard. She and Yalt spoke together.

How Iben wished he could hear their conversation. He didn't think they were arguing as there was no show of anger on either side. He willed the talking to last a long time to allow him to gaze more on Lyta's face.

Nirk tugged his arm. 'What in Sun is the matter? You're standing like an idiot with your mouth open and your eyes all vacant.' He stared hard at Iben and then grimaced. 'Oh no! Please tell me you haven't fallen for that wench?'

Iben spoke without taking his eyes from Lyta. 'Isn't she the most beautiful girl you have ever seen?'

'No,' said Nirk. 'As wenches go, she's pretty enough but too skinny and tall for my taste.'

Iben clenched both fists. 'Skinny! How can you say such a thing? She's as slender as a willow wand in spring and exactly the right height.'

'Taller than you,' said Nirk bluntly. 'Iben, you've seen the girl and that's the reason we came to Aldea. Now let's go home before we get more involved in this rabble's affairs. Matters could get messy.'

But Iben ignored him. Too soon for him, Lyta and Yalt walked back to Druck. Iben was surprised that after Yalt crossed the bridge, it stayed down. Had Lyta ordered this?

The townsfolk crowded around Yalt. 'What news?' asked the old man.

'The Falgan will be sentenced to death tonight in the great hall. I'm permitted to bring ten witnesses to the ceremony. Unarmed, of course.'

Iben wished he could be one of the ten but as a stranger, he had no standing in Aldeton.

'Who will go with you?' sked the man who'd thrown the dung.

'I'll decide back at the tavern. Let's go. I've worked up a thirst doing this business.'

When the mob surged after him, Iben and Nirk dropped back. 'Well,' said Nirk. 'Are we going returning to Parian on the morn?'

'Not before I've got inside the castle.' said Iben.

Nirk shook his head. 'By the True Sun, instant love has turned your wits. Iben, this isn't wise. One of those nobles up there might recognize you. As Tela said, you bear a strong resemblance to your father and they all know him.'

Iben glared at his companion. 'I must see Lyta again. Whatever the risk.'

Chapter Forty-Eight

Lyta entered the great hall behind Magian Domen and her erles. Although she stared straight ahead, she caught glimpses of the scene from the corners of her eyes. A large log blazed in the hearth and flaming torches lined the walls. The flickering light was reflected in the long row of battle shields hanging from the rafters. The banners on the walls stirred in the puffs of warm air, rising from the fireplace.

The tables had been pushed back to allow standing room for those present. Except for some kitchen staff, the castle workers were in attendance. Lyta caught a glimpse of Yalt in the middle of his townsfolk. The Falgans in their red and black garments stood in one area with a row of Aldean guards facing them. Like Lyta, her men were dressed in the green and silver colours of Aldea.

Lyta stopped at the end of the hall. The Kedura's large carved throne stood empty. It would not be occupied until she had received the Moon Crown in a sevenday. She moved toward the chair placed at the right side of the throne. Out of the corner of her eye, she glimpsed her aunts seated at the end of the row of officials. They had assured her they wished to attend. .

Into the silence, Lord Wilus's voice rang throughout the hall. 'I declare that this sentencing court is now in session.' With a rustle of silk clothes, Lyta sat down followed by Magian Domen and the erles.

A murmur rose from the crowd as the massive door opened with a crash. Archis Druck strode into the hall. Two guards followed him with the prisoner shackled in chains between them. Lyta could hardly bear to watch the man's white face and dragging feet. Trul fell to the floor when the guards released their hold on his arms. He lay there face down, without moving.

Wilus stood up. He pointed at the prone figure and ordered the guards to raise him. Trul was yanked up to stand on unsteady feet, his head lowered to his chest.

Wilus asked, 'Prisoner Trul, do you confess to the murder of Borut? Answer yea or nay.'

His affirmative answer was barely audible.

'Since you have confessed, before all these witnesses, you are declared guilty of the crime.' Wilus paused before pronouncing the sentence. 'Trul of Falga, you are hereby sentenced to death by the sword. Your execution will be carried out tomorrow at mornbreak.'

Trul drooped still lower between his two guards. Only their firm grasp kept him upright.

Josik took over. 'Trul, is there anything you wish to say?'

Although the prisoner lifted his head and opened his mouth, no words emerged. His eyes rolled wildly in his head. Lyta felt a wave of pity for his distress. The pity was increased by the fact that she could do nothing to alleviate it.

Then her eyes shot wide open. She'd caught a thought from the anguished man's mind. 'I'm innocent,' he'd said. He tried again to speak aloud. 'I wish…

The words floated in the air, doomed to remain unfinished. A sudden commotion in the row of Falgans caught everyone's attention. A man brandishing a blade leapt from the line and rushed at Trul. 'Brother, you should die honourably at the hands of a Falgan.'

The blade flashed in the firelight as he thrust it into Trul's chest. The prisoner uttered a choking sound before slumping to the floor. Blood spurted from his wound.

Lyta stared in horror at the sight and gasps rose from the spectators. The guards and Druck stood frozen to the spot in disbelief. Taking advantage of this reaction, the killer rushed through the open door with a wild yell and slammed it shut behind him.

That noise was the signal for everyone to respond. Josik and Quilin jumped from their seats while Magian Domen hurried to kneel down beside the injured prisoner. Druck, the erles, and the Aldean guards dashed for the door in a clatter of boots, yelling threats and instructions.

Wilus took Lyta's hand. 'I fear the man is dead.'

Domen looked up from his position beside Trul. 'Yes, he is indeed dead. The blade pierced his heart.'

Stor had stayed in the hall with his men. He ordered them to remain at their posts before striding to meet Wilus and Lyta. 'Needless to say, I do not endorse that action and I regret that one of my men has prevented justice being carried out in your demesne. I will investigate this last murder.'

Druck returned alone to the hall. His scowl deepened as he reached Lyta, Wilus and Stor. 'This act and the escape were well planned,' he said. 'He had a horse waiting at the door and he wounded two of my men at newgate as he passed. And of course, the bridge was down.'

'Can we follow the attacker?' she asked.

'I've sent out a search party, Kedie Lyta. If the culprit is still in Aldea, we will capture him but I fear he may flee to Falga by water.'

Quilin and Josik were the next to report back. The townsfolk and castle workers had quietly disappeared. 'He got clean away,' said Quilin, wiping his brow. 'He must have had help outside the castle.'

'It wasn't a spur of the moment action,' Josik added. 'I bet the fellow is already on a ship.'

Stor looked at each face in turn. 'If the man reaches Falga, then he will be punished by Kedur Ulit.' He turned to regard Trul's body. 'I hope we can take him back with us.'

'Of course,' said Lyta. 'Do you know yet when Lord Darik can travel?'

'Your magian says another two morns will make the difference. He'll journey by water as it will be easier for him than riding.'

Lyta looked for her aunts. They were still seated, hands clutched together with shocked expressions on their pale faces. She ordered Jer to escort the two women to their chambers. Wilus had been speaking with Druck and now the commander gave orders to remove Trul's body from the hall. Soon after, Godit and his staff arrived to remove the stained rushes from the floor and to restore the tables and benches to their normal places before supper was served.

As she left for her chambers, Lyta knew she had no appetite for her meal. . However, she realized castle life must continue as usual. She'd take the next opportunity to consult Magian Domen about the latest thought-catching episode. She was deeply upset by receiving Trul's declaration of innocence. Her powerlessness to do anything about it was even more disturbing.

Preparations for Lyta's crowning began in earnest the next morn. She had chosen the gown her mother had worn for her own ceremony. Wea, the castle seamstress, said that the fabric was in good condition although the style was sorely dated. 'My Lady, I'll change it to make it more fashionable and alter it to fit you better. It will be admired by everyone.'

The erles consulted each other, Magian Domen, and Godit about the correct protocol for the crowning ceremony. The actual crowning would take place in the chapel with the old salvan presiding while the rest would take place in the great hall. A large celebratory banquet would end the day.

Two morns ago, Darik had been strong enough to leave his bed and Lyta had asked Magian Domen if she should visit and received his agreement. She was glad to see Darik sitting in a chair, looking more like his old self. Although he'd lost weight during his illness, he'd lost none of his disagreeable spirit.

'So, Trevin escaped after he stabbed me,' he said with a mocking grin. 'His disappearance simply proves his guilt. The man should be arrested.'

Lyta's voice grew cold. 'He left here because his wife and son became ill. We have just heard that both of them died.'

Darik shrugged. 'Both unfortunate and lucky for him.' He went on, 'I've been thinking while I lay in bed. The goodwill between our two demesnes has been sadly tested. To repair matters, I suggest you change your mind and invite our kedir here for your crowning or soon after it.'

Lyta knew she would not extend such an invitation. 'Our two peoples need separation to allow the ill-feelings to dissipate. And as my lords said earlier, all eligible kedirs will be invited here at the time of our next council meeting. That is when I would be pleased to welcome Kedir Ardul.'

'Well, your answer isn't pleasing but I'll take it back to Kedur Ulit. I know he won't be happy either.' He drank from a glass of red wine. 'Thank the Stars, we will leave this cursed place in the morn. I can't wait to return to Falga's more civilized court.'

Lyta clenched her fists to keep her anger under control. As she swept from Darik's bedchamber and returned to the castle, she was exceedingly glad that the Falgans would depart soon. Darik was insufferable and his men were no better. She had reached the steps when loud voices and yells from beyond oldgate startled her.

Lyta peered in the direction of the commotion but the inner walls prevented her from seeing further. 'Jer, find out what's happening down there.'

She waited on the steps until her guard returned. 'Another fight,' he said between gasps for breath. 'They claimed one of our horses as theirs. Nin is so angry he can only splutter.'

'Then he must be exceeding angry.' Lyta's head groom was seldom lost for words. 'Should someone settle this latest dispute?'

'No need, My Lady. Lord Stor has already resolved the argument.'

In her mind, Lyta thanked Mother Moon for Stor's presence in the Falgan delegation. While she had lost the last shred of any respect for Darik, she had gained much respect for Stor. The man had behaved wisely and calmly in every difficult situation and she wouldn't mind dealing with him in the future.

She continued to her chambers where Wea waited with the altered crowning gown. When her maids had dressed Lyta in it, the seamstress adjusted the hem. 'I have added another piece here, Lady. You are taller than your mother. I wonder if you will grow more.'

'I hope not,' said Lyta. 'I am taller than some men around here already and would not like to turn into a giantess.'

When Wea lifted the surcoat from the bed, Lyta caught her breath. The spring green garment was richly embroidered with the birds and beasts of Aldea. She looked first for the icecat design on the left side. Facing it, the oak spread its branches and leaves down the length of the garment. She lifted the garment to examine the rell, salmon, boar, wolf and stag stitched across the back. Flowers and plants shone between each symbol and each silver thread sparkled like diamonds in the afternoon light.

She had already tried on the tall silver Moon crown. It was high and difficult to balance but by concentrating, she could manage. With matching silver jewels on her neck and arms, she'd gleam like a real kedura. Now, she hoped with all her heart that she'd rule her demesne like a true kedura. As Wea tugged at a fold, Lyta sent a silent prayer to Mother Moon for her help in the morns ahead.

Her maids had tears in their eyes as Lyta turned slowly around. 'Your Lady Mother would be so proud,' Amia said. Obela simply sniffed. She shook her head and mopped the tears running down her cheeks.

'You've done well,' Lyta told the seamstress. She pulled the surcoat towards her eyes to examine it. 'Your workers have mended these designs so cleverly I can't tell which ones were damaged.'

Wea smiled and bobbed a curtsey. 'I will pass on your words to my embroiderers. They will be happy to hear your praise of their stitching.'

As Amia helped her from the garments, Lyta wondered how her mother had felt when she was crowned. Halia's situation was different. She had the support of a husband but she must have felt the same mixed tingle of excitement and apprehension as she prepared for her future role.

The sound of raised voices from the antechamber made Lyta pause. She nodded at Caza to open the door. Jer was standing there with Aunt Vea's woman behind him.

'What's the matter?' Lyta asked. 'Is my aunt ill?'

'She cannot rise from her bed,' said the woman, 'and would see you when you have the time.'

'Tell my aunt I'll be there as soon as possible.' Lyta turned to her maids. 'Remove these garments and dress me in my regular gown.'

The shutters had been closed across Vea's window and only the light of a single lamp allowed Lyta to grope her way toward the bed where her aunt lay.

'What ails you, Aunt? Should I send for Magian Domen?'

'No,' said Vea in a weak voice. 'He cannot help me. I will simply lie here until I die.'

'But you must not give up like this. I am expecting you and Aunt Jona to attend my crowning.'

Vea raised her head from the pillow. 'Jona can attend but I will not be there. But my heart will not stop beating until I hear that the Moon Crown has been placed on your head.'

Lyta held her aunt's hand. 'I am sure you will recover from this sickness. Domen will visit if you change your mind. And if you need anything at all, please send your woman to me.'

'You're a good child.'

Lyta left her aunt's chamber with a heavy heart. She didn't like to see spirited Vea lying in bed with such a defeated expression on her face. She'd better visit Aunt Jona while she was in this wing of the castle to make sure she was as well as possible.

Jona's chamber was also shrouded in darkness. Lyta grimaced in annoyance. It was so like Jona to wish to appear more ill than Vea. Sickness was Jona's demesne.

Jona's woman appeared from the gloom. 'My lady is not feeling well.'

'What is her complaint?'

'She says her whole body aches so much she might die.'

Lyta bit back her reply. 'Aunt Jona?'

'Yes, child.' Her voice was a faint whisper.

'I am relying on you to attend my crowning.'

'I do not think I will be able to move from my bed.'

'Please do your best. I would like you to be in the chapel if you cannot attend the feast.' Lyta had no more patience for her aunt. She left Jona's bedchamber and went to her own.

Chapter Forty-Nine

Next morn, Darik was able to mount his horse to lead the Falgan delegation from the castle. Since his face was pale and his forehead beaded with sweat, Lyta had no doubt that riding was painful. Stor rode beside him, one hand ready to grab Darik's reins if necessary. The men at arms followed, looking tidy and clean in their red and black tunics and jerkins. Quilin and Wilus brought up the rear as the official Aldean escort. Lyta lifted an arm in salute as the party trotted through oldgate and disappeared from her view. She willed them to ride quickly to the harbour and then to board the waiting ship.

She breathed out in relief and turned to Josik. 'Lady Moon be praised. I thought they'd never leave.'

'Don't be thankful yet. Let's wait until Darik has sailed beyond our harbor walls.'

'You're right. I should have waited to give thanks. Send word to me when the ship is out of sight.' Lyta turned toward the castle door. 'Now all we have to do is prepare for the ceremony and feast.'

Josik stopped her with his hand. 'Kedie, are you absolutely sure you wish to rule Aldea? We've all assumed you'll take the crown without ever asking you this direct question.'

'I'm Halia's daughter. She'd expect me to follow in her footsteps. And she did her best to train me for the role. I know I'm young and inexperienced but I'm willing to learn.'

'As long as you are certain.' Josik shook his head. 'It's a huge task governing a demesne even with guidance.'

Lyta patted Josik's sleeve, touched by his concern for her welfare, even though it was a concern he'd expressed so belatedly. How could she change her mind at this point?

When Quilin returned from the harbour, he came to Lyta's solar. Since neither of her aunts was stitching there, it had become a convenient place to receive people. Jer announced Quilin and he entered with an anxious expression on his face. 'The atmosphere in town is still disturbed. I don't know what's behind it now that Trul is dead.'

'They did want to hang him in the square. Mayhap folk are still angry.'

Quilin rubbed his chin. 'Something more is going on. I've sent one man to drink at The Grey Goose and a second to The White Swan. They may be able to collect scraps of information from the inn patrons.'

'Won't your men be recognised?'

Quilin's sudden grin made him look ten summers younger. 'They're in disguise. One in a shaggy black wig and the other with a grey beard. Their own mothers wouldn't know them.'

'Then please tell me if they hear anything useful. I don't like to have continuing strife between the townsfolk and us.'

'I'll do that, Kedie.' He rose and then stood looking down at Lyta. 'In three more morns, you'll be my kedura. That will seem strange after all these summers of being my kedie.' He paused. 'I will regret the change.'

After he strode away, Lyta took several deep breaths to calm her heartbeat. She'd been caught unawares by the intense look in Quilin's grey eyes. They'd always had a close relationship and she, too, didn't want her crowning to alter it. Would everybody she had known in her life treat her in a different manner when she became kedura? Her mind told her that this might be so.

As the senior member of the council, Wilus was in charge of the crowning arrangements. The nobles and Lyta had decided to keep the occasion an Aldean concern because of Halia's death. The kedurs and keduras from the other demesnes hadn't been invited. At Domen's suggestion, the magians of the land would represent their masters and mistresses. Lyta was looking forward to meeting these people. She'd always felt a sense of strangeness about magians with their mystic powers. Mayhap some of them would even resemble the magians of the old tales with straggling long beards and hair and piercing eyes that could freeze words in the mouth and cast evil spells. They'd certainly be the opposite of Domen with his close cropped hair although he did have grey eyes that demanded the truth.

The closer they came to the ceremony, the busier the occupants of the castle grew. Lyta was reminded of the buzzing around the hives at the end of the grazing fields. As a child, she'd been fascinated by the activity as the bees flew in and out. So fascinated in fact, that one morn she'd been stung on her arms and neck after venturing too close.

The human bees hunted deer and boar for the crowning feast; they distributed new tunics or jerkins to all the castle workers; they baked bread, pies, and cakes; they cleaned and polished every corner and sewed new banners in celebration of her crowning. Everywhere Lyta looked, her people were busy.

She seized the chance when nobody was asking her questions to visit Magian Domen. Now that his patient had left, he might also have time for her. She left Jer at the gate when she saw Domen bending over a row of Salusy. He stood up to greet her. 'I thought you'd be occupied with preparations.

'I'm not as busy as everyone else. I wanted to talk to you.'

'Of course.' He wiped his hands on the edge of his robe like a small boy.

Inside the workchamber, the magian poured his favourite peach juice for them both. 'What is on your mind, Kedie?'

Lyta took a sip from her cup. 'In the hall, I caught a disturbing message from Trul. I believe he was innocent.'

Domen said in his usual grave tone. 'I caught the same message and I'd opened my mouth to ask Wilus to stop the sentencing. But before I could say one word, the man was slain.'

'I feel angry that an innocent man died and we may never catch the one who did slay Borut. And I don't really understand why I caught the message. My lofting doesn't take place regularly. A person must be in extreme distress before I catch a thought.'

The magian nodded. 'Your training reached only a certain level. Because of your position, I could never work enough with you. And as kedura, your time will be taken up with other matters.'

'So I should be satisfied with the skill I have now?' Lyta asked.

'I am sure that even at your level, it may be useful. Very few people can loft. In my lifetime, I have met only three others and one of them is dead.'

'I didn't realise it was such a rare skill. I believed all magians could send and catch thoughts.'

'Thank Lady Moon it isn't so. I would never want my fellow magians to know exactly what I am thinking about them at all times. And with young ones in training, that would be a disaster.'

'Will you tell me who else can loft besides you?' Lyta finished her juice and placed the cup down.

Domen shook his head. 'I am sworn to secrecy. But who knows what might happen? You could discover them for yourself.'

Lyta asked, 'Are you looking forward to being reunited with your fellow magians?'

'Most of them are here already.'

When he saw Lyta's surprise, Domen said, 'Magians don't go anywhere with a lot of fuss. We slip into places unnoticed. They have asked to meet with you after your crowning.'

'Are you all close friends?'

'Our hyalas keep us close. I studied with many at the Erudence and then actually trained the rest.'

Lyta left the magian's dwelling with their conversation running through her head. She felt slightly better knowing that Domen had caught Trul's thought and that like her, he'd lacked the time to do anything about the man's innocence. At least the burden of guilt was not only hers to bear. But on future occasions, would she be able to take action? No wonder that Josik and the other erles had told her how difficult wearing the Moon Crown might be.

She sighed. One of her present and future responsibilities was visiting her aunts. After climbing the castle steps she turned right to take the passage to their chambers.

***

Obela wakened her early. 'Rise and shine, kedie.' A tear slipped down her wrinkled cheek and she sniffed loudly. 'Next morn, I will call you kedura. You will never be my little kedie again.'

Her words were almost an echo of Quilin's and Lyta wondered who else would be having similar thoughts.

Obela handed Lyta a silver platter. 'Prala has baked special cakes for you. She says they'll be named crowning cakes from now on. Taste one and see what you think.'

Lyta took a bite and chewed thoughtfully. 'I taste honey and nuts and something different. This delicious spice is new to me. What is it?'

'Prala did tell me but I forget the name. She said it comes from Sevvir. '

'No matter what it's called, the cakes are delicious. Prala can bake them any time for me, not just for my crowning.'

Lyta went through the elaborate preparations. Hot water was brought for her bath, which was perfumed with attar of roses. As she lay in the scented water, she tried to stay calm. But it was difficult to steady her thoughts with the shining crowning robes hanging beside the window and the silver Moon Crown sitting near her on a table.

Dressed in regular clothes, she went to the meeting chamber for her last gathering with the erles and magian. Lyta hoped they wouldn't get sentimental about her imminent change in status. The men rose when Jer opened the door and then they applauded her entrance. She bent her head to hide a tear. Lyta lectured herself about not crying as she sat down. If I start now, she thought, I will be awash in tears and red-eyed before the evening.

Wilus displayed the documents she would sign after the Salvan had pronounced her the Kedura of Aldea. 'Then down here, we will all sign as witnesses to the event.'

'What's this space for?' Lyta asked.

Wilus looked rather uncomfortable as he glanced at the other men. 'Didn't anybody tell you? That is where you place the impression from your thumb. Like sealing a letter with wax.'

'Do I use my mother's special green wax?'

Quilin spoke. 'I don't know why you weren't informed earlier, Kedie. Sealing wax isn't used for this document.' He cleared his throat. 'The Crowning Oath is always sealed in blood.'

'Blood? Then I must be cut. How does that happen?'

'One of us will use a blade. It will be fast and as painless as possible.'

Domen said, 'If you wish, I will dab the area with Hort to deaden the skin.'

Lyta thought for a moment. 'Is the idea behind this tradition to show me that I am prepared to bleed to preserve the demesne?'

'I believe that might be the original aim,' said Wilus. 'But I can't be sure. The ideas behind many of our traditions have been lost over time.'

'No Hort,' said Lyta. 'I will cut the left thumb with my own blade. How do I do it without bleeding on my gown?'

The Salvan is meant to hold a silver bowl under the wound,' said Quilin. 'But I don't think the man can keep it steady without trembling. If you wish, I can hold it for you.'

Lyta nodded. 'I'd like that. What else should I know?'

Wilus explained some further details and then he paused. 'I know you wished to ride through the town after the ceremony as your mother did, Kedie. But with the recent unrest, I'm not sure that plan is wise. It's not too late to change your mind.'

'I will ride through town,' said Lyta in a firm tone. 'I must show the people that I care for them. And also that I do not fear them and they have no need at all to fear me.'

Josik gave a half smile. 'I knew you would say that. We will make sure you are well guarded.'

'I will have the same number of guards that I use on my normal rides.'

Quilin frowned. 'Then will you allow us to accompany you? I will feel easier if I am nearby. Just in case.'

Lyta said, 'Very well but you won't surround me so that I can't be clearly seen by the townsfolk. You will ride behind me.'

At the sound of a rap on the door, Quilin rose. Lyta heard several voices talking together outside. The erle left the door open as he returned and spoke to her. 'Good news,

Kedie. Lord Trevin has returned in time for your crowning. And you'll be exceeding pleased to learn that he's brought his daughter, Lady Adina, with him.'

He stopped. His whole demeanour and tone changed. 'Along with her husband Firt.'

Chapter Fifty

Lyta gave an involuntary gasp. Firt? Why had Trevin brought his son-in-law with him? She'd never wanted to see the kedir from Delis again. Their only meeting had been a disaster from start to finish. His father had bought Firt to Aldea as a prospective husband but Lyta soon discovered Firt was cruel and cowardly with a roving eye. He didn't like her either. Lyta hoped Adina led a happy life with her husband but she doubted that Firt's miserable nature would have changed over the last two summers. .

When Trevin ushered his daughter into the chamber, she rushed toward Lyta and fell against her shoulder with loud cries and noisy tears. 'I thought that dreadful Rurrik would lock you up for ever and ever. You were so clever to escape from him! You must tell me all about it.'

Lyta patted Adina's back. She was made uncomfortable by this unseemly display of emotion. When she caught Quilin's eye, he winked at her.

'That's enough, girl,' Trevin said, tugging his daughter's arm. 'Stop weeping over Kedie Lyta. Her kidnapping and all such stuff is long past.' He pulled out a spotted kerchief to wipe her eyes as he steered Adina to an empty chair. Lyta took her usual chair beside the girl.

Firt strolled through the door. His long cloak was thrown back to reveal a green tunic shining with gold embroidery and a sword hilt glittering with jewels. He stopped beside Lyta and stared down at her. She moved both hands to her lap to avoid a kiss from those wet red lips. 'Greetings, Firt. And Trevin, you are most welcome. It's good to have you and Adina back again.'

Firt murmured a reply and then without an invitation to sit, dropped into the chair next to his wife and nodded at the men facing him. They had all risen at Trevin's and Adina's entrance. Josik's lips were set in a firm line and Lyta knew he'd be annoyed by Firt's rudeness in not waiting for Lyta's permission to be seated.

Since Lyta didn't wish to discuss any business with Firt and Adina in the chamber, their council meeting was effectively over. 'I will see you all at the crowning,' she said. 'Adina, do you wish to accompany me to my solar?'

When Adina nodded and smiled, they left the chamber. As they walked through the passages, Lyta remembered how annoying Adina had been when she spent time at the castle two summers ago. The girl's head had been stuffed with nothing but thoughts of robes, jewels, hair styles, and handsome men. The only thing they had in common was a love of horses.

'It's so nice to be here again and in time for your crowning. I thought we would be too late and my new gown would be wasted. It is blue silk and the gold embroidery on it was worked by my new seamstress. She's exceeding clever with her needle. I can't wait to see what robe you will be wearing.'

Adina clasped her hands together when she was shown the gown and surcoat. 'Oh, it's quite wonderful.' She fingered the surcoat and peered closely at it. 'The stitching is very fine.' Then she turned to view the Moon Crown. 'That is just magnificent. You are so lucky to be able to wear it.'

Lyta reflected that Adina probably had little concept of the considerable responsibilities that went with the stiff robe and the uncomfortable crown. To her mind, they were simply costly items of dress. Adina hadn't changed much over the last two summers either.

'I hear you have a baby,' Lyta asked. 'How old is he now?'

Adina beamed with pleasure. 'Belid's just reached one summer and he looks so much like his father. I hated to leave him but he has two nursemaids who simply dote on him. He's exceeding intelligent and already walks on his own.'

Lyta summoned Godit to take Adina to her bedchamber. She was sure her castlian had prepared suitable accommodation as soon as he saw their guests arrive. After a light meal, she dismissed Obela and her maids. She needed time to herself to prepare her mind for the ceremony. She sat in the solar by the window and tried to remove all the thoughts which were making her feel nervous.

Her robing an hour later was accompanied by tears. As Amia and Obela took turns to slip the garments over her body, the other maids sniffed or sobbed, Lyta finally stopped them with a raised hand. 'This is meant to be a happy event. If you all cry, I'll start as well.'

Amia gulped several times and then managed a watery smile. 'Forgive me, Lady. You know why I was weeping.'

Lyta did know. Amia had been her mother's maid for many moons. She'd dressed Halia for her wedding and for her crowning. Seeing Lyta in the same robe must be difficult for her.

Obela wiped tears from her own face. 'I am not sorry for weeping. My babe is now all grown. She won't need me any longer and I'm sad.'

Lyta hugged her nurse. 'You should be happy that I'm grown and following in my mother's footsteps. I owe much to your care.'

'I was trying to be happy for you but it didn't work.' Obela mopped her face.

When Lyta was dressed, she summoned Jer to the chamber. His task was to inform Archis Druck that the Moon Crown was ready to be carried to the chapel with an escort of guards. Outside her door, Lyta found the erles and Magian Domen waiting, wearing their finest garments. Her eyes were drawn to Quilin's silver tunic bearing the black emblem of an icecat. The beasts were numerous in the highlands of his estate. Quilin bowed his head and smiled at her.

The castle officials had assembled in the great hall where Godit was arranging them in order of precedence. They would lead the procession, followed by the erles and the magian. Archis Druck and four guards would precede Lyta who would be the last to enter the chapel. Because the chamber was not large, only those people involved in the ceremony had been invited.

Torches in holders at the sides and front lit the chapel. Lyta waited until everyone had filed inside before she stepped into the flickering light. She set her eyes on the bent figure of the Salvan, clad in his silver robes beside the Moon Altar, which bore the crown and other sacred objects.

When Lyta reached Elon, she remained standing when everyone except Archis Druck took their seats. As the official protector of the demesne, he stood several steps away from Lyta with his right hand on his sword hilt, the only armed man in the chapel. The Salvan began the introductory prayers to Mother Moon. His mumbles were so indistinct that Lyta wondered how many more ceremonies he should conduct.

She stood still until all the prayers and ritual words had been spoken. The Salvan recited the Oath of Office and Lyta repeated it. Then she took one step forward. With shaking hands, the priest lifted the crown and held it high in the air. Those in the chapel drew in an audible breath as the crown swayed back and forth before it landed askew on Lyta's head. She pushed it straight with one quick movement.

The Salvan called out, 'Long live Kedura Lyta!'

Lyta faced her people. Immediately, the chapel walls echoed with the sounds of men's voices repeating the words and their feet stamping on the stone floor. Her heart thumped in her chest as she fought for control. Tears would be exceeding unseemly. Starting with Druck, each man knelt before her to swear fealty. Wilus's knees creaked audibly and as he raised his head, he gave a rueful smile before heaving himself to his feet.

When Quilin bent his dark head and took the oath, Lyta heard a slight tremor in his voice. She forced her own voice to remain steady as she uttered the formal response. She had an urge to smooth the single curl that lay against his neck. Luckily, the moment passed and Quilin rose to his feet. His face was unusually serious as he backed away.

After each official had sworn fealty, the erles came forward again to sign the written version of the Oath of Office. Lyta drew her blade from its hidden pocket in her surcoat. Quilin came forward to hold the silver bowl, his grey eyes steady on hers. When he nodded slightly, she ran the sharp tip over the flesh in her left thumb. Blood immediately welled from the skin and dripped into the bowl. Quilin handed her a linen square to blot the wound before she placed her thumb print on the foot of the document. Having signed in her own blood, she was now responsible for the entire demesne.

Quilin mouthed the words. 'Well done,' before he stepped away with the bowl and Lyta drew in a sigh of relief at completing the tasks of her crowning without any difficulties. As she walked from the chapel at the head of the procession, she pressed the linen against her thumb to staunch the bleeding.

The rest of the day passed in a blur. Some of the castle workers were lined up in the great hall to cheer her as she left the chapel; others had gathered in the courtyard outside the keep. Loud shouts followed her as she walked through oldgate and into the outer ward where Nin and all the stable hands waited with her mount. Silver wore a gleaming saddle and cover to match her name.

When Lyta was mounted, Druck and two guards preceded her across the drawbridge and down the hill into Aldeton. Two guards followed her and the erles rode two by two behind them. Smiling people waved flowers and green branches on each side of the streets. Lyta stopped in the square to receive a scroll from the mayor and to give a brief speech of thanks. She saw Yalt's head above others in the crowd. He caught her eye and nodded.

Back at the castle, Lyta went to her solar for a brief rest before the feast began in the great hall. Adina had accompanied her. She fluttered around Lyta, exclaiming at the beauty of her robes and jewels. 'And your hair under the crown is so becoming. Which maid did it? She has excellent hands.'

Lyta asked to be left alone. She stood looking down into the courtyard where people ran back and forth, performing their duties. Now, if things went wrong, she must see they were mended; if things went right; she must give praise where it was due. Could she learn to govern well? Would petitioners have faith in her decisions? Could she ever be as well-respected as her mother? So many questions flooded her mind. And she could provide so few answers.

Before she went into the hall, she went to show her crowning finery to the aunts. She frowned when saw Vea's pallor and drawn face. The magian must see her as soon as possible whether she agreed or not. Lyta was less concerned about Jona. Although her other aunt was still lying in bed, Jona looked much the same as usual. She fingered Lyta's gown. 'I remember your dear mother wearing this robe. And she looked exceeding beautiful. Your father too was such a fine man in his silver and green tunic. I will never forget how kind he was to my own dear husband and me when we attended the crowning.'

The black rafters of the high hall had been decorated with garlands of purple, blue, and red flowers threaded through the battle shields. More blooms hung among the banners. The wide hearth was empty of logs but a display of fragrant pine boughs and yellow daisies filled the space.

Lyta was escorted by her erles to the throne at the centre of the table. It too had been adorned with blue and white flowers. Cheering and stamping diners greeted her entrance. She sat between Wilus and Josik with Druck, Magian Domen, Trevin, and Quilin at the head table. Firt, Adina, and the most important castle officials sat at the nearest table. The group of strangers at the same table must be the visiting magians.

Prala had created crowning pies; some were sweet with fruit and nuts while others were savoury with fowl, shellfish, and egg fillings. Servers brought in steaming platters of venison, boar, and whole fish. Trevin had brought the special cheese his estate produced while Wilus had sent for honey from his lands. He drizzled this on slices of bread for Lyta to eat and described its famed healing properties to her.

Singers, dancers, and story tellers provided the entertainment. Lyta was grateful that no jugglers had been hired. She remembered the feast where the juggler had thrown a blade at Firt and she'd caught it, preventing serious injury. Firt had snarled at her instead of giving thanks. Now, Lyta watched him, sitting beside his wife but fondling the pretty serving maid behind him with his left hand. The man was quite despicable.

A black-haired singer with a lute took the place of a story teller. Since Lyta didn't recognize him, she assumed he was one of the new entertainers hired by Godit for the feast. He began to play his instrument, impressing Lyta with his considerable talent.

Then he said, 'I wrote a song about a man who fell in love at first sight. The maid was young and slender with long black hair and eyes as brown as the deep pools in a mountain stream. Do I have your permission, Kedura, to sing my ballad?'

All eyes were fixed on Lyta. She heard Wilus mutter, 'Impudent young dog,' and felt heat rise in her cheeks. She leaned forward and smiled. 'You may sing.'

When his voice rose so clearly and sweetly into the ancient rafters, all sounds of serving, eating, and drinking ceased. The song was tender and true with a sorrowful catchy melody. By the third verse, people were singing the lilting refrain. 'Will she ever love me? I will love her until I die.'

After five verses, the singer stopped, laid down his lute, and bowed low. Lyta called out to him. 'Well sung, my friend. What is your name?'

The man lifted his head and deftly caught the purse Josik threw to him. 'I will speak my name on the morn my love gives me her hand.'

Lyta laughed. 'Then I hope, Lord Anonymous, that her heart softens soon and she agrees to have you. You cannot wish to be nameless forever.'

The singer touched his chest. 'I hope so too, Kedura. If not, my heart will surely shatter.' He bowed again and left the hall.

Wilus stared after him. 'I know that face. Where have I seen it before?' He shook his head. 'The name will come to me in the middle of the night.' He turned to Lyta. 'But. Kedura, I won't come to your chamber and wake you.'

The hour was late when Lyta finally rested her aching head on the pillow. Sights and sounds from the last twelve hours whirled together in a series of dizzying and memorable pictures. She'd never forget her crowning even if she lived to reach one hundred summers.

Chapter Fifty-One

The morn seemed unchanged. The sun rose in the east and the clumsy maid dropped yet another platter. Obela woke Lyta with the same admonition to eat a good repast while dogs continued to bark and howl in the kennels. And, as usual, the sweet smell of baking cakes wafted through the chamber window. But one thing was different and inescapable. Lyta was now the Kedura of Aldea. Before she rose, she prayed silently to her own mother and to Mother Moon to get her safely through this morn and the next ones. She would need all their help and wisdom.

After the lords had greeted Lyta for the first time as their kedura, an important decision had to be made. Who would stay to advise Lyta and who would return to his own lands? Before any discussion, Trevin spoke frankly. 'I would prefer to go home. I brought Firt with me, Kedura, because I could not trust him to be left behind alone. We'll stay for the tournament because he's determined to be champion but after that we'll leave.'

Lyta nodded. 'I understand your concerns but regret that you must leave. Will we see you at the winter council meeting?'

'If things go well, I'll return.' Trevin grimaced. 'I was such a fool to allow this marriage to Firt but Adina and my wife nagged me morn and night until I agreed to it. On his side, Firt was desperate to get out of Delis after Baldus replaced him as heir with his younger brother. The reward was helpful as his father was exceeding grateful to see him depart.' He rubbed an imaginary coin between his fingers. 'And now I have severe regrets and must live with them.' He ended with a heavy sigh.

Wilus said, 'I can stay here until the next meeting if necessary. My grandson is governing well in my absence and eager to continue.'

Josik spoke next. 'I'd prefer to return home as well. I'm arranging a marriage for my youngest daughter. She's the only child unwed in my household and dear to my heart. I have been negotiating with an erle in Parian who has an eligible son.'

Wilus thumped the table, startling everyone around it. 'That's it! I knew I'd seen the singer's face before. He's the spitting image of Gerit when he was a young man. He's the kedur of Parian. We used to hunt together.'

'Then surely he's baseborn,' said Josik. 'Why would a kedir be here unescorted? We'd have been informed by Parian's magian of any visit.'

'Unless he's here in secret,' said Quilin with a frown. 'That lovesick song might have expressed his true feelings. Kedura, we must find out.'

'Of course,' Lyta said.

Quilin turned to Magian Domen. 'Please send a message to Kedur Gerit asking if one of his sons is absent from the castle and his demesne. I believe his heir is named Iben.'

'Then is it decided?' Lyta asked. 'Trevin and Josik wish to return to their estates. Are you able, Quilin, to remain here with Wilus to give me advice?'

Quilin nodded. 'I would be honoured, Kedura, to stay as long as you wish. I can contact my officials through my own magian if any problems or questions arise.'

Lyta was happy to be supported by the men she preferred. When the meeting ended, Quilin asked to speak with her and followed Lyta to her solar.

She smiled at him when they were both seated. She had no idea why he wished to talk with her.

'I am able to stay here because my steward governs well in my absence. But I miss my son. May I bring Jilik here? He'd come with his nursemaid, tutoran, and man at arms.'

Lyta said, 'He'd be most welcome. It's a pity no other noble children live here to be his friends.'

'I'm sure that will change after you're wed.'

Lyta willed her cheeks not to flush without success. She didn't like to discuss marriage at any time, most of all with Quilin.

She cleared her throat and deliberately changed the subject. 'I wish to follow my mother's tradition and receive any petitioners after midday dinner. When shall I start having these audiences?'

'As you know, we've already dealt with some petitions in our meetings but you may have others. I'll ask your clerks for a list. After the tourney when folk leave the castle, you can decide to resume this tradition.'

'The tourney! How I wish there wasn't one. Will you joust against Firt? You know what happened last time.'

Quilin smiled. 'Don't worry, Kedura. He won't get a second chance to injure me. I'll make sure of that.'

'Is Firt really a danger to Trevin?'

'I believe so. Trevin told me about a plot he uncovered. Luckily, his own men remained true to their lord and his steward told him about it. Firt denied the whole thing, of course. He said it was a misunderstanding.'

'You warned me that governing wouldn't be easy.' She frowned. 'Closer to home, did your men discover any trouble in town?'

'Yalt seems to be the key to the unrest but I am unsure what he's doing now. My men reported they met two strangers at The Grey Goose, the son of a Parian erle and his man.'

'From Parian? Could he be that black-haired singer?'

Quilin's face darkened. 'That song was discourteous to you.'

'He did no harm,' said Lyta. 'And the melody was very pleasing.'

***

After Quilin left, Lyta went to Domen's dwelling to meet with his fellow magians. She was shown into his workchamber where seven people were gathered. Lyta smiled to herself when she looked at the assembled faces. Not one was the doddery magian of the tales Obela had told her. In fact, half of the magians looked young and three of them were women.

They bowed at her entrance and Lyta welcomed them to Aldea. Then Domen led her to a chair and took the stool beside her. He introduces each of his guests who, in turn, told her something of the demesne where they lived. Four lived at the court of the various kedurs in the land but three were part of an erle's household.

When Hela was introduced, Lyta paid extra attention. This magian was a tall woman with deep green eyes and long white hair. Lyta knew that she lived on Quilin's estate, the latest one to live there. Quilin had told Lyta that his great-grandsire had agitated to get a magian when the Erudence had produced the first trained people. He had been unusual in his desire. The high cost of purchasing a hyala had been a deterrent for most erles. The other two magians to be part of an erle's estate lived in Delis and Sevvir.

The magian of Falga also caught her attention because Domen had trained her. Gila had brown hair and rosy cheeks in an unlined face. Her hazel eyes studied Lyta closely and she wondered if this magian was one of the three people who were also skilled in lofting.

After an hour of conversation, Lyta rose to leave. 'I am sure you have many things to discuss among yourselves like the best uses for Salusy and how to dry Bright-Ease. I hope you will attend the tourney on the morrow.'

***

Clear blue skies and sunshine promised a fine day for the tournament. Firt had suggested an archery contest as well but Lyta had refused to hold the competition. After the disastrous end to the last one, she didn't want to stir up more ill feelings.

When Lyta took her place in the pavilion, she waved to the crowds of cheering people. Adina sat beside her with a white scarf in her hands. 'Last time we were both here, I had no idea I'd soon become a married woman,' she said. 'Now I must award this token to my own husband.'

She smiled at Firt as he arrived at the pavilion on his white charger. He nodded without meeting her eyes and then caught the scarf on the tip of his lance.

Lyta waited for Quilin's approach to bestow her own token which bore the silver and green colours of Aldea. He reached up as she leaned down, bringing her hand to his warm lips before receiving the scarf. Then he smiled and trotted back to the lists.

'Lord Quilin is so handsome in his black mail.' Adina clasped both hands to her bosom with a loud sigh.

Lyta turned to Wilus on her other side. At least, she might hold a sensible conversation with him. 'Did you attend many tourneys in your youth?' she asked.

His eyes lit up. 'Indeed I did. And I watched my own father take part in them when I was a child.' He shook his head. 'Tourneys were vastly different then.'

'How did they differ?'

'The joust was only a minor event often held the night before. The melee was the true purpose of the tournament.'

'I read about that in a history book,' Lyta said. 'Wasn't the melee like a mock battle between two armies?'

Wilus smiled. 'It was. The fighting was fast and furious until one side drove the other back and won the prize. But we lost our appetite for mock battles after the Freedom War with its real battles and copious bloodshed. The melee fell out of popularity and the joust became the main aim of a tournament.'

The jousting began at last with a bugle call and the crowd lining the lists forgot about buying and eating their meat pies and surged forward. The canvas walls on either side kept people at a safe distance as the first horses thundered toward each other. A lance shattered on the chest of the left hand rider. .

'That's one point to Josik's squire,' said Wilus. 'The first time he's ridden in a real tourney too. He should have aimed for the helm and won two points but he shows promise.'

When both riders trotted back to their respective ends, Josik's squire was handed a new lance. On the second bout, neither lance touched mail.

Wilus continued with his explanation. 'The lad's called Sard and his equipment is all borrowed. Just as well this isn't a serious tourney. If it was and he lost, his mail and helm would be forfeit.'

The promising lad was victorious after the third bout. Sard raised his helm in response to the crowd's shouts and bowed to Lyta. Through the rounds that followed, three riders remained undefeated: Quilin, Firt, and Sard. Josik who was arranging the tournament placed Sard against Firt. The winner of that contest would joust against Quilin for the prize.

Lyta held her breath as the men and their horses readied themselves. As kedura, she was obliged to be gracious to the winner regardless of her personal opinion but she hoped Sard would defeat his more experienced opponent. Adina clutched Lyta's arm as the two lances met in the middle of the lists. Since both men remained seated and neither lance connected, they trotted to their ends and turned around.

The bugle announced the next bout. Lyta watched closely as the horses approached the centre. Adina grabbed Lyta's arm with both hands. 'I'm closing my eyes. I can't watch.'

Once again, both riders were safe and they prepared themselves for the third and final bout. 'Tell me when it's over.' Adina moaned, her eyes still screwed shut.

Lyta kept her own eyes firmly on Sard, holding her breath as the men and horses met. With a sudden jab of his lance, Sard unseated Firt who crashed to the ground and then lay still.

Adina opened her eyes and gasped. Then Firt's arms moved and he was soon able to sit up with the help of his squire. 'I thank you, Mother Moon,' said Adina clasping both hands to her bosom. 'You have saved my dear husband.'

Subdued applause greeted Firt as his squire led his horse away and he limped to his tent. Many in the crowd had seen him stab Quilin two summers ago and remembered the occasion well. Sard, however, received loud yells and cheers for his fine performance.

The final match was between Sard and Quilin. The latter was the better and more experienced jouster but the young squire put up a brave fight. When he was unhorsed in the third bout, he threw off his helm and staggered to his feet. Quilin turned his horse and removed his own helm before trotting to the pavilion to receive his prize.

Lyta smiled at him, observing his damp face and curling hair. She undid the clasp from her surcoat. It was the representation of a leaping icecat made of silver with sapphires for eyes. 'Lord Quilin, I congratulate you on your victory,' she said. 'This prize is most appropriate for you.'

Quilin took the clasp and studied it. His voice was a little breathless as he said. 'Thank you, Kedura. The workmanship is fine but I'll treasure it because of the giver.' He bowed deeply and rode away without another word.

Lyta drew in a shaking breath. Mayhap it would have been better for her peace of mind if Sard had won. The unsettling thought was driven from her mind when she glimpsed Firt outside his tent at the end of the field. He was thrashing an attendant with a whip. Lyta was not surprised that his defeat would have violent repercussions for everyone around him; she trusted that Adina would stay out of her husband's way until he grew calmer.

***

In the morn, Lyta opened her eyes to the sound of running feet and slamming doors. When she turned her head, Amia bent over the bed. Her dark eyes were wide with alarm. 'Thank Lady Moon that you're awake, Kedura. There's bad trouble afoot.'

Lyta stretched her arms and legs. She was more tired now than she'd been yestermorn after her crowning and the feast. 'What kind of trouble?'

'Lord Trevin died in the night.'

Lyta's own eyes widened in shock. 'Trevin? But I sat beside him at supper last night. He dined well and was in excellent health.'

'Lady, his man and the magian both say he's dead.'

'Then send Magian Domen to me at once. I'll see him in the solar. Hand me that robe.'

Lyta pushed her arms into a bedrobe and took the platter of food from the clumsy maidservant. For once, Fluva hadn't dropped her repast. When Domen arrived, Lyta was chewing a nut in a desultory fashion. The shocking news had driven away her appetite. She gestured at the full platter but Domen shook his head. 'I've eaten already.'

'Tell me what happened?'

Domen sat beside her. 'I'm not exactly sure. He ate a large dish of pickled eels last night but his man told me that he often ate eels with no stomach trouble.' The magian sighed. 'I am considering some type of slow-acting poison.'

'Poison? Who in the name of Mother Moon would want to kill him?'

'I can think of the man who'd benefit the most.'

'Firt, of course. But why here?'

The magian looked hard at her. 'Plenty of witnesses at the castle. If Firt was responsible, then the act was better done in full view rather than far off at Trevin's estate. There, you would have to take his word for the cause of death and be full of suspicion. Here, you take the blame especially if he accuses your cook.'

'You're correct. Can you test for poison in his body? You can ask the magians for assistance.'

'Even if we found poison, what does that prove? Godit told me he has hired extra help from the town for all the meals while we have guests. For two morns, the castle has been full of strangers.'

Lyta nodded. Prala had also used more workers in her kitchen to prepare the food. She shuddered as she recalled the gusto with which Trevin had attacked the eels cooked especially for him. He'd rubbed both hands and smiled when the dish was brought to the table. 'Your cook knows my taste well. And eels from that stream in the Dark Forest are the best in the whole demesne.'

Remembering this scene at dinner, Lyta blinked away her tears. 'Who else knows this sad news?'

'When the Lady Adina heard about her father's death, she was so distressed that everyone in the chambers around her learned what had happened. I have given her a calming potion.'

'Then please inform my lords that we will meet in the council chamber in one hour to discuss this matter.' As Domen rose, she placed a hand on his arm to halt him.

'Don't tell Firt of this meeting. I will speak to him afterwards.'

The magian nodded and left the solar. Lyta pushed the platter away and called for her maids. She must be ready for this difficult meeting.

Chapter Fifty-Two

An hour later, Lyta studied the pale faces of her erles. Wilus's beard was uncombed and straggly while Josik's eyes were red rimmed. He and Trevin had been close friends for many summers. She knew they'd been squires together in her grandsire's household.

Quilin's spoke in a strained voice to Domen, 'Are you certain that poison killed Trevin?'

'The magians and I have examined his body closely and that is what we all believe. Prala has provided a small portion of the pickled eels that were not served to Trevin and they are free of any poison. We assume that a substance was added to the dish after it left the kitchen and before it reached Trevin.'

'Do we know which servant handed the eels to him?' Wilus asked.

'Druck is investigating that matter,' said Lyta. 'I spoke to him and Godit before I came here. He will report to us when he has any information.'

The words had barely left her mouth when the door was flung open and Firt strode into the chamber. He stared at Lyta with both hands on his hips. 'Kedura, why was I not informed of this meeting?'

Lyta smothered a gasp of fright, 'Because it was intended for my erles and Magian Domen,' she said.

'But with Trevin gone, I am the person responsible for his estate. His eldest son and wife are dead and the heir is just a boy. Do you expect Eldin to become a council member immediately and to govern the land in his father's place?'

Quilin rose and closed the door. He faced Firt with a hard gaze. 'The circumstances of Trevin's death are unclear. Everyone who served him or benefited is suspect. We were meeting to discuss that very matter.'

'Then is my poor wife, prostrate with grief, also a suspect?' Firt's sarcastic smile exposed his square teeth. He reminded Lyta of a wild beast at bay. 'Will you order Adina to rise from her bed for questioning?'

'Of course not,' said Wilus. 'We extend our condolences to the Lady Adina. She has already been treated by Domen.'

'Then I hope the potion he gave her is free of poison. By the Lady, I refuse to eat or drink anything more in this castle unless my man tastes it first.'

Although his voice was cold and his face set, Lyta sensed the rage behind his words. She flinched slightly as she received the dark message.

'You can be assured that the potion was safe,' said the magian with a frown. 'If necessary, I shall take a draught myself from the same flask.'

When Josik glanced at Lyta, she leaned forward to speak. 'Firt, I'll tell you what my lords and I have discussed. Both Archis Druck and Godit will talk to those who served food to Lord Trevin. It seems a fatal substance was added to the dish of eels between the kitchen and the hall.'

Firt sat down next to her and after a minute Quilin took the seat beside him. Firt placed both hands on the table and turned to Lyta. 'Are you certain you can trust Druck and Godit? One of them may have wanted to get rid of Trevin.'

'That's absurd,' said Wilus, his voice rose as he added. 'Both men respected Trevin and are completely trustworthy.'

'How can you be so certain about their loyalty?' Firt raised both eyebrows. 'They could have paid another person to do the deed.'

'So could you,' said Josik. He stared at hard at Firt. 'Right now, you are loudly accusing everyone else of this crime. Prove to us you are guiltless.'

Firt spread out both hands. 'And how is that possible? I'm the chief suspect but clearing my name might be near impossible. I ask permission, Kedura, to take my poor wife and her dead father home as soon as possible. I also ask you to appoint me as advisor to Trevin's heir until he is old enough to govern on his own.' He pushed himself from his chair. 'I'll leave you to consider these matters without my presence.'

At the door, Firt swung around to face the council. 'Kedura Lyta, I expect to hear from you as soon as you and your esteemed and loyal lords have reached a resolution.' He marched from the chamber leaving the door open behind him.

Quilin rose but before he closed the door, he stood for a moment looking along the passage. 'He's gone.'

Wilus sighed. 'We might have expected him to behave like that. I doubt whether Druck or Godit will find the servant who poisoned the eels. By now, that villain has probably taken the coin and travelled far from the castle.'

'I agree,' said Josik. 'And, Kedura, I don't see how you can avoid appointing Firt as Eldin's advisor. The boy is too young and inexperienced to govern. And only our Lady knows if the poor lad will reach a suitable age.'

'Josik, your land adjoins Trevin's,' said Quilin. 'Is it possible, Kedura, for Josik can visit the estate on a regular basis to watch over Eldin?'

'Would Firt be content to accept this arrangement?' Lyta asked.

'Probably not,' said Wilus, 'but as kedura, you can command it.'

'That might cause more trouble,' said Lyta. 'Mayhap, you could visit the estate occasionally, Josik, to see what's happening. If Firt becomes the official advisor, he has every right to govern as he thinks best for Eldin and his younger brothers and sister.'

She paused to judge the reactions of the men around her. 'Do you agree that I have to appoint Firt as the official advisor?' When she looked at the men around the table, they all nodded in agreement.

'However, I won't give him permission to leave until we've investigated the matter of Trevin's death.' She received murmurs of assent from her council. 'Then this meeting is over. We will resume our deliberations if new information is revealed. Thank you, my lords.'

When she rose, they followed suit and Quilin escorted her to the solar. Lyta paused outside the chamber door. 'Quilin, please leave your son at home until Firt has left here. I've never trusted the man and I truly believe he's responsible for Trevin's death.'

Quilin nodded. 'I'll leave Jilik where he is meanwhile. And I agree with you, Kedura, Firt probably paid somebody to poison Trevin. I dearly wish we could prove his guilt but unless Druck finds good evidence, that may not happen.'

He stood back to allow Jer to open the door and then bowed and walked away. Lyta stood for a minute, staring after him. She wondered if his small son had dark hair like his father or if he resembled his mother. The hair of Quilin's wife was as red and gold as the evening sunset and she had the green eyes that often accompanied such hair colour. She'd been a most beautiful woman.

Lyta mentally shook herself and entered the solar. She shouldn't be wasting time thinking about the past. The present day at the castle with Trevin's death was worry and sorrow enough.

Lyta was preparing for dinner when Druck was announced. 'Kedura, I have a description of the servant who gave Lord Trevin the dish of eels.' The commander stood stiffly despite's Lyta's invitation to be seated. 'The servant was young and short with fair hair and either blue or grey eyes.'

'That description fits many young men in our demesne.'

'It does, Kedura. Godit hired him to work in the kitchen and to serve at the feasts. And Prala recalls handing him the dish. All the other workers have received their pay for last night except this man. He seems to have vanished. I have guards searching the town and the harbor.'

'But you don't think he'll be found in Aldeton?'

Druck shook his head. 'I believe somebody paid him well and then arranged for him to leave the castle as soon as he gave Lord Trevin the eels. The hall was crowded that night and it would have been easy to slip away.'

'Is there anything more we can do to find the culprit?'

'Nothing more at the moment. If my men have any news after their search, I will report it to you.' He cleared his throat. 'Kedura, I think there may be an obvious culprit in the castle but I have no proof.'

'I understand, Archis. Please tell me of any developments in this matter, however small they may seem.'

Druck turned and bowed twice on his way out the door. Lyta knew she was probably ungracious but she could not like her commander. Her mother had said he was a dedicated and hard-working man and mayhap, he was. Lyta might be unfair in her critical assessment but to her mind, Druck had always worn too many insincere smiles.

Druck returned to the castle after dinner and was shown again into the solar. 'I have news, Kedura. A body was found in the harbor. I've had it brought to the castle for Prala and Godit to view. It fits their description,'

He bowed low and coughed. 'And one more disturbing thing about this body. Several townsfolk told my guards that the dead man is a relative of our annoying friend, Yalt.'

Chapter Fifty-Three

Nirk threw up his hands in exasperation. 'Iben, you're doing no good sitting here like some blasted broody hen. Be sensible, Kedir. You can't ask Lyta for her hand for another five moons. Let's go home.'

Iben plucked a few more notes on his lute. He'd spent the morn composing a second song to his fair lady. But the refrain was all wrong. He needed an air catchy enough for the listeners to sing along with him.

'Have you heard a single word I said?' Nirk slammed his left hand against the chamber wall.

'What?' Iben's dark eyes lost their dreaminess and he focused on his companion. 'Don't damage that wall. The landlord will charge me extra coin if you punch holes in it.'

'Damn the landlord. And damn the morn you set eyes on that girl.' Nirk sighed and rubbed his hand. 'Exactly what are you intending to do next?'

'Well, I'd like to sing this new song to Kedura Lyta but first I have to get into the castle.'

Nirk dropped onto a stool. 'Be very careful about going there again. Even from the back of the hall, I noticed Lord Wilus staring hard at you. He's seen your father often enough. What if he's recognised you?'

'Then mayhap he thinks I'm a distant relative. People know I come from Parian so it's a logical conclusion.'

Nirk snorted. 'Not logical enough. Please put down the lute. I'm tired of that mournful tune.' He stood up. 'Why don't we have a drink?'

'We might as well. I'm stuck on the refrain.' Iben placed the lute on a table. 'The right notes might come to me after a few cups of ale.'

Downstairs, the two men looked around for Yalt. For once he was sitting alone in a corner, his fair head bent low over his cup.

'Not another broody hen,' said Nirk as he carried three cups toward Yalt's table. 'Lord Sun, deliver me from drinking with sad men.'

When Nirk set the cups down, Yalt raised his head. He didn't speak but simply stared at them.

'Friend, what's wrong?' Iben asked. 'You look like a man in trouble.'

Yalt sighed. 'You could say that. Did you hear that Trevin is dead? They're saying he was poisoned.'

Iben gulped in shock. His father was a friend of the lord and had often travelled to Trevin's estate on hunting expeditions in the hills. He licked his lips and asked, 'Who could have poisoned him?'

'My guess is the one who has most to gain. My friend, Belia, is maid to the kedura and she says it was Firt. But he didn't dirty his own hands. He paid another to do the deed.'

Nirk leaned forward. 'Do you know the culprit?'

'The castle guards fished my drowned cousin from the harbor. Apparently, Citil fits the description of the man who served Trevin.'

'Is there any proof of your cousin's involvement?' Iben asked.

'A purse of coin found in his house. My aunt says Citil was paid for boots he made for someone at the castle.' Yalt shook his head. 'The guards took the body up there. Druck claims Citil was serving in the hall last night but his mother said he was courting a girl in town.'

'What's the girl's story?'

'Her father took her early this morn to the country. He didn't approve of the match. She isn't around to back up my aunt's words.'

Iben sipped his ale and pushed a full cup to Yalt. 'Will Druck question you? There's no love lost between the two of you.'

Yalt grimaced. 'That could happen if he believes I'm involved. The timing of this murder is so bad.'

'Why so?' Nirk asked.

Yalt looked around at the nearest drinkers and lowered his voice. 'You two were involved in the march to the castle so you're sympathetic to the cause of justice. If I tell you something, will you promise to keep silent? I need your advice.'

Iben and Nirk both nodded.

'I'm working on a plan to give power in the demesne to ordinary townsfolk.'

Iben wasn't sure if he'd heard correctly. 'What do you mean?'

'Why should the erles and Kedura Lyta make all the laws for us? Just because we don't have titles doesn't mean we're stupid. We should be able to have our voices heard. As a youngest son, Iben, you already know how little influence you have on any of your father's decisions.'

Iben felt an uncomfortable clenching in his belly. He was listening to treasonous words. Surely Yalt wasn't proposing to overthrow the traditional form of governance? Iben believed he was destined by Father Sun to rule Parian when Gerit died. He'd been trained from birth for that role. Townsfolk had no such guidance and no experience. What dreadful mistakes they would make if they acquired the power to create laws! His voice was much calmer than the tumultuous thoughts in his head as he asked. 'How would this work?'

'We would select townspeople to join the erles' council. Four lords and the magian advise the kedura at the moment so five of us could also advise her. The kedura could listen to every point of view before making her decisions.'

Nirk cleared his throat. 'What about Aldeans from the countryside? Would their voices also be heard?'

Iben heard Yait mention words like education and reading and writing but he was unable to get past the fact that noblemen like him would have to take a seat beside ordinary folk in this new council. They had no birth right to govern.

'Are women included?' Nirk asked.

'Few people are as wise as my mother. I'd trust her to make laws for me.'

Iben cleared his throat. 'It's certainly a new idea. How would these councillors be selected?'

'By ballot,' said Yalt. 'All grown people with reading and writing could cast a vote.' He leaned forward with both elbows on the table. 'Do you like my plan? Can you see anything wrong with it?'

Iben didn't know how to reply. Every thread in his being recoiled from the ridiculous idea of giving power to common folk who did not deserve the privilege. He could see unrest, anarchy, and even war developing as a result. Everything was wrong with this plan.

Instead he forced a deliberate steadiness into his voice. 'It's a very different way of governance.'

Yalt smiled for the first time. 'It certainly is different. But life would be better for everyone in this demesne.'

Iben finished his ale, looked hard at Nirk, and they both rose from their stools. 'I will consider your idea and we'll talk later.'

Back in their chamber, Iben fell back on the bed and rubbed his forehead as if he was wiping Yalt's plan from his mind. 'I've never heard such nonsense in my whole life! What if these opinions spread throughout the land? My father would behead anyone who even voiced such thoughts in Parian.'

Nirk folded his arms and leaned against the wall. 'I'm not so sure this is a bad idea. Nobody ever asks my opinion about any laws. I just go along with what's told to me.'

Iben stared at him in astonishment. 'But you aren't trained in the art of governance! How could you possibly choose the wisest path in a troublesome matter?'

'Like Yalt said, I'd think about it and discuss it with others. I'd be just as thoughtful about the proposal as an erle.'

Iben raised himself on both elbows. 'In all the years we've known each other, I never knew you harboured such dangerous ideas. Does this mean I can't trust you to do my bidding?'

'No, Kedir. I took an oath before your father to serve and protect you with my life. I am a man of my word.'

'I'm glad to hear it.' Iben frowned and bit his lower lip. 'Now I must get to the castle to talk to Wilus.'

'Surely, you won't tell him about Yalt! He hasn't done anything wrong except tell us about this idea.'

'But the idea is wrong and what's more, it's treasonous. I need to warn Kedura Lyta and her council. The man must be stopped before his seditious words become dangerous acts.'

Chapter Fifty-Four

Both Prala and Godit viewed the body taken from the harbor. Unfortunately, the man's head had been battered when waves carried it against the seawall and his features were unrecognizable. However, the cook and the castlian agreed the height and figure of the man were similar to the measurements of the servant who'd carried the dish of eels.

Wilus voiced his doubts to Lyta. 'Waves might not have done that damage to his face. What if the man was beaten to make his identification difficult? And then slain and thrown into the harbour? '

'True,' said Lyta. 'And his mother's story about him courting might also be correct. Has Druck found the girl?'

'Not so far. His men are still searching for her.'

'I don't think we'll ever be certain of the facts,' said Lyta. 'With reluctance, I'll allow Firt to leave. His stay is getting more difficult with each passing morn.'

Lyta had visited Adina in her chamber but Firt had forbidden the magian to dose her with any more of his remedies and he had posted an armed man on the door to prevent others from entering her chamber. Adina had scarce stopped weeping since her father's death and she was a sorry sight with her red swollen eyes and white face. Lyta noted that the girl was even neglecting her appearance. Before his meals, Firt questioned Prala and Godit about the preparation and serving of his food and he did not eat or drink anything until his man had tasted it first. Lyta had grown disgusted with his playacting.

When permission was given to leave the castle, Firt said he was glad to hear it and he'd go as soon as he could arrange for a suitable ship. Lyta asked Quilin to make sure one was readily available. 'I can't wait to see the last of him.'

'You'll have to see him again at our next council meeting.'

Lyta sighed. 'I know but at least I will be spared from his face for a while.'

Quilin said, 'Did you raise the topic of visits with Firt?'

'Firt said Josik could visit to discuss Eldin's wellbeing but he wasn't happy about my command.'

Two morns later, Adina and Firt left for the harbour. Trevin's body in a lead-lined coffin had been taken on board the ship. Wilus acted as an escort for the party and reported to Lyta that her troublesome guests had sailed away. She was in two minds about their departure; she felt grief for the loss of Trevin but relief for the absence of Firt.

Josik and his men departed the following morn. He took formal leave of Lyta, promising to return for the next council meeting. 'Firt is in a strong position now. He can justify all his decisions as benefitting Eldin and his younger brothers.' He sighed. 'Oh well, we will see what happens in the next moons.'

The magians also departed to their various homes. The castle should have settled into its normal routine except that Vea's woman came to Lyta's bedchamber early one morn.

'My lady has died in her sleep.' She dabbed her eyes with a corner of her apron. 'When I went to wake her, she seemed to be at peace.'

Lyta threw back the bed covering and called for her maids. 'I'll dress and come to see her at once.'

As her clothes were pulled over her head, Lyta thought about her aunt's background. Vea had been born in Falga and she had remained true to her Star faith. She still had a nephew and his wife who lived on an estate near

Naris. Magian Domen would know the best way to tell them about Vea's death. She could receive the correct Asteriki funeral rites if her body was returned to Falga.

Vea's woman was right. Her aunt's face had lost its haggard appearance and she looked younger and very peaceful. Lyta kissed her cheek and murmured words of farewell. 'Has the Lady Jona been informed?' she asked the maid.

'Yes, Lady. She did not take it well.'

'Not surprising, thought Lyta. Despite the spats that often arose between the two women, Jona would be lost and lonely without her stitching companion.

'I will visit Lady Jona.' She paused at the bedchamber door. 'Magian Domen will contact Lady Vea's family. Then I will arrange to send my aunt's body to Falga.'

'Lady, I would like to go with the body. I came from Falga and have family in Naris. Now that Lady Vea has passed, I will live with my daughter.'

Jona seemed to have shrunk in her bed. Her small face looked tiny on the pillow. She stared up at Lyta with her pale blue eyes. 'I will die soon too.'

'The magian will come and see you.'

She shook her head with its ring of red and grey curls. 'There's no need for his visit. His potions won't do me any good now.'

'He could mix a tonic for you.'

'I wouldn't swallow it.' Jona clutched Lyta's hand. 'Promise me you'll send me home.'

'To Parian?'

'I want the correct rites performed in the Sun Temple and then to be laid at rest beside my husband.'

'I promise.' Lyta looked down at her aunt and felt a pang of sorrow and regret. She could have been kinder to Jona. When she died, Lyta would lose the last links to her mother.

'Inform me each morn of Lady Jona's condition,' she said to the maid.

Lyta had resumed her mother's practice of being available in the great hall after dinner to hear any petitions. Either Wilus or Quilin accompanied her but each man had said he would listen but not voice an opinion unless she asked for one.

Wilus sat with her the first time when she pronounced judgment in a case where two men claimed ownership of one cow. Lyta decided on the rightful owner when one petitioner was unable to describe the exact colouring of the animal. The clerk had given her the details of the animal in the written copy of the petition. Lyta hoped all cases would be as easy but knew from attending her mother's audiences that this was unlikely.

Before supper, Lyta received a message from Nin the head stable groom. Her mount, Silver, was ailing. When she arrived at the stall, Silver was standing listlessly in her stall with her head hanging low. Lyta had brought an apple with her but even this treat didn't tempt the horse to take the fruit from Lyta's palm.

'How long has Silver been like this?' she asked Nin. The groom looked uneasy, and shuffled his feet in the straw.

'Since yestermorn, Kedura. She didn't eat her oats.'

'Why didn't you inform me she was ill? What treatment have you used so far?' When Lyta ran a hand down Silver's neck, the horse shivered and turned her head away.

'I used one of Virr's potions but it didn't restore her appetite.'

For the thousandth time, Lyta wished that Virr was still alive. As the head of the stables before Nin, he'd been an expert at diagnosing complaints. His skill had been enhanced by the fact that he was able to communicate with the animals under his care. Using this talent he'd saved many horses. Lyta remembered his cure of Midnight, her mother's horse, and Bold, the mount of Archis Druck.

Now, she sighed as she looked at Silver. 'Please continue to watch her closely,' she said to Nin. 'And if her condition becomes worse, send me a message, even if it's nighttime.'

Nin gave his assent and Lyta patted her horse once more and left the stables. At supper she asked Wilus if he would go to the stables to observe Silver. With his long experience at raising and riding horses, he might have some suggestions for her care.

Wilus took his captain with him as the man was also adept at treating horses. Afterwards, he told Lyta they both thought Silver had a belly ache which would soon resolve itself.

'Don't worry, Kedura. Nin said the horse seemed a little better. We both agreed that your groom had done what was needed. With Silver on the mend, you can rest lightly tonight.'

But everyone was wrong. At repast, an urgent message came from the stables. Silver had died.

Lyta pushed her platter aside and called for her clothes. Then she sped to the stables. Nin was crouched in the stall with one hand on Silver's neck and tears streaming down his cheeks. The other grooms and stable boys huddled close by, silent and pale.

Nin raised his tear-stained face. 'I had no idea, Lady. She ate some oats and even took your apple. We all thought she was improving. Then as I was holding a pail of water for her to drink, she shuddered and fell down.'

Lyta stared at the body of her dear friend. It was impossible to accept that she would never ride the horse again.

'I'm sorry, Kedura. I did all I could.' Nin rubbed a hand over his eyes. 'She was a fine horse.'

Lyta knelt in the straw, heedless of her robe. She bent down to lay her head against Silver's nose. 'I don't blame you, Nin. Lord Wilus also thought she was recovering.'

Lyta kissed her horse and stood up. 'Please ask Magian Domen to examine her. Then I want her buried at the end of the grazing fields. Send for me when she has been placed in the grave.'

Lyta walked back to her chambers, determined not to cry until she was alone. In the solar, she stared at the hanging on the far wall, which displayed a meadow of wild flowers with two black horses and a grey one. She recalled the many moons her mother, aunts, and maids had taken to stitch the tapestry, which depicted Halia's horses, Nighthawk and Midnight, along with Silver. Only then did Lyta allow her tears to flow. Virr was dead. Her mother and aunt were dead and so was Silver. Links with the past were being severed, one by one.

Wilus came to see Lyta, his eyes full of sympathy. 'I know, Kedura, you have lost a good friend. I always grieved exceedingly much when a favoured horse or dog died.' He patted her hand.

Lyta had decided to finish weeping for her losses. 'Thanks for your kind words. You're right. Silver was my friend. I will sorely miss her.'

Wilus shuffled his feet. When he looked as though he had more to say, Lyta said, 'Please be seated my lord. Did you have another reason to seek me out?'

'Well, yes, Kedura, but this may not be the right time to discuss it with you.'

'Go ahead. Right now, I need to think of other business.'

'Remember I said that the young singer looked like Kedur Gerit of Parian?'

Lyta nodded.

'Domen found out that Kedir Iben is not in his demesne. He's meant to be visiting his sister in Delis but instead, he's here in Aldeton. He was that very singer who entertained you. He came to see me on a matter of some importance.'

'What is it?' Lyta asked.

'He's concerned that Yalt has seditious ideas. The man proposes that common folk should be part of our council to give them a voice in making new laws for Aldea.'

For a moment, Lyta wasn't sure she'd understood his words. 'But it is treason to try to change the natural order of governance.'

'Of course it is. I am very grateful that Kedir Iben came to me with this startling news. We must tell Quilin and Domen as soon as possible.'

Lyta said, 'Please send for them. We'll meet in the council chamber.'

Wilus bowed and left her solar.

At the meeting, Wilus explained to Quilin and Domen what he had heard from Kedir Iben.

'Do you think that Yalt is serious? His words may be mere puffs of smoke in the wind,' Quilin said. 'Men often say things they don't mean just to rile others.'

'Iben thought Yalt intended to carry out his ideas. To create a new council, he'd need support from the townsfolk first and then others in the demesne.'

Quilin said, 'That would involve holding meetings and men going out into the countryside to spread the word.'

'But people in this demesne seem content,' said Domen. 'I wonder if they realize that changing the natural order can lead to bloodshed and loss?' '

Wilus said, 'I've asked Iben to keep me informed. We're lucky to have his ears to learn more about Yalt's next step. I also warned him to take care that his true identity is not discovered. He's put it about that he's the young son of an erle from Parian.'

Lyta had remained silent throughout the discussion. After the first shock of hearing Yalt's ideas, she was now wondering what dreadful things would happen to the demesne if a small group of the common folk did advise her. Would such a change automatically lead to violence and disorder? She needed to think more about it before she voiced an opinion. She ended the meeting with a request to hear everything Kedir Iben reported from Aldeton.

In the evening, Lyta donned a cloak and escorted only by Jer, went down to the grazing fields. At the far end, a small group of people stood near a pile of earth. As she walked closer Lyta recognized the stable boys and grooms and Magian Domen. They parted to allow her to stand on the edge of the yawning grave where Silver lay on her side. Amia had gathered a bunch of wildflowers and Lyta dropped them one by one onto her beloved horse. Red, blue, gold, and orange, they created a bright blanket to cover her.

'Sleep well, my good friend,' she murmured as she threw the last flower, a pink wild rose. Then she turned to the stable boys. 'Cover Silver well with earth. She must lie undisturbed in this patch of ground.'

She walked away abruptly and as she did, four young horses from the other side of the rough fence thundered toward her, tossing their heads and lifting their tails. The pure white one seemed to be the ringleader in their play. Lyta stopped to watch them gallop in a wide circle, nudging each other and snorting. Their wild spirits were strangely comforting.

Chapter Fifty-Five

Magian Domen told Lyta he'd examined Silver's body and seen no sign of poison. 'But I don't know what killed her. She must have suffered from an ailment that nobody recognized.'

Lyta frowned. 'Are other horses likely to fall ill?'

'To prevent any sickness, the stall straw should be removed and burned. Then the stones scrubbed and allowed to dry before new straw is laid down.'

'I will give the orders at once.'

When Domen had left, Lyta wondered if she would ride again. It seemed wrong to replace Silver with another animal. But then she remembered her pleasure at the sight of the young horses galloping toward her. And Nin may have already chosen a new mount.

When Quilin arrived in the antechamber, Amia admitted him to the solar. He greeted Lyta and then said, 'With your permission, Kedura, I will instruct my people to bring Jilik here. Now that Firt has gone, life is peaceful here.'

'Yes, of course, he may come,' said Lyta. She paused. 'I was wondering whether your son resembles your wife in appearance or you.'

Quilin smiled. 'One glimpse will show you the truth. Such bright hair means he can always be seen from a distance. Which is very useful as he likes to roam on foot and on horseback.'

'Does he ride well?'

'My wife loved horses and Jilik was almost born on one. He rides exceeding well for his age. I hope we can find a suitable mount in your stable while he's living here.'

'Nin will be pleased to suggest one.'

Quilin's face turned serious. 'I heard about your own horse. You must be grieving for Silver.'

Lyta nodded. She didn't want to discuss Silver for fear she might weep in front of Quilin, despite her resolve. She changed the subject to Aldean matters. A petitioner was asking for judgment in a theft. He claimed his neighbor had stolen coin from its hiding place in a chimney. The neighbor claimed the man's own son had taken the coin and gambled it away. Lyta and Quilin would hear both sides when petitions were heard.

Before Jilik could arrive, the old salvan collapsed on the chapel floor during morn prayers. The magian said Elon was unable to speak. 'His mind has been struck as if he'd been hit on the head. At his great age, he is unlikely to linger very long.'

Lyta gave orders that Elon should be kept in a comfortable state and sent for the head of the Salvence.

She had not met him before. Salvis Hurd was a tall man with a bald head, piercing blue eyes, and a lofty manner. Lyta wondered if he would look down his nose in quite the same way if his ruler were a man.

She greeted him in courteous fashion but his returning bow was merely perfunctory. 'Ah, Kedura, I hear Salvan Elon cannot continue with his duties. No doubt you wish me to select a new man who has completed training at our school to replace him.'

'Do you have any women priests who would be suitable?'

Hurd visibly recoiled. 'For such an important position here, women are not fitting. Their shrill voices don't carry well in prayers and rites. You need a man's commanding tones to fill your chapel.'

'You obviously haven't seen my chapel. It's in the oldest part of the castle and holds only fifty souls.'

'But the right voice is essential to maintain the dignity of our Moon faith.'

Lyta studied him for a moment before she spoke. 'My mother had no trouble maintaining the dignity of her position as Kedura with her woman's voice. And so far no man or woman has complained about the quality of mine.'

For the first time in their audience, Hurd looked flustered. 'Kedura, of course I'll find suitable candidates for you, both men and women. Would you like to see them here or at the Salvence? You could visit our new school.'

Lyta hadn't been to the Salvence for many summers. The priestly school was attached to the Moon Temple and she knew a building had been erected recently to replace one that had burned down last summer.

'I will visit you,' she said. 'In a sevenday.'

Salvis Hurd agreed that it was very suitable and left with a bow that was much lower than the one he'd performed earlier. Lyta wondered if her mother had encountered similar opinions about women during her reign as Kedura. Possibly so, she thought. Old ideas were exceeding slow to change.

Two morns before she left for the Moon Temple, Jilik and his little party were due to arrive. Lyta had told Godit to prepare her old tower quarters for the child. He would have a bedchamber and a workchamber there with sufficient space to house his attendants.

As soon as word came from the harbour that the ship had been sighted, Quilin rode down to meet his son. From her solar window, Lyta saw them return. The boy was seated on the saddle in front of his father. Lyta smiled when Jilik threw back the hood of his green cloak. That shining copper hair could easily rival a torch flame.

Before Lyta changed for dinner, Quilin brought his son to meet her. The child had been schooled in courtesy. His bow was so low he almost overbalanced.

Lyta bent down to raise the child. 'Welcome, Jilik, I trust you'll be very happy here.'

'It's a big castle,' he said.

'You'll enjoy exploring all the inner passages and chambers and the outer buildings. When I was young, I knew every part.'

The child stared around the solar until his eyes landed on the bright horse tapestry. 'I like that,' he said, walking closer. 'My horse at home is called Rusty. She is chestnut in colour.'

Quilin had been watching his son with a proud look on his face. 'Now we must allow the Kedura to dress for dinner.' He moved to Jilik's side. 'Bow again and we will leave.'

'Do I walk backwards like my tutoran said?'

'In your case, you might be safer bowing and turning,' said his father. 'Then you can walk forward to the door.'

Jilik performed a second shaky bow. When he surfaced, he grinned up at Lyta. 'Thank you for receiving me.'

Then he looked at his father. 'Did I say that right?'

'Indeed, you did,' said Quilin.

His eyes twinkled at Lyta as he made his own bow, and took Jilik's hand to lead him through the door. Lyta thought that life might become lively with the boy at the castle. She told herself to ask Godit to move the wall hanging of the horses to Jilik's work chamber. It could replace the tapestry with the peasant begging for mercy from his lord. As a child, she'd been disturbed by the frantic expression on the petitioner's face and the cold expression on his lord's face.

Two morns later, Druck and six guards escorted Lyta and the magian from the castle. Domen had asked to accompany her to the Salvence.

'I have heard good reports of the new building,' he said. 'I may get some ideas from it to improve our magian school in Aldeton.'

Nin had provided a new mount for her journey. The horse was light bay in colour and known as Spirit. She had an energetic nature but none of the sweet disposition of Silver. Lyta told herself it was unwise to make comparisons. This horse would serve her until she had time to search for a more fitting mount.

The Moon temple was situated in the town of Caldis, ten leagues east of the castle. Lyta and her party arrived as dusk was falling. The air was cooler now with the approach of harvest time. Red and gold leaves carpeted the road leading to the temple. It perched on a rise above the town with a commanding view of the countryside. Although it was an impressive building of four stories in height, Lyta considered it was an inferior sight to the Asteriki Temple in Falga with its array of silver spires. She'd visited that place after her escape from Erle Rurrik. The Asteriki Temple was acclaimed throughout the land for its wonderful ceiling which depicted several sparkling constellations.

Lyta was welcomed by Valin, the chief Moon priest and by Hurd. She and Domen were taken to the guest quarters behind the temple where they washed and changed from their dusty travelling clothes. They were served a simple meal of fish, bread, cheese and wine.

Domen sipped from his glass of wine. 'This is very fine wine.'

Valin said, 'We have our own vineyards, which the priests tend as part of their training. We believe that hard work using the hands is as important as hard study using the mind. And the coin the vines generate keeps our Salvence and Temple running well.' He lifted his glass in a toast to Lyta. 'I will send you home, Kedura, with a cask of this particular vintage. We are very proud of its high quality.'

Lyta asked about her former tutoran. 'How is Cordon? I'd like to see him.'

'I will make sure he comes to see you,' said Hurd.

Lyta spent a busy day. She met four candidates for the position of castle salvan. She was shown over the new building and when she sat down for her meal at noon, Cordon joined her.

'You look well,' she said to him. She remembered her tutoran as pale and weak but now he looked tanned and healthy.

Cordon smiled. 'I work in the vineyards each morn. The remaining hours, Kedura, I attend classes.'

They talked about Cordon's studies and recent events at the castle. He nodded and muttered his condolences when she informed him of Lady Vea's death. They had never got on well because Vea expressed her own ideas about Lyta's education to Cordon. He was more upset to hear about Trevin's death. 'He was a good man who should not have died in such a terrible manner.'

In the evening, Lyta attended prayers at the temple. The ceiling of this building depicted a series of images of Lady Moon. At the edges, she was shown as delicate silver curves which gradually increased in size until she became a glorious full orb, beaming down from the very centre. In the light of large candles set on metal stands, The Lady shone, casting a golden glow over the people below. Lyta prayed that the guidance of Mother Moon would be as constant as her regular passage across the heavens.

When Lyta and Domen returned to the castle, they took the new salvan with them. Mena was a woman of thirty summers, older than the usual priests in training. She'd explained that she'd been married to a fisherman from Caldis who'd lost his boat and his life in a fierce spring storm. Then her only child, a boy of six summers died suddenly of the spotted fever. Instead of becoming a melancholy recluse after these tragedies, Mena was comforted by her devotion to Mother Moon and she had helped others seek the right path.

Lyta was impressed by the woman's forthright nature and good sense. Mena believed in offering practical help as well as prayers. And her voice was clear and carried well. Her first duty would be to conduct the funeral of her predecessor. The old salvan had died on the very morn that Lyta left on her journey

When they reached the castle, Druck stopped the escort party on the far side of the moat. He frowned as he studied a cluster of guards talking in an agitated manner outside the gatehouse.

'Something's wrong,' he said. 'Please wait here with my men, Kedura, until I discover the cause.'

He crossed the bridge and spoke to his guards. When he returned to Lyta he said, 'The child is missing.'

'Child?' repeated Lyta. 'Do you mean Jilik, Lord Quilin's son?'

'That's the one,' said Druck. 'A party has been searching the town while others scour every corner of the castle.'

'How long has he been gone?' Lyta asked.

'He was seen just after supper last night,'

Lyta spurred Spirit across the bridge. 'This is dreadful news. I must learn as soon as possible exactly what has been done to find Jilik.'

Chapter Fifty-Six

The castle was in chaos when Lyta set foot inside the great oak doors. Groups of servants huddled together speaking in low voices while others hurried by with frowning faces. Godit came to meet her, his chubby red face creased with distress. 'What a homecoming for you, Kedura. We're at sixes and sevens here. I'll send for Amia.'

'Do you know where Lord Quilin is?' Lyta asked.

'Last time I saw him he was off with his men to search the Dark Forest.' Godit shook his head. 'I certainly hope the poor little lad isn't lost in that dreaded place. Wild beasts could attack him.'

'Was Jilik on foot or mounted?'

'Nin says he didn't take the pony he's been given.'

'Then he can't have gone too far,' said Lyta. 'Send Amia or any of my maids to me.'

In her chamber, she stripped off her cloak and washed her face and hands. Then she stood by the window, looking down into the inner courtyard. She wondered where an adventurous child might go. The castle had so many nooks and crannies and since Jilik was small in stature, he might have squeezed into a place where an adult wouldn't fit. Now, which ones had been her favourite spots to hide when she was young?

Amia hurried into the solar. 'Forgive me, Kedura, for not being here to receive you. We've all been looking for Jilik. Lord Quilin is exceedingly worried.'

'I can imagine so. The child will be hungry and thirsty by now. He may be asleep and not hear people searching for him.'

Amia nodded. 'Lord Quilin said that same thing before he left for the forest.'

'I've been thinking of places I used to go,' said Lyta. 'Whenever there were puppies, I always went to the kennels. And although I was scared of ghosts and rats, I explored the old dungeons in the Prison Tower.'

'But Kedura, it would not be fitting for you to look for the boy,' Amia said as she pulled Lyta's dusty robe over her head. 'Godit can send men to the kennels and the dungeons if they have not been searched already.'

But Lyta wasn't listening to her maid's counsel. If Jilik was distressed enough, she might be able to use her lofting power to receive a mind message from him. It was worth a try.

Once she was dressed in a clean gown, Lyta slipped on her cloak and went into the antechamber. 'Jer can escort me,' she said to Amia. 'If I see Godit on the way, I'll ask him about the kennels and the tower.'

On her way to the Prison Tower, Jer expressed his concern about the safety of the place. 'Those steps down to the unused dungeons are old and crumbling. You must let me go first, Kedura, for fear you could fall.'

Jer opened the door to the tower. 'And there might be rats.' He peered into the gloom and swept his lit torch from side to side. 'Nobody here.'

'Let's look at all the steps.' Lyta moved to walk past him.

Jer shook his head. 'Let me, Lady.' He pulled the blade from his belt and strode across the chamber to stop at the foot of the steps. 'The boy hasn't been here, Kedura. The dust is thick and undisturbed.'

He crossed to the lower steps and looked down. 'And he hasn't been here either. A fall of stones has blocked the way.'

'Then we will try the kennels.' Lyta turned and left the tower.

'Mayhap the kennel master has already searched there.'

'Jer, we will look again. There's a secret passage at the very back that leads into the wall. Mayhap the kennel master doesn't know about it'

Jer hurried to keep up with her as she crossed the courtyard. Sek, the kennel master, bowed low when he saw her enter the door. 'The boy is not here, Kedura. I have taken out all the dogs and looked in every space.'

'What about the passage that leads into the wall? Virr said that I should hide there if the castle was ever attacked by an enemy.'

Sek shook his head. 'I didn't know about this passage, Kedura. I came here after Virr died.'

The master calmed the dogs as Lyta walked through the kennels. He followed her through the little chambers. At the very rear, she pushed against a section of wall. The lower stones swung open like a door, just wide enough for a child or a dog to squeeze through.

Lyta called Jilik silently. No response.

She tried again. This time she received a faint reply. Jilik was definitely in the passage and he must have been in great distress to receive her mind message. Mayhap he had discovered like her that the secret door was difficult to open from the other side.

When Lyta called aloud, a tearful voice answered her. 'I hurt my leg and can't walk.'

Sek grasped the situation at once. He sent for the smallest boy in his employ. When the child came, he wriggled into the hole and disappeared. Lyta heard a brief conversation.

The boy reappeared. 'Kedura, I need a cloak or some such to put beneath Lord Jilik. Then I can pull him forward.'

Lyta was pleased with the kennel lad's quick thinking. She started to undo her own cloak before Jer stopped her. 'Take mine, Kedura.' He undid the clasp at his neck and handed the garment to the boy.

Within minutes, Jilik had been wrapped up and tugged along to the narrow opening. Jer and the kennel master yanked him into the light.

Jilik's face was grubby from dirt and tears. 'I want my nurse,' he said through loud sobs.

Lyta said to the stable boy. 'Please tell Magian Domen that Lord Jilik's been found with an injured leg.'

After the boy had left, Sek summoned a burly worker to carry Jilik from the kennels. When Lyta followed, they met Domen in the courtyard. He gave directions for the child to be taken to his dwelling for treatment. Finally, Lyta ordered Jer to send a mounted messenger to Lord Quilin telling him the good news.

Before she returned to the castle, Lyta spoke to the kennel master. 'Please block that passage with large stones. We don't want any more mishaps.'

Sek shook his head. 'I didn't see him, Kedura. And I didn't know about that there passage.'

'I understand.' Lyta sighed. 'I'd better remember the other places I hid when I was young. Lord Jilik is an adventurous boy who may find every spot.'

The master bowed and Lyta heard him mutter under his breath some words about Lord Jilik being a troublesome brat. She ignored the comment.

Quilin was almost overcome with his feelings when he returned from the forest. His face was drawn and his eyes were underlined with purple shadows. He tried to smile at Lyta but it was a shaky effort. 'I can't thank you enough, Kedura. Jilik could have perished in that passage. Thank Lady Moon you knew about it.'

'How is his leg?'

'Domen says a bone in his lower leg is broken. He has strapped it to a straight board to allow it to heal. That should curtail his exploration for at least one moon, if not longer.'

When Lyta smiled at him, Quilin seized her hand and kissed it. 'I am in your debt for ever, Kedura. How can I repay you?'

Lyta let her hand rest in his warm grasp for a minute. 'No need, my lord. I was happy to help Jilik. Now we must all take care to keep him safe at the castle.' With some reluctance, she reclaimed her hand.

Quilin shook his head. 'That may not be a simple task.'

***

Mena conducted Elon's funeral with every eye on her to assess her command of the correct prayers and sacred rituals. Amia had said some of the castle officials disapproved of a woman in the role of salvan. The new priest was dignified in her green robe; her bearing was stately, and her words were clearly heard throughout the chapel. As she listened to the service, Lyta hoped that Mena would, in time, win everyone's support. Elon's body was taken from the castle by wagon with an escort of guards. It was carried to the Moon Temple for burial in the graveyard reserved for salvans.

Wilus had arranged to meet Iben on a secluded track near the Dark Forest. He left for the meeting, taking only his captain. When he returned to the castle, he came to see Lyta.

'What news about Yalt?' she asked.

'He is meeting folk in his own house rather than in the tavern. They gather in secret at night.'

'Did Iben attend these meetings?'

'He's been to three so far. Different people come each time to hear Yalt. But we have a difficulty. Kedur Gerit has discovered his son is in Aldea and he's sent a messenger to his son ordering him to return to Parian.'

'Then we'll lose our ears and eyes.'

'True. And Gerit's letter said a ship will arrive in the harbor in a sevenday with an escort to take Iben home.'

'How can we discover what Yalt is doing?'

'Quilin told you earlier he has men in disguise in Aldeton. One of them may be able to befriend Yalt.' Wilus shook his head. 'But it won't be the same.'

Lyta sat in silence for a few minutes. Then she said, 'I don't wish Quilin's man to be placed in danger.'

'We would try our best to keep him secure. But, Kedura, no situation can be made completely safe.' Wilus rose to leave the chamber.

'Lord Wilus?' Lyta spoke hesitantly. 'Is it such a terrible thing to listen to the common folk to learn what they think?'

Wilus stared hard at her. 'Are you saying this because you distrust the counsel of your erles?'

'No, of course not. I trust you completely. But I will never know what other folk think unless I ask them.'

'My dear Kedura, our form of governance is what Mother Moon has ordained for us. I inherited land from my father and grandsires with all its right and privileges. I govern my people fairly and protect them against their enemies. In turn, they serve me and pay me tithes. Your situation is the same on a larger scale. And most importantly, we have been trained from birth to rule with all diligence and care.'

'I know that,' said Lyta. 'And I would never ignore your wise advice. But what if the people I govern have good ideas too?'

'I can't believe you are raising this matter. Nothing is wrong with the traditional ways of making laws. You are young and inexperienced and you've let Yalt's wrong ideas take root in your mind. The man must be stopped right now. We know enough already to arrest him for treason.'

His brow was creased with worry and his mouth set in a straight line. 'Kedur, remove these seditious ideas from your mind. They have the power to destroy our demesne.'

Lyta met his stare with one of her own. She felt troubled at disturbing Wilus. He'd been faithful and true to her mother and now he'd sworn fealty to her. But was she so wrong in considering a different way to rule Aldea? Traditions might sometimes benefit from change. She wondered if Josik and Quilin would be equally adamant in their opinions.

'Forgive me, my lord. As you say, I am young and inexperienced. But my schooling with Cordon taught me to think for myself. And my mother encouraged me to consider new ideas.'

'I would be happier if you didn't consider this particular idea at all. However, I can't stop you from thinking about it. But please be guided by men who have many moons of governance under their belts and have seen foolish ideas come and go. Do not make rash decisions without consulting us.'

'I would never undertake any important action without consulting you.' She gave Wilus her hand. 'You have my word on it.'

He drew her hand to his lips and bent to kiss it. As he rose, Lyta saw the flicker of doubt in his eyes and knew Wilus had serious misgivings about the direction of her thoughts. This could be the first real rift between them.

Chapter Fifty-Seven

Lyta stared at the faces of her advisors. The three men around the table had fixed expressions on their face as they listened to Wilus's arguments about detaining Yalt. From his previous comments, she'd expected Domen to agree but she'd hoped that Quilin who was younger than the other two would be more receptive to change. However he also thought Yalt should be arrested.

'He might destroy the stability of your demesne, Kedura. And if his ideas spread beyond our borders, they could disrupt peace in the whole land.'

Lyta raised her eyebrows but bit back her answer. She didn't think that listening to ordinary folk expressing their opinions would cause civil war but she wouldn't achieve anything by supporting Yalt at this point. She wanted to speak to the man as she'd found him to be intelligent and thoughtful in their previous encounter on the castle wall.

'Kedura, he must be detained at once,' Wilus said. 'This treasonous behavior has gone on long enough.'

'I agree,' said Domen.

Quilin glanced at Lyta for a minute before he too nodded his assent. They all looked at Lyta for her permission. She said, 'He can be detained on one condition.'

'And what is that, Kedura?' Wilus asked.

'That Yalt not be mistreated in any way. When he is brought to the castle, I wish to talk to him and I'll ask him about his confinement. If I see a single bruise or a cut on him, I'll demand to know who was responsible.'

She looked at each man and received reluctant nods in return. 'Then he will be picked up this morn.' said

Wilus, barely hiding his satisfaction. He cleared his throat. ‘You should know, Kedura, that Iben set sail yestermorn. His father wants no mention made by us of his stay in Aldea. As far as Gerit is concerned, his son was never here.’

‘That makes no sense. Iben will be recognized at once when he returns here as a suitor.’ Lyta said.

‘I\m sure he’ll concoct some story,’ said Quilin in a sour tone. ‘I just hope he won’t put the tale to music and sing it to us.’

After dinner, Lyta went to Jona’s chamber. Apart from brief spells in a chair, her aunt stayed in bed. Occasionally, she did some stitching but even her favoured needlework couldn’t hold her interest for long.

‘I am waiting to die like dear Vea,’ she said to Lyta. ‘But it is taking so long for me to go.’

Magian Domen had visited Jona. She submitted to his examination in resigned silence. Afterwards, Domen told Lyta said he could do little to improve her health. ‘I’ve given her a tonic but she may not take it. Once a person has decided she does not wish to live, then that is it. I have seen it happen many times.’

When she returned from her visit to Jona, Druck was shown into Lyta’s solar. He came to attention before her chair and bowed. ‘Bad news I’m afraid, Kedura. Yalt has disappeared. My men have searched the town but no sign of him.’

‘Could he be hiding in the countryside?’ she asked.

‘I’ve sent out a party beyond the town. It looks as though he left in a great hurry. His tools were set out on his table as though he was in the middle of working on some task.’

‘Yalt might have learned he was going to be detained,’ said Lyta.

‘Kedura, I’m not sure how he discovered that. We kept the arrest a secret.’

'What does his family say?'

'Yalt lives with his mother and grandsire. He spent much time away from home. They didn't realize he hadn't slept in the house until repast this morn.'

'Let me know if you find him.'

Druck bowed and left the solar. Strange, Lyta thought, that both Iben and Yalt had left Aldeton. Surely no connection existed between the two departures. Yalt was unlikely to make a sudden journey to Parian to spread his ideas. She hoped he hadn't come to harm.

As often happened at harvest time when Lady Moon shone bright and full, a storm arose in the late afternoon. At the first sign of black clouds building in the west, fisherfolk pulled their boats high on the sand away from the punishing waves. Farmers shut their animals up to keep them secure and mothers called their children home to be safe inside. .

This storm was a strong one. Wind howled around the castle all night, squeezing through cracks in the stone walls, pushing cold fingers through gaps in the windows and blasting through the doors whenever they were opened.

Lyta huddled under extra coverlets in her bed, loathe to leave the warmth. Rising meant she would brave the chamber, which was frigid even with the braziers her maids kept burning in every corner. She pulled on a heavy cloak to eat her repast in bed. The wind and rain had awakened her several times during the night, rattling the heavy shutters latched across her windows.

When she did dress, she kept the warm cloak drawn around her body and sat beside a brazier, holding her hands to the warm coals. Amia announced Druck and he almost blew into the solar when the door from the antechamber was opened.

The commander's nose was red from the cold and his eyes watered. He strode near Lyta. 'A cool morn, Kedura,' he observed.

'It's more than cool. Please tell me if anyone has been hurt. And is there much damage?' Lyta blew on her fingers.

'That old oak in the outerward came over with a mighty crash in the night. We all heard it from the gatehouse. And branches and loose articles lie scattered everywhere. But I came to tell you that a ship has been wrecked on the other side of the seawall. It lies on the rocks.'

'Was anyone saved?'

'Four bodies washed ashore and four swam there. Fisherfolk rescued six others.'

'Then it was a large ship with so many men. Do you know where it came from?'

'From Falga, Kedura. But the important matter is that one of the men is Kedir Ardul.'

'Ardul? Is he living or dead?'

'Barely alive. He's been taken to Domen's dwelling. The magian is not sure he can be saved. He asks your permission to send a message to Kedur Ulit informing him of the sad event.'

'Yes, of course. Was Ardul on his way here?'

'One of his men said they were going to Sevvir when they were caught in this storm. They tried to take shelter in our harbour but the easterly wind blew them beyond it. Luckily the ship was seen from the shore or Kedir Ardul would certainly have perished in the cold water.'

'When you talk to the magian, ask him to come to me when he gets a chance. And I would like to be informed of any return messages from Kedur Ulit.'

'Yes, Kedura.' Druck bowed low and left the solar. Lyta shivered in the blast of cold air from the door as it opened and closed.

Fluva added more coals to the brazier beside Lyta. 'Kedura, I hear tell that Kedir Ardul is very handsome,' she said. 'Rina who works for the magian came to the kitchen for soup. She says he has fine white skin and golden hair.'

Lyta reflected that so far she had been visited by two eligible suitors: Iben from Parian and now Ardul from Falga. Could she expect to see Merik from Sevvir and Fultis from Delis in the next moons? She certainly hoped not. Ardul was an added complication in her life. If he died in her demesne, Darik would be sure to tell his kedur that the death was part of a sinister plot against all Falgans who ventured into Aldea.

When she was visited by Wilus and Quilin later in the morn, they discussed Ardul and agreed that it was important for everyone that the kedir should live. Domen joined them just before dinner.

'What news?' Lyta asked.

'His life is in the balance,' said the magian. 'He swallowed a large quantity of seawater and when that happens, the lungs are affected. He is having difficulty breathing.' He looked at Lyta. 'So far, I have treated him with a mixture of Fredul and Salusy. He has also broken a bone in his left leg. All I can do is to dose Ardul and keep him warm and rested.'

'What are his chances?' Wilus asked.

'The kedir is young and strong so that works in his favour. If he'd been any longer in the sea, he would have drowned.'

Lyta nodded. 'Then I will pray to Mother Moon to save him although mayhap, I should also ask the Stars for aid. Ardul must be a child of the Asteriki.'

'Certainly,' said Domen, 'He was wearing the Star around his neck.'

'Did you hear back from the magian in Falga?' she asked.

'Kedur Ulit was deeply distressed by the news and grateful to the people of Aldea for the rescue. He asks to be kept informed of any change in his son's condition.' The magian rose and bowed to Lyta. 'I must return to my patient. Rina is very competent but I do not like to leave her alone for too long.'

When Domen had left, Lyta and her two lords decided not to eat in the great hall. Its cavernous space would be cold and exceeding draughty in the present weather. They ate the simple meal that Prala had sent from the kitchen. The hot vegetable soup and bread with cheese were welcome. Lyta finished her soup and put down her bowl. She crossed to the window, opened one of the shutters, and peered outside.

The wind had abated a little and the rain showers grown less frequent and lighter but signs of the storm were obvious. Debris littered the courtyard. She saw several water barrels, assorted pieces of wood and stone, and an entire door as well as numerous branches and drifts of leaves.

Quilin opened the other shutters and secured them both against the wall. He too stared into the courtyard. 'The storm is moving off,' he said. 'I'll ride into town in an hour to see what damage has been caused.' He turned to Lyta. 'It's exceeding strange that Yalt had gone before Druck reached his dwelling. I wonder if he knew he was going to be brought in.'

'Druck says the capture was kept a secret,' said Lyta.

'Yes, but it's almost impossible to keep secrets at this castle. I'd be surprised if your maids hadn't described the rescued kedir of Falga to you by now.'

Lyta laughed. 'Indeed Fluva did. I already know Ardul is handsome with white skin and golden hair. I don't know about the colour of his eyes as no doubt they were closed.'

'Then if he lives, let's hope he doesn't like to play the lute and compose melancholy love songs.'

'I'm sure he does. Every accomplished kedir is taught to play and sing but his songs may not be as tuneful as Iben's.'

She enjoyed Quilin's reaction to her words. He grimaced and shook his head. 'Then it's just as well I'm not a kedir. I can't carry a tune or play the lute.'

'How is Jilik?' Lyta asked.

'Bored with his inactivity. His man carries him from one chamber to another and of course this storm has kept him inside today. He complains much about not being able to ride his new pony.' Quilin paused. 'Thank you, Kedura, for placing that hanging of horses in his workroom. He likes looking at it. Sometimes he takes more notice of it than his tutoran.'

'I am glad it pleases him. My mother and her aunts stitched that piece and I have always found it pleasing.'

When Wilus and Quilin had left her, Lyta also longed for fresh air. She wore her warm cloak and accompanied by Jer went to inspect the storm damage at the castle. The barrels had been returned to their positions by the well and the door had been collected. The carpenter was already fastening it to the kennel entrance with Sek supervising his work. Other folk were picking up branches and twigs and two men were sweeping the leaves into a single heap.

Lyta walked through oldgate into the outer ward. The damage here was more severe with less protection from the wind gusts. The old oak tree had barely missed one of the large storechambers and her stable boys were helping to chop up the trunk. The logs would feed the fires that blazed day and night during the winter in the hearth of the great hall.

When she saw Nin watching the workers, Lyta went to stand beside him. The head groom bowed low when he saw her. 'Quite a bad night, Kedura.'

'How did the horses fare during the storm,' she asked.

'We moved many of them into the back part of the stables where the sound was not so loud,' he said. 'But Spirit has never liked strong winds and she had to be kept calm. Saxo stayed with her all night.'

'I don't feel the same bond with Spirit that I felt with Silver,' Lyta said. 'I'd like you to find me another horse.'

Nin stroked his beard. 'I have one in mind for you. A young filly, still being broken in.'

'Then I will come and see her one morn.'

Magian Domen sent a messenger to Lyta as she sat at supper asking her to come to his dwelling a once. Ardul had taken a turn for the worse.

Quilin touched Lyta's hand. 'I will escort you, Kedura. Domen will want witnesses if the kedir dies.'

They hurried from the hall following Jer with a torch. Domen met them at the door, his usually calm face tense with worry. 'Kedura, Ulit will want to know details. I don't wish Darik dropping hints into his ear about our bad healing treatment in Aldea. We already know he wasn't happy about his own accident.'

'I do understand.'

'Follow me.' Domen took them into one of the chambers behind his workspace. Ardul lay on a bed in the far corner where a young woman was wiping his brow with a cloth. She rose and curtseyed.

'Please continue your work,' Lyta said in a low voice. Harsh gasps filled the chamber as Ardul struggled for every breath. His chest rose and fell unevenly with each effort.

'I fear his lungs are much damaged,' said the magian. He paused to look at Lyta. 'Do you remember that I mixed a potion to help Tibir the stable boy with his breathing? I haven't used it yet. The problem is that Dasty, the herb I distilled it from, is poisonous.'

'I do recall that potion,' said Lyta. 'You wouldn't allow me to even touch the flask that stored it.'

Domen pointed to a flask wrapped in straw on the table. 'Should I try it on Ardul? It may be his last chance but I cannot be certain of the effects.'

Lyta took a deep breath as she watched the pale face before her. Ardul looked as though he were dead already. She glanced at Quilin's grave face. 'What do you think?'

'Will my opinion help you to decide?'

'I'd value your counsel.'

'For what it's worth, I believe Domen should use the potion if he thinks this might be his only chance to save Ardul.'

The magian nodded. 'That is my belief.'

Lyta took a second deep breath. 'Then, I say yes. Magian Domen, I am ordering you to give Dasty to Ardul. Then, if it fails to cure him, the fault is mine.'

When her knees felt suddenly shaky, she dropped onto a stool. 'Mother Moon, pray for me,' she murmured.

Quilin echoed her words. 'Mother Moon, pray for all of us.'

Lyta watched the magian lift the flask and pour a tiny amount into a wrapped cup. She wondered how his hands remained so steady. Then he crossed to the bed and with both Quilin and Rina supporting the kedir, he dripped a tiny portion into Ardul's open mouth.

Domen's hand shook slightly as he lowered the flask and the cup to the table. 'Now we wait.'

Quilin asked in a low voice. 'What do you expect to happen?'

'If the potion works, then his lungs will clear. If not…' His voice cracked and he stopped, unable to continue.

Chapter Fifty-Eight

Lyta held her breath as she watched Ardul. He choked when the potion dripped down his throat and then his whole body twitched so violently it lifted from the bed. She jumped to her feet. Was the kedir about to die?

When Quilin stepped back from the bed and held out his hand, Lyta clutched it. Domen bent down with his ear close to his patient's chest.

Suddenly Ardul opened his eyes. Even in her distress, Lyta noted they were bright blue. He groaned and flailed his arms. Then he took one loud gasp and lay very still.

'Is he dead?' whispered Quilin to the magian. He dropped Lyta's hand as he stepped forward to stare intently at Ardul.

'No, he's still breathing and I am cautiously optimistic,' said Domen. 'The rattle I was hearing earlier has lessened just a little.'

'So do you think he might live?' Lyta asked, knowing her question was foolish. How could Domen assure her that his potion would save Ardul?

The magian straightened up and gave her one of his rare smiles. 'I am hopeful that the kedir will survive this ordeal. However, I am far more certain that I can mend his broken leg.'

For the first time, Lyta noticed that the kedir's leg extending beyond the covers was strapped with bandages to a long board.

Quilin's eyes followed her gaze. 'Isn't that the left leg like Jilik?'

Domen nodded. ‘If Ardul recovers, they can complain together.’ He bent down again over the kedir and listened again to his chest. ‘Yes. His lungs are starting to clear. We have been lucky tonight.’

‘I don’t think luck helped him.’ said Quilin. ‘Your skill as a healer was the essential matter.’

Domen shook his head as he lifted Ardul’s wrist. ‘I didn’t know the Dasty potion would be effective. We can thank luck or Lady Moon if you prefer it.’ He placed the kedir’s wrist back under the covers.

‘Kedura and Quilin, thanks for coming here. Rina and I will watch over Ardul for the rest of the night.’

Outside the magian’s door, Jer sprang to his feet. ‘Is the kedir dead?’ He pulled the lit torch from the ground.

‘No,’ said Lyta. ‘Magian Domen believes he will recover his strength.’ She stared into the sky where Lady Moon shone in full splendor over the castle towers and walls.

Quilin grasped her arm above the elbow. ‘Watch your step, My Lady, the stones are raised here in places.’

Lyta felt the warmth of his grip even through her cloak. It was strange that the pressure of his hand was so comforting. She could feel safe on any uneven ground if Quilin held her arm. The thought sent a rush of blood to her cheeks and she was grateful for the dark shadow from the Prison Tower that hid her blushes. Would any of the kedirs vying to be her husband have the same effect on her?

***

Over the next morns, Ardul improved rapidly. As his breathing became more normal, his strength returned. Soon he could sit on a chair and eat the food Prala sent from the kitchen. He had a constant twinkle in his blue eyes. Rina and Domen’s other healers were enslaved by the first smiles Ardul gave them.

When Lyta visited him, Ardul struggled to stand. She waved him down into his chair. 'Please remain seated. You must rest your leg.'

'So I am told, Kedura, but it's discourteous of me to sit in your presence.

'Then I'll sit beside you. I'm happy to see you're getting well.' She looked at the large square board he held in his hand. 'Is that part of a game?'

'A game from Falga,' Ardul said. 'Your carpenter, Kedura, has made the board to my directions but I'll add the numbers myself. Now he's carving the playing pieces. This game is known as Threes in my demesne.'

'Are the rules difficult?' she asked.

'They can be adapted for many ages.' He smiled at her. 'And older people place wagers on the outcome. Kedura, do you want to play with me?'

Lyta hoped her cheeks hadn't reddened. 'I was thinking of your fellow captive. Jilik, Lord Quilin's son, also has a broken leg and is chafing under the restrictions of staying inside.'

'I sympathize with him. How old is the boy?'

'He has almost five summers.'

'Then he's able to play the simple version of this game. When the counters are ready, he can be brought here. We will entertain each other.'

As Lyta walked back to the castle, she thought about Ardul. He certainly did have a most engaging smile and he was kind in offering to amuse a child.

The next time, Lyta went to the magian's cottage, she found Domen's two patients engaged in a lively game of Threes. They each had a left leg supported by a low stool with the board set between them on a table.

As she walked over to study the game, Ardul looked up and smiled. 'You are here, Kedura, to watch this little imp beat me in our third game. I should never have taught him the rules.'

Jilik grinned at Lyta. 'I am winning because of my lucky counter.' He waved a miniature horse. 'It always beats the fish, the icecat, and the bear.'

'Will you join us, Kedura? We can play with three people.'

Lyta pulled up a stool and sat down. 'I'll use the icecat.' She picked it up and examined the clever detail of the wide ruff around its neck and the flowing tail. 'This is fine work. Who carved these pieces?'

'The carpenter's son. I've hired him to make a large icecat piece from oak for me.'

Jilik said, 'I will ask Father if Kivo can make me a bigger horse.' His mouth dropped. 'I wish I could ride my pony, Cloud.'

To divert his attention, Lyta said, 'Jilik, tell me the rules so that I may win the next round of this game.'

The boy's face brightened as he explained how the counters moved. His directions were not always clear but Lyta reckoned that Ardul would set her straight if she erred.

An hour later, she rose from the stool. The game had been most entertaining and she admired Ardul's tact in dealing with the boy when he lost the round. She suspected that the kedir might have let Jilik win previous games. Ardul was probably right however, in teaching the boy about losing. Children had to learn to deal with defeat. She was surprised to realize that she remembered her mother uttering that exact saying. Did this mean she was growing older? And if so, was she also growing wiser?

Chapter Fifty-Nine

Lyta's first visitor of the morn was Druck. He strode into the solar and bowed low before her. 'Kedura, Captain Stor has arrived by ship from Falga. I've sent an escort to the harbour to meet him.'

'No doubt he's come to see how his kedir is faring.'

'Yes, My Lady. I'm sure he'll report to Kedur Ulit.'

Lyta was grateful Stor had been sent rather than Darik who would cause only trouble. 'When the captain reaches the castle, bring him to the council chamber.'

Druck hesitated. 'Do you know, Kedura, that Stor is not a mere captain?' Lyta nodded. 'Lord Wilus told me that he's the commander of the army in Falga and related to Kedir Ulit.'

'True, Kedura. I can't understand why he doesn't use his rightful title when he travels here.'

'Falga often does things differently than us. Thank you, Archis.'

Druck allowed himself a narrow smile at her comment about Falga before he bowed and left the chamber.

By the time Stor arrived in the council chamber, Lyta had been joined by Wilus and Quilin. After the captain marched through the door, Lyta gave him her hand, which he kissed in a brisk fashion. 'You are very welcome,' she said. 'I am sure you're here to see the recovery of Kedir Ardul with your own eyes.'

'Thank you for receiving me, Kedura. My lord is most anxious to hear my opinion of his son's health. However, I have no doubt at all that Ardul has been well cared for by Magian Domen.'

'My magian is a most accomplished healer but it wasn't easy for him to save Kedir Ardul. He had to take a large risk and give him a new potion.'

Stor nodded. 'I am charged by my kedur to give the magian our grateful thanks. I already knew from his treatment of Lord Darik's wound that he's exceedingly skilled.'

'Lord Wilus will escort you to the magian's dwelling for you to see Ardul and judge his condition. He's been confined there because of his broken leg.'

As she spoke, Lyta heard noises outside the council chamber and Jer opened the door. He looked flustered. 'Forgive me, Kedura, but Kedir Ardul is outside and wishes to speak with you.'

'Ardul is here?' Lyta asked in surprise.

'I am definitely here.' Ardul swung into the chamber. He was balanced on two long poles and supported by cross pieces resting under his armpits.

Wilus exclaimed aloud. 'Kedir, should you be walking?'

Ardul grinned at them before dropping onto a chair and propping his poles beside him. 'Greetings, Kedura.' He nodded to the others and smiled at Stor. 'I'm pleased to see you, Captain. Isn't this a wonderful device! I can keep my leg straight and still move around.'

Quilin lifted a pole. 'I have seen single sticks used as a crutch but not double ones. Who made these for you?'

'Magian Domen and I came up with the plan. Then the carpenter built them to the right height.' He rubbed his armpits. 'I do get a little sore from walking.'

'Why not use cloth to bind the wood?' Quilin asked.

'Domen suggested the same thing this morn.' Ardul looked at Quilin. 'The carpenter measured Jilik and is making a small set for him. I can instruct him on getting around safely.'

'He won't be able to ride,' Quilin observed, 'but he'll be happy to move by himself.'

'Your father will be pleased to hear about your progress,' Stor said to Ardul. 'You'll travel home more easily when your leg has healed. Does Magian Domen know how long it must be bound?'

'At least a moon and mayhap longer,' said Ardul. 'I hope, Kedura, I can trespass on your hospitality for that time?'

'Of course,' Lyta said, smiling at him. 'Now you can reach the hall, I may require you to sing for your supper.' She stole a look at Quilin and noticed the quick frown that appeared and then disappeared from his face.

'I'll certainly sing for you but I'll need a lute. Mine sank with the ship.'

'We can find one for you,' Lyta said. 'Would you and Captain Stor like to talk together about Falgan affairs? The little chamber next door is empty.'

Ardul nodded and rose to his feet. 'Many thanks, Kedura.' He tucked the poles under his arms and stood still for a minute. 'I need to consider which leg should move first before I start.' He bent his head to her and then swung himself from the chamber with Stor following him.

'A fine young man,' Wilus remarked as soon as the door closed. 'An admirable suitor for you, Kedura. He has both good looks and a good mind.' He glanced at Quilin. 'Don't you agree?'

'Mayhap,' Quilin answered shortly. 'The kedura doesn't need to choose a husband yet.'

'She does in three more moons,' said Wilus in a cheerful tone. 'But in my mind, Ardul is favoured over Iben. What's your opinion, Quilin?'

Lyta noticed that Quilin did not respond. Instead, he stared at his boots and then cleared his throat. 'With your permission, Kedura, I will visit my son.' He bowed and left.

Wilus stared after him. 'What's the matter with him? Ardul is ideal for you. And the marriage would improve our relationship with Falga.'

Lyta rose. 'As Lord Quilin said, I don't have to decide the matter now. I will retire to dress for dinner.'

She walked back to her solar with mixed thoughts in her mind. Ardul did meet the requirements for a husband. But even though she enjoyed his company, was a pleasant nature enough for her to live happily with a man and bear his children? Her mother, Halia, had told her that she herself was very lucky in her own choice of a partner. She and Lyta's father had fallen in love at their first meeting and their marriage had been exceedingly happy. .

'I know we were fortunate, child,' she'd said. 'Kedies and kedirs do not choose their marriage arrangements. You always hope to be wed to a man you can like. I always praised Mother Moon for selecting exactly the right man for me.'

The right man, Lyta thought. But how would she recognize him? That was the problem. To her surprise an image of Quilin popped into her mind. She shook her head to drive it away. At least she had time before she must make a decision about a husband.

Before supper, Lyta walked to the stables. Nin led her to a stall where she met a pure white horse. The green eyes were lively and full of interest as they surveyed her.

Nin handed Lyta a carrot. 'Kedura, this is her favourite treat.'

The horse took the carrot delicately between her teeth and then allowed Lyta to stroke her neck. 'I've seen this horse in the grazing fields.' She smiled. 'Her coat is as white as clean snow. And I like the intelligent look in her eyes.'

'In fact, we've been calling her Snow,' said Nin. 'She has an amiable nature, Kedura, and is quick to learn. I think she'd make you a good mount.'

'Then I will ride her when you have finished her training and see if we are suited. Thanks, Nin. Snow might be a fine replacement for Silver.'

Lyta stroked the horse again; she wished it was as easy to select a husband as it was to choose a mount. And the advantage here was that she could try out a horse to see if they were compatible.

On her way back to the castle, Lyta passed Domen and Stor talking together in the courtyard. Their faces were serious.

'Ah, Kedura,' the magian said. 'I was coming to find you when I met Captain Stor. I have received a message from Falga. Bad news, I am afraid.'

A jolt of anxiety caused Lyta to stand still. What had gone wrong now? She glanced at Stor's grave face.

'It seems that the ship carrying Kedir Iben has been wrecked off the Falgan coast. Everyone is presumed lost.'

Lyta's hand shot up to cover her mouth. 'Iben can't be dead! Are they sure he was aboard this particular ship?'

The magian nodded. 'Part of the prow with the figurehead washed ashore and was recognized by several seamen.'

'I can't believe it. Was everyone drowned?'

'No living soul has been found but folk will search now the seas are calmer.'

'What dreadful news.' Lyta shook her head. 'Do we know if Kedur Gerit has been informed? After all, the voyage was undertaken in secret.'

Domen nodded. 'I'm not sure how Falga knew he was aboard this ship. They may have informed his father but in case he doesn't know, I can send a message. And give him our condolences.'

Lyta nodded in assent, still upset by the unexpected news.

Stor regarded Lyta with a sympathetic look. 'Mayhap we shouldn't give up all hope, Kedura. There's a chance Iben could have come ashore on an isolated stretch of our coast.'

'Mother Moon, please answer my prayer that this happened.' Would Lyta never hear again Iben's fine voice soaring into the rafters of her great hall? And she would miss seeing the warmth in his dark eyes as they rested on her.

'The news about Iben is indeed saddening.' said Domen, 'but we must also think practically. Stor, who's next in line in Parian?'

'Iben has three younger brothers. Netin is the oldest but I'm not sure if Gerit will appoint him as heir.'

'Why not?' Lyta asked.

Stor said, 'Netin was born with a crooked back and walks with a severe limp. But I've met him and there's nothing crooked about his mind. He's very clever.'

'No doubt we'll soon discover the facts. Magian Domen, please inform me of any messages from Kedur Gerit. And also, if you hear more about the shipwreck.'

As Lyta left the two men, she had more to contemplate than her sorrow over Iben's death. Some folk in her demesne did not accept children born with deformities. They said that the mother must have offended Mother Moon when the child was still in the womb. The crooked back or misshapen head was a clear punishment for evil-doing.

She wondered if the same ideas were abroad in Parian. They believed in Father Sun. Was he also likely to punish folk who ignored him or offered up the wrong prayers? Her only contact with a priest of the Sun had been when she was in Falga escaping from Erle Rurrik. The priest who had given her a ride had stripped off his robe to expose his scrawny body to the sun's rays. Then he'd tried to get Lyta to do the same. She recalled how thankful she'd been to leave his wagon.

But then, her heart grew heavy as her thoughts returned to Iben. Although she'd known him only a short time, like all young men, he had deserved to enjoy a long and happy life.

As Lyta walked toward the great hall, she met Quilin hurrying in her direction. 'One minute if your time, Kedura.'

Lyta stopped. 'You look concerned. Is something wrong?'

'I am worried about a message from Cela. Domen has just given it to me.'

Lyta put out a hand to draw him into an antechamber. 'Let us talk in here.' She led him to chairs and bid him to be seated.

Quilin drew in a deep breath. 'Two matters. Or rather three matters. I knew about the first two. Cela and I had discussed them. '

'Tell me more.'

'A landslide last moon swept away three huts in a highland village. That's not unusual. Heavy rain storms often cause landslides with tragic results.'

'Bad news indeed. What is the second matter?'

'An icecat has been terrorizing another village. It has taken three children and everyone is afraid to venture from their homes.'

'Then that cat must be taken even though it is regretful.' An image of Seta romping in the snow flashed through Lyta's mind.

'Yes,' said Quilin. 'I never like to slay such a fine beast and the symbol of my land as well. But this event has happened before. My father slew a beast that developed a taste for human flesh about twenty summers ago.'

'You said three matters.'

'Fire has raged through the town of Tirin near my home. At least a score have been killed or burned. Cela is caring for survivors with bad burns.'

'That is indeed tragic. I am exceedingly sorry to hear the news.'

Quilin drew in a deep breath. 'I must go home, Lyta. An old wife is spreading the tale that my land is cursed because of my absence.'

'I suppose she refers to the power of threes. My nurse, Obela, also believes in that particular omen.'

'Well, I don't believe in it but still I need to allay the fears of those who have faith in superstition. Cela says there's much unrest after the fire. .And, what's worse, there's been two cases of the spotted fever in Tirin. '

'Will you take Jilik with you?'

Quilin said, 'I'd like to leave him here, especially with the reports of the fever. He hasn't had the sickness and I had it as a child. Besides, I intend to ride and he can't sit on a horse.' He paused. 'Is that a problem for you?'

'Not at all.' Lyta reached forward to touch his arm. 'We will all care for him. You must go speedily. My good wishes will travel with you.'

'My thanks, Lyta. You still have Wilus to provide guidance.'

'Do you how long you will be away?'

Quilin shook his head. 'I have no idea but I will try to return when matters have calmed down. And I'll have to find that icecat.'

Lyta rose. 'I will be exceedingly sorry to see you go.'

He rose as well. Then he turned to face her, with an intent gaze in his grey eyes. 'Will you be truly sorry, Lyta?'

She felt the flush rise to her cheeks. 'Of course. I don't like to see any of my good lords leave the castle.'

He nodded. 'I shall find Jilik. Farewell, Kedura.'

When he strode from the chamber, Lyta felt an unfamiliar hollow in her chest. Her heart seemed to have ceased besting and dropped from its usual position. She was suddenly dizzy and clutched the chair back for support.

Was it possible that Quilin's absence could provoke such strange feelings in her body? She pushed herself away from the chair and stood upright waiting for her heart to resume its regular rhythm and place. This was unseemly conduct for a kedura. She nodded to Jer to follow and went into the great hall for her supper.

Chapter Sixty

'You know Yalt won't be welcome in Parian.' Nirk scowled down at Iben.

'I removed him from Aldea to help Lyta.' Iben waved a weak hand. 'Let's not discuss this again. I can't think straight with the ship pitching so much.'

'We shouldn't have set sail in this weather.'

'The captain was more afraid of my father than the approaching storm.' Iben held his head and groaned. 'I never thought I'd die at sea.'

Nirk moved a large bowl closer to his kedir's head. 'Try to puke in here.'

Iben shuddered as he leaned from the bunk. 'I don't have anything left in my belly to bring up.' He vomited a stream of green bile.

'I'll see what's happening on deck.' Nirk climbed from the little cabin.

An hour later, the ship was dropping even lower into the trough between one wave before rising almost vertically up the next one. Iben was still wishing for death and it seemed more likely that he'd be granted his request. Nirk reported that the captain had lashed himself to the wheel. The man was concerned about the mast, which swayed and creaked alarmingly with each violent movement of the vessel.

'If the mast goes, we're in big trouble,' Nirk said. 'Let me remove Yalt's fetters. We might all have to swim for our lives.'

Iben's face grew even whiter. 'Go ahead. I didn't intend to kill the fellow.' He looked at Nirk. 'I'm not much of a swimmer. How about you?'

'I can keep afloat in a calm sea but what's out there is another matter.' He turned to the ladder again. 'I'll free Yalt and then come back for you.'

He'd no sooner returned than a tremendous crash shook the whole boat. It lurched forward and then swung around in dizzying circles.

'There goes the mast.' Nirk grabbed his kedir in both arms and tugged him across the floor. 'Just as well you're not a big fellow.' With Iben slung over his shoulder, he clambered up the ladder.

Iben opened his eyes and then wished he hadn't. The deck was strewn with broken wood and twisted sails. An angry green and white sea surrounded them with waves crashing down on the ship.

The captain staggered toward them. He pointed at the small boat, which three seamen were struggling to launch. 'Get into it, Kedir, before my ship breaks up.'

A gigantic wave washed the boat, throwing Iben and Nirk off the deck. Iben bounced like a cork on the surface before sinking and rising again. He spat out a mouthful of seawater and knew he was facing his last minutes on earth. He yelled at the Stars to save him even though he knew rescue was unlikely.

Then Nirk yelled. 'Into the boat. Now!'

Iben felt hands on the back of his tunic lift him into the air. As he landed in the boat, his man said something but the words were lost in the roar of the storm. .

Iben crashed onto his hands and knees and turned his head to make sure Nirk was also safe. Before he could catch sight of his man, Iben was whacked on the head by something heavy and sank into blackness.

***

When he opened his eyes, rain was spattering his face. He squinted up at the sullen grey sky before lifting his head. He couldn't see anybody close. Where in the Stars was he? And how did he get here?

The back of his head was very painful and when he explored the spot with the tips of his fingers, they came away red with blood. How had he been injured? No answers came to him and when he tried to think, his head ached even more. After a struggle, he rose to his hands and knees. He seemed to be in a rocky place with a shore lashed by a wild sea. Broken pieces of wood washed in and out with each wave. Had he arrived here in a boat that had shattered on the black rocks?

Iben used the large boulder near him to heave himself upright. He paused until his head stopped spinning and then looked around. He needed to find people and shelter from the weather. A sturdy stick lying at his feet allowed him to move at the pace of an elderly tortoise to the top of the hillock behind him.

His heart sank as he surveyed the scene. He was on a small island. Scrubby bushes grew among the grey rocks and to his left, he glimpsed a small hut that might protect him from the rain. As he staggered toward it, Iben realized he was very thirsty. He wondered if the pool nearest his feet held fresh or salt water. Planting the stick in the ground, he knelt down, scooped up a handful and tasted it gingerly. What a relief to discover fresh water. He gulped several cool handfuls and washed his face.

Since the door of the hut was wedged tight, Iben used his shoulder to force it open. Not a good idea, he thought as black spots swam before his eyes. He clutched the door while he waited for his sight to clear. The hut was a single chamber with containers set against one wall and a window opposite it. A low cot occupied the wall opposite the door with a small table and two stools below the window. He stumbled to the cot and sank down on it with a groan. Although the blanket felt damp and smelled musty, this lowly cot might be the best bed he'd ever lain upon. Iben turned on his side and closed his eyes.

When he woke, he became conscious of gnawing hunger pains in his belly. When had he last eaten? He searched his mind and found a large gap in his memory. His heart raced when he realized he didn't even remember his name or his birthplace. Was he a simple person or a nobleman? He looked down at his clothes and noted that they were of good quality. So he probably wasn't a peasant. Iben used the support of the wall to stand. Food was his first priority.

He wrenched open the containers. The first one held hard flat cakes; the second, flour and the last, dried fruit and nuts. At least he wouldn't starve. He fought down a surge of panic as he wondered how often this island was visited. Would he be alone for many moons? This food cache would be used up and he'd need to catch fish and gather shellfish from the rocks. Mayhap, he could eat eggs if seabirds nested here.

After he'd eaten cakes and nuts, Iben felt calmer. He tipped the fruit and nuts into the cakes to gain an empty container for water. Stumbling outside, he returned to the pool where he used the lid as a scoop. Then he took the water back to the hut. The effort involved to collect it had exhausted him. He lay down again on the cot and slept.

He woke to darkness and wondered how long he'd been asleep. Water and another cake allayed his hunger. It made sense to sleep in the night and explore the island in the morn. Iben dropped back on his cot. When he opened his eyes again, sunlight streamed through the window. The weather must have improved. Using his stick as support, he ventured from the hut.

The sea was more peaceful than it had been earlier although waves still broke over the long lines of twin reefs that stretched from the shore. He didn't have hooks or lines for fishing but he could gather any shellfish from the rocks.

He must regain his strength before he navigated the reefs. With difficulty he walked around the whole island while large white birds wheeled above him uttering plaintive cries. He wondered when they laid their eggs as there was no sign of nests on the shore.

***

Iben made another mark on the wall. He'd been on the island for ten morns. His head no longer ached and his mind felt clearer. He tried not to think about the probable length of his confinement and its problems and to concentrate of his new routine. He'd found three more pools of fresh water and he refilled the container whenever the level grew low. He rationed the cakes and nibbled a few pieces of dried fruit or nuts at each meal. The seabirds had begun to nest on the shore. He found the first eggs in a circle of stones and waved his stick over his head and yelled to ward off attacks from the parents while he stuffed the eggs into his tunic.

The ring of blackened stones outside the door had indicated where fires for cooking were laid. He'd found two pieces of flint under the rough covers of the cot and experimented with them until he was able to coax a small flame. Now he lit the fire and placed the flat cooking stone on top. Then he mixed a rough fritter from flour and eggs. As it cooked, the smell made his mouth water. When Iben burned his lips with the first mouthful, he waited until the fritter had cooled a little before he consumed it with gusto.

At low tide, Iben had been gathering shellfish on the reefs. He opened the long green shells with a rock and then scooped out the flesh inside. As he was wary of illness from eating it raw, he cooked the shellfish. On one morn, he'd found several small fish stranded in a rock pool and they'd been a great addition to his sparse diet. He wished he had a net to catch them from the sea.

On the eleventh morn, Iben noted that most of the birds were nesting. He collected eggs and brought them back to the hut. He went back to gather shellfish from the most exposed reef. He was careful to avoid the clusters of golden seaweed, having learned the hard way that it was difficult to keep his footing on the slippery mass. He was bending down to scrape a shellfish from the rock with his special flat stone when a sudden wave rose to thigh height and swept him into the sea.

What a foolish way to die, Iben thought as his head sank below the surface. He rose up, spluttering and coughing, and waved his arms and kicked his legs in an effort to return to safety. He'd made a little progress before being sucked back into the sea. Then a second wave lifted him and swept him forward. At the last minute, he realized he might hit the rocks with enough force to injure himself.

***

Iben felt a strange rocking motion and heard voices speaking above him. He was almost afraid to open his eyes in case he was imagining being in a small boat with rescuers. Above him, a green sail waved. Then a red face framed by a grey beard peered down at him. 'So you're awake at last. Lucky for you, we were nearby when you landed on the reef.'

'You'll likely have a sore pate,' said a second man. When Iben turned his head, he noticed a younger person with brown hair and green eyes. 'Them rocks are hard.'

Iben realized the back of his head had been hit again. He hoped he'd not gashed it in the same place as before.

'What's your name, lad?' asked the older man.

'Nirk.' Iben wondered why that particular name had popped into his mind. It seemed familiar but not his own.

'We're on our way home,' said the older man. 'We've been collecting eggs but didn't expect to collect a lad.' He chuckled as he adjusted the tiller.

The younger man said, 'They call me Evir. My mother will treat your head but rest yourself now. We'll be back soon.'

Iben did as he was bid. He woke only when the boat slid onto a sandy shore. Evir helped him out. 'Lean on me. We're going up there.' He nodded toward the thatched roofed cottages nestled above a stone sea wall.

They stopped before the third house on the narrow street. 'Here we are.' The door opened and a stout woman with curly hair who reminded Iben of his old nurse looked out. 'You found this on Gull Island?' she asked.

'He's in need of healing, Mother.'

'Bring him closer to the fire so I can see him better.'

Iben was placed on a stool near the hearth. The woman stood behind him and gently parted his hair. 'You've hurt your head here before.'

'I think I was injured when I first landed on the island,' he said. 'And then this morn, a wave carried me onto the rocks.'

The woman was silent as she fetched water and cloths. 'Now I'll clean your head. I might need to stitch the edges of this wound together.'

Iben sucked in his breath as she dabbed the skin and hair. She must have added some potion to the water to make it so painful. 'Do I need stitches?'

'You're lucky, lad. I don't need to find my needle.'

Evir had been watching her work. 'Mother, his name is Nirk.'

'They call me Runa,' said the woman. 'I'll give you a bowl of soup and a sleeping potion. Then you can rest.' Her shrewd eyes looked Iben up and down. 'You're well-born by your dress and speech. How did you get to the island?'

Iben shook his head. 'I have no memory of the events but I hope to recall them soon.'

'We'll ask around,' said Evir. 'You probably came off a ship in that bad storm. Father and I couldn't fish for three morns.'

As he spoke the older man came into the house, rubbing his hands together. 'The wind's getting up strong again. Mother, where do you want the eggs?' He smiled at Iben. 'Just as well we found you, lad. The sea's getting up and we won't be launching our boat tomorrow morn.'

Iben drank the hot soup and then the potion with some reluctance. Bruna pulled back a curtain at the rear of the chamber to reveal a cot. 'Nirk, you'll rest here to be close to me. Evir can sleep next door with my kin.'

Iben didn't argue about taking Evir's bed. His eyes were growing too heavy to care. Runa helped him to the cot and covered him. 'Sleep now,' she said, smoothing the hair from his forehead with a warm hand.

'Just like my old nurse, thought Iben before his eyes closed.

Chapter Sixty-One

Domen was shown into Lyta's solar. 'I heard back from Parian,' he said. 'Kedur Gerit thanked you for the condolences. He said that Kedir Netin is now the heir in his demesne. That surprised me given his infirmity.'

'Mayhap in Parian a man is judged by his mind and not his body.'

Domen nodded. 'We will see for ourselves what manner of man Netin really is when he arrives in Aldea.'

'Magian, I was about to send for you to ask about the spotted fever in town. Has anyone else been taken ill?'

'Two children and an old man since yestermorn. The young ones should recover but I fear the old man may not.'

'So that's two deaths and ten sick folk altogether?'

'Correct. I am concerned the sickness may soon spread to the castle. I had it as a child and so did two of my prentices. But Ardul has never caught the fever and neither have you or young Jilik. Wilus has no memory of being ill with it.'

'Then should I order that anyone who hasn't had the sickness must stay away from town?'

'That would be my counsel,' said Domen.

'Easier ordered than obeyed since supplies are carried back and forth but I will give the command.'

When Domen had left, Lyta attended prayers in the chapel. Wilus and a handful of officials and castle workers were present. After the salvan had conducted the service, Wilus and the others left but Lyta stayed behind to speak to Mena. 'No doubt you've heard about the spotted fever in town.'

‘Two morns ago, I was at the burial of a child the same age as my son. The ceremony was difficult for me.’ Mena blinked tears from her eyes.

Lyta placed a hand on her arm. ‘Since you lost your own son, I am sure you were distressed. Did you catch the fever when your boy was stricken?’

Mena shook her head. ‘I had the sickness as a child and apparently, you cannot get it a second time.’

‘So Magian Domen tells me but please take care when you visit the town.’

As Lyta walked back to her solar, she turned to Jer. ‘Have you had the spotted fever?’

He shook his head. ‘And my sweetheart in town hasn’t had it either.’

Lyta frowned. ‘Have you seen her since folk became sick?’

‘I saw her last night, Kedura, when I was off duty.’

‘Then obey my new order to stay away from town until the fever passes.’

Jer bent his head. ‘Yes, Kedura,’ he said in a low voice.

Over the next morns, Domen and Wilus reported on the number of sick folk in the town. Twenty had been counted with eight deaths, mainly of young people and older ones.

One of the kitchen maids was the first case of illness in the castle. Domen placed the girl in a chamber by herself. ‘She has a mild attack and should recover without problems. But a lad in town had the fever and now has difficulty with his sight. This illness can affect the eyes.’ Domen shook his head. ‘He is a prentice to the blacksmith. An unfortunate complication for him.’

Lyta turned to Wilus. ‘Make sure the boy is looked after. His family may need extra coin for his care.’

The presence of the fever had prevented Lyta from riding Snow. However, she visited the stables carrying carrots to allow the horse to become accustomed to her. She met Jilik there, balanced on his double crutches. He had learned to get around the castle on them and was a constant visitor to Cloud, the grey pony Nin had selected for him.

'I like Cloud very much,' Jilik said. 'And I like Ardul too. But I like my pony, Rusty, back home more than Ardul and Cloud.'

Lyta was amused by his the order of his ranking and wondered if his father rated higher or lower than both ponies and the Falgan kedir.

A second kitchen maid came down with the spotted fever and she joined her fellow worker in the separate chamber. Lyta wondered how the sickness was spread and asked Domen.

'There's some dissension about that,' he said. 'Some healers think the fever is contained in a miasma. Like a fog in the air, it drifts around and covers people who then get sick.'

'What is your opinion?' Lyta asked.

'I believe that several things are involved. Mayhap an infected person touches food and then the person who eats it becomes ill. I also wonder if the fever can be passed in sneezes and coughs but other healers think I am wrong. In fact, they think I am mad.'

'But if you are right, then what is in a sneeze to make someone sick?'

Domen smiled. 'I do not know the answer. It could be that the substance is too small to be seen with our eyes.'

'There is much to be discovered,' said Lyta.

'More than I could ever discover in my lifetime but your children will learn things that we cannot imagine.'

Lyta did not want to hear him mention her children. The time for her suitors to arrive was coming closer and she didn't want to contemplate husbands, marriage, and subsequent children.

The numbers of sick folk in the castle increased. Two stable boys caught the fever and one died. The first kitchen maid to come down with the fever also died and Wea, the castle seamstress became seriously ill. Domen feared that she would not survive.

Druck reported one morn that Jer was ill. 'And his girl in town also has the fever. His brother, Kel, will guard you in the daytime and I'll assign another man for the night watch.'

The ill workers were placed together in a larger chamber where Domen and his prentices who'd had the fever could tend them. 'There's not much I can do except wait for the illness to pass,' Domen said to Lyta. 'Salusy reduces their fever but they still complain of aching heads and limbs. Wea's eyes pain her. I bound them to prevent the light from bothering her.'

The next person to fall ill was Obela. Lyta urged Domen to keep her old nurse as comfortable as possible. 'I cannot imagine life without her.'

She felt guilty when she remembered the times she had become annoyed with Obela's scolding and admonitions to eat better repasts. Then she recalled being a child and sitting next to Obela to hear old takes about icecats rescuing beautiful ladies and magians with wonderful spells. 'Lady Moon, if it is your wish, please allow my nurse to live.'

The magian's morn habit was to visit Lyta to report on the progress of his patients. She had usually eaten and dressed before he arrived. This morn he wore a very grave expression.

'Lord Wilus has been taken ill during the night. Rina is caring for him as well as his man. I have sent the others away but they may also fall ill.'

Lyta caught her breath. She could not imagine ruling Aldea without her wise advisor. 'Is his fever severe?'

'He was burning up when I arrived in his chamber but I have reduced the fever a little.' Domen shook his head. 'Older people seem less able to fight this illness. I am going to visit Lady Jona. Her woman said she was ill last night.'

'Please keep me informed.' The shock of hearing about Wilus had almost driven thoughts of the other sick people from her mind. 'How is Obela? Are Jer and Wea still very ill?'

'I regret, Kedura, that Obela may not survive the morn. Wea is slightly better but I fear Jer may not recover either. I heard that his sweetheart died yestermorn.' Domen looked sharply at Lyta. 'Kedura, please do not even consider visiting any of these people. It is too dangerous for you.'

Lyta nodded. She had thought briefly about going to see Obela, Jona, and Wilus but she knew the magian was correct about the great risk.

He kept her informed throughout the next hours by sending messages through her maids. Lyta lost her appetite when she learned that Obela had died. In her mind, she heard the nurse rebuking her for pushing the platter of food away. She sat by the window mourning Obela, her head in her hands.

A strange lethargy gripped her all afternoon. By dinner time, her throat felt sore and swollen and her head ached. Amia looked at her in concern. 'My Lady, I will ask the magian to come. Your face is very flushed.' '

Lyta did not have the strength to argue with her maid. 'As you wish,' she said. 'Please help me to undress. I will not eat supper in the hall tonight.'

Domen held Lyta's wrist and then listened to her chest. He peered into her throat and opened the top of her bedgown. What he saw there caused him to frown and purse his lips.

'I have the spotted fever, don't I?' she asked.

'I believe so. Now you must rest and take this potion I have mixed for you.'

Lyta winced as the liquid passed down her throat. 'It hurts to drink.'

The next hours passed in a series of nightmares. Her eyes were so painful in the candle light that she called out for relief. Someone bound them with a soft cloth and she sank into a frightening world peopled with evil magians and ferocious icecats, snarling bears and lurking wolves. In her feverish dreams, both Obela and Wilus visited her. She told stories about golden-haired kedies and he told her to arrest Yalt for his treasonous ideas. She argued with both of them.

Domen lifted her and made her swallow sour potions while others wiped her burning face and hands with cool cloths. Hushed voice spoke constantly above her in a confused babble of sounds. Lyta wondered if it was morn or night.

Then just as fast as it had arrived, the burning sensation in her body passed. Her limbs and head were still heavy and strange but the aches had gone.

'What morn is it?' Her voice was croaky and faint.

'Thank you, Lady Moon.' Amia sounded both tearful and happy. 'Magian, she is herself again.'

Domen's cool hand lifted her wrist. 'The Kedura will recover,' he said in a choked voice. Surely Domen wasn't tearful as well.

Lyta wanted to see them. When she touched her eyes, she was surprised to feel cloth. 'Please untie this band.'

Hands undid the cloth and Lyta blinked several times. 'Is it night?'

After a pause, Amia said. 'It is dinner time, Kedura.'

'Then why is everything black?'

The pause this time was lengthy enough to frighten her. ‘Why can’t I see anything?’ Lyta’s voice rose in panic.

Domen cleared his throat. ‘The fever has damaged your eyes.’

‘But will the darkness pass?’

‘I don’t know, Kedura. We will have to wait and see.’

Chapter Sixty-Two

By the second morn, Lyta's eyesight had not returned. And Domen said she should prepare herself for the prospect of staying blind for life. She lay in bed with the hangings pulled around her, cursing her blindness. Lady Moon had deserted her. What use was a kedura who could not see her people? What use was a woman who would never see her husband or her children? It would have been better for everyone if she had died like Obela, Jer, and Wilus.

When she heard about the death of her faithful advisor, Lyta lacked the tears to grieve for Wilus. His men had taken the body back to his home and his grandson was now lord of the estate. Aunt Jona had also died and, as she had requested, her remains had been taken to Parian.

Domen came every morn to assess her health. Lyta remained silent as he counted her pulse and listened to her chest. At the end of a sevenday, he said in a stern voice, 'Enough is enough. You are well able to rise from this bed, sit in a chair, and eat a proper repast. Amia, please assist your mistress to get up and dress in a warm robe. I will return soon to talk to her.'

Shocked by his harsh tone, Lyta allowed Amia to help her from the bed and dress in a loose robe. The maid guided her to a chair and placed the platter of food close by on a table. 'Kedura, you have here four honey cakes and some fruit and nuts. Prala asked if you want to eat anything special.'

Lyta shook her head. She felt across the platter for a honey cake and took a small bite. She was chewing it when Domen returned.

'Ah, I am glad to see you up and eating. You need to build up your strength after this illness.'

'Why?' she asked. 'I can no longer be a ruler.'

'Why not?'

Lyta felt a spurt of anger. 'I should think that was obvious. A ruler who cannot see her people is one who cannot guide and protect them. I intend to give up my position.'

'You are thinking with your heart and not your head. Of course, you can continue to be the kedura of Aldea.'

Lyta let her head fall against the high back of the chair. 'So, have you invented a special potion to restore my sight?'

'Of course not but you have a special skill to help you rule.'

'You refer to my lofting skill.'

'I do and you now must develop it further to assist you.'

Lyta was silent as she thought about his words. 'Then,' she said. 'Even if I do, lofting cannot take the place of eyes.'

'I understand that but you don't know yet to what degree more training will assist you in governing this demesne.'

After another long pause, Lyta said, 'I will consider your words but they may not change my mind.'

'Then consider this as well. If you give up the throne, who will you name to take your place?'

Lyta sensed him watching her but remained quiet. After a few minutes, he said to Amia. 'Help your mistress back to bed. She looks tired.'

The next morn, she asked to be dressed and taken into the solar. She picked at her repast and then pushed the platter away. A shaft of sunlight coming through the window was comforting on her face. She turned her head toward it and did not hear someone approaching until he spoke.

'My poor girl, I came as soon as I could. How are you?' Quilin caught her hands and lifted them both to his lips.

Lyta's heart beat wildly. She breathed out and said, 'I'm blind.'

'So I heard. And I was exceedingly sorry. But at least you lived unlike Wilus, and the others. Too many good folk have died from this fever.'

Lyta drew her hands from his grasp. 'I should have been one of them.'

'How can you say that? Lady Moon obviously wanted you to live.'

'A blind kedura is no use on the throne.'

'You still possess wisdom and that is more useful than sight.'

Lyta made her tone formal. 'Please sit down, Lord Quilin. I need advice on protocol. Now that Wilus has gone, I'm without an expert to consult. Will you study the old documents to discover if and how I may resign my throne and appoint someone to take my place?'

She heard his swift intake of breath. After a pause, he said, 'Lyta, you can't make such an important decision in a hasty manner. Since your strength hasn't returned, you're bound to feel unsure about ruling.'

'But I am sure about one thing. No matter how strong I become, I'll remain blind. No other ruler of Aldea has suffered from this infirmity.'

'Then you can be the first one. Your mother overcame the obstacle of ruling as a woman to become a wise and beloved kedura. Your obstacle is to conquer your blindness in order to become an equally wise ruler.'

'Words! Words! They mean nothing. How can I make a judgment when I can't see the faces of the people before me? Why should I ride through Aldea if I cannot observe the state of the town or the countryside? How can I believe what people tell me without the confirmation of my own eyes? Quilin, your words are empty.' She forced down the sobs that rose in her throat.

He took her hands again. 'Don't you trust me, Josik, and Domen? Why would we lie about any matter? We will be your eyes.'

'It's not the same.' She felt a single hot tear roll down her right cheek.

'I know that, my dear, but I also know your true nature. You are the girl who escaped from kidnappers and found your way home. Lyta, you're so much stronger than you realize. Rely on that inner strength.'

Lyta gulped and felt for her kerchief. Before she could use it, Quilin had loosened her hands and wiped the tear from her cheek with a finger.

His tone was gentle when he said, 'Your people won't reject you because you cannot see them. They already admire the competent way you've stepped into Halia's slippers.'

Lyta said, 'Mayhap, I was starting to be competent before this illness.' She sighed. 'But please, I beg of you, discover the protocol of resigning my throne.'

He sighed. 'Very well. I will do as you bid even though I will never agree with it. Is there anything else?'

'That is my only wish. I will not rest easy until I know what I should do.'

***

Two morns later, Amia announced a visitor to Lyta's solar. 'Kedura, Lord Josik has arrived from his estate. He wishes to see you.'

Lyta guessed that Quilin or Domen had summoned Josik to use as extra ammunition in the struggle to persuade her to keep the throne. When his firm footsteps had crossed the floor and halted before her, she held out a hand to be kissed. 'I hope this visit was not too inconvenient for you, Lord Josik.'

'Not at all, Kedura. My daughter is married now to a fine young man. And my eldest son is very happy to run the estate without my head popping over his shoulder.' He gave a short bark of laughter. 'In fact, he told me to stay away as long as I wished.'

'Please sit down.'

She waited until he had seated himself in the chair opposite hers. 'So, are you here to persuade me to remain as ruler?'

He coughed and then cleared his throat. 'Am I able to do that, Kedura?'

'I don't know what arguments you will use. Domen and Quilin have done their best but they haven't yet convinced me. I think the demesne needs a better ruler than I can be with my blindness.'

'Then name that better ruler.'

'You or Quilin would be more suitable than a sightless woman.'

'But I would refuse the offer. I'm quite content with my present rank and way of life. And I'm too old to take on such heavy responsibility. The throne needs a young and spirited person.'

'Quilin is young and he has plenty of spirit.'

'He does but I already know he wouldn't accept the role either. And Domen is content to remain here as the castle magian. Of course, there are others who'd jump at the chance. Firt, for one, would be delighted to be kedur of this demesne. '

Lyta heard her voice rise. 'Firt? I would never give him my throne. Not even if he were the last man in Aldea.'

'But you may have to search the length and breadth of the demesne for someone appropriate.' Josik's tone changed. 'I believe you should wait until the kedirs arrive in one moon's time. You can measure their qualities. The right man to be your husband and help you to rule could be among them.'

Lyta knew his advice was wise but she didn't want to wait for one more moon to shed the unwelcome responsibility of ruling. She sat for a while in silence before she said in a reluctant voice. 'Very well, but if I do not find the right man among the kedirs, I will resign my throne.' '

'Delaying this important decision is a sound move.' Josik's knees creaked as he stood up. 'With your permission, Kedura, I will leave you.'

He had no sooner left the solar than Amia said, 'Lord Jilik is here. Do you want to receive him?'

Lyta suspected the child would question her about her eyes. She was ready to deny him but then she changed her mind. She'd have to face Jilik sooner or later so it might as well be now. 'Let him come in.'

Jilik's rapid steps crossed the chamber and then stopped near her. 'I can tell your leg is mended, Jilik, by the fast way you walk.' ' she said.

'And Ardul's leg is better too.' When he paused, Lyta sensed that he was studying her. 'Can you see anything?'

'No, my eyes don't work now.'

'What's it like?'

'Close your eyes and tell me what you see.'

'Everything is black'

'That's what I see too.'

Jilik said, 'I don't like not seeing things.'

'Neither do I but I must get used to the feeling.'

Jilik said, 'Kedura, you don't know if I bowed when I came in.'

'That's true. Did you bow when you came in?'

'Yes, I did.'

'Then you should still continue. You bow your head because I am kedura of this demesne. It doesn't matter if I am blind or not.'

She heard him move closer to her chair. 'How will you go around without tripping?'

'I'll have to remember the position of furniture and doors.'

'I have a good idea. You could lean on me and I will tell you where all the chairs and stairs are.'

Lyta smiled. 'You aren't big enough for me to lean on you.'

'Kedura, can you stand up.'

Amused by his request, Lyta rose to her feet. 'Now what?'

'Put out your hand. Can you touch my head or my shoulder?'

Lyta stretched out her hand until she felt hair. 'I can reach the top of your head. You must have grown, Jilik.'

'Father says I'm like a weed and my legs are hollow. But Magian Domen said I have blood running around my bones. That's funny.'

When he giggled, Lyta thought he must be imagining the blood moving through the interior of his legs. 'Kedura, if you rest your hand on my head, I can walk beside you. I will guide you to the window.'

Lyta let him lead her across the chamber. 'There,' Jilik said in a triumphant tone. 'We didn't trip over anything. We could go to the stables and you could see Cloud, my pony.' Then he paused. 'Oh no, you can't see Cloud but you could put your hand on his nose. It is very soft.'

'Jilik, thanks for the offer but I must get better at walking inside the castle first before I go outside.'

'Then I will practice walking with you. My tutoran says I must always practise my writing and reading but I'd rather help you.'

'Your schoolwork comes first. Now, take me back to my chair.'

When she was seated again, Lyta said, 'I hear Magian Domen's voice at the door so you must leave now.'

'Then I'll go to the stables by myself.' His footsteps moved away. 'I am bowing, Kedura, even though you can't see me.'

Lyta laughed as he left. The child's visit had lightened her mood. Domen came into the chamber. 'I am glad to see you are sounding happier. Does Jilik have something to do with it?'

'It's hard to be cross with him.'

'He's an imp.' said Domen, 'but quite an amusing imp. I have brought something for you.' He placed a smooth stick into the fingers of Lyta's right hand. 'This cane will help you in two ways. You can lean on it when you walk and wave it before you to feel if there is an object in your path.'

'Jilik offered his head for the same reason.'

'Try the cane out by crossing the chamber to the door. You will recall that the door is on your left.'

'I also remember a round table near my chair.' Lyta poked the cane forward until it touched a solid object. 'Ah, it's here.' With caution, she edged past the table with her empty hand trailing along its smooth surface. 'Now, I should be in a straight line to the door.' She took several steps before feeling for the carved oak panel. 'And I've reached the door.'

'Well done,' said Domen. 'I have taken the liberty, Kedura, of ordering your maids and Godit not to move any piece of furniture from the place you last remembered seeing it. That way, you will feel more confident walking alone around your chambers.'

Lyta retraced her steps without accident and sat down again. 'I feel as though I ran a long race.'

'You will tire more easily at first because you are relying so much on your other senses. Sound, smell, and touch will become much important than before.'

'I understand that better now.' She leaned the cane against the chair. 'Thanks for bringing this.'

'I also came on behalf of Ardul. Now that his leg is mended, he wishes to take a journey to see The Moon Temple and the Salvence. After discussions with Mena, he has become interested in exploring the Moon faith.'

'Of course he has my permission to travel there. He will enjoy the wine they serve at meals.'

'Thank you, Kedura. I will tell him.' The magian said in a tentative tone, 'If you are up to studying, we can start lessons on the morrow. Kel can bring you to my dwelling.'

Lyta's throat tightened. Was she ready to venture outside where everyone could see her and whisper together about her lack of sight? 'I will think about that and send you word.'

She heard Domen stand up. 'Kedura, don't think for too long. Every morn you don't study is a morn lost.' He touched her hand, an unusual gesture for him. 'I will do anything in my power to help you, Kedura. Never doubt that fact.'

Chapter Sixty-Three

Iben had found an occupation in the village of Hortis. When Runa asked if he could read and received an assent, she handed him an official-looking document. 'What does it say? These papers with a seal on them are from Lord Darik. They always say he wants more taxes.'

He scanned the words. 'And you're right. Your village will pay Lord Darik two more pieces of silver coin in the next tax collection.'

'Two!' Runa's voice rose in agitation. 'We couldn't afford the last taxes. Lord Darik's man took two cows as payment.'

'Can't anyone in this village read and write?'

'Only one old man and his head is cloudy. We've had nobody to teach us for many summers.' Runa paused and studied Ihen's face. 'Could you teach the children and mayhap, some of their parents? I'd like to learn.'

'I'm no tutoran.'

'But you learned to write and read when you was young.'

Iben shrugged. 'I don't have any books to use.'

'I can help with that.' Runa opened the battered chest by the door. 'I have two books that belonged to my grandsire. Can you use them?' She rubbed the books against her apron to remove some of the dust.

Iben took the volumes from her. They smelled musty and when he opened the first one, a collection of dead spiders and flies fell onto the floor. He shook them both hard before reading the titles. 'These are old histories of Falga.'

'Can you teach us with them?'

Iben sighed. 'I suppose I can do it as payment for your food and care. But we need a place for teaching.' He glanced around the cluttered chamber. 'The children can't meet with me here.'

'There's an empty house at the far end of the village. I'll find some women to brush away the cobwebs and wash the floor.' She gave Iben an enormous gap-toothed smile. 'I'm so glad you'll help us.'

Just like my old nurse when she persuaded me to do something I didn't want to do, thought Iben.

So began his busy days as a tutoran in his new workchamber. Iben had seven children to teach before midday dinner, five women including Runa after the meal, and six men at night. Because of a lack of ink and paper or even slates, he arranged for the local carpenter to build eight flat wooden boxes. These he filled with sand. By sprinkling water over the sand to keep it damp, his pupils could write their letters on the surface with sharpened sticks. It was easy to smooth the surface and start again.

Like all tutorans, Iben had some pupils who lacked concentration, some who were slow to learn, and some who absorbed rapidly everything he said and then asked for more letters to learn. The ultimate prize was the ability to read the history of their demesne from one of Runa's books.

At the end of each session, he told his students a tale but never reached the end. They all sighed in frustration at his methods but the final part remained a challenge like a carrot held before a donkey. Evir, his most diligent pupil, was the first to discover an ending to a tale.

At night, Iben had no trouble falling asleep but he often woke during the night and wondered how he'd arrived on Gull Island. Presumably, he'd come off a wrecked ship but where had he boarded the vessel and what was his destination.

As he lay staring at the ceiling above him one night, a thought drifted into his mind, as gently as a floating feather. His name wasn't Nirk; it was Iben. He sat bolt upright. Nirk was somebody close to him but who was he? He sighed in frustration when the answer to that question eluded him. Then he lay back on the lumpy cot. If he'd recalled this important fact, surely he'd recall others. He decided to keep answering to Nirk. For all he knew, Iben might be an escaped prisoner with a large reward for his capture.

The morn of taxation arrived. Luckily, the fishing had been excellent since the last storm and the sale of fish to townsfolk further inland had been lucrative. Among them the villagers had scraped up enough silver coins to pay the extra taxes to Lord Darik's steward.

The arrival of the taxing party was a big occasion. Lord Darik's men were fed in the house of the village head and the women joined forces to bake sufficient bread and to cook fish in their own houses. Extra ale had been brewed for the feast. Iben thought providing this meal was like imposing an extra tax but he kept his opinion to himself.

The children were scrubbed from head to toe and dressed in their least ragged tunics and hose. At Runa's request, Iben tied his straggly hair back off his face. He'd been wearing a simple brown tunic and grey hose but Runa urged him to don the clothes he'd been wearing when he was rescued. She'd managed to clean the worst of the seawater stains from the garments.

A small boy was posted outside the village to watch for the party. Just before noon, he rushed back to announce the men were on their way.

'How many?' asked the headman.

'Lord Darik's steward, four men at arms, and another big fellow I never seen before. They'll be here soon.'

A table and chair had been set in the shade of a tree in the village square. There, Iben was told, the steward would take the coin from each villager and mark the amount down in a large red book. Afterwards, the men in the party would eat and drink before they moved to the next fishing village.

Reluctantly Iben joined the crowd gathered in the square. He stood at the back, unwilling to be part of the ceremony. As a newcomer, his name wouldn't be entered in the account book and he hoped nobody would add it to the list of villagers. He'd earned only a few copper coins from his tutoran duties. Most payment had been in the form of platters of food and jugs of ale.

The party clattered down the only street in the village and stopped at the square. Iben saw a fat man wearing a large hat seated in the wagon that was driven by a man at arms. Three others on horseback accompanied the wagon. In its tray lay four large oak chests bound with stout cord. He couldn't see the face of the last man in the group but somehow the back of his head looked familiar.

Then the man turned to survey the crowd and Iben lost his breath. His loud gasp brought the stranger's eyes to him. A broad smile broke out on the man's face and he leapt off his horse and pushed his way through the people. He hugged him so hard Iben was lifted from his feet.

'Found you at last.' He dropped Iben and whacked him on the back. 'You don't know how many miserable places I've searched.'

'Nirk? That's you, isn't it?'

The halting voice sharpened Nirk's gaze. 'What's the matter? I can't have changed that much since you last saw me.'

Iben's voice continued to be hesitant. 'I lost my memory for a long time. I seemed to have been shipwrecked.'

Nirk pulled Iben away from the listening villagers. 'You're Kedir Iben of Parian and you're right. You were shipwrecked on the way home from Aldea. I never believed you were dead. Kedur Ulit suggested I accompany Darik's tax men along this coast to search each village.' He stopped and stared at Iben. 'Has that information helped your memory?'

Pictures of his former life flooded into Iben's mind. Yes, he did recall Parian. And the faces of his father and brothers were coming back to him. 'Does Father think I am dead?'

Now it was Nirk's turn to sound hesitant. 'I heard he appointed Netin as his heir. So, yes, he believed you were dead.'

'I was in Aldea, wasn't I? I do recall meeting Kedura Lyta.'

Nirk grinned. 'You met her all right? Don't you remember anything more?'

'It's all coming back to me.' He paused. 'Isn't she meeting with her suitors soon to choose a husband?'

'Within one moon. Netin will be there representing Parian,'

Iben felt his heart thud at the very idea. 'Well, I'll be there too. I'll need new garments, a horse, and a lute. But I'm without coin. '

'Then you're in luck. I had a fortunate run at the dice and Kedur Ulit says he would fit you out. ' Nirk jiggled his coin pouch as he spoke. 'I think the first step is to buy a horse. One of Darik's men may be persuaded to ride home in the wagon. There's only one more village to visit.'

'That sounds good.'

'Leave it to me,' Nirk clapped him on the shoulder. 'Wait here while I negotiate.'

Iben had been conscious of village eyes looking curiously at him as he and Nirk spoke together. He'd have to talk to Runa and Evir about any future plans.

Before he could choose the right words, Runa came up to him. 'Do you know that man?'

'Yes, he's an old friend of mine.' Iben had suddenly realized he couldn't use Nirk's name. 'He's been looking for me ever since I was shipwrecked. My father wants me to come home.'

While he was talking, Iben watched Nirk bargain with one of the men at arms. He had to hope Nirk would not reveal either of their names to the villagers. This situation was getting complicated.

Nirk returned wearing a broad grin. Iben spoke before his man could open his mouth. 'This is Runa who's been so good to me. Meet my friend, Iben. He's been scouring the coast for me ever since I was shipwrecked.'

Nirk lifted an eyebrow but accepted the switch in names. 'Nirk's father wants him to return home.'

Bruna's expression grew anxious. 'But what about our reading and writing lessons?'

Nirk looked from one to the other. 'So you've been a tutoran here?'

'He's very patient,' said Runa. 'I know all my letters and my son, Evir, can read whole sentences in books.'

'Evir has done well and can continue the lessons,' said Iben. 'I'm sorry, Runa, but I must leave the village.'

'And I've acquired a mount for you. The bay horse is yours.' Nirk nodded towards the group around the table. 'They will be finished with the taxes soon.'

'Then is it farewell?' Runa asked.

Iben clasped both her hands. 'I'll never forget your kindness.' He nodded at Nirk. 'Mayhap some coin may show my gratitude.'

Nirk grimaced as he dug into his pouch to produce two silver coins. When he dropped them into Runa's hand, she stared open-mouthed at the contents of her palm. 'Oh, many thanks, Sir, but we never tended Nirk for coin. He repaid us many times over with his reading and writing lessons.'

'But you did mend my head,' said Iben.

Nirk touched his arm. 'Are you ready to go?'

Iben was surprised to feel a pang of regret. He'd enjoyed the peaceful village ways. Now he must return to the world of kedurs and kedirs and he'd probably never experience the simple life again.

'Say farewell to everyone for me,' he said to Runa. 'My friend wants to leave now' He watched the steward close the account book and one of the men of arms unbind a chest to drop a pouch of coin inside. The collection part of the morn was over.

Runa grabbed Iben in a swift hug before standing back with tears in her eyes. Iben patted her shoulder and then followed Nirk to where the horses stood under the tree. He'd miss the woman's rough and ready kindness and he'd miss living like a villager. Now he must become a kedir of Parian once more.

Chapter Sixty-Four

Lyta took a deep breath. Clutching Kel's arm with one hand and her new cane with the other, she'd left her bedchamber and walked with great caution through the winding passages of the castle. Now she stood at the top of the stone steps that led down to the courtyard. 'I've forgotten how many there are.'

She heard Kel count in a whisper. 'A score, Lady. Will I say each number out loud as we go down?'

'Yes. Is anybody approaching?'

'Not a soul, Lady. Shall we start?'

Lyta negotiated both the steps and the uneven stones of the courtyard. When Kel had delivered her to the magian's door, Lyta twisted her shoulders to release the tension that had built up during the journey. Domen opened his door and ushered her inside. Lyta used her cane to make her way to her stool. She let her breath out and tried hard to relax.

'You have done well to reach here.' Lyta heard the magian pour some liquid into a wooden cup. He moved the cup across the table until it touched her right hand.

'What is it?'

'Smell it carefully.'

Lyta bent her head and filled her nose with the rich aroma of golden summer. She knew at once what was in the cup. 'Your special peach juice!' she said with pleasure. 'I haven't drunk this for many moons.'

'Then enjoy it,' said Domen. 'Until I make more, this is from my last flask.' He waited while she drained the cup before he took his seat. 'Now, let's explore the range of your present lofting power.'

'I can sense extreme emotion. Rage is the easiest for me but when Jilik was trapped in the kennel, I also caught his great distress.'

'Hmm,' said the magian. 'I don't want to encourage you to catch the private thoughts of the folk near you. We must work toward a balance. What would be the most useful thing for you to know?'

'Since I can no longer see the expressions on faces, I'd like to know whether the words of the person talking to me are true or untrue. If I remain as kedura, I'll want to hear petitions.'

'So you need to distinguish between truth and untruth. I have never tried to explore that area using lofting skills.' When he paused, Lyta heard the tiny sounds that indicated he was rubbing a hand across his bearded chin.

She folded her hands in her lap and waited. Since Domen had always stressed patience, he might appreciate her effort now.

At last, the magian spoke, 'I must think more about this matter but in the meantime let us try an exercise. I will make two statements and you can decide whether I am telling the truth or not. You must judge by the subtle changes in the tone of my voice.'

'Very well.' Lyta prepared herself to focus on the sound of his voice.

'Empty your mind and then we will start. 'Domen cleared his throat. 'I am wearing a green robe this morn.' He waited and then spoke again. 'I am wearing a blue robe this morn.'

Lyta concentrated with all her might on the manner he delivered each statement. She detected a barely imperceptible difference in the second one. But was she right? She knew Domen owned both a blue robe and a green one. She went with her first thought.

'You're wearing a green robe.'

'I am indeed. What indicated the true statement?'

'Your voice changed just a little. If I had not been focusing hard, I wouldn't have caught it.'

She heard the smile behind his next words. 'I can tell you used great effort by the fierce scowl on your face. Shall we try again?'

'I had berries on my platter for repast.' Then a pause. 'I had no berries on my platter for repast.'

Lyta was caught. From the tiny alteration in his tone, she believed that he did not have any berries. On the other hand, she had been given berries for her repast. When she was sorting truth from untruth, should she use all the information available to her or just decide on the tone alone?

'I believe you did not have berries on your platter.'

'You are right again. But why did you wait so long to tell me?'

Lyta explained her dilemma.

'I think that if you are making a judgment in a case then you should get all information possible ahead of time and study the facts carefully. Quilin, Josik, or your clerk can help there. But when you are listening to the voices of the folk before you, you must use your lofting skill to catch differences in tone. It will be harder when more than one person is speaking to you.'

They completed four more exercises. Lyta was wrong in three which may have been, as Domen said, because she had become tired. He poured more peach juice at the end of their session.

'That's enough work for now. Shall we try this again on the morrow?'

Lyta agreed. 'I will meet you at the same time.'

Kel walked her back to the castle and she sank into the usual seat in the solar. The journey seemed easier this time. Why should it be so hard to listen carefully? She leaned her head against the back of the high chair and dozed.

Amia woke her. 'Lady, Lord Quilin is here.'

'Show him in.'

She recognized his quick and sure steps. 'Kedura, were you resting?'

'I have been working with Domen and it was tiring.'

'I see.' She was pleased that he didn't ask what she was doing with the magian. As far as Lyta knew, nobody else was aware of her lofting skill and she'd like to keep the talent as a secret. 'Kedura, I've brought some sad news. Lady Adina has died in childbirth.'

'Oh, no! She was too young to die. Only one summer more than me.'

'Apparently the child lived for only two morns.'

Lyta recalled Adina's happiness with garments and jewels, her pleasure with marriage to Firt, and her delight at riding Silver. She should ignore the times the girl had annoyed her with ceaseless talk about trivial matters. That aspect of Adina's nature was not important now.

'Please send my condolences to Adina's mother and to Firt.' It was politic to remember Firt even though she wondered how much he would mourn his high-spirited wife.

'One thing to bear in mind, Kedura, is that Firt will be seeking another wife.'

Lyta sat bolt upright. 'Surely he won't offer for my hand?'

'Knowing Firt and since he'll be here when your other suitors arrive, I'd say that was a certainty.' Quilin voice held a wry touch.

'Lady Moon protect me! At least I get to choose my husband and he is definitely last on the list.'

Quilin paused. His tone was neutral as he asked. 'Kedura, who would be first on your list?'

She was warned by his colourless voice to be cautious. 'I don't know yet. I've met only two of them and Iben has been drowned. Firt is beyond my consideration.'

'I see. Well, I'll leave you to your deliberations.'

When Quilin had left, Lyta ate her dinner. She preferred to eat this meal in her chambers but she had started to appear in the hall for supper at night. In the kitchen, Prala arranged the food on her platter in separate areas. Then Amia indicated where each item was by referring to the markings on a sundial. As she was finishing her meal, Jilik was announced.

She heard him bounce into the solar and halt near her. 'I am bowing to you Kedura.'

'You don't have to tell me each time, Jilik.'

'Then how will you know?'

'I'll expect you to do the right thing.'

'Then I'll do the right thing and say nothing next time,' said Jilik. He walked closer. 'Are you going to eat that bread on your platter?'

Lyta laughed. 'I can tell your legs are still hollow.' She touched the edge of the platter. 'Go ahead and take it.'

She heard Jilik take the piece of bread and chew it with gusto.

'Did you come here just to finish my meal?'

Jilik swallowed hard before he said, 'I came to bring you to the stables to meet my pony. The sun is shining and it's nice outside.'

Lyta was ready to refuse his offer but then she changed her mind. Visiting the stables would take her mind off Adina's sad death.

'I'll come with you and Kel will accompany us.'

'But I'm big enough to take you by myself,' Jilik protested.

'I know you're big enough but a kedura must always have an armed guard with her. It's a rule. '

'Oh,' said Jilik. By his voice, he was clearly disappointed. 'Well, if it's a rule, then I suppose he can come with us.'

'You can guide me through the castle but Kel will take me down the steps and across the first part of the courtyard.'

Jilik said nothing.

'Is that satisfactory?' Lyta asked.

'I was nodding but you couldn't see me.'

'It's better for me if you speak. If you've finished the bread, we can go.'

Lyta grasped the cane in her right hand and rested the left on the top of the boy's head. The hair felt warm and springy under her fingers. Then Jilik took her to the door and opened it. Lyta told the guard in the antechamber that they were all leaving for the stables and he would take her down the steps. 'And please escort me over the uneven ground.'

With Kel, she navigated the steps and the cobblestones near them before once again trusting herself to Jilik's head. He walked with great care, which made Lyta feel reasonably safe but she found it difficult to realize that folk watched her progress and no doubt felt very sorry for her. She was reminded of the time of her mother's death when she'd had equal problems with accepting sympathy.

They were almost at the stables door when she heard Druck's short cough beside her. 'Kedura, I'd have sent an escort to the castle if I'd known you intended to venture here.'

'But, Commander, I do have an escort. Lord Jilik is beside me and Kel is walking closely behind me.'

Then she recognized Nin's plodding steps and deep voice. 'Kedura, I didn't know you were visiting the stables. Can I help you?'

Lyta forced her own voice to remain calm. 'I have all the help I need. Lord Jilik wants me to meet his pony,

Cloud. And I should give a carrot to Snow to curry favour with her.'

She heard Druck march away but sensed Nin hovering near her. She knew his round face would be screwed up in his anxiety to do and say the right thing.

When they stepped inside the stables, Kel warned Lyta in a low voice to be mindful of the water barrels on her left. She used the cane to pinpoint their location and moved past them.

Jilik's head was quivering with excitement as they neared Cloud's stall. Lyta discovered that the pony was housed beside Snow. First she patted Cloud and ran her hand over his shaggy head and back. From what she could gather from his movements and sounds, Jilik had bent down to hug his horse and kiss its nose.

'Doesn't Cloud have the softest nose you ever felt?'

Lyta felt the pony nuzzle her palm. 'Yes, it's exceeding soft. Now I must talk a little to Snow or she'll think I don't care for her.'

After Nin placed a carrot in Lyta's hand, she fed it to Snow. The head groom said in a tentative voice, 'Lady, you could still ride. I would accompany you on a long rein.'

Lyta had been considering riding but Snow was a young filly and not used to her and she didn't fancy being led by anyone. 'If I do decide to ride, it must be on a more experienced horse. Snow and I are not accustomed to each other.'

'Yes, Kedura,' said Nin. 'You will let me know when you are ready for riding again and I'll find you the best horse.'

Lyta felt suddenly weary and sorry for herself. 'Jilik, if you wish to stay with Cloud, then Kel can take me back.'

'I'd like to stay and ride Cloud.' He paused. 'But I can take you back to your chambers instead.'

Lyta smiled. 'Please ride Cloud. And, Jilik, you were very helpful getting me safely here. Many thanks.'

As she and Kel crossed the courtyard, Lyta heard Quilin's steps approaching. 'Kedura, if you'd mentioned it, I'd have escorted you to the stables.'

Lyta bit her lip to prevent a howl of impatience escaping her mouth. 'If I want an escort, I'll certainly ask for it. As it was, your son brought me down here.'

'Then where is Jilik? Why didn't he complete his task?'

'I permitted him to stay and ride his pony. Please don't scold him. He offered to return me to my chambers.'

'Very well. But, Kedura, please allow me to bring you up the steps and into your solar.'

Lyta gave in with as good a grace as she could manage. Her problem was not her inability to move around the castle and its grounds but that too many folk would be trying to help her.

Chapter Sixty-Five

On her second lesson with the magian, Lyta found it easier to distinguish between true and false statements. Of the eight exercises they attempted, she was correct in seven of them.

'Now comes the difficult part,' said Domen. 'You might hear someone make a true statement followed by an untrue one and once again, must rely on the fine changes in tone. I will make a single statement and you must focus hard to assess if it is true or not.'

He cleared his throat and then said, 'This morn, I collected some herbs before you arrived.'

Lyta concentrated so hard her ears rang. She tried to judge the truthfulness by tone alone but she knew Domen liked to collect herbs in the cool of the morn and she could smell fresh Salusy in the workroom. Then Domen often cleared his throat before he said something significant. These facts and her senses told her he was speaking the truth.

'You did pick herbs this morn. But I didn't guess by your voice alone.'

'Since you could probably smell the herb, mayhap that was too easy a test. I will give you a more difficult one. Through my window, I can see Quilin and Josik talking together in the courtyard.'

Lyta decided that was a likely occurrence but this time she had no clues to assist her. Only a minute hesitancy in Domen's voice alerted her to the fact that he was not telling the truth. 'That is a false statement.' She rubbed her brow as she spoke. 'I'm getting an ache in my head.'

'Then I'll prepare a draught for you.' Lyta heard the magian cross to his shelves and take down a flask. He poured something into a cup and handed it to her. 'This will help the concentration. You are using considerable mind power to complete these exercises. We must take care that you do not become weary.'

He paused and then said, 'What is in the potion?'

Lyta tasted it. 'A mixture of Bright-Ease and Flenny.'

'Correct,' said Domen. 'I won't ask you for the proportion of each.'

'But I do remember it should be half and half.' Lyta placed the cup on the table. 'Now I'm ready to continue.

In the next six exercises, she identified four statements correctly. When Domen praised her, she said, 'I'm getting used to the changes in the tone of your voice. How well will I do when a stranger appears before me?'

'Mayhap, ask questions of the person first. Ask where he lives and what family he has. If your clerk has provided you with those answers beforehand, then you may be able to tell if his later words about the case ring true.'

Lyta sat silent, pondering his advice. 'That might be helpful but it will mean I must remember many things and focus hard for a long time.'

'Yes, it will be difficult at first. But I believe the task will get easier with more practice. And I should stress again that this skill of yours should be used with caution. Folk have a right to keep their private thoughts to themselves.'

'Of course. I promise to use my lofting skill in matters of justice or governance.'

Domen rose from his stool. 'Then I am content. We shall continue on the morrow.'

Lyta agreed and left his dwelling. Josik intercepted her as she crossed with Kel to the steps. 'Kedura, Druck did not wish to disturb you but he has just learned that a ship from Delis has entered the harbour.'

'Who would be arriving now from Delis?'

'The ship flies the stag banner of Baldus. I hope I'm wrong, Lady, but it would be just like him to send Fultis here early. He'll want to gain an advantage over the other kedirs.'

'I suppose he knows that one kedir is already at the castle. When will Ardul return from his visit to the Moon Temple?'

'On the morrow. We can expect many battles between the Delis boys when Firt comes for the council meeting. There's no love lost among Baldus's four sons. He raised them to compete with each other in every field. I understand they can scarcely occupy the same chamber without coming to blows.'

Lyta sighed. She'd hoped that the remaining kedirs would arrive together at the appointed time but obviously this was not to be. 'You and Druck should meet Fultis if he is on board and escort him here. Please come to my solar on your return to describe the kedir before I meet him.'

Josik agreed and hurried off. Lyta noted the slight limp in his step as he walked over the stones.

Kel accompanied Lyta to her chamber where she asked Amia to choose a robe and surcoat in which to receive Fultis.

'Lady, the apple green would be suitable for the occasion.' Amia moved efficiently around her, taking off her present garments and replacing them.

'I have selected silver jewels, Kedura.'

A necklet was put in place and a tiara arranged on her head. Fultis would be the first stranger she'd encountered since her blindness and Lyta felt her lips and mouth grow dry with nervousness. She asked for wine, which she sipped in the wait for Josik.

When Kel knocked on the door, Amia answered it. She heard her guard say that Kedir Fultis was being shown to his bedchamber. Josik followed in the next minute and entered the solar.

Lyta said, 'Please sit down and give your impression of the kedir.'

'In looks, he resembles his father and brother with the same chestnut hair and brown eyes although he is taller than both Baldus and Firt.'

'What about his manner?'

Josik was obviously annoyed. 'Fultis is an arrogant puppy, Kedura. He declared that a full guard of honour should have met his ship. I explained that his visit was unexpected. He replied that the stag banner indicated he was aboard and we should have noted it. '

'Then you were right. We can probably expect warfare when Firt gets here. Do we know when he's due?'

'He's left his estate and we should see him within two morns.'

'While you are here, Josik, please tell me about our new council member. I've never met Wilus's grandson.'

'Ronin's a sound man, very like his grandsire in many ways. And he's mayhap a suitor for you. He hasn't had much luck with getting a wife. He was first betrothed to a girl who died in a fire before their marriage. Then he was betrothed to a kedie from Sevvir. She drowned in a shipwreck on the way to their wedding. Wilus was arranging another wife for Ronin when he himself died.

'Such bad luck.' Lyta sighed. 'Then I am quite deluged with choice.'

She wondered which suitors would regard her blindness as a hindrance to marriage. On the other hand, some kedirs might prefer to have a blind wife and to be able to make decisions without her knowledge. It was now important than ever to choose an honest man.

'Would you please stay, Josik, when I receive Fultis?'

'Of course, Kedura, and I've asked Quilin and Domen to join us in the council chamber. With your permission, I'll take you there.'

In the chamber, Josik led Lyta to the chair with the symbol of Aldea carved into it. The spreading branches and sturdy trunk of an oak tree formed the back rest of the seat.

Commander Druck swung open the heavy door and announced the entrance of Kedir Fultis in a loud voice. Lyta listened for the sound of the kedir's steps. They sounded brisk and confident on the stone floor.

When Fultis came near her, Lyta held out her hand. The kedir kissed it and then stood before her. 'My father, Kedur Baldus, wishes me to send his good wishes for your return to health after your illness. And I would like to say that it's a great pleasure for me to attend your court and to meet you.'

Lyta decided she'd be able to recognize Fultis in future by the musky perfume that clung to his garments. 'Thank your father for his wishes. I am glad to say that I have regained my health. Please be seated, Kedir.' She indicated the empty chair on her right and waited for Fultis to take it. 'I trust you had a comfortable sea journey.'

'We were lucky to avoid any severe storms. I heard that the unfortunate Iben of Parian was lost and Ardul was rescued. I expected to see the kedir from Falga here as we received word he was recovering from his sickness.'

'Kedir Ardul is indeed well again. He expressed an interest in seeing the Moon Temple and the Salvence but should return soon.'

'Then I'll be glad to meet him. I trust we will have the opportunities when all the kedirs are present to demonstrate our prowess in sporting contests.'

'That has been arranged. I'm sure your brother when he arrives would like to take part. If the weather holds, we may stage a tourney although it's very late in the season to hold one.'

'I look forward to competing against Firt in any sport like archery or jousting. Since he last saw me, my skill has increased and I am fully confident of any victory.'

The two brothers were well matched in arrogance, Lyta thought. She wondered if the other kedirs were equally proud of their abilities. If so, it might be difficult to endure a gathering of talkative braggarts.

The meeting in the chamber ended after more polite exchanges and Quilin escorted Lyta to the great hall for the first of many banquets that would be held in the next sevenday. Quilin sat beside Lyta and in a low voice gave her instructions about the position of her silver platter and wine glass. He described the contents of the platters before her and served food and drink. Fultis, who was seated on Lyta's right, indulged himself in a long monologue about his many talents and fine character. The man seemed to have no other topic of conversation but himself.

Lyta was glad to escape from Fultis and the great hall. Eating in public with a stranger beside her had been an ordeal but she had to get used to the feeling of being closely observed by her guests and her people. She dreaded dropping food or spilling wine on herself, the table, or her guests. Quilin had been helpful and tactful in his quiet guidance.

Next morn over repast, Amia informed Lyta that Lord Firt and his party had just entered the castle gates. He'd wasted no time. She hoped for a peaceful meeting of the two brothers even though confrontation seemed more likely. As she ate berries and nuts, she thought that once Ronin arrived, they could hold the first council meeting.

When Lyta was dressed, she sent a message to Nin that she wished to ride. She wanted to test her nerves before the council meeting. She'd remembered an old horse called Gentle. Surely the name alone was an omen for success.

Once Kel had escorted her to the stable, Lyta explained her choice of mount to Nin. 'I know she'll move slowly but she's highly unlikely to buck me off.

'I agree, Lady. I should've thought of her.'

'I'll visit Snow while you prepare Gentle. Can one of the boys find a carrot for her? Please tell the commander that I intend to ride.'

'The message's been sent, Lady. He will accompany the escort party.'

So, Druck was taking no chances with her safety. Lyta couldn't blame him. The responsibility of taking a blind kedura out of the castle was a heavy burden. And he would have in mind the accident to her mother who'd had her sight and more experience with horses.

After she'd talked to Snow and fed her the carrot, Nin said Gentle was ready and Druck was waiting outside when Kel brought her into the sunshine. It was a fine morn with crispness in the air but no hint of rain. Lyta allowed herself to be boosted into the saddle like a small child. As she gritted her teeth, she knew this was a small price to pay if she was able to enjoy riding again.

Lyta shook her head when Nin placed a long rein into her fingers. She could imagine the resignation on the groom's face as she dropped it on the ground. If Gentle behaved like her name, she would be as safe as possible.

Druck coughed to get her attention. 'Kedura, I will post two men before you and I will ride beside you. Then the rest of the guards will follow.' He paused. 'We have another rider accompanying our party.'

Lyta heard the sudden clatter of hooves and the sound of a high voice. 'Jilik is coming with us?

'Yes, Kedura, I'd already promised him an escort before I knew you wished to ride this morn. He will be directly behind us, ahead of the rear guard.'

'That sounds satisfactory.'

'Will you ride through the town?'

'I wish to be away from the town and I don't want to go too far on this first outing. We will take the Forest road and then circle back home.'

'Very good, Kedura. Lord Jilik, bring your pony over here.'

Druck gave the orders to his men while Lyta tried to appear calm. But her heart was thudding as she waited to begin. Mayhap, this idea was folly. All she would experience was movement in the fresh air. The point of also viewing her demesne on a ride was lost.

Druck must have been aware of anxiety and melancholy thoughts. 'Lady, if it pleases you, I could describe what I see on the way.'

'That does indeed please me, Commander. You could start once we cross the bridge.'

Druck was as good as his word and Lyta had never felt more kindly toward the man. He pointed out several fallen trees and speculated on whether a wild boar had dug up the pile of earth near the track. 'Should I tell the kennel master to bring his dogs to catch the scent of the beast?'

'I want to see the boar,' Jilik called out. 'Can't we wait until it comes back?'

'No, my lord,' said Druck. 'The kedura wishes to continue.'

Lyta could sense Jilik's disappointment. 'You might see a boar on another ride. There are many in the forest.'

'I saw a stag yestermorn. The commander said I had quick eyes.'

'And a quick mouth,' Druck commented in a low voice.

'Tell the kennel master about the beast,' Lyta said. 'With so many guests arriving soon, Prala will need as much meat as she can get. I understand that several deer have already been taken.'

'The late wildflowers are in bloom here, Kedura. I don't know their name but they're tall with red leaves and purple blooms.'

'That sounds like Purple Cloak.' Lyta said. 'Please inform Magian Domen when we return. He might want to use the seeds for a potion.'

'I'd like to mix potions,' said Jilik overhearing their conversation. 'Then I could kill the people I don't l like. Not you, Kedura,' he added hastily. 'I like you almost as much as Cloud.'

The ride was pleasant but unexciting. In fact plodding along on Gentle's back was like being seated on a rocking horse. But Lyta realized she was able to continue her favourite activity if someone accompanied her to describe what she couldn't see any longer. It was the best outcome she could expect.

'Are we near the end of the track?'

'Yes, Kedura. The gates will come in sight beyond this bend.'

But never for me, thought Lyta as they clattered back across the bridge and through the gates. She sensed the tension in her commander as they passed between the stone posts. Her body tightened too and she knew they'd both hold their breath at that particular point in a ride, remembering only too well the morn when Halia had slipped from her saddle.

Once they'd crossed the outer ward and come through oldgate, Druck halted his horse. He said, 'Kedura, there are guests dismounting in the courtyard. Kedir Ardul has returned from the Moon Temple. And the rell banner tells me Lord Ronin has also arrived here from his estate.'

Chapter Sixty-Six

Druck's strong arms assisted Lyta to dismount from Gentle's back. ,As her feet touched the ground, someone took the reins from her hands. 'Did the horse behave herself?' Nin asked.

'The ride was exceedingly uneventful,' Lyta said, 'but she got me there and back in one piece. I will ride her again when I have the time.'

She heard Jilik chattering to one of the stable boys. As Kel took her arm, Lyta said, 'Do my guests wait for me?'

'Yes, Lady. They stand a few steps away.'

'Ardul spoke first, 'Kedura, I bring you greeting from the Moon Temple and the Salvence. They welcomed me most kindly. And I have a gift for you.'

I can guess what it is. Wine?'

'A whole cask.'

'Then you and your red companion are doubly welcome.'

'Did you have a pleasant ride?' Ardul asked.

'It was good to be out in the fresh air.' Lyta held out her hand and hoped the erle was near it. 'Lord Ronin, I am pleased to greet you.'

Her hand was swallowed up in an enormous one and then kissed. His voice was quiet but so low it rumbled like a wagon passing over rough stones. 'Thanks, Kedura. I am exceeding honoured to be here. I hope to fill my grandsire's place on your council without disgracing his name.'

'Ronin, are you a large man?'

He chuckled. 'Behind my back, they call me The Giant. I am taller and wider than most men in the demesne.'

'Taller and wider than two men,' said Ardul. 'I feel like a child standing next to you.'

Ronin chuckled again. When Ardul exclaimed and moved away, Lyta wondered if Ronin's large hand had ruffled the kedir's hair.

'We will meet again at dinner,' said Lyta. 'Godit will show you to your chamber, Lord Ronin.'

She nodded at Kel to lead her to back to her own chambers. Once there, she asked him to take a message. 'Please tell Lord Josik I wish to see him.'

Josik arrived shortly. When he'd taken a seat, Lyta asked him about the matters usually discussed by the winter council.

'At this meeting, we start with estate reports and then discuss any business that arises from them. As you already know, the drought in the eastern part of the demesne is causing serious problems for Firt. He will have found it difficult to collect all the taxes from his people. And the big storm resulted in the loss of fishing boats on the coast. Others may have their own concerns, which we will need to discuss.' He cleared his throat. 'Forgive the question, Kedura, but have you decided to stay on as our ruler. I haven't heard you mention the question of resigning for a while.'

'I really didn't make a formal decision. It just seemed the right thing after I thought about what my mother and Virr would expect me to do. I believe they'd both want me to continue even though I'm sightless.'

'Well, I'm glad to hear those words. I have been unsure of your intentions ever since your illness.' She heard him rise. 'Now, did we cover the demesne concerns?'

Lyta nodded. 'Taxation matters may occupy most of the time for the first meeting. We'll begin after we've eaten. And, Josik,' she added. 'You may tell the other members about my decision.'

Josik was replaced by Quilin. 'I examined the archives for any information about resigning your throne.' He paused and then added. 'But before I mention what I found, it seems to me that you might have decided to stay as our ruler. Your manner and actions now are quite different from your behaviour after the illness.'

'You should have spoken to Josik. I just told him I was remaining as kedura. I still feel that Aldea deserves better than a blind ruler but I won't resign after all. I hope you're content with my decision.' She paused to drink from her wine glass. 'As you searched, did you find any information about a kedura choosing her own husband?'

'There's no guidance for that. You will establish a precedent.'

'I feared that might be the case.'

Quilin leaned forward so that she caught his breath against her cheek. 'Lyta, I'm relieved that you will remain our ruler. Despite your concerns, you are wiser than you know. Your mother would have been exceeding proud to see how you govern. Serving you faithfully all my life will be my pleasure and not just my duty.' He took her hand and kissed it. The imprint of his warm lips lingered on her skin long after he'd left the solar.

***

On the morrow, Lyta dreaded the prospect of presiding over the meeting. Firt would be sure to dispute the amount of tax due to be paid to the demesne. As she was preparing to leave for the council chamber, Quilin met her outside her bedchamber.

His voice was terse. 'Trouble already. Firt drew his blade on Fultis.'

'What happened?'

'Josik intervened to prevent bloodshed. This time we were lucky but who knows what will happen if they get into another argument. It's a difficult task for you, Kedura, but you must make it clear they can't behave in this manner.'

Lyta began the council meeting by welcoming Ronin. He replied in his deep strangely peaceful voice. Her heart was quaking as she admonished Firt about drawing a blade under her roof. 'I will not tolerate an abuse of my hospitality from any guest, no matter what his rank may be.'

She imagines the pout on his face as Firt answered. He sounded like a sulky child being rebuked by a parent. 'Fultis started it. He always does. I don't know why he's come here ahead of the other suitors.'

Lyta detected the false note in his voice. She knew that Firt had begun the argument. She hoped it wasn't wrong to use her lofting skills to discover the truth in this matter. It did concern governance of the demesne.

The meeting began with the reports from each estate. Ronin's account was brief and clear. He acknowledged that some parts of his land had become dry but so far the grain, fruit, and vegetable crops had been unaffected and he'd received the required coin in taxes.

Quilin said much the same along with a reference to the damage to fishing boats, which had been a severe loss for folk in the coastal villages. He had assisted in the repair and rebuilding by providing the necessary timber. Josik did not report any dryness; in fact he had been lucky that his land in the higher elevations had received the normal amount of rainfall. His crops and animals had done well.

Last came Firt's report. He said he'd been forced to take strong measures to exact taxes from his tenants. 'We took animals, goods, and chattels but I am still short of the coin you expect.'

His absence of feeling for the hardship of his people chilled Lyta. Something must be done for the folk who lost their livelihood. 'What are the prospects of the drought ending now that winter has arrived?' she asked Domen.

The magian said, 'The word from Sevvir to the west of the continent says that the rains have begun there already. I am confident the wet weather will soon spread into Aldea in its usual pattern.'

'Then, Firt, your people should be able to reap their crops of winter wheat,' said Josik.

Wishing she could look directly into Firt's eyes, Lyta turned her head to face his chair. 'I am willing to forgo the taxes from your estate this one time.' She was mindful of the fact that she hadn't discussed the plan with the others and hoped they'd agree with her sudden decision. 'Please restore everything you collected to their owners.'

She could almost imagine the shock on Josik's face at the idea of the demesne's coffers not being filled to their normal amount. He oversaw the coin in her realm along with her steward. Firt didn't sound as relieved as she expected. Mayhap he would have difficulty returning the collected animals and chattels to his people.

'Very well,' he muttered at last, 'but is there a precedent for your decision? Goods collected instead of coin are legal in every demesne.'

'As kedura of the demesne, I'm permitted to make an exemption. Josik, what is the state of our coffers without the addition of Firt's taxes?'

'At the moment, we can manage,' said Josik. 'But we may not be prepared for a catastrophe like a wide-spread famine or severe flood.'

'Then let's hope we avoid one.'

Ronin said, 'Would it help, Lord Josik, if my estate provided a little more in taxes? We've done exceeding well for the last five summers.'

Lyta imagined the reaction of her erles to his words. They would either be dismayed, surprised, or relieved at his unusual suggestion.

'Josik, is that needed?' she asked.

'As I said, we can cope,' said Josik.

Quilin added in a dry tone, 'It's heartening to know that Ronin's land is doing so well. I may ask him for a contribution to cover the costs of my boat building.'

Lyta said they would meet again next morn to discuss other affairs of the demesne and Kel took her back along the passages to the solar. Before they reached the door, she heard Druck's heavy steps approaching.

'Kedura, another guest has arrived. Kedir Merik and his large retinue have been admitted to the courtyard.'

'Large retinue? How big is it?

'A score of men, Lady.'

'One score? We might have trouble accommodating that number.'

'We have space in the guard's rooms at oldgate, Kedura.'

'Then tell Godit he can bed them there. We are still expecting Kedir Netin from Parian and his party. No doubt, Godit will manage. I will receive Kedir Merik in the great hall.' She sent a servant to inform the council members of his arrival.'

Although Lyta disliked the formality of a welcome in the hall, it was wise to show respect to guests from another demesne. After Druck had departed, she called Amia to change her robe. She liked to wear the green and silver colours of Aldea when greeting foreign guests.

Lyta wished she could see Merik and judge his appearance for herself. The kedir's imposter who'd kidnapped her two summers ago had been said to resemble Merik. She recalled her mother saying that not only did the false kedir resemble Kedur Petrin of Sevvir closely but he also had the same silver tongue. That man had the skill of telling entertaining stories and singing sweet ballads. Would the real Merik be equally endowed?

She was seated on her carved throne when Merik was announced and she heard footsteps approaching from the far end of the hall. 'Does he look like the imposter?' she whispered to Josik.

'You'd be hard put to tell the two men apart,' he whispered back.

When the footsteps halted, she presumed Merik was bowing before her. 'You are most welcome in Aldea.'

'Kedura, I am most pleased to be here.'

Lyta resisted a strong urge to laugh. The kedir's voice was as high as an unbroken boy's. It could hardly be more different from the imposter's pleasant tenor tones. She bit her lip before replying in the expected manner and bidding Merik to be seated beside her. Now that she could not see faces, voices had taken a more important role in her assessment of people.

After some polite exchanges, Merik asked leave to change his clothing before the meal. Lyta waited several minutes until she couldn't hear any steps, before she asked, 'Josik, has he left the hall?'

'Yes, Kedura. He's gone.'

'I shouldn't laugh at Merik or judge him by his voice but, Quilin, he sounded more like your Jilik than a grown man.'

'I agree,' said Quilin. 'Most unfortunate for a kedir to squeak, I mean speak, like that.'

His mistaken word gave Lyta a most unfortunate picture of Merik as a brown mouse. Would she be able to dismiss that image from her mind? After all, she'd have to listen to Merik's voice for the next sevenday.

'His garments are too fancy,' said Josik in a disapproving voice. 'I wouldn't like to rely on him in battle.'

'I'm sure he'd be exceeding brave,' said Quilin. 'Josik, you shouldn't judge the boy by his clothes. Your garments should definitely be fancier. You're always wearing an old grey tunic.'

Lyta heard the smile in his voice. She said, 'I'm sure Josik looks most respectable. Now we only await Netin from Parian.'

'Mayhap he'll come by sea,' said Josik. 'It would be easier for him with his infirmity than travelling on horseback. The magian in Parian said he's left their demesne but not how he will journey.'

Godit came to see Lyta about the arrangements for dinner. 'We have three kedrirs who must have precedence over the erles. But which kedir has the most precedence? He should be seated next to you.'

'I wish to have Lord Josik on my left and the kedirs on my right. We could change the order for each meal. Ardul should be first as he's been here the longest time. The other kedirs can take turns.'

Godit sighed. 'These matters are awkward, Lady.'

'But I know I can always rely on your good judgment,' Lyta said. She thought that the man almost purred at her compliment.

No wonder Mother's face looked strained at times, Lyta thought. While Godit assigns beds and chairs, managing a household full of guests is complicated, especially with ill will between them. And that is not my only concern. I have put off asking my lords for advice on choosing my husband but with the selection so close in time, I can avoid it no longer. I will discuss the matter with Josik and Quilin on the morrow.

That night she was unable to fall asleep. Then when she did close her eyes, the faces of the people who'd died recently appeared in her dreams. Each gave her conflicting advice on suitable husbands. Her uneasy slumber left her drowsy and dispirited in the morn.

Chapter Sixty-Seven

Iben and Nirk sat on the side of the road under the shade of a wide-spreading elm and let the horses graze. The morn's ride had left men and horses hot and dusty. 'I'm aware Ulit might help me,' Iben said, 'but if I attend his court, he'll contact my father. I'll probably be ordered home.'

Nirk chewed a blade of grass as he spoke. 'It's mighty confusing having two heirs at once. I wonder what he'll do in this case.'

'He might stick with my brother. Although Father had difficulty accepting his body, he said Netin had a better head on his shoulders than I did.'

'True,' said Nirk. 'He's the power behind the throne, the man who keeps the peace and fills Gerit's coffers.' He spat out the grass.

Iben flinched at his candid words. 'So we'll avoid Ulit.'

'But you know Darik's steward will tell him you're alive. And Darik's likely to inform Ulit.'

'Then we'll avoid Darik too.' Iben batted a pesky fly from his face. 'How much coin did you win? Enough for presentable clothes, a better nag and a lute?'

'Forget the lute but I've got plenty to fit you out and me too.' Nirk regarded his brown jerkin with disgust. 'This is stained with salt water. And I think it shrank during my little swim in the sea.'

Iben glanced along the empty road and across at the fields of golden wheat, ready for harvest. 'Does all this land belong to Darik?'

'Right down to the coast. You can see Aldea from one point.'

'We want a town large enough to sell both clothes and horses. What's near here?'

'I came through the town of Letil with the steward's party. It's big enough to have several merchants and our best bet.'

'Then Letil it is. Which way and how far?'

'This way and we should reach it by evening.' When Nirk pointed north, they took the next road in that direction. His estimate was correct. By nightfall, they saw lights shining through the gathering gloom indicating a large building at the side of the road. They peered at the sign swinging above the door.

'It's The Red Fox,' said Iben. 'A change from the usual ducks, geese, and swans. We'll stop here. I'm in dire need of ale, meat, more ale, a pretty serving maid, and a bed. In that order.'

They'd stayed in worse inns on their travels. The landlady was plump and welcoming; her daughter, blue-eyed and willing, the meat, tender and the ale, strong. Even the bed seemed relatively free of bugs.

After a pleasant night, daylight revealed the rest of Letil beyond the inn. Their landlady told Iben he could buy clothes on Tunic Lane and a horse in the town square market. When Iben and Nirk ventured into the town they found that Tunic Lane was part of a warren of twisting alleys lined with shops selling hose, hats, cloaks, jerkins, and boots as well as tunics.

The garments Iben finally chose were plainer than he desired but when he complained about their lack of decoration, the tailor said, 'I'll add silver embroidery here, here, and here.' He pointed to the relevant places. 'My wife is skilled with her needle but, Sir, you'll have to pay more coin and wait an extra morn for the work.'

Since the ale at the inn was so drinkable and the daughter so bedable, Iben decided he could spend the time profitably.

A suitable horse was not so easily found. Those tied together in the town square looked as though they were more used to carrying sacks of turnips and cabbages than men.

'My present nag is better than any of these.' Iben poked the sway-backed animal beside him in disgust and turned to the dealer. His oily smile had slipped a little at Iben's words. 'Don't you have anything else?'

'The portly man stroked his chin. 'Lord Darik might have a horse he could part with. For a price, of course.'

Iben exchanged glances with Nirk. 'Then please ask him.'

'Your name, Sir?'

'Gerit,' said Iben. 'Gerit of Aldea.'

'Very good. If you return here on the morrow, I'll have news for you.'

Iben and Nirk whiled away some of the time by drinking ale and playing dice with the locals. Iben quickly lost the stake Nirk had provided while his man added more coin to his pouch. When he also lost that, Iben leaned back against the wall to watch the game. He noticed that Nirk stopped playing as soon as those around him began to scowl and murmur together about the constant luck.

'We don't want to be knifed in our sleep,' Nirk muttered to Iben, before offering ale to all those seated at the table. 'Smile sweetly at the landlady and see if she can find a roast fowl for our meal.'

On the morrow, the horse dealer made good on his word. The chestnut horse from Darik's stable was a superior animal with a glossy coat and an intelligent look in its eye. Iben handed over his own horse as part payment and Nirk counted out more coin into the man's sweating palm. He said in aside to Iben, 'I hope the horse hasn't been stolen from Darik's stable.'

'With a bit of luck, we'll have left Falga before the truth is discovered.'

Then they visited Tunic Lane to collect their new clothes. The merchant's seamstress had decorated Iben's tunic, jerkin, and cloak with silver patterns of branches and delicate sprays of leaves.

Iben spread out the garments on a table to admire the work. 'This has been excellently done. Please thank your wife.'

Nirk paid with a grudging expression. 'I'll have to win more coin if you keep buying more goods.'

'Now I need only a lute and the landlady has promised to find me one.'

'I don't mind if she's unsuccessful,' said Nirk. 'You'll only invent another mournful love song to offend my ears.'

'Kedura Lyta enjoyed my singing. And I do intend to create a new song for her before I reach Aldea.'

The landlady presented Iben with a lute which she said belonged to her uncle. It was a battered instrument with a broken string that her relative mended, much to Nirk's annoyance.

'The tone is good despite the wear,' Iben said, plucking the opening notes of a new ballad. 'By the way, you need to pay the old fellow.'

'I'll go into town to avoid this noise and find out the best route from here to Aldea,' said Nirk.

'I'll try out this new tune on the girl. She likes love songs.'

Two hours later, Nirk returned to tell Iben what he'd found. 'By sea's the quickest way but I'm loath to board another boat, even on a short trip. We'll spend three days riding there.'

'I agree with you about avoiding another sea voyage. I know Aldea's quite close but I'd like land under my feet not water. We'll ride there'

After Nirk had paid for their lodgings, the landlady bade them farewell with a broad smile. Iben kissed the pretty daughter for the last time and drank a final cup of ale. Then they mounted their horses and took to the road.

They covered many leagues before evening and stopped at a small inn for the night. When Nirk opened the door, the chamber was full of men drinking ale and listening intently to a tall fair-haired fellow.

Nirk dug Iben in the ribs. 'Look who's here.'

'Yalt,' said Iben with a sigh. 'I might have known he'd survive the storm. It's exceeding hard to get rid of that man.'

Since Yalt had his back to them and was occupied with his speech, Iben and Nirk were able to enter the inn without being seen by him. They asked the landlord if he had room.

'I've got a few empty chambers. That lot,' he said nodding at the crowd, 'all live around here. '

'Do you know the fellow talking to them? Iben asked.

'Name of Yalt. He's been here for three nights and I'm in two minds about telling him to move on. I'm selling plenty of ale but I don't like what he's saying. If word gets to Kedur Ulit, we're all in trouble.'

'What's he saying?' Nirk asked.

The landlord dropped his voice to a mutter. 'He says common folk should have a say in Falgan laws, not just the nobles. I don't agree with him but as you can see, some of them do.'

Iben saw this was true. More listeners were nodding their heads in agreement than shaking them in disagreement. Yalt was continuing with the same message he had preached in Aldea, stirring up ordinary folk to believe they had a right to take part in demesne affairs.

While Yalt was still talking, Iben asked if the landlord could feed them in another part of the inn. The man took them into the cramped, steamy kitchen where a gaunt woman in a red kerchief stirred a copper kettle of stew. At a gesture from the landlord, she ladled portions into two bowls and nodded at the table. Iben and Nirk sat down on two stools and tore large pieces from a loaf of warm rye bread.

'Eat up but don't bother speaking to her. She can't hear.' The landlord tapped his ears.

Nirk took a cautious spoonful. 'If she can't hear, she can't spread gossip or talk about her husband,' he said. 'A wife like that would suit me fine.'

'But she couldn't tell you how much she loved you.' Iben sopped up the tasty gravy with a chunk of bread.'

Nirk's stew had disappeared at a fast rate. 'If she cooked as good as this, I wouldn't care whether she loved me or not.' He touched the cook's arm and held out his bowl to be refilled.

The landlord took them up the back stairs to a chamber under the eaves. It was oddly-shaped with a sloping ceiling but it did contain two narrow cots. Iben took one look at the greasy blanket and decided he would sleep wrapped in his cloak. As he lay down on the lumpy bed, he heard a knock on the door. He waved at Nirk to answer it.

'Well, well, if it isn't Yalt,' Nirk said. 'What do you want?'

'To talk to both of you.'

When Iben nodded, Nirk opened the door and stood back for Yalt to enter the chamber.

Once in, Yalt filled the remaining space. He sat down on the single stool by the window and stared from one to the other. 'You thought I'd drowned, didn't you?'

'Obviously you didn't,' said Iben.

'We three were the only ones who survived.'

'And you really didn't deserve to survive,' said Iben.

Yalt scowled. ‘Kedir Iben, why did you kidnap me? Oh yes, I found out who you were after the wrecked ship was identified’

‘I wanted to remove you from Aldea where you were causing trouble for Kedura Lyta,’ Iben said. ‘And I won’t apologize for that action.’

‘So, you pretended to be in sympathy with my ideas and all along you were telling them up at the castle what I said and did.’

Iben sat up and folded his arms. ‘You’ve got it right. What are you going to do about it?’

‘I’d like to run a blade through your false heart.’

Nirk stood up. Looming over Yalt, he said in a low growl, ‘Watch your mouth, boy. You’ll have to stick me first.’

‘Oh, do sit down,’ said Yalt with a casual wave of his hand. ‘I’m a peaceful fellow. Where are you two going? Back to the castle for the gathering of suitors?’

‘Yes, we’re off to Aldea.’

‘You can take me with you.’

‘But Druck will lock you up as soon as you appear in Aldeton,’ Iben said.

‘If you want to keep me quiet in the town about the spying and the kidnap, you’ll let me tag along with you.’

Nirk laughed. ‘Even though you’ll be recognized?’

‘I’ll turn my hair and beard black, get a horse, and pose as your groom from Parian.’

Nirk and Iben exchanged glances.

‘I’ll consider it,’ Iben said. ‘See me in the morn for my answer.’

‘Right,’ said Yalt. ‘I’ll await your reply.’ He stood up and walked to the door where he paused. ‘And don’t even think of creeping away without me. I have friends in the inn stable.’

When he’d left, Iben sighed heavily. ‘The townsfolk won’t forgive me for the way we treated Yalt. And they have more friends and family at the castle. My life could be at risk. I think we should take him to keep an eye on his movements. He'll get to Aldea by himself eventually.'

'Unless I use my blade tonight,' said Nirk. 'I could discover where he sleeps and solve our problem with one quick thrust.'

'It could be dangerous to kill him in a place where he's been so well received. Let me think about it.'

Nirk threw himself back on the cot. 'Don't take too long. In this case, action is more useful than thought. If you don't want him slain in this inn, I could dispatch him on the road in a lonely spot.'

Chapter Sixty-Eight

Mindful of her old nurse's constant advice, Lyta forced herself to eat repast. But after her restless night, she had little appetite. The marriage decision was weighing heavily on her mind. Once Kedir Netin arrived from Parian, all the eligible suitors would be present and she'd have to make her choice within the following sevenday.

Domen had suggested another training session. Although Lyta wondered how effective it would be after little sleep, she went to his dwelling. She was right to be concerned. Out of the eight exercises Lyta tried, she was wrong in six.

'You lack concentration.' The magian paused. 'What ails you?'

'Many things but especially this matter of choosing a husband. I must make the decision by myself.'

'Then you are fortunate. Most noble women don't have any say in the choice of a husband. '

'I'd feel more certain if I could see the men I've never met.'

'Would it help if you told me your thoughts?'

Lyta thought for a minute. 'Yes, it might.'

'Which men are not worthy?'

'Firt for one and his brother Fultis who sounds and acts like him.'

'That's two out of the way. Who's next?'

'Merik might be a worthy suitor but I could not live with his squeaky voice. Iben, on the other hand, had a fine voice. But he's dead.'

'What about his brother?'

'Netin may be rejected by many because of his infirmity but since I can't see his crooked back, I'll judge him by his nature. Apparently, he has a clever mind and takes much interest in the governance of his demesne.'

'So we've eliminated Firt, Fultis and Merik. Of the kedirs, that leaves Ardul and mayhap Netin.'

'I think Ardul would make a kind husband but I'm not really sure about being so closely allied with Falga. They have been an uneasy neighbor for too many summers for me to feel that Aldea would be stay as a separate demesne.'

'Of course there are others to consider?'

Lyta was sure her surprise must be evident. 'Who?'

'Lord Ronin for one'

'He seems an exceeding pleasant man and I know he's in need of a wife. But I haven't known him long enough to be sure of his character.'

'Well, there's someone you have known most of your life. In fact, he's your most loyal supporter. Do you know whom I'm talking about?'

Lyta hoped her cheeks had not reddened. 'I think you refer to Quilin.'

'He'd make an admirable husband.'

Lyta was silent as she absorbed his words. She needed to be alone to think more fully about choosing Quilin. Despite her expressed doubts, Ardul was still a candidate for her hand. She stood up and tapped her cane against the wall to guide her to the door. 'Many thanks for your help and your counsel, Magian Domen. You've given me much to consider.'

As Kel led her across the courtyard, he said, 'Lady, Archis Druck is approaching and indicating he wishes to speak to you.'

She heard Druck halt before her. 'Kedir Netin's vessel has landed at the harbour, Kedura. Lord Josik and Lord Quilin have gone to meet him.'

'Bring him to me when he reaches the castle.' She heard the sounds of horses' hooves on the stones. 'Is he here already?'

'No, Kedura.' Druck paused before saying with wonder in his voice. 'I don't believe it!'

'What's the matter?'

'He's back from the dead. It's Kedir Iben.'

'Iben?' cried Lyta. 'Surely not!'

'He and his man are dismounting from their horses. I'll bring him to you, Kedura. Please wait here.'

As his steps moved away, Lyta asked her guard. 'Kel, are you certain he is Kedir Iben?'

'Yes, Lady. I recall him singing in the great hall before we knew he was a kedir. It's the same man and that big fellow with him.'

When she heard several sets of footsteps, Lyta turned. She recognized Iben's voice as soon as he spoke.

'Kedura Lyta, you don't know how happy I am to see you again.'

Lyta smiled. 'I'm amazed that you're alive. Does your father know you've been rescued?'

'He will by now. But Netin probably sailed for Aldea before Father got the news. His ship was in the harbor. I knew it by the wolf banner.'

'Commander Druck had just told me about your brother. You'll be pleased to meet him.'

'He'll certainly be surprised to see me,' said Iben in a dry tone. 'But I'm not sure how happy he'll be about it, Kedura.'

'Yes, of course. Your presence complicates the situation in Parian. You should meet Kedir Netin before I see him. I'll receive you both later on.'

Back in her solar, Lyta considered the situation. Now she must add Iben with his fine voice to her list of possible suitors. But was a good singing voice enough qualification in a husband? She remembered telling Adina three summers ago that a fine voice didn't last while a fine mind did. She'd been wiser than she knew.

Lyta had been discomposed by the magian's remarks about Quilin. Was his faithfulness to the throne merely a duty or was something more personal behind it? It was true that she'd known him most of her life. She remembered being impressed as a small child by the black-haired boy with the steady grey eyes who practiced so diligently at the tilt post in the castle courtyard. He'd been kind to her, even then. The other boys who trained with him called her a foolish babe and pushed her away from their games but Quilin always protected her and answered her questions. Could she know his true intentions toward her now without asking him directly?

Before supper, Lyta received the Parian kedirs. She sensed the uneasiness between them as soon as they spoke to her although their behavior was courteous. She hoped they'd been given chambers a distance apart. However this set of brothers had cooler heads and better manners than those from Delis. They were unlikely to brawl under her roof.

In the solar, Josik and Quilin met Lyta to discuss whether a tourney was possible. They were not normally held in the winter months but lately the weather had been exceeding warm and fine for the season. The two erles suggested that the jousting should go ahead.

'We have also planned contests in archery and wrestling,' Josik said.

'To allow your suitors to demonstrate their skills to each other,' said Quilin in a caustic tone.

Lyta asked, 'Surely, Quilin, you'll enter the jousting?'

'If you request it, Lady.' His voice now was serious.

'I do. The honour of Aldea must be upheld.'

At each meal in the hall, Godit placed a different kedir beside Lyta at the high table. Ardul was the easiest companion. He talked about a wide range of subjects and was quick to notice if Lyta needed her glass refilled or her platter replenished. Netin was more awkward in manner but he asked pertinent questions about the demesne of Aldea and explained how it differed from Parian.

She endured Fultis and his conversation, which still centred around his many accomplishments and talents. Much to Lyta's disgust, the man even spent a considerable time describing every detail of his appearance from the top of his head down to his feet.

Iben, however, told her about his shipwreck and his ordeal on the deserted island of gulls. He made her laugh at his trials of being a tutoran in the fishing village where he'd been given shelter. 'I wished every morn that I'd listened more closely to my own tutoran as he taught me to read and write instead of dreaming about hunting or practicing in the tilt-yard.'

Godit had arranged a variety of entertainers. One night an old fellow from the town recited Aldea's most popular poem, which described the accomplishments of Lyta's heroic grandsire. He had slain scores of wild beasts with only a short blade, dispatched multiple enemies with a single blow of his battle-axe, and won the heart of the fairest lady in the land.

'Hard for anyone to live up to that man,' murmured Quilin in Lyta's left ear.

'Luckily, a woman isn't expected to wield a battle-axe,' she whispered back.

'You will need to make your mark in some other way to have a poem written about you.'

'You forget I already have a song written about me.' Lyta wished she could see the expression on his face when he recalled Iben's ballad.

And Iben was another entertainer. He dedicated a new song to Lyta, which proved to be as tuneful as the first one. He also sang in answer to requests from the people in the hall. Ardul too used his lute and light tenor voice to sing two songs from Falga.

Lyta spent another restless night, thinking about her options. At night, the choice seemed harder to make than during the hours of light. Her breathing rate increased and her heart beat faster every time she thought about the approaching morn when her new husband must be named.

Druck arrived at repast. He came to attention before Lyta as she ate a honey cake. 'Kedura, I'm exceeding sorry to disturb you so early but I have just discovered Yalt is back in Aldea.'

'Where has he been?'

'I have no idea. My men didn't know him at first as his hair and beard are now black. Should I arrest him at once?'

Lyta considered the matter. 'Only if you can take him without anyone knowing. I don't want a disturbance in the town.'

'Yes, Kedura. I'm sure we can take him privately. I've assigned a guard to watch his movements.'

'Make sure your watcher is discreet.'

'Yes, Kedura. He's a good man. I'll inform you when Yalt is taken.'

After Druck had marched from the solar, Lyta reflected on his news. She had not changed her mind about wishing to talk to Yalt about his ideas. But a further complication might arise if her future husband was not receptive to considering new notions. Kedirs like Ardul and Netin might be traditionally bound in their views on governance and more in agreement with her council members.

She wondered about sharing the power when she was wed. How would it work when there were two people on the throne? Would they divide the principal duties and if so, which responsibilities would remain as hers? She might find it hard to compromise on ruling with a virtual stranger.

The magian's words came to mind again as she ate the last honey cake. There was one person eligible for her hand who was not a stranger. Lyta pushed the platter away and took a long swallow of cider. Enough thinking for one morn. She had a wrestling contest to attend.

As the air was cool on the field, Lyta was glad of her warm cloak. A small pavilion had been erected for her and various officials. Quilin appointed himself as her eyes for the occasion.

'You must have seen many wrestling contests.' He settled Lyta in her seat and placed something before her. 'Rest your feet on this box. The grass is very damp here, Kedura.'

'I remember attending wrestling matches with my mother.'

'Our Druck was a champion in his youth. I recall seeing him win several prizes. He is in charge of this contest. For fairness, he's asked a man from Parian and another from Delis to act as judges with him.'

'A wise move,' said Lyta, trying to control a shiver as a breeze hit her face.

Quilin must have caught the quick movement as he said. 'Why not raise your hood against the wind?'

When he leaned forward to tug up the hood, she caught his scent, a mixture of honey and a spice she couldn't instantly identify. Cinnamon? Nutmeg? No, it was definitely cloves. She breathed it in while he was close. Once his sure hands had adjusted the fur around her face, he moved away.

'The first contestants are getting ready. Druck has ordered a ring of grass to be cut low for the action. We have a man from Sevvir and one of our own guards.'

Druck announced the two names in a loud voice. From the cheer that followed, Lyta guessed a large crowd was present.

'Are there many watchers?' she asked.

'I'd say about four score are present.'

During the next two hours, he provided Lyta with a full description of each bout. At the end, the final wrestlers were the two brothers from Delis. .

'I'd hoped we'd avoid this particular combination,' said Quilin. 'There'll be more bad feeling no matter who wins. Fultis might be a more generous loser.'

'I doubt it,' said Lyta. 'And for the first time since my sickness, I'm grateful I can't watch this match. You can spare me the details.'

Quilin laughed. 'You can't miss a match as important as this. At least let me tell you who wins.'

'You probably will inform me whether I want to know or not.'

Lyta heard the sounds of the match as well as the occasional chuckle from Quilin. When she heard yells and shouts, she said, 'What am I missing now?'

'Druck had raised Fultis's arm to indicate he was the winner. Firt is objecting to the last move by his brother.'

'Of course he is.'

'Druck was prepared for trouble. Guards have stepped forward to form a ring around the champion. Oh, that's good. Firt is marching off the field.'

'It didn't matter who won this match,' said Lyta. '.I just hope we'll be spared any trouble in the next contests.'

'Let's get you out of the wind.' Quilin helped Lyta from her seat. 'Place your arm into the crook of my elbow. You'll keep warmer walking close to me.'

And she did feel more comfortable. Lyta reflected that Quilin always seemed warm when she was beside him and she felt sure that he'd always lead her along a clear path.

Chapter Sixty-Nine

'The brothers are at it again.' Josik announced. 'When Fultis won that wrestling match, it must have made matters worse. Apparently, Ronin saw them shoving each other against the wall. I arrived on the scene just as he picked each man up by the back of his tunic. It reminded me of separating a pair of snarling puppies. A most unusual sight.'

'But they didn't draw a blade?'

'Not this morn but it's only a matter of time before one of them completely loses his temper.'

'I wish we could keep them apart,' Lyta hoped that if Firt won the archery or the jousting, he might be satisfied. She never thought that governing a demesne would involve her in such matters

'Mayhap,' said Josik in a gloomy tone. 'I don't trust either of them as far as I can kick them.' He asked permission to leave her for a consultation with Quilin and Druck about the next contest.

Amia placed a heavy cloak over Lyta's shoulders before Kel escorted her to the archery field. After the cold conditions of the previous morn, Quilin had ordered the larger pavilion to be erected to shelter the spectators from the wind. Lyta was grateful for the extra protection.

Once again, Quilin provided an account of the contest. 'Druck, Josik, and a man from Delis will be the judges. Before you arrived, they'd weeded out many of the entrants and now the best ten are left to shoot it out.'

'And I suppose Firt and Fultis are among them?'

Quilin sighed. 'Unfortunately they are. In fact, all your suitors are here, even Netin. He manages to shoot straight despite his twisted body. He must have endured many hours of practice to become so proficient with his bow.'

After several rounds, four bowmen were left: Ardul, Netin, Firt, and Fultis. The two who missed the target in the next match would be eliminated. Quilin described the scene to Lyta.

'They are testing their bows and lining up. Josik should have separated the Delians instead of letting them stand side by side. That's not wise. Right, here we go. Ardul's arrow has hit the mark. And so has Netin's. Firt is aiming now. And yes, he's hit the mark too. We're waiting for Fultis who's taking extra time.' He paused. 'And he is also through to the next round.'

'Firt has started.' Quilin suddenly halted. 'Ah, he's missed the mark. Fultis laughed at him and now they're exchanging angry words.'

Lyta heard the sounds of a scuffle with blows and yells. 'What's happening?'

'Firt whacked his brother with his bow and knocked him to the ground.'

'Oh no. Is he conscious?'

'He's groaning so he's alive. His head is bleeding.'

'Does it look serious?'

'Head wounds always bleed exceedingly much. I'm sure he'll recover but if the flesh around his eye swells, he won't be able to continue. ' Quilin paused. 'And Josik has disqualified Firt so neither of them will win the archery.'

'Have they both entered the joust?'

'They have and so have I. Josik must be more careful with his combination of entrants in the bouts. Oh, the magian has just arrived and he's examining the wound.' He waited for a minute. 'Domen's guiding Fultis from the field.'

Ardul was the victor at the end of the archery contest and Lyta awarded him a golden chain. 'Many thanks, Kedura. I'll remember your kindness every time I wear this.' He kissed her right hand and then her left one.

At the meal that followed, Ardul was placed beside Lyta. He made a point of telling her that the chain was around his neck. 'I may never remove it, even to bathe or joust,' he said with laughter in his voice.

***

Next morn, Druck was an early arrival in Lyta's solar. She had finished her repast when he was shown into the chamber. 'Kedura, we have Yalt in the cells. Do you still wish to speak to him?'

'Yes, I do. Please escort me to the gatehouse.'

'I'll have guards close by to make sure he doesn't harm you.'

Lyta didn't want their conversation to be overheard but she kept silent. She could arrange matters as she wished when she met Yalt.

She went with Druck from the castle. At the gatehouse, the commander escorted her through several doors and into a chamber where he assisted her to sit down. 'Kedura, there's a brazier beside you and a table in front. A stool for Yalt is placed opposite. He'll be brought here in fetters and I'll have four armed guards standing behind him.'

Lyta threw off her cloak. 'Bring Yalt in.'

She heard shuffling feet as Yalt was brought through the door and across the floor and clanking sounds when he sat down. Druck was still standing beside her.

'Yalt,' she said. 'Will you swear not to attack me if your fetters are removed?'

His voice was amused. 'Yes, Lady. I swore that oath earlier and you were quite safe with me then. I'll swear again if you wish it.'

'I believe you. Archis Druck, have the fetters removed.'

Druck protested but she ignored his comments. 'Remove them.' She waited in silence for the noises that indicated Yalt was being unbound.

'I wish to speak to this man alone. Take your guards from the chamber.'

'But, Kedura, I must stay. I'm sworn with my life to protect you.'

'I have his word and that is sufficient. There is no need for concern.'

Druck snorted but he didn't argue further. After the door closed with an angry click, Lyta was alone with Yalt.

'My Lady, I was exceedingly sorry to hear about your blindness,' Yalt said in a soft one. 'It must make your position and duties difficult.'

'I'm becoming accustomed to my infirmity.' Lyta leaned forward. 'Now, tell me what changes in governance you are suggesting.'

Yalt took a deep breath and described the details of his idea. He was clear and brief in his explanation of the people who would be eligible for election.

'I see,' said Lyta. 'Then your council would consult with my erles but would not overrule their decisions.'

'We want to express our opinion on a law while it is being discussed not just complain about its unfairness when it is imposed on us. For example, I don't think your nobles realized how difficult it was to restrict the types of animals permitted in towns.'

'I understand. Then we should work out new rules for a new council.'

'Yes, Lady.' He paused. 'So, are you willing to consider my idea?'

'I am willing to consider it and I will also raise it again with my erles. You've probably guessed they are opposed to it. And they will have to agree before any action is taken.'

Yalt said, 'At least you will take the next step.'

'But not until I have wed my future husband. You'll have to wait for discussion at our next council meeting at midsummer.'

Yalt sighed. 'Very well, Kedura. This is better than nothing and I'm much further than I was before this meeting. I accept your conditions.'

'There's one more. Will you swear to keep the peace in the meantime? That means not stirring up strong feelings in the town and countryside.'

'Kedura, you strike a hard bargain but yes, I will swear to it.'

When Lyta held her hand across the table, he kissed it.

'We are in agreement. I will keep my part of the bargain. I'll order you to be released from custody. But if you break your word, the commander will arrest you once more.' Lyta began to rise from her chair.

'Kedura, let me help you.'

'Please go to the door and call in the commander.'

Druck arrived so quickly that Lyta wondered if he'd been listening with one ear to the door. He gave her his arm but she waited until Yalt had been taken from the chamber.

'I am ordering Yalt's release. He has sworn to keep the peace and to refrain from stirring up trouble in the town.'

'I will obey your command, Kedura.' Lyta knew from Druck's tone of voice how unwilling he was to free Yalt and how skeptical he was of a peaceful outcome. But she heard him pass on the order to guards who entered the chamber.

'Now please escort me back to my chambers.'

As they walked through the gate and across the courtyard, Lyta thought the meeting had gone well. Yalt was a reasonable man. The hardest task would be to convince her erles that his idea was worth considering.

When Amia dressed Lyta for the joust, she handed her a fur lined cloak that had belonged to Halia. 'Lady, it's even colder this morn. You will need this extra warmth.'

Lyta heard her opening another chest. 'What else are you searching for?'

'Your Lady Mother had boots lined with fur as well. Ah, here they are.' She slipped them on Lyta's feet. 'Luckily your feet are much the same size.'

Josik arrived to speak to her. She heard him rubbing his hands together as he entered the chamber. He moved close to Lyta who was seated by a brazier. 'Is it still really cold outside?' she asked him.

'Exceeding brisk. I've been looking over the arrangements in the lower field. The lists are ready and your pavilion is being moved from the archery grounds as we speak. I'd suggest that we put braziers in it to keep you warm.'

'Amia has already given me a fur cloak and boots.'

'Since Quilin will be occupied this time, Domen will keep you informed of the proceedings.'

'A good idea.'

'With your permission, Kedura, I'll go back to the field to make certain that the pavilion has been soundly erected. The wind is blowing in gusts.'

Later in the morn, Domen escorted Lyta to the lower field. She heard the confused babble of sound from crowds of people as soon as she came through oldgate. The tantalising smells of roast meat and spiced cider reached her nostrils.

Like the wrestling and the archery contest, attending this tourney would be a novel experience. Lyta would hear the horses thundering toward each other and the clang when one lance met another. She would also catch the roars of approval or disapproval from the crowd and the shouts from the hawkers of food and drink. But she'd have to remember the sights from watching previous tourneys. She recalled the bright flags and banners waving from the tops of striped tents, the colourful garments of the young squires, the horses prancing nervously before a bout, and the intent faces of the spectators lining the lists.

The magian handed her to a seat in the pavilion. 'You have a brazier behind you and one on your left,' he said. 'Kedura, I'll sit on your right.'

Lyta pulled the cloak tight around her body. Although she felt the heat from both braziers, the wind blowing through gaps in the canvas held a sharp edge. She was glad that her feet would stay warm in her mother's boots.

Domen said, 'The kedirs except Netin will take part in the tourney. Fultis insists he can wear a helmet over his head bandage but I am sure it will be painful for him. Josik was careful to avoid pitting Fultis against Firt. He also didn't want to place Firt and Quilin in the same match.'

'Please describe what you can see.'

'Before I do, Kedura, a problem is fast approaching. Three men are trotting toward you to beg for a token. Quilin, Firt, and Ardul.'

Lyta smiled. 'Oh dear! I will award my token to the man who reaches me first. Mayhap, Ardul is the most diplomatic choice.'

She was in luck. With a yell of triumph, Ardul pulled up his mount before her seat. 'Kedura, I won the race to receive your token.'

'Kedir Ardul, I'm delighted to award it to you.' Lyta leaned forward hoping she was near enough for him to take the green scarf.

'I will carry this with great pleasure after beating two worthy opponents to reach your side first.'

Domen said, 'They are all moving away. Firt has a scowl on his face but our Quilin is congratulating Ardul on his win.'

Lyta suddenly experienced doubts. Now that Ardul had won a chain and a token from her, was he expecting to be a winner in the husband contest? Mayhap, he would lose the joust.

Domen's description of the match was very precise and clear. However it lacked the interesting details that Quilin had provided for the wrestling and archery. He gave his opinion of the number of points each competitor was likely to be awarded by the judges.

The magian described each bout. In one of them, Firt unseated Iben who was also unseated by Merik. When everyone had taken part, four riders were undefeated: Quilin, Merik, Firt, and Ardul.

'Firt and Ardul are matched in the first bout,' said Domen.' They are preparing their horses now.'

The magian announced each winner. In the first match, Ardul was victorious. Since Firt won the second, all interest was focused on the last bout.

Lyta felt Domen lean forward, intent on the scene before him. 'They are starting. They are reaching the centre. Oh, well done!' he exclaimed. 'Ardul is the winner.'

'I shouldn't feel glad but I am,' Lyta said. 'Now Quilin and Merik will face each other.'

'Yes,' said Domen. 'They are donning their helmets and gauntlets as I speak. You will hear the horses soon.'

The hooves started pounding and Lyta imagined Quilin in his black mail on his black destrier with his lance in hand, intent on his opponent coming toward him. Merik had proved himself to be skilled in this sport.

'No points were awarded in this bout,' said Domen. 'Now they are each preparing for the next bout.' The magian paused.

'What's happening now?' Lyta asked when Domen didn't continue speaking.

'Kedura, there might be a difficulty. Merik has dismounted and removed his helmet. And he's fallen to the ground. I must go and aid him.'

Lyta heard him clamber down from his seat. Without his body blocking the breeze, she felt colder than ever. She rubbed her hands in their gloves together and stretched them out toward the brazier. A stronger gust shook both the sides and back of the pavilion. A thud told her that the brazier might have been blown over. If so, where had the hot coals scattered?

She felt sudden rush of heat near her boots and smelled smoke. Why hadn't the others in the pavilion noticed the danger? A sudden scramble from those around her indicated they had seen and smelled smoke, but no hands were helping her to leave.

'Fire!' Lyta yelled.

Chapter Seventy

When Lyta stretched out a hand, she touched familiar hangings. How had she reached her bed? The last thing she remembered was being seated in the pavilion at the jousting tourney. Her head ached when she moved it on the pillow. Then she winced as recent memories rushed back. One of the braziers had fallen over and she'd sensed both smoke and flames and she didn't know which way to turn to escape. What had happened after that moment? Lyta struggled to sit up.

'Please be calm,' said Domen, placing hands on her shoulders. 'You need to lie there and rest. How do you feel?'

Lyta's throat was swollen and painful. 'How did I get here,' she asked in a strange hoarse voice.

'Quilin carried you from the pavilion when the fire broke out.'

'Wasn't he jousting at the time?'

'When Merik collapsed, Quilin dismounted too and took off his helmet and gauntlets. He told me he looked over and caught a glimpse of flames shooting from the top of the pavilion and people hurrying from their seats. He didn't see you among them.'

'So he rescued me?'

'To his cost. His hands were burned.'

'Oh,' Lyta was lost for words for a few minutes. 'I must thank him. Why did Merik fall?'

'He'd been hit on the helmet in the previous bout. I have seen this sort of damage before. Sometimes a blow does not take effect at once. A man can fall to the ground an hour later.'

'Is he seriously hurt?'

'No, but I have ordered him to rest and avoid any type of sport until his aching head recovers.'

'I will pray to Lady Moon for his return to good health.' Lyta grimaced and lifted a hand to her throat.

'Don't speak any more, Kedura. You must also heal. I have prepared a sleeping potion of Sweet-Ease and Wister for you.' He supported her head while she drank from the cup.

When Lyta woke again, her head felt better. She sat up with care and swung her legs over edge of the bed. She heard Amia rush forward. 'My Lady, the magian said you were to stay in bed until he returned.'

'What is the hour?'

'You have slept the whole night through.'

'I feel much better,' Lyta said although her voice still sounded strange to her ears. 'I'm thirsty but I wish don't wish to drink in bed. Help me to my chair.'

Amia continued to protest but she helped Lyta into a robe and then to sit down. She poured a glass of ale. 'My Lady, are you also hungry?'

'I fear my throat will hurt to eat anything. Swallowing this ale is difficult enough. Don't fuss, Amia.'

'Should I admit anyone to your chamber?'

'Only the magian.' Then she added, 'And Lord Quilin if he comes.'

Her hair stank of smoke and she wondered if it has stained her skin. 'Are my face and hands black?' she asked Amia.

'A little, Lady. We'll prepare a bath when the magian says you may wash.'

'I don't need anyone's permission to bathe.'

Amia's voice trembled. 'I worry for you, Kedura. You might have died in that horrible place.'

Lyta heard Quilin in the antechamber, speaking to Kel. Her hands flew to her hair to pat it into place. 'Tidy me quickly!' she ordered Amia. 'Wipe my face before he sees me.'

'Lord Quilin begs leave to speak with you,' Kel announced as he opened the chamber door.

'Wait a moment.' Lyta swallowed hard. After Amia had wiped her face and hands, she pushed away the cloth. 'Let him enter. Amia, Caza, and anyone else in the chamber, you may leave.' Quilin's quick steps crossed the floor and stopped near her.

She spoke quickly. 'Quilin, thank you for saving me. I am exceeding grateful.'

'It was nothing. Lyta, I hope you are not in too much discomfort.'

'No, I'm almost recovered.'

She sensed his smile. 'Not by the sound of that voice.'

'I could pass for a frog croaking in the moat,' Lyta said. 'But what about you? Domen said you were injured. Is the burn exceeding painful?'

'It'll mend,' he said in a dismissive tone. 'Domen has applied a thick layer of his special salve. I smell like a flower.'

'A flower and a frog. We make a good pair.' Lyta's cheeks flushed as she realized the implications of her words.

All levity had vanished from Quilin's voice when he next spoke. 'Lyta, when I saw those flames, I thought I'd lost you.' She heard him drop to his knees beside her and then he touched her arm with a bandaged hand. 'I couldn't bear a life without you in it.'

Both her hands covered Lyta's cheeks. 'Why do you say this? Is it because you swore fealty to me as your ruler?'

'Fealty has nothing to do with it. I spoke as a man to a woman.'

Lyta was robbed of speech. Her feelings about him were too jumbled to express. When he too was silent, Lyta wished she could see his face.

Then he spoke again in a cool, controlled voice, 'Please forgive me, Kedura. I shouldn't have spoken thus. My words were uttered in a moment of madness.' He got to his feet. 'I will leave you now to rest.' She heard him turn to move away.

'But Quilin, those words sounded as though they came from your heart.'

'Forget them.' His tone became harsh. 'And forget me as a man. From now on, I'm only your devoted servant. Take Ardul for your husband. He's younger than me, handsome and strong. And he plays the lute.'

He marched to the door and flung it open. As his footsteps faded away, he could not hear Lyta's quiet reply. 'But I don't want Ardul.'

She lay back against the chair and let Quilin's words sound over and over in her head. She knew which ones were true.

When she heard noises in the antechamber, she sat up again. Josik was speaking and he sounded agitated. She called out, 'Kel, let Lord Josik enter.'

'Thank you, Kedura.' Even Josik's footsteps sounded disturbed.

'What's the matter?'

'Firt has been slain in his bed.'

Lyta drew in a sharp breath. 'By his brother?'

'I believe so because we can't find any trace of Fultis. I'm sure he and his men are on their way back to Delis.'

'I thought Firt would be protected by his own men at arms.'

Josik snorted. 'Two were found lying drunk on the floor. The other three have disappeared.'

'How was Firt slain?'

'With a single blade thrust through the heart.' He sighed. 'Trevin would have approved of such a death.'

'His body must be returned to lie beside Adina and we must discuss the governance of his estate.'

'Kedura, I'm sure you've talked too much. Your voice is exceeding hoarse.'

'I know but I must raise the matter of his estate and my choice of a husband with you. Please sit beside me that we may talk more easily.' She patted the seat next to her.

***

After Josik had left, Domen arrived to visit his patient. He agreed that Lyta might bathe. When enough water had been carried from the kitchen, she was helped into the bath. She lay there, enjoying the sensation of the silken water against her skin. Amia said she'd scrubbed away all traces of soot before she and Caza poured jugs of water over her hair and used perfumed soap to scrub it clean.

Lyta felt refreshed when she stepped from the bath to be wrapped in sheets and dried. Once she was dressed, she called for Kel. 'Please summon my lords. We will meet in the council chamber within an hour.'

***

Lyta settled into her chair at the head of the table. Her council members had expressed pleasure at her speedy recovery but concern about the state of her voice.

'It'll mend,' she said, imagining Quilin's face at the repetition of his previous comment. 'I won't pretend to be sorry that Firt is dead although I do not like the manner of his passing. Domen, please let me know as soon as we hear from Delis. I have no idea what Baldus will think about one of his sons killing another.'

'He'll say good riddance,' muttered Josik.

Lyta ignored his comment. 'We are here to discuss the governance of the estate. Eldin is inexperienced to govern on his own. We'll need someone in place to guide him.'

'I could do that,' said Quilin. 'My steward manages my estate well. And once you'll have a husband, Kedura, you won't need me to advise you.'

'But your land lies far from his estate,' said Domen. 'Josik is closer and I'd suggest him for this role. He won't be needed here either.'

'I agree,' said Ronin. 'If problems arise on Lord Josik's estate, he can easily get home.'

'Kedura,' said Domen, 'what is your pleasure?'

'Josik would be the most suitable person. And he's the boy's moonfather. Before Trevin died, Eldin was about to become a squire at Edgemere. My Lord Josik, are you in agreement with this proposal?'

'I'll be happy to supervise the estate. Eldin is a quick-witted lad, eager to learn. The younger children will benefit from guidance too. And my son will be even happier to keep me away from my own land.'

'Then that is agreed.' Lyta took a deep breath. 'I am ready to select my husband. Because I have no father or uncle, Josik will announce my choice tonight. It's appropriate that this is the time of Moonfest so we'll have another reason to celebrate.'

'Kedura, can we know the man's name?' Ronin asked.

Lyta shook her head. 'I wish to speak privately to him beforehand.'

'Of course,' said Domen. 'Kedura, we will be delighted no matter which man you may choose.'

Murmurs of assent rose from around the table. Lyta listened hard to catch Quilin's voice but did not hear it.

When she left the council chamber, she heard Druck striding toward her. She was learning to identify many of the men by the sound of their steps on the courtyard outside or the floors inside. Druck marched briskly and solidly like the soldier he was.

‘Kedura, is Lord Quilin still inside the council chamber?’

‘He has just left. Lord Josik and Magian Domen are still inside and mayhap one of them knows where he was going. Is there a problem?’

‘There was a problem but it has been solved. His son fell into the moat. He was looking for fish in the water.’

’ ‘Was the boy hurt?’

‘Luckily no, Kedura. Just exceeding wet and dirty. Lord Jilik was fished from the water by one of my guards and taken into the gatehouse. We gave the lad a warm drink by the fire and I have just delivered him to his nursemaid.’

Lyta smiled. ‘I suppose we can look forward to many other escapades. He has an adventurous streak in his nature.’

‘He’s a likely lad,’ said Druck in a surprisingly warm voice. ‘I’ve met many boys like him. He will need good training to control his high spirits but he could grow into a fine man. He should go as a squire when he’s older.’

‘Who would you suggest should train him?’

‘Lord Ronin might be suitable, Kedura. He seems a patient man but one who wouldn’t tolerate any impudence.’

‘Thank you, Archis, for the rescue. You should voice your opinions about Jilik to Lord Quilin.’

‘I will when the chance arises.’

Before she dressed for the Moonfest banquet, Lyta asked Kel to take her to the castlian. Godit was in the small chamber where he kept his accounts. When she entered, he said, ‘My Lady, you should not have come to me. I am always happy to be summoned.’

He led her to a seat. ‘I need to discuss two matters. First, has Druck seen to the removal of Firt’s body?’

‘Yes, My Lady. He has been taken away.’

‘What about the men at arms?’

'The commander threw them in the cells to sober up. After that, he will do with them whatever you desire.'

'I will consult him. Second, please provide extra decoration in the hall tonight. Fir boughs or some such.'

She sensed Godit regarding her curiously. 'Do you want more boughs than are usually cut for the Moonfest?'

'Yes,' said Lyta. 'The announcement will be made tonight about my future husband.'

'My Lady, let me be one of the first to offer my best wishes. This will be indeed a happy occasion. Do you know yet when you will be wed? We must plan for the wedding.'

'We haven't decided on the date but we'll give you sufficient time.' She rose to her feet.

'Very good, My Lady.' Godit took her hand to lead her to the door when Kel waited.

Chapter Seventy-One

Now that Godit knew a wedding announcement was imminent, the word would soon spread from him to the kitchen to the stables to the kennels and to every chamber. Lyta knew that her maids in dressing her would recognize that this was a significant night.

'Lady, will you wear the golden robe?' Amia asked.

'I am sure you've already taken it from the chest and shaken out the folds.'

Caza giggled. 'She has, My Lady, and it hangs on the wall along with the surcoat. Now my sister is taking out the matching necklet and tiara.'

'Don't forget the golden bracelets,' said Belia.

Lyta said, 'Then I don't need to tell you that I wish to look as fine as possible.'

'No, My Lady, we all know why and we're exceedingly pleased for you,' said Amia. 'We can't wait to find out who you have chosen. Now, let's remove the gown you have on and dress you. We will make sure you look as fine as possible for your betrothal night.'

Lyta stood still while her maids fussed around her. She was glad that she knew how she looked in the golden gown and surcoat from wearing it before she lost her sight. The trouble with future new clothes would be that she'd have to rely on her maids to describe the robes and her appearance in them. Lyta smiled when a sudden thought hit her. Her new husband could also tell her whether a garment was flattering. She was glad to have chosen an honest man.

Finally the maids stopped poking and pulling at Lyta's clothes and hair and she was robed and ready.

'Oh, My Lady,' said Amia in a choked voice. 'You look exceedingly beautiful.'

When Lyta entered the hall, the scent of pine mixed with wood smoke greeted her nose. In her mind's eye, she saw the deep green boughs hanging from the rafters, the shields shining above her head, and the brightly-coloured banners stirring in the heat from the torches and the fire in the hearth. Her hand trembled on Josik's arm as she remembered her lucky rescue from the pavilion fire. Fire would always be a concern and a danger for her now that she'd lost her sight.

A herald blew a horn blast as Lyta neared her seat. She remained standing while Josik left her and moved forward in the sudden silence. His voice was loud and every word was clear in the quiet hall.

'Greetings to you all on this happy Moonfest. I am honoured tonight to be asked to make an important announcement.' When he paused, Lyta could sense the atmosphere in the hall became tight with anticipation.

'Kedura Lyta will give her hand in marriage to the man who will now step forward.'

Loud applause and shouts met his words. Lyta waited until she felt the warm pressure of his familiar body next to hers. He took her hand in his comfortable grasp and stood beside her. Lyta was certain his smile was as wide as hers.

'I prefer the older man who cannot sing or play the lute,' she whispered. 'The one who smells like a summer flower.'

'And I will plight my troth to the lady who croaks like a frog in her moat,' he whispered back.

They were both laughing when Josik led them around the table to be met with thunderous applause, claps, calls, stamping on the floor, and the ringing of blades on the tables.

'I believe this choice is most welcome,' Josik yelled in Lyta's left ear.

'Better the man they know than the stranger,' Quilin yelled in return.

'You are both wrong,' Lyta called back. 'The man I have chosen for my husband is the best.'

Quilin raised her hand to his lips. His lingering kiss promised a wonderful life together.

The End

About Molly Fraser

Molly Fraser was born and raised in New Zealand where she attended university and became a secondary school teacher. Following her family's move to Canada, she taught at a community college. Now, she spends six months in Canada and six in New Zealand, avoiding the winter in both. While she enjoys reading and gardening, writing has always been a vital part of her life.

Social Media Links:

Website: www.barbarawinterandwood.com

Acknowledgements:

Thanks to Sheila Gale, Donna Kirk and Linda Shales, members of the Fiction Highway Guild. Without their critiquing skills and friendship, the manuscript might have languished on my laptop. And I'm grateful to my husband for enduring my writing schedule.

77835552R00275

Made in the USA
Columbia, SC
06 October 2017